T0352185

The**NAGUIB MAHFOUZ**Reader

The NAGUIB MAHFOUZ Reader

Edited by
Denys Johnson-Davies

The American University in Cairo Press
Cairo   New York

Copyright © 2011, 2016 by
The American University in Cairo Press
113 Sharia Kasr el Aini, Cairo, Egypt
420 Fifth Avenue, New York, NY 10018
www.aucpress.com

First paperback edition 2016

All rights reserved. No part of this publication may be reproduced, stored in a retrieval system,
or transmitted in any form or by any means, electronic, mechanical, photocopying, recording,
or otherwise, without the prior written permission of the publisher.

Exclusive distribution outside Egypt and North America by I.B.Tauris & Co Ltd., 6 Salem Road,
London, W4 2BU

Dar el Kutub No. 14395/15
ISBN 978 977 416 759 1

Dar el Kutub Cataloging-in-Publication Data

Johnson-Davies, Denys
        The Naguib Mahfouz Reader / Edited by Denys Johnson-Davies.—Cairo: The
    American University in Cairo Press, 2016
            p.   cm.
        ISBN 978 977 416 759 1
        1. Mahfouz, Naguib, 1911–2006
        2. Authors, Arab—Egypt
        3. Arabic Fiction—History and Criticism   I. Johnson-Davis, Denys (edit)
        892.7309

1 2 3 4 5   20 19 18 17 16

Designed by Jon W. Stoy
Printed in Egypt

Contents

—∿—

Acknowledgments

—⟋⟋⟋—

I n the course of putting together this book I had recourse to many works that have been written about Naguib Mahfouz; I would mention in particular Dr. Rasheed El-Enany's short but highly perceptive book, *Naguib Mahfouz: His Life and Times*, and Gamal al-Ghitani's *The Mahfouz Dialogs*, translated from the Arabic, which contains numerous entertaining personal observations about the author's day-to-day life and his work.

My thanks are of course also due to my friend Neil Hewison at the American University in Cairo Press for editing the book and for his many useful suggestions.

Introduction

———◊———

S ome time in the 1980s, I remember receiving a telephone call with the news that a woman from Sweden was in Cairo and that she wanted to see me. We met up for coffee in a hotel and she told me that she had come from Tunis, where—if my memory serves me right—she was the wife of an ambassador. She told me that the purpose of her visit was to discuss with me and others the possibility of an Arab writer being awarded the Nobel Prize in Literature.

"We feel it is high time an Arab writer was awarded the prize. What are your thoughts about that?"

I agreed with her and said that there was now a new modern movement in Arabic literature that should be recognized. I was also delighted to find out that the Nobel Prize might be awarded to an Arabic-language writer. She then read out the names of possible candidates on a list she had. These included Naguib Mahfouz, the leading short-story writer Yusuf Idris, the Sudanese writer Tayeb Salih, and a well-known poet. The name of Tawfiq al-Hakim was not included in the list because he had already passed away. I immediately suggested that if the prize were to be awarded to an Arab writer, Naguib Mahfouz was the obvious choice.

I then forgot about this meeting and was only reminded of it in 1988, when I learned that Mahfouz had been awarded the prize. Mahfouz himself later wrote that he thought his wife was joking when she told him he had won the prize. He was only convinced when the Swedish ambassador visited him at home to deliver the good news.

Born in 1911, Naguib Mahfouz began his writing career relatively late in life, publishing his first novel in 1939. At first, he decided to devote himself to writing fictional accounts of Egypt's remarkable ancient history. Having done considerable research on the subject, Mahfouz wrote three novels and several short stories set in pharaonic times. He then, fortunately, decided that the time in which he was living was even more deserving of serious attention by the novelists and short-story writers who had become part of the new literary movement in Arabic. It was thus that in 1945 his novel *Khan al-Khalili* appeared in print. Its title is the name of the famous bazaar district of Islamic Cairo, near Mahfouz's childhood neighborhood. The events of this novel and most of his early work, including his recognized masterpiece, *The Cairo Trilogy*, take place in and around this historic part of Egypt's capital.

Then in 1947 his novel *Midaq Alley* was published. Shortly after it appeared, Mahfouz gave me a copy of it. I was greatly impressed by it and felt that no novel of equal stature had been written in Arabic. I also thought that it ought to be translated. I set about the task but, halfway through the translation, I was discouraged by the thought that there would be little chance of finding a publisher for it. At that time, I had already translated and published a volume of short stories by the then pioneer of this form of literature, Mahmoud Teymour, but had had to have it printed at my own expense in Cairo, the time having not yet come when translations from the Arabic were thought worthy of attention by publishers in the west. *Midaq Alley* was, however, later translated by someone else and published in Beirut in 1975.

What I had particularly liked about the novel was the way in which the author had been able to capture the atmosphere of this typical Egyptian middle-class quarter in the old part of Egypt's capital city, and the lives of its inhabitants. I especially liked the extraordinary character named Zaita, who makes his living by bringing about bodily defects in people so that they are better able to make a living as beggars.

Mahfouz was to continue his career as a writer by producing no fewer than thirty-three novels and sixteen collections of short stories and plays, as well as various other publications. In addition to his prolific work as a writer of fiction, Mahfouz also wrote scripts for twenty-five films—and all this on top of his day job as a civil servant between 1934 and his retirement in 1971.

Mahfouz had studied philosophy at university but somehow acquired enough proficiency in English to be able to read many great classics, by writers such as Tolstoy, Mann, and Proust, in English translation. He even learned enough French to be able to read French classics by writers such as Flaubert. He also read widely in the extensive literature of Sufism. This is evident in some of his later books, such as *Echoes of an Autobiography* and *The Dreams*. Even more remarkable—and something I learned only when I was researching this collection—was that Naguib Mahfouz had once indicated that his favorite poet was Hafiz al-Shirazi. Yet in all of our meetings it had never occurred to me to ask him if he had ever read any of the great Persian poets, since the only Persian poet to have been effectively translated into English was Omar Khayyam. In fact, one of Mahfouz's masterpieces, *The Harafish*, contains a number of verses from Hafiz in the original Persian.

And yet with all this activity, Mahfouz enjoyed nothing so much as sitting around in his favorite cafés with his literary friends. How was it then that he was able to write such an extraordinarily large body of work? The answer is that he was a man of great self-discipline, able to keep himself to tight schedules where his work was concerned.

Mahfouz's greatest work is perhaps *The Cairo Trilogy*, which is now available in one volume of over 1,300 pages. Its preparation and writing took some seven years of hard work. In *The Mahfouz Dialogs*, the novelist Gamal al-Ghitani, a friend of Mahfouz's for many years, records how the writer, having eventually finished this vast book, had taken it to his usual publisher, whose only reaction was shock at the manuscript's excessive length, and who refused to publish it. Mahfouz was greatly disappointed, but the work was later serialized in a literary magazine, and eventually—divided up into three separate volumes under different titles—came out in book form. Later, the three volumes were brought together under the title *The Cairo Trilogy* and enjoyed wide sales throughout the Arab world.

The Cairo Trilogy deals with the fortunes—and misfortunes—of the Abd al-Jawad family, covering a period of some twenty-eight years in the history of modern Egypt, beginning in the middle of the First World War. The novel contains, over a period of three generations, a remarkable portrait of Ahmad Abd al-Jawad, an authoritarian patriarch ruling over his family with an iron hand, though at the same time something of a libertine. Time takes its toll and reduces him to little more than a helpless old man, who soon meets his death. Among the most interesting characters in the *Trilogy* is Kamal, one of the sons of Ahmad Abd al-Jawad, who rebels against the conservative religious beliefs of the time. After reading Darwin, Kamal publishes an article on evolution, and is roundly scolded by his father for putting forward such a heretical explanation of the world's origins.

It is interesting to note that Naguib Mahfouz's next work of fiction, *Children of the Alley*, deals with the history of man's religious beliefs from the beginning of time up to the present day. The characters include Gabalawi (representing God), others representing Moses, Jesus, and Muhammad, and another named Arafa who represents knowledge and science (the Arabic root from which the name is taken means 'to know').

The novel was first serialized in *al-Ahram* newspaper in 1959, but was later banned from appearing in book form in Egypt. On one of my visits to Cairo, I remember Mahfouz telling me about the difficulties he was having because of the book. He had been asked to meet with some of the sheikhs at al-Azhar University so that they might question him about it. He asked me what I thought about this, and I answered that he should refuse to grant such a meeting and should say it was not the responsibility of an author to explain his work.

The book nevertheless was widely attacked, and led to an assassination attempt by a Muslim extremist in October 1994. Earlier, Naguib Mahfouz had been among eighty Arab personalities who lent their signatures to a document censuring the fatwa issued against Salman Rushdie for his book *The Satanic Verses*. It was the death threats made against Mahfouz for blasphemy by the blind Sheikh Omar Abd al-Rahman that led his young assailant—who had not read the book—to attempt to murder him. Though the writer escaped with his life, the wound he received from the attacker's knife left him incapable of using his right arm for the purpose of writing. Thenceforth his writings, shorter but no less important, were all dictated.

While Mahfouz is known primarily as a novelist, he also published no fewer than sixteen volumes of short stories. *Zaabalawi* and the very short *Half a Day*, for instance, spring to mind immediately as masterpieces in this genre. During one gathering with Mahfouz and his friends, someone mentioned the fact that I had included *Zaabalawi* in the Oxford University Press book *Modern Arabic Short Stories*. Mahfouz himself then mentioned that many years before that, as early as 1946, I had translated a story of his from his first volume, *Whisperings of Madness*, and that I had had it broadcast over the local English-language radio station. While I no longer possess a copy of the story, it was good to be reminded of the fact that I was the first to translate something by this famed writer.

My meetings with Naguib Mahfouz always took place in one of the several cafés he frequented. Our conversations invariably dealt with literature, and I well recollect several heated discussions about the form of Arabic that writers of fiction should adopt in their work. I was all for having the narrative part of a work of fiction written in the classical language, while resorting to the colloquial language for the dialogue. Mahfouz, however, insisted that the whole work should be in the classical language. His argument for this was that this would ensure that the book was read throughout the Arab world.

"But how can you have an illiterate peasant speak like a university professor?" I would protest, and he would answer that this could be done by using a simple form of the classical language. I was unconvinced, and only in these last few days, while reading material for writing this introduction, I came across a piece in his book *The Dreams* admitting that some of the conversations in his earlier novels were unrealistic because they were written in the classical language. Today the trend is for many of the younger generation of Egyptian writers to employ the colloquial language for the dialogue—some have even written complete works in the colloquial idiom. The situation has changed to some extent since the days when Naguib Mahfouz was writing. These days, Egyptian radio, television, and films are widely broadcast throughout the Arab world, and many Arabs find no difficulty in understanding the spoken form of Egyptian Arabic. I was nevertheless recently given proof of Mahfouz's argument when an Iraqi friend gave me a copy of a novel he had written in which he had employed the Iraqi dialect for all the dialogue. With only a limited knowledge of Iraqi Arabic, I found the novel a difficult read and gave up after toiling through only the first two or three chapters. The issue of which form of Arabic to employ still exists for the Arabic writer.

I remember, while living for a period in Beirut, hearing from a visiting friend that Mahfouz had given all the translation rights to his books to the American University in Cairo (AUC) Press, and had done so without receiving an advance on royalties. I was shocked by the news, and on my next visit to Cairo, I expressed my astonishment to him that he had done such a thing. "At least this way my work will get translated and read in English," he told me, "and for me that is more important than money." And of course he was right. Mahfouz wrote because that was his passion in life, and up until that time his rewards from the sale of his books had been minimal. Now, for the first time, the AUC Press set about getting his major works translated into English. For the first time an organization was commissioning translators so that Arabic books could be published in English.

Not only did Mahfouz's decision to allow the AUC Press to translate his works into English mean that his books were now available to a much wider audience, it was also partly responsible for his Nobel Prize. No one on the Nobel Prize committee in Sweden could read Arabic, so the fact that some of his work had been translated into English and French made him eligible for the prize. Through the AUC Press's efforts, some of Naguib Mahfouz's books have now appeared in no less than forty languages.

Miramar was one of the first of Mahfouz's novels to appear in English translation. This occurred before he was awarded the Nobel Prize, when he was virtually unknown outside the Arab world. The English novelist John Fowles wrote the introduction in the original English edition. No doubt the reason the introduction was not included in later editions was that Mahfouz, with his usual humility, was quoted as ranking himself, in relation to European literature, as "fourth- or fifth-rate." When asked to give his ideas of writers who could be classed as first-rate, he suggested Shakespeare, Joyce, and Tolstoy. John Fowles's introduction shows that, before receiving any official recognition, a very talented fiction writer had found Naguib Mahfouz to be "a considerable novelist."

Before ending this introduction to Naguib Mahfouz, let me give two more small examples of the singularly generous nature of this remarkable man, who, in a world where money holds pride of place, continued to live a life unchanged by money and fame.

When Mark Linz became director of the AUC Press in 1995, I suggested to him that the publications of the Press would gain prestige and a boost in sales if they instituted a literary prize bearing Naguib Mahfouz's name. "Do you think he would agree?" Mark Linz asked me. "I am quite certain he would," I replied. So we drove to the writer's modest apartment in the suburb of Agouza, the same apartment in which he had long lived with his wife and two daughters, and to which the Swedish ambassador had gone to tell him he had been awarded the Nobel Prize. And so was instituted a prize in Naguib Mahfouz's name, to be awarded yearly to an Arabic-language writer who had distinguished himself or herself in the field of letters. While the monetary award was a modest one, the prize carried the name of the only Arab writer to be awarded the Nobel Prize. It also made it possible for the winning book to be translated into English and published by the AUC Press in Cairo and in the English-speaking world.

Shortly before his death, the AUC Press asked Mahfouz if he would write a short introduction to a book of mine entitled *Memories in Translation* that was about to be published. The answer was, as usual, "Yes, of course."

With this present publication, it is my hope that readers will be encouraged to take a plunge into modern Arabic literature through a selection of the writings of a man who showed that the same language that had produced a world classic like *The Arabian Nights* is also capable of making a worthwhile contribution to the literature of today.

Novels

from *Thebes at War*, 1944

This is the third of the novels that Naguib Mahfouz wrote about pharaonic Egypt early in his career. Thereafter, he turned his interest to the Egypt in which he was living.

More hours passed and the sun started to incline toward the west. Commanders Mheb and Deeb approached the king, Ahmose Ebana following in their footsteps. They bowed to Ahmose respectfully and congratulated him on the victory. Ahmose said, "Before we congratulate one another, we must perform our duty toward the bodies of the heroes and soldiers, and the women and children, who were martyred for the sake of Thebes. Bring them all to me!"

The bodies, begrimed with dust and stained with blood, were strewn at the sides of the field, on top of the wall, and behind the gates. The iron helmets had fallen from their heads and the terrible silence of death hung over them. The soldiers picked them up respectfully, took them to one side of the camp, and laid them side by side, just as they brought the women and children whom their soldiers' arrows had cut to pieces, and put them in a separate place. The king proceeded to the resting place of the martyrs followed by Chamberlain Hur, the three commanders, and his entourage. When he got close to the rows of bodies, he bowed in silent, sorrowing reverence, and his men did likewise. Then he walked on with slow steps, passing before them as though he were reviewing them at some official occasion before spectators. Next, he turned aside to the place where the women and children lay, their bodies now wrapped in linen coverings. A cloud of sadness cast a shadow over the king's face and his eyes darkened. In the midst of his grief, he became aware of the voice of Commander Ahmose Ebana, crying out despite himself in a choking voice, "Mother!"

The king turned back and saw his commander kneeling in pain and agony beside one of the corpses. The king cast an enquiring look at the body and saw that it was Lady Ebana, the terrifying shadow of extinction sketched on her visage. The king stopped beside his kneeling commander, humbled and with sad heart. He had had a great respect for the lady, and knew well her patriotism, her courage, and her merit in raising Ahmose to be, without contest, his best commander. The king raised his head to the heavens and said in a trembling voice, "Divine Lord Amun, creator of the universe, giver of life and arranger of all according to His high plan, these are your charges who now are returned to you at your desire. In our world they lived for others and thus they died. They are dear fragments broken from my heart. Grant them your mercy and compensate them for the ephemeral life that they lost with a happy eternal life in the Hereafter!"

The king turned to Chamberlain Hur and said, "Chamberlain, I wish that these bodies all be preserved and placed in Thebes' western cemetery. By my life, those worthiest of the earth of Thebes are those who died as martyrs for its sake!"

At this point, the messenger whom the king had sent to his family in Dabod returned and presented his lord with a message. Surprised, the king asked, "Have my family come back to Habu?"

The man replied, "Indeed not, my lord."

Ahmose spread open the message, which was sent by Tetisheri, and read:

My lord, aided in triumph by the spirit of the Lord Amun and His blessings, may the Lord grant that this letter of mine reach you to whom Thebes has opened its gates so that you might enter at the head of the Army of Deliverance to tend to its wounded and make happy the souls of Seqenenra and Kamose. For ourselves, we shall not leave Dabod. I have thought long about the matter and have found that the best way for us to share with our tormented people in their pain is to remain in our exile where we are now, living the agonies of separation and homesickness until such time as we smash the shackles that bind them and they are relieved of their trials, and we may enter Egypt in security and take part with them in their happiness and peace. Go on your way aided by the Lord's care, liberate the cities, suppress the fortresses, and cleanse the land of Egypt of its enemy, leaving it not one single foothold on its soil. Then summon us and we shall come in safety.

Ahmose raised his head and folded the message, saying discontentedly, "Tetisheri says that she will not enter Egypt until we expel from it the last Herdsman."

Hur said, "Our Sacred Mother does not want us to cease fighting until we have liberated Egypt."

The king nodded his head in agreement and Hur asked, "Will my lord not enter Thebes this evening?"

Ahmose said, "I will not, Hur. My army shall enter on its own. As for me, I shall enter it with my family when we have thrown out the Herdsmen. We shall enter it together as we left it, ten years ago."

"Its people will suffer great disappointment!"

"Tell anyone who asks after me that I pursue the Herdsmen, to throw them beyond our sacred borders; and let those who love me follow me!"

The army passed the daylight hours dressing its wounds and taking its share of rest and recreation, song, and drink. Those soldiers who were from Thebes raced one another to get to their homes, where hearts embraced and souls mingled. So great were the joy and emotion, that Thebes seemed as though it were the beating heart of the very world. Ahmose, however, did not leave his ship, and, summoning the officer charged with guarding the princess, asked him about her. The man told him that she had gone the night without tasting food. It occurred to him to put her on another ship, under the charge of trustworthy officers, but he could not arrive at a definite decision. He had no doubt that Hur was displeased at her presence on his ship and sure that the chamberlain found it difficult to understand why the daughter of Apophis should be given this honored status in his eyes. He knew the man inside out and that his heart had no place for anything but Thebes' struggle. He, on the other hand, found his emotions athirst and overflowing. He was making himself sick with the effort of holding himself back from hovering about the chamber and its occupant or of distracting himself from his obsessive desire for her, despite his displeasure and anger. Anger does not destroy love, but conceals it briefly, just as mist may cloud briefly the face of a polished mirror, after which it is gone and the mirror's original purity returns. He did not, therefore, give in to despair and would say to himself consolingly that maybe it was remnants of defeated pride and fallen conceit from which she suffered, that maybe her anger would go away and then she would discover the love that lay behind the outward show of hatred and relent, submit, and give love its due, just as she had anger. Was she not the one in the cabin, who had saved his life and granted him sympathy and love? Was she not the one who had become so upset by his absence that she had written him a message of reproof to hide the moans of suppressed love? How could these emotions of hers wither just because of an upsurge of pride and anger?

He waited until the late afternoon, then shrugged his broad shoulders, as though making light of the matter, and went to the chamber. The guard saluted him and made way, and he entered with great hopes. He found her seated unmoving and silent, dejection and ennui showing in her blue eyes. Her dejection pained him and he said to himself, "Thebes for all its vastness was too narrow for her, so how must she feel now that she is a prisoner in this small chamber?" He stood unmoving before her and she straightened her back and raised her insolent eyes to him. He asked her gently, "How was your night?"

She did not answer and lowered her head to look at the ground. He cast a longing look at her head, shoulders, and bosom and repeated the question, feeling at the same time that his hope was not far off, "How was your night?"

She appeared not to want to abandon her silence, but raised her head sharply, and said, "It was the worst night of my life."

He ignored her tone and asked her, "Why? Is there anything you lack?"

She replied without changing her tone, "I lack everything."

"How so? I gave orders to the officer charged with guarding you to . . ."

She interrupted him with annoyance, "Don't even bother to speak of such things! I lack everything I love. I lack my father, my people, and my liberty. But I have everything that I hate: these clothes, this food, this chamber, and these guards."

Once again he was stricken by disappointment and felt the collapse of his hopes and the disappearance of all he longed for. His features hardened and he said to her, "Do you want me to release you from your captivity and send you to your father?"

She shook her head violently and said vehemently, "Never!"

He looked at her in amazement and confusion but she resumed in the same tones, "So that it not be said that the daughter of Apophis abased herself before the enemy of her great father or that once she needed someone to comfort her."

Aroused by anger and exasperation at her conceit and pride, he said, "You are not embarrassed to display your conceit because you feel sure of my compassion."

"You lie!"

His face turned pale and he stared at her with a harsh look and said, "How callow you are, you who know nothing of sorrow or pain! Do you know the punishment for insulting a king? Have you ever seen a woman flogged? If I wished, I could have you kneeling at the feet of the least of my soldiers begging for pardon and forgiveness."

He looked at her a long time to ascertain the effect of his threat on her and found her challenging him with her harsh, unflinching eyes. Anger swept over her with the same speed that it overtook all those of her race and she said sharply, "We are a people to whose hearts fear knows no path and our pride will not be brought low though the hands of men should grasp the heavens."

He asked himself in his anger, should he attempt to humiliate her? Why should he not humiliate her and trample her pride into the ground? Was she not his captive, whom he could make into one of his slave girls? However, he did not feel at ease with this idea. He had had ambitions for something sweeter and lovelier, so that when his disappointment caught up with him, his pride rose up and his anger grew sharper. He renounced his desire to humiliate her, though he made his outward demeanor conceal his true thoughts, saying in tones as imperious as hers, "What I want does not require that you be tortured and for that reason you will not be tortured. And indeed, it would be bizarre for anyone to think of torturing a lovely slave girl like you."

"No! A proud princess!"

"That was before you fell into my hands as a prisoner. Personally, I would rather add you to my harem than torture you. My will is what will decide."

"You should know that your will may decide for you and your people, but not for me, and you will never put a hand on me alive."

He shrugged his shoulders as though to make light of this, but she went on, "Among the customs passed down among us is that if one of us should fall into the snares of abjection and has no hope of rescue, he abstain from food until he die with honor."

Contemptuously he said, "Really? But I saw the judges of Thebes driven to me, and prostrate themselves before me, groveling, their eyes pleading for pardon and mercy."

Her face turned pale and she took refuge in silence.

The king, unable to listen to more of her words and suffering the bitterness of disappointment, could stay no longer. As he got ready to leave the chamber, he said, "You will not need to abstain from food."

He left the chamber angry and depressed, having decided to transfer her to another ship. No sooner, however, had his anger died down and he was alone in his cabin than he changed his mind, and he did not give the order.

Translated by Humphrey Davies

from *Khan al-Khalili*, 1946

This was the first of Mahfouz's novels to be set in the district after which the novel is named. It deals with a year in the life of a Cairene family during the Second World War. The passage chosen features the younger son, Rushdi, and his first meeting with the beautiful Nawal.

Rushdi went back to his room, lit a cigarette, and started to smoke by the window. His gaze was riveted to that particular window, all in the hope of catching a glimpse of his lovely neighbor once in a while. His hopes were rewarded when she did indeed appear at the window, wearing her new outfit and with a gray coat over her shoulders. However, she quickly withdrew, almost as though she needed to escape from his piercing stare. The young man had taken due note of the coat and surmised that she was on the point of going out. He quickly took out some clothes and started getting dressed. Within minutes he was out of the apartment.

He wondered where was the best place to wait. Just then he remembered the narrow passageway that connected the quarter to the New Road. He rushed over there, then stopped on the sidewalk at the spot where it joined the main road. The entire street was teeming with people. Carts had come down from the Darrasa district loaded with boys and girls singing, dancing, and banging drums. He stayed where he was, one eye happily watching the crowds in the street and the other glued hopefully to the passageway. He was an old hand at this type of situation, so he was not worried.

As it turned out, he did not have long to wait. The girl soon appeared at the entrance to the passageway accompanied by a young boy who closely resembled her. He avoided looking straight at her by lighting another cigarette. He had no doubt that she had spotted him, but he still wondered whether she had realized that he was actually waiting for her. As she made her way toward al-Azhar, he followed close behind and was able to get a good look at her for the first time. She was sixteen at the most, of medium height, and nicely turned out. However, it was her face that was the loveliest part of her, and her honey-colored eyes were its loveliest feature.

He did not manage to enjoy looking at her for very long, because she soon reached the trolley stop and got on the women's carriage along with her brother—that was his assumption about the young boy. He too got on the trolley, one carriage back so he could see where she got off. The trolley began to move, and he had no idea where this particular chase was going to take him. He now started an assessment: a young girl, seventy-five percent for face; sixty-five percent for figure; and it wouldn't take long to find out whether she was easy prey or would present more of a challenge. Would she get swept up in the romance, or was she dreaming of getting a wedding ring? We'll know soon enough, he told himself. If it's the wedding ring she's after, then things might rapidly become tricky; even worse, annoying. At this stage, however, the most important thing was to cajole her into chatting and then see what happened.

When the trolley reached Queen Farida Square, they all got off—the girl and her brother first, and then him. Just then she happened to look round and noticed him staring directly at her. She immediately turned away and pretended to be deep in conversation with her brother. Now he was sure that she realized he was deliberately following her.

The pair boarded the first trolley that came, the one going to Giza. He immediately boarded it as well. "Are they going to visit a relative," he wondered to himself, "so they can celebrate the Eid with him?" At that moment he decided, out of the sheer goodness of his heart, that he would leave the day to her. But at just that moment they both alighted at the Imad al-Din stop. He now realized that they were going to the cinema, a thought that delighted him. They all crossed the road to Imad al-Din Street, the pair first, then him behind them, poised and ready to respond to a smile or any kind of gesture she might make if she looked behind her. But instead, she kept staring straight to the front, grasping her brother's hand as he hurried to keep up with her. Rushdi kept his gaze firmly on her back and legs, her gait, and the way she walked. He was happy to discover that the view of her from the back was just as nice as from the front. Her rear view earned her a solid eighty percent. It all took him back to the old days. "Well, well," he told himself, "these days there's beauty to be had in Egypt."

When they got to the Ritz Cinema, she looked behind her and noticed him still staring hard at her. Quickly looking away, she hurried off in the direction of Studio Egypt, leaving him flummoxed by the lack of any clear signal. He regretted the fact that their eyes had not had a real conversation, and yet her choice of cinema pleased him a lot. It was showing the film, *Dananir*. He realized that this little chase he had embarked upon would now offer him a double pleasure. He was eager to sit next to her, so he managed to work his way to a spot right behind her in the queue at the box office; that way he could select a seat right next to hers. The young boy was standing to one side, looking at the pictures. Rushdi moved up close behind her, so close that it felt as though his breaths were actually touching her ponytail; it gave him the same sensation as the purest of scents. He watched her fingers as they picked out two seats on the cinema chart for herself and her brother. He noticed that there would be a single vacant seat to the right and three to the left. Which side would the girl be sitting on? he asked himself. To find out, he used the old guessing game, "eeny meeny miny mo," and came up with the seat on the right. He chose it with a degree of confidence and then moved away. Looking around he could find no sign of either the girl or her brother, but that did not bother him. After all, he had the ticket in hand; that was enough to put him next to her, no matter where she had disappeared. He had no idea why, but it all reminded him—the power given him by the ticket, that is—of the sanctity and magic of marriage, all of which gave his heart a jolt.

He was still feeling the effects as he entered the cinema. As the usher escorted him to his seat, he was hoping that his choice had been the right one, but he discovered that the boy was sitting between himself and the girl. The girl saw him coming and looked away in alarm; she refused to even glance in his direction. He sat in his seat, delighted, and kept stealing glances in her direction. On two occasions he noticed that she was staring straight in front of her; the way she was blushing and looking thoroughly awkward made him fully aware of how bashful and agitated she was feeling. That made him feel sorry for her, and he decided then and there not to bother her any more. Instead, he contented himself by looking around at the boxes and rows of seats and fondly surveying the bosoms, necks, mouths, and wrists on display. He did not have long to wait. A bell sounded, lights were dimmed, and the screen prepared itself to unwrap the world of dreams. He was happy enough to be sitting close to the girl with whom he had fallen in love, even though his heart was actually not fully involved as yet. The heavenly voice started to sing the spring song, "How sweet the gentle breeze!" and he allowed himself to float off into another world. He had always loved singing, so much so that one day it had even occurred to him that he had been born to be a musician. As the film continued, he felt himself swept up in a divine melody.

When the film came to an end, the lights went up. Rushdi looked over at the girl and saw that she was standing up with her eyes closed, shielding them from the bright lights after spending so long in the dark. He stood there waiting until she opened them and saw him staring at her. Once outside the cinema, he made a point of looking carefully at her fingers and noticed that she was not engaged. That made him smile. He then proceeded to trail her all the way back, just as he had on the way to the cinema. However, he decided not to follow her to al-Azhar since he did not want to reveal his little secret to anyone from his new quarter. Returning to the family apartment, he found his family waiting to eat. It was not long before his mother was happily summoning the family to the table with the words, "It's time for the Eid stew!"

Translated by Roger Allen

from *Midaq Alley*, 1947

Midaq Alley is one of Mahfouz's most popular novels, set in the same quarter as his earlier *Khan al-Khalili*. Two films have been made of it, one in Egypt and the other in Mexico.

As soon as Mrs. Afify left the room, Hamida came in combing her black hair, which gave off a strong smell of kerosene. Her mother gazed at her dark and shining hair, the ends of which nearly reached to the girl's knees, and said sadly, "What a pity! Imagine letting lice live in that lovely hair!"

The girl's black eyes, framed with mascara, flashed angrily and took on a determined and intent look. "What lice? I swear by the Prophet that my comb found only two lice!"

"Have you forgotten that I combed your hair two weeks ago and squashed twenty lice for you?"

The girl answered indifferently, "Well, I hadn't washed my hair for two months. . . ."

She sat down at her mother's side and continued combing her hair vigorously.

Hamida was in her twenties, of medium stature and with a slim figure. Her skin was bronze-colored and her face a little elongated, unmarked, and pretty. Her most remarkable features were her black, beautiful eyes, the pupils and whites of which contrasted in a most striking and attractive way. When, however, she set her delicate lips and narrowed her eyes, she could take on an appearance of strength and determination which was most unfeminine. Her temper had always, even in Midaq Alley itself, been something no one could ignore.

Even her mother, famous for her roughness, did her best to avoid crossing her. One day when they had quarreled her mother cried out to her, "God
will never find you a husband; what man would want to embrace a burning
firebrand like you?" On other occasions she had said that a real madness
overcame her daughter when she got angry and she nicknamed her tempers
the khamsin, after the vicious and unpredictable summer winds.

Despite all this, she was really very fond of Hamida, even though she
was only her foster mother. The girl's real mother had been her partner in
making and selling sweet and fattening potions. She was eventually compelled by her poverty to share Umm Hamida's flat in Midaq Alley and had
died there, leaving her daughter still a baby. Umm Hamida had adopted her
and placed her under the care of the wife of Kirsha, the café owner, who had
suckled her along with her son Hussain Kirsha, who was therefore a sort of
foster brother to the girl Hamida.

She went on combing her black hair, waiting for her mother to comment
as usual on the visit and visitor. When the silence remained unbroken unusually long, she asked, "It was a long visit. What were you talking about?"

Her mother laughed sardonically and murmured, "Guess!"

The girl, now even more interested, asked, "She wants to raise the rent?"

"If she had done that, she would have left here carried by ambulance
men! No, she wants to lower the rent!"

"Have you gone mad?" Hamida exclaimed.

"Yes, I have gone mad. But guess . . ."

The girl sighed and said, "You've tired me out!"

Umm Hamida twitched her eyebrows and announced, winking an eye,
"Her ladyship wants to get married!"

The girl was overcome with astonishment and gasped, "Married?"

"That's right, and she wants a young husband. How sorry I am for an
unlucky young woman like you who can't find anyone to ask for her hand!"

Hamida gazed at her derisively and commented, now braiding her hair,
"Oh yes, I could find many, but the fact is that you are a rotten matchmaker
who merely wants to hide her failure. What's wrong with me? Just as I said,
you are a failure and you only go to prove the saying: 'It's always the car-
penter's door that's falling apart.' "

Her foster mother smiled and said, "If Mrs. Saniya Afify can get married, then no woman at all should despair."

The girl stared at her furiously and said, "I am not the one who is chasing marriage, but marriage is chasing me. I will give it a good run, too!"

"Of course you will, a princess like yourself, a daughter of royalty."

The girl ignored her mother's sarcasm and went on in the same severe tone: "Is there anyone here in Midaq Alley who is worth considering?"

In fact, Umm Hamida had no fear that her daughter would be left on the shelf and she had no doubts about the girl's beauty. Nevertheless, she frequently felt resentful about her vanity and conceit and she now said bitingly, "Don't slander the alley like that. The people who live here are the best in the world!"

"You're the best in the world yourself, aren't you? They are all nonentities. Only one of them has a spark of life and you had to go and make him my foster brother!"

She was referring to Hussain Kirsha, with whom she had been suckled. This remark annoyed her mother and she objected angrily, "How can you say such a thing? I didn't make him your brother. No one can make you a brother or a sister. He is your brother because you both suckled the same woman just as God ordained."

A spirit of devilment seemed to take possession of the girl. She said jokingly, "Couldn't he have always sucked from one breast and me from the other?"

At this her mother punched her hard in the back and snorted, "May God punish you for saying that."

The girl replied by muttering, "Nothing Alley!"

"You deserve to marry some really important civil servant, I suppose?"

"Is a civil servant a god?" retorted Hamida defiantly.

Her mother sighed deeply and said, "If only you would stop being so conceited. . . ."

The girl mimicked Umm Hamida's voice and replied, "If you would only be reasonable for once in your life."

"You eat and drink my food but you are never grateful. Do you remember all that fuss you made about a dress?"

Hamida asked in astonishment, "And is a dress something of no importance? What's the point of living if one can't have new clothes? Don't you think it would be better for a girl to have been buried alive rather than have no nice clothes to make herself look pretty?" Her voice filled with sadness as she went on: "If only you had seen the factory girls! You should just see those Jewish girls who go to work. They all go about in nice clothes. Well, what is the point of life then if we can't wear what we want?"

Her foster mother replied cuttingly, "Watching the factory girls and the Jewish women has made you lose your senses. If only you would stop worrying about all this."

The girl took no notice of what Umm Hamida said. She had now finished plaiting her hair and she took a small mirror from her pocket and propped it up on the back of the sofa. She then stood in front of it, bending down slightly to see her reflection. In a wondering voice, she said, "Oh what a shame, Hamida. What are you doing living in this alley? And why should your mother be this woman who can't tell the difference between dust and gold dust?"

She leaned out of the room's only window, which overlooked the street, and stretched her arms out to the open shutters, drawing them together so that only a couple of inches of space was left between them. She then sat resting on her elbows placed on the windowsill and gazed out into the street, moving her attention from place to place and saying as though to herself, "Hello, street of bliss! Long life to you and all your fine inhabitants. What a pretty view and see how handsome the people are! I can see Husniya, the bakeress, sitting like a big sack before the oven with one eye on the loaves and one on Jaada, her husband. He works only because he is afraid of her beatings and blows. Over there sits Kirsha, the café owner, his head bowed as if in a deep sleep, but he is really awake. Uncle Kamil is fast asleep, of course, while the flies swarm over his tray of unprotected sweets. Look there! That's Abbas Hilu peeping up at my window, preening himself. I'm sure he thinks that the power of his look will throw me down at his feet. You're not for me, Abbas! Well now, Mr. Salim Alwan, the company owner, has just lifted up his eyes, lowered them, and raised them once again. We'll say the first time was an accident, but the second, Mr. Alwan? Sir? Watch now, he's just started a third time! What do you want, you senile and shameless old man? You want a rendezvous with me every day at this time? If only you weren't a married man and a father, I'd give you look for look and say welcome and welcome again! Well, there they all are. That is the alley and why shouldn't Hamida neglect her hair until it gets lice? Oh yes, and there's Sheikh Darwish plodding along with his wooden clogs striking the pavement like a gong."

At this point her mother interrupted. "Who would make a better husband for you than Sheikh Darwish?"

Hamida remained looking out the window, and, with a shake of her behind, she replied, "What a powerful man he must have been! He says he has spent a hundred thousand pounds on his love for our lady Zainab. Do you think he would have been too mean to give me ten thousand?"

She drew back suddenly, as though bored with her survey. Now she moved in front of the mirror and, gazing into it searchingly, she sighed and said, "Oh, what a pity, Hamida, what a shame and a waste."

In the early morning Midaq Alley is dreary and cold. The sun can reach it only after climbing high into the sky. However, life begins to stir early in the morning in parts of the street. Sanker, the café waiter, begins activity by arranging the chairs and lighting the spirit stove. Then the workmen in the company office start coming in ones and twos. Presently Jaada appears carrying the wood for baking the bread. Even Uncle Kamil is busy at this early hour, opening his shop and then having his nap before breakfast. Uncle Kamil and Abbas, the barber, always have breakfast together from a tray placed between them containing plates of cooked beans, onion salad, and pickled gherkins.   .

They each approach their food in a different manner. Abbas devours his roll of bread in a few seconds. Uncle Kamil, on the other hand, is slow and chews each piece of food laboriously until it almost dissolves in his mouth. He often says, "Good food should first be digested in the mouth." So it is that Abbas will have finished eating his food, sipping his tea and smoking his pipe while his friend is still slowly munching his onions. Kamil, therefore, prevents Abbas from taking any of his share by always dividing the food into two separate sections.

In spite of his portly build, Uncle Kamil could not be considered a glutton, although he was very fond of sweets and extremely clever at making them. His artistry was completely fulfilled in making up orders for people like Salim Alwan, Radwan Hussainy, and Kirsha, the café owner. His reputation was widely known and had even crossed the boundaries of the alley to the quarters of Sanadiqiya, Ghouriya, and Sagha. However, his means were modest and he had not lied when he complained to Abbas that after his death there would be no money to bury him. That very morning he said to Abbas after they finished breakfast, "You said you bought me a burial shroud. Now that really is something that calls for thanks and blessings. Why don't you give it to me now."

Abbas, the typical liar, had forgotten all about the shroud. He asked, "Why do you want it now?"

His friend answered in his high-pitched adolescent voice, "I could do with what it's worth. Haven't you heard that the price of cloth is going up?"

Abbas chuckled. "You are really a shrewd one in spite of your fake simplicity. Only yesterday you were complaining that you hadn't enough money for a proper burial. Now that I have a shroud for you, you want to sell it and use the money! No, this time you won't get your way. I bought your shroud to honor your body after a long life, if God wills."

Uncle Kamil smiled in embarrassment and shifted his chair nervously. "Suppose my life lasts so long that things get back to the way they were before the war? Then we'll have lost the value of an expensive shroud, don't you agree?"

"And suppose you die tomorrow?"

"I hope to God not!"

This made Abbas roar with laughter. "It's useless to try to change my mind. The shroud will stay in a safe place with me until God works His will. . . ." He laughed again so loudly that his friend joined in. The barber now spoke teasingly. "You're completely without profit for me. Have I ever managed to make a penny out of you in your whole life? No! Your chin and upper lip simply don't sprout and your head's quite bald. On all that vast world you call your body there's not a single hair for me to cut. God forgive you!"

"It's a fine clean body which no one would mind washing down," said Uncle Kamil with a mock seriousness.

The sound of someone yelling interrupted them. Down the street they saw Husniya, the bakeress, beating her husband, Jaada, with her slippers. The man collapsed in front of her, offering no defense at all. His wails reverberated from each side of the alley and the two men laughed uproariously.

"Have forgiveness and mercy on him, madam!" shouted Abbas loudly.

The woman continued pummeling him until Jaada lay at her feet weeping and begging forgiveness.

"Those slippers could do your body some good," said Abbas, turning to Uncle Kamil. "They'd soon melt that fat away!"

Just then Hussain Kirsha appeared; he was dressed in trousers, a white shirt, and a straw hat. He made an ostentatious show of looking at his gold wristwatch, his small darting eyes filled with pride of possession. He greeted his friend the barber in a friendly fashion and seated himself in a chair. It was his day off and he wanted his hair cut.

The two friends had grown up together in Midaq Alley. Indeed, they had been born in the same house, that of Radwan Hussainy, Abbas three years before Hussein. Abbas lived with his parents fifteen years before he and Uncle Kamil met and decided to share a flat and had remained close friends with Hussain until their work separated them. Abbas went to work as a barber's assistant near New Street, and Hussain took a job in a bicycle repair shop in Gamaliya.

From the first, they were of entirely different character: perhaps it was this dissimilarity which strengthened their mutual affection. Abbas was gentle, good-natured, and inclined toward peace, tolerance, and kindness. He was content to fill his leisure time with card playing and idle gossip with his friends at the café.

He avoided participation in quarrels and all unpleasantness by waving both aside with a smile and a kind word for the contestants. He conscientiously performed the prayers and fasted and never missed Friday prayers in the mosque of Hussain. Lately he had tended to neglect some religious duties, not from indifference, but rather out of laziness. However, he still attended Friday prayers and faithfully fasted during the month of Ramadan.

Sometimes disputes occurred between him and Hussain Kirsha, but whenever his friend became too excited Abbas yielded and thus avoided a serious quarrel.

He was known to be easily satisfied and he was often rebuked because he continued to work as a barber's helper for ten years. He had only opened his own little shop five years ago. In that time he thought that he had prospered as well as could be expected. This spirit of satisfaction with his lot was reflected in his quiet eyes, his healthy and vital body, and his perpetually even disposition.

It was agreed that Hussain Kirsha was one of the cleverest people in the alley. He was known for his energy, intelligence, and courage, and he could be most aggressive at times. He had begun by working in his father's café, but because their personalities conflicted he had left to work in a bicycle shop. He remained there until the war broke out and then went to work in a British Army camp. His daily wages were now thirty piasters compared to the three piasters in his first job. All this was apart from what he made by applying his philosophy: "For a decent living you need a nice quick hand!" Thus his standard of living and his finances had increased.

His new wealth afforded him undreamed-of luxuries. He bought new clothes, frequented restaurants, and delighted in eating meat, which he considered a luxury reserved especially for the rich. He attended cinemas and cabarets and found pleasure in wine and the company of women. Frequently his drinking kindled his hospitality and he would invite his friends to the roof of his house, where he would offer them food, wine, and hashish. On one occasion when he was a little drunk he said to his guests, "In England they call those who enjoy my easy life 'large.'" For some time after this his jealous rivals called him "Hussain Kirsha the Large"; later this became corrupted to "Hussain Kirsha the Garage."

Abbas began to tidy up carefully and quickly the back and sides of Hussain's head. He did not disturb the thick mass of wavy hair on top. Meetings with his old friend now usually had a sad effect on him. They were still friends, but life had changed and Abbas missed those evenings when Hussain used to work in his father's café. Now they met only rarely. Then too, Abbas was aware that envy was a part of the wide gulf that now separated them. However, like all his emotions, this new one was under careful control. He never said an unkind word about his friend and he hoped for the same in return. Sometimes, to ease the gnawing envy, he would say to himself, "Soon the war will end and Hussain will return to the alley as penniless as when he left."

Hussain Kirsha, in his usual prattling manner, began telling the barber about life in the depot, about the workers, their good wages, the thefts, about his adventures with the British, and the affection and admiration the soldiers showed him.

"Corporal Julian," he related proudly, "once told me that the only difference between me and the British is that of color. He tells me to be careful with my money, but an arm" (and here he waved wildly) "which can make money during the war can make double that in times of peace. When do you think the war will be over? Don't let the Italian defeat fool you, they didn't matter anyway. Hitler will fight for twenty years! Corporal Julian is impressed with my bravery and has a blind faith in me. He trusts me so much that he has let me in on his big trade in tobacco, cigarettes, chocolate, knives, bedcovers, socks, and shoes! Nice, isn't it?"

"Yes, very," Abbas muttered in reply.

Hussain peered at himself carefully in the mirror and asked Abbas, "Do you know where I'm going now? To the zoo. Do you know who with? With a girl as sweet as cream and honey." He kissed the air noisily. "I'm going to take her to see the monkeys." Roaring with laughter, he continued: "I bet you wonder why the monkeys. That's just what one would expect from someone like you who has only seen trained monkeys. You must learn, you fool, that the zoo monkeys live in groups in the cages. They're just like humans in their actions. You can see them making love or fighting, right in public! When I take this girl there, she'll have as good as opened up the doors for me!"

"Very good," muttered Abbas without interrupting his work.

"Women are an extensive study and one doesn't succeed with wavy hair alone."

"I'm just a poor ignorant fellow," laughed Abbas in reply, looking at his hair in the mirror.

Hussain threw a sharp glance at his reflection in the mirror and asked, "And Hamida?"

The barber's heart skipped a beat. He had not expected to hear her name mentioned. Her image rose before him and he flushed red. "Hamida?"

"Yes. Hamida, the daughter of Umm Hamida."

Abbas took refuge in silence, a look of confusion on his face, while his friend went on: "What a bashful simpleton you are! Your body is asleep, your shop is asleep, your whole life is sleeping. Why should I tire myself out trying to wake you up? You're a dead man. How can this dreary life of yours ever fulfill your hopes? Never! No matter how much you try, you'll only make a bare living."

The barber's pensiveness showed in his eyes as he said half aloud, "It's God who chooses for us."

His young friend said scornfully, "Uncle Kamil, Kirsha's café, smoking a water pipe, playing cards!"

The barber, now really perplexed, asked, "Why do you make fun of this life?"

"Is it a life at all? Everyone in this alley is half dead, and if you live here long, you won't need burying. God have mercy on you!"

Abbas hesitated, then asked, although he could anticipate the reply, "What do you want me to do?"

"The many times I've told you," shouted Hussain. "The times I've given you my advice. Shake off this miserable life, close up your shop, leave this filthy alley behind. Rest your eyes from looking at Uncle Kamil's carcass. Work for the British Army. It's a gold mine that will never be exhausted. Why, it's exactly like the treasure of Hassan al-Basary! This war isn't the disaster that fools say it is. It's a blessing! God sent it to us to rescue us from our poverty and misery. Those air raids are throwing gold down on us!

"I'm still telling you to join the British Army. Italy is finished but Germany isn't defeated and Japan is behind her. The war will last at least another twenty years. I'm telling you for the last time, there are jobs to be had in Tell el-Kebir. Go and get one!"

The barber was so excited he had difficulty in finishing his job. Abbas had a lazy dislike for change, dreaded anything new, hated traveling, and if he were left to himself he would make no choice other than the alley. If he spent the rest of his life there, he would be quite happy. The truth was, he loved it.

Now, however, the image of Hamida rose before him. His hopes and desires and her image formed one indivisible whole. Despite all this, he feared to reveal his true feelings. He knew he must have time to plan and to think. He said aloud, feigning disinterest, "Oh, traveling is such a bore."

Hussain stamped his foot and shouted, "You're the real bore! Going any-where is much better than Midaq Alley, and better than Uncle Kamil. Go and put your trust in God. You've never lived. What have you eaten? What have you drunk? What have you seen? Believe me, you haven't been born yet. . . . Look at your dreary clothes. . . ."

"It's a pity I wasn't born rich."

"It's a pity you weren't born a girl! If you were born a girl, you'd be one of Midaq Alley's many old maids. Your life revolves only around the house. You never even go to the zoo, or to Mousky Street. Do you know that Hamida walks there every afternoon?"

Mention of her name redoubled his confusion and it hurt him that his friend should talk to him so insultingly. "Your sister Hamida is a girl of fine character. There's nothing wrong with her strolling occasionally along the Mousky."

"All right, but she's an ambitious girl, and you'll never win her unless you change your life. . . ."

Abbas's face burned with outrage. He had finished cutting the young man's hair and he set about combing it silently, his thoughts in a turmoil. Eventually Hussain Kirsha rose and paid him, but before he left the shop he discovered that he had forgotten his handkerchief and he hurried back home for it.

Abbas stood watching him and was struck by how purposeful and happy Hussain seemed. It was just as though he was witnessing these things for the first time. "You'll never win her unless you change your life." Surely Hussain was right. His life was mere drudgery. Each day's work scarcely paid for that day's expenses. If he wanted to save in these hard times, it was clear he must try something new. How long could he continue to feed on hopes and dreams? Why shouldn't he try his luck like the others? "An ambitious girl." That's what Hussain had said and he was certainly in a position to know. If the girl he loved was ambitious, then he must acquire ambitions himself. Perhaps tomorrow Hussain would think—and he smiled at the thought—that it was he who had awakened him from his stupor. He knew better, however. He realized that were it not for Hamida, nothing could stir him from this life. Abbas now marveled at the strength of love, its power and its strange magic. He thought it right that God had created mankind capable of love and then left the task of developing life to the fertility of love.

The young man asked himself why he should not leave. He had lived in the alley almost a quarter of century. What had it done for him? It was a place that did not treat its inhabitants fairly. It did not reward them in proportion to their love for it. It tended to smile on those who abused it and abused those who smiled on it. For example, it had barely kept him alive, while it rained wealth on Salim Alwan. There was Salim, a short distance away, piling up bank notes so high that Abbas could almost detect their seductive smell, whereas this palm clutched at what was scarcely the price of bread. Why shouldn't he leave in search of a better life?

These thoughts ran their jagged course as he stood before his shop, gazing at Uncle Kamil, who was snoring loudly, a fly whisk in his lap. He heard steps coming from the top of the alley, and he turned to see Hussain Kirsha striding back down again. He looked at him as a gambler beholds a turning roulette wheel. Hussain approached and almost passed; just then Abbas put his hand on his shoulder. "Hussain, I want to talk to you about something important. . . ."

The alley lay shrouded in darkness and silence. Even Kirsha's café had closed and the customers gone their separate ways. At this late hour Zaita, the cripple-maker, slipped through the door of the bakery, making his rounds. He went down the alley to Sanadiqiya and turned in the direction of the mosque of Hussain, almost colliding with another figure coming toward him in the middle of the road. The man's face was barely visible in the dim starlight.

Zaita called out, "Dr. Booshy! . . . Where did you come from?"

Panting slightly, the "doctor" replied quickly, "I was coming to see you."

"You have some customers who want to be disfigured?"

In a near-whisper, Dr. Booshy answered, "It's more important than that. Abdul Hamid Taliby is dead!"

Zaita's eyes shone in the dark. "When did he die? Has he been buried?"

"He was buried this evening."

"Do you know where his grave is?"

"Between Nasr Gate and the mountain road."

Zaita took him by the arm and walked with him in the direction he was going. To make sure of the situation, he asked, "Won't you lose your way in the dark?"

"Oh no. I followed the burial procession and took particular note of the way. In any case, we both know the road well, we've often been on it in pitch dark."

"And your tools?"

"They're in a safe place in front of the mosque."

"Is the tomb open or roofed?"

"At the entrance there is a room with a roof, but the grave itself is in an open courtyard."

In a faintly sarcastic tone, Zaita asked, "Did you know the deceased?"

"Only slightly. He was a flour merchant in Mabida."

"Is it a full set or just a few?"

"A full set."

"Aren't you afraid his family might have taken it from his mouth before he was buried?"

"Oh no. They are country people and very pious. They would never do that."

Shaking his head sadly, Zaita commented, "The days are over when people left the jewelry of their dead in the grave."

"Those were the days!" sighed Dr. Booshy.

They walked in darkness and silence as far as Gamaliya, passing two policemen on the way, and then drew near Nasr Gate. Zaita took a half cigarette from his pocket. Dr. Booshy was horrified by the lighted match and reminded his companion, "You couldn't have chosen a worse time to have a smoke."

Zaita paid no attention. He walked along, muttering as though to him-self, "There's no profit in the living and very few of the dead are any good!"

They walked through Nasr and turned along a narrow path lined on both sides with tombs, enshrouded in awesome silence and heavy gloom. After they had gone a third of the way down the path, Zaita said, "Here's the mosque."

Dr. Booshy looked about carefully, listening a moment or two, and then moved off toward the mosque, taking care not to make a sound. He exam-ined the ground near a wall at the entrance until he came across a large stone. From under the stone he lifted a small spade and a package contain-ing a candle. He then rejoined his companion and they continued on their way. Suddenly he whispered, "The tomb is the fifth one before the desert path." They hurried on, Dr. Booshy gazing over at the graves to the left of the path, his heart pounding wildly. Presently he slowed down and whis-pered, "This is the tomb." Instead of stopping, however, Dr. Booshy hurried his friend along while giving instructions in a low monotone. "The walls of the burial place overlooking this path are high and the path isn't safe. The best thing for us to do is to skirt through the graves from the desert side and then climb over the back wall of the tomb to where the grave is in the open courtyard."

Zaita listened carefully and they walked in silence until they reached the desert path. Zaita suggested they rest on the roadside curb, from where they could see the path. They sat side by side, their eyes searching the terrain. The darkness and desertion were complete. Behind them as far as the eye could see graves were scattered over the ground, and although this adven-ture was not their first, Dr. Booshy's nerves and pounding heart were weighted with fear. Zaita remained quite calm. When he was sure the path was clear, he instructed the doctor, "Leave the tools, go to the back, and wait for me there."

Dr. Booshy rose quickly and crept between the graves toward the wall. He kept close to it, feeling his way carefully along in the darkness that was broken only by starlight. He counted the walls until he reached the fifth. He stood still, looking about him like a thief; then he sat down cross-legged. His eyes could detect nothing suspicious nor did he hear a sound. However, his uneasiness increased and he grew more and more anxious. Soon he saw Zaita's shape appear a few arm's lengths away and he rose cautiously. Zaita eyed the wall for a moment and then whispered, "Bend down so I can get on your back."

Putting his hands on his knees, Dr. Booshy did as he was told, and Zaita climbed on his back. He felt the wall, gripped the top, and sprang up lightly and easily. He dropped the spade and the candle into the courtyard, extended his hand to Dr. Booshy, and helped pull him to the top of the wall. Together they jumped down and stood at the base gasping for breath. Zaita picked up the spade and the package. Their eyes were now accustomed to the dark and they could see fairly well by the faint light from the stars. They could even see the courtyard quite clearly. There, not far from them, were two tombs side by side, and on the other side of the courtyard they could see the door leading out to the road along which they had come. On each side of the door was a room, and Zaita, pointing toward the two sepulchers, asked, "Which one?"

"On your right . . ." whispered Dr. Booshy, his voice so low that the sound scarcely left his throat.

Without hesitating, Zaita went to the sepulcher, followed by Dr. Booshy, whose whole body was trembling. Zaita bent down and found the ground still cold and damp. He dug his spade carefully and gently into the earth and set to work, piling up the soil between his feet. This was not new to him, and he worked briskly until he had uncovered the flagstones that formed a roof over the entrance to the vault of the sepulcher. He drew up the hem of his gown, gave it a good twist, and tied it up around his waist. Then he grasped the edge of the first flagstone and pulled it up, straining with his muscles until it stood on edge. With Dr. Booshy's help, he drew it out and laid it on the ground. He then did the same with the second flagstone. The uncovered hole was now sufficient for the two of them to slip through and he started down the steps, muttering to the doctor, "Follow me!"

Numb and shivering with fright, Dr. Booshy obeyed. On such occasions Dr. Booshy would sit on the middle step and light a candle, which he would place on the bottom step. He would then close his eyes tight and bury his face between his knees. He hated going into tombs, and he had often pleaded with Zaita to spare him the ordeal. However, his colleague always refused him and insisted he participate in each separate stage. He seemed to enjoy torturing Dr. Booshy in this way.

The wick of the candle was burning now, lighting the interior. Zaita stared stonily at the corpses laid out in their shrouds side by side throughout the length and breadth of the vault, their order symbolizing the sequence of history, the constant succession of time. The fearful silence of the place spoke loudly of eternal extinction, but brought no echo from Zaita. His gaze soon fixed on the new shroud near the entrance to the vault and he sat down beside it cross-legged. He then stretched out his two cold hands, uncovered the head of the corpse and laid bare its lips. He drew out the teeth and put them in his pocket. Then he covered the head as he had found it and moved away from the corpse toward the entrance.

Dr. Booshy still sat with his head between his knees, the candle burning on the bottom step. Zaita looked at him scornfully and mumbled in sarcasm, "Wake up!" Dr. Booshy raised his trembling head and blew out the candle. He raced up the steps as though in retreat. Zaita followed him quickly, but upon emerging from the vault he heard a fearsome scream and the doctor yelping like a kicked dog, "For God's sake have mercy!" Zaita stopped short and then rushed down the steps, icy with fear and not knowing what to do. He retreated backward into the vault until his heel touched the corpse. He moved forward a step and stood glued to the floor, not knowing where to escape to. He thought of lying down between the corpses but before he could make a move he was enveloped in a dazzling light that blinded him. A loud voice shouted out in an Upper Egyptian accent, "Up you come, or I'll fire on you."

In despair, he climbed the steps as ordered. He had completely forgotten the set of gold teeth in his pocket.

The news that Dr. Booshy and Zaita had been apprehended in the Taliby sepulcher reached the alley the next evening. Soon the story and all its details spread, and everyone heard it with a mixture of amazement and alarm. When Mrs. Saniya Afify heard the news, she was overcome with hysteria. Wailing in distress, she pulled the gold teeth from her mouth and flung them away, slapping hysterically at both cheeks. Then she fell down in a faint. Her new husband was in the bathtub, and when he heard her screams, panic struck him. Throwing a robe over his wet body, he rushed wildly to her rescue.

Uncle Kamil was sitting in his chair on the threshold of his shop, lost in a dream, his head resting on his chest. The fly whisk lay in his lap. He was awakened by a tickling sensation on his bald head, and he lifted his hand to brush off what he thought was a fly. His fingers touched a human hand. Angrily he seized it and groaned audibly, lifting his head to seek the prankster who had wakened him from his pleasant slumber. His gaze fell upon Abbas, the barber, and he could scarcely believe his eyes. He stared in blind confusion. Then his bloated red face beamed in delight and he made as if to get up.

His young friend protested at this gesture and hugged him tightly, shouting emotionally, "How are you, Uncle Kamil?"

"How are you, Abbas?" the man replied in delight. "Welcome indeed. You made me very lonely by going away, you bastard!"

Abbas stood before him smiling while Uncle Kamil gazed at him tenderly. He was dressed in a smart white shirt and gray trousers. His head was bare and his curly hair gave him a decidedly appealing look. All in all, he seemed extremely fit.

Uncle Kamil looked him up and down admiringly and said in his high-pitched voice, "My, my! Oh, Johnny, you do look good!"

Abbas, obviously in the best of spirits, laughed heartily and replied in English, "Thank you. . . . From today on Sheikh Darwish is not the only one who can chatter away in English!"

The young man's eyes roved up and down his beloved alley and rested on his old shop. He could see its new owner shaving a customer and he stared longingly in greeting. Then his gaze lifted to the window. He found it closed just as it was when he had arrived. Abbas wondered whether she was home or not, and what she would do if she opened the shutter and saw him there. She would stare at him in delighted surprise while his eyes feasted on her dazzling beauty. This was going to be the happiest day of his life. . . .

His attention was once again drawn to Uncle Kamil's voice asking, "Have you quit your job?"

"Oh no. I've just taken a short holiday?"

"Have you heard what happened to your friend Hussain Kirsha? He left his father and got married. Then they fired him and he came back home, dragging his wife and her brother along behind him."

Abbas looked sad. "What rotten luck! They're firing a lot of people these days. How did Mr. Kirsha welcome him home?"

"Oh, he's never stopped complaining. Anyway, the young man and his family are still in the house."

He sat quietly for perhaps half a minute and then, as though he had just remembered something important, said, "Have you heard that Dr. Booshy and Zaita are in prison?"

Then he related how they had been captured in the Taliby sepulcher and been convicted of stealing a set of gold teeth. This news staggered Abbas. He would not have put it past Zaita to commit the most dreadful evil, but he was amazed that Dr. Booshy was a participant in this ghoulish crime. He recalled how Dr. Booshy had wanted to fit him with gold teeth when he returned from Tell el-Kebir. He shuddered in disgust.

Uncle Kamil continued: "Mrs. Saniya Afify has got married. . . ." He almost added, "Let's hope you do the same." But he stopped suddenly, recalling Hamida. In days to come he was often amazed at his frequent lapses of memory.

However, Abbas noticed no change in Uncle Kamil, as he was quite lost in his dreams. He stepped back a couple of paces and said, "Well then, good-bye for now."

His friend was afraid the news might shock him terribly if it came too suddenly, and he asked hurriedly, "Where are you going?"

"To the café to see my friends," replied Abbas, moving along.

Uncle Kamil rose with some difficulty and shuffled off after his friend.

It was late in the afternoon, and Kirsha and Sheikh Darwish were the only ones in the café. Abbas greeted Kirsha, who welcomed him, and he shook hands with Sheikh Darwish. The old man stared at him smilingly from behind his spectacles but did not speak.

Uncle Kamil stood to one side, gloomily obsessed with thoughts about how he could broach the painful news. At last he spoke: "How about coming back with me to the shop for a while?"

Abbas hesitated between accompanying his friend and making the visit he had dreamed of these past few months. However, he wanted to please Uncle Kamil and he saw no harm in staying with him. He accompanied him, hiding his impatience with small talk.

They sat down and Abbas talked cheerfully. "You know, life in Tell el-Kebir is perfect. There's plenty of work and plenty of money. I haven't been flinging my money about either. I've been quite content to live as I always have. Why, I've only smoked hashish occasionally, even though out there it's as common as air and water. By the way, Uncle Kamil, I even bought this; look at it."

He drew a small box from his trouser pocket and opened it. Inside was a gold necklace with a small dangling heart.

"It's Hamida's wedding present. Didn't you know? I want to get married while I'm on leave this time."

He expected his friend to comment, but Uncle Kamil only turned his eyes away and settled into a heavy silence. Abbas looked at him in alarm and for the first time noticed his friend's gloominess and worried expression. Uncle Kamil's face was not the kind that could camouflage emotions. Abbas was alarmed now. He frowned, shut the box, and returned it to his pocket. He sat staring at his friend, his happy mood extinguished by a strange emotion which he neither expected nor could account for. The gloomy look on his friend's face was so obvious now that he asked suspiciously, "What's wrong, Uncle Kamil? You're not yourself. What's made you change like this? Why won't you look at me?"

The older man raised his head slowly and gazed sadly at him. He opened his mouth to speak, but no words came.

Abbas sensed disaster. He felt despair smothering the last traces of his high spirits and suffocating all his hopes. Now he shouted, "What's wrong with you, Uncle Kamil? What are you trying to say? Something's on your mind. Don't torture me with your silence. Is it Hamida? Yes, by God, it's Hamida. Say it. Tell me. Tell me!"

Uncle Kamil moistened his lips and spoke almost in a whisper: "She's gone. She's not here anymore. She's disappeared. No one knows what's happened to her."

Abbas listened to him in stunned silence. One by one the words engraved themselves on his brain. Thick clouds seemed to swirl over his mind, and he seemed suddenly to have been transported into a whirling, feverish world. In a quivering voice, he asked, "I don't understand a thing. What did you say? She's not here anymore, she's disappeared? What do you mean?"

"Be brave, Abbas," Uncle Kamil said soothingly. "God knows how sorry I am and how grieved I was for you from the very first, but nothing can be done about it. Hamida has disappeared. No one knows anything. She didn't return after going out as usual one afternoon. They searched everywhere for her, but without success. We tried the police station at Gamaliya and Kasr el-Aini Hospital, but we found no trace of her."

Abbas' face took on a vacant stare and he sat rigidly, not saying a word or moving, not even blinking. There was no way out, no escape. Hadn't his instincts warned him of disaster? Yes, and now it was true. Could this be believed? What had the man said? Hamida had disappeared. . . . Can a human being disappear, like a needle or a coin? If he had said she was dead or had got married, then he could foresee an end to his agony. At any rate, despair is easier to accept than torturing doubt. Now what should he do? Even despair was a blessing he could not hope for. Suddenly inertia subsided and he felt a surge of anger. Trembling all over, he glared at Uncle Kamil, and shrieked, "So Hamida has disappeared, has she? And what did all of you do about it? You told the police and looked in the hospital? May God reward you for that. Then what? Then you all returned to work as if nothing had happened. Everything came to an end and you simply returned to your shop and her mother went knocking on brides' doors. Hamida's finished and I'm finished too. What do you say to that, eh? Tell me all you know. What do you know about her disappearance? How did she disappear and when?"

Uncle Kamil was visibly distressed by his friend's outburst of hostility, and he replied sorrowfully, "Nearly two months have passed since she disappeared, my son. It was a terrible thing and everyone was deeply shocked by it. God knows we spared no efforts in searching and inquiring after her, but it was no use."

Abbas slapped the palms of his hands together, his face flushed and his eyes bulging even more. Almost to himself he commented, "Nearly two months! My God! That's a long time. There's no hope of finding her now. Is she dead? Did she drown? Was she abducted? Who can help me find out? What are people saying?"

Gazing at him with sad affection, Uncle Kamil replied, "There were many theories, and people finally concluded she must have had an accident. Nobody talks about it anymore."

"Of course. Of course," the young man exclaimed angrily. "She's not the daughter of any of you and she has no close relatives. Even her mother isn't her real one. What do you think happened? In the past two months I've been dreaming away, happy as could be. Have you ever noticed how a man often dreams of happiness while disaster waits nearby to snatch it? Perhaps I was just having a quiet conversation with a friend while she was being crushed under a wheel or drowning in the Nile . . . two months! Oh, Hamida! . . . There is no power or strength except in God."

Stamping his foot, he rose and made for the door. "Goodbye."

"Where are you going?"

"To see her mother," Abbas answered coldly.

Walking out with heavy dragging feet, Abbas recalled that he had arrived tingling with anticipation and joy; now he left crushed and broken. He bit his lips and his feet came to a halt. He turned and saw Uncle Kamil gazing after him, his eyes filled with tears. Suddenly Abbas rushed into the shop and threw himself on the older man's chest. They stood there whimpering, weeping and sobbing, like two small children.

Did he really have no suspicion of the truth of her disappearance? Did he experience none of the doubts and suspicions common to lovers in similar circumstances? The truth was that whenever a shadow of suspicion had crossed his mind he dismissed it immediately, refusing to harbor it for an instant. By nature Abbas was trusting and always tended to think the best of people. He was tenderhearted and belonged to that minority who instinctively make excuses for others and accept the feeblest excuses for the most fright-ful deeds. Love had not changed his good nature except, perhaps, to make it even stronger; consequently, the whisperings of doubt and suspicion within him went unheard. He had loved Hamida deeply, and he felt completely secure and confident in this love. He truly believed this girl was perfection, in a world of which he had seen so little.

That same day he visited her mother, but she told him nothing new, merely repeating tearfully what Uncle Kamil had said. She assured him that Hamida had never stopped thinking about him, anxiously waiting for his return. Her lies only made him feel sadder, and he left her as heartbroken as he had arrived.

His leaden feet slowly led him out of the alley. Dusk was falling now; it was the time when, in days gone by, he would catch sight of his beloved going out for her evening stroll. He wandered aimlessly, unaware of what was going on about him, but seeming to see her form in its black gown, her large and beautiful eyes searching for him. He recalled their last farewell on the stairs and his heart seemed to stop dead.

Where was she? What had God done with her? Was she still alive or in a pauper's grave? Why had his heart had no warning all this time? How could this happen? And why?

The crowds in the street jolted him from his dreams and he stared around him. This was the Mousky, her favorite street. She loved the crowds and the shops. Everything was just the same as before, except for her. Now she was gone. It was almost as if she had never existed. He wanted to cry out all the tears in his swollen heart but he would not give way. His weep-ing in Uncle Kamil's arms had unknotted his nerves a bit. Now he only felt a deep, quiet sadness.

He wondered what he should do next. Should he go to the police stations and the hospital? What was the point? Should he walk the streets of the city calling out her name? Should he knock on the doors of all the houses one by one? Oh God, how weak and helpless he felt. Should he return to Tell el-Kebir and try to forget everything? But why go back? Why bear the additional strain of being away from home? Why go on working and saving money? Life without Hamida was an insupportable burden and completely without purpose. His enthusiasm for life was gone now, leaving him with nothing but a numbing indifference. His life seemed a bottomless void enclosed by a black despair. Through his love for her he had discovered the only meaning of his life. Now he saw no reason for living. He continued walking, bewildered and purposeless. Whether he knew it or not, life still had a hold on his consciousness, for he was quick to notice the factory girls coming toward him, returning from work. Before he knew it he had blocked their path. They stopped in surprise and immediately recognized him. Without hesitating, he spoke: "Good evening, girls. Please don't be angry with me. You remember your friend Hamida?"

A vivacious pretty girl was quick to reply, "Of course we remember her. She suddenly disappeared and we haven't seen her since!"

"Do you have any clues to her disappearance?" A different girl, with a look of spiteful cunning in her eyes, answered him, "We only know what we told her mother when she questioned us. We saw her several times with a well-dressed man in a suit, walking in the Mousky."

An icy shudder shook his whole body, as he asked, "You say you saw her with a man in a suit?"

The cruel look now left the girl's eyes as they registered the young man's anguish. One girl spoke softly: "Yes, that's right."

"And you told her mother that?"

"Yes."

He thanked them and walked away. He was certain they would talk about him all the way home. They would have a good laugh about the young fool who went to Tell el-Kebir to earn more money for his fiancée, who left him for a stranger who appealed to her more. What a fool he had been! Probably the whole quarter was gossiping about his stupidity. Now he knew that Uncle Kamil concealed the raw truth, just as Hamida's foster mother had. In a state of complete confusion he told himself, "I was afraid this might happen!" Now all he could remember were those very faint doubts.

Now he was moaning and muttering, "Oh God! How can I believe it? Has she really run off with another man? Who would ever believe it?" She was alive, then. They were wrong to look for her in the police station and the hospital. They had not realized she was sleeping contentedly in the arms of the man she had run off with. But she had promised herself to him! Had she meant to deceive him all along? Or was she mistaken in thinking she was attracted to him. . . . How did she meet the man in the suit? When did she fall in love with him? Why did she run off with him?

Abbas' face had now turned ghastly white and he felt cold all over. His eyes glowered darkly. Suddenly he raised his head, gazing at the houses in the street. He looked at their windows and asked himself, "In which one is she now lying at her lover's side?" The seeds of doubt were now gone and a burning anger mixed with hatred took its place. His heart was twisted by jealousy. Or was it disappointment? Conceit and pride are the fuel of jealousy and he had little of either. But he did have hopes and dreams and now they were shattered. Now he wanted revenge, even if it only meant spitting at her. In fact, revenge took such possession of him that he longed to knife her treacherous heart.

Now he knew the true meaning of her afternoon walks: she had been parading before the street wolves. Anyway, she must be in love with this man in the suit; otherwise how could she prostitute herself rather than marry Abbas?

He bit his lip at the thought and turned back, tired from walking alone. His hand touched the box with the necklace in his pocket, and he gave a hollow laugh that was more an angry scream. If only he could strangle her with the gold necklace. He recalled his joy in the goldsmith's shop when he selected the gift. The memory flowed through him like a gentle spring breeze, but, meeting the glare of his troubled heart, it was transformed into a raging sirocco. . . .

Perhaps the only hour of her past life that Hamida missed was her late-afternoon walk. Now she spent that hour standing before the huge gold-trimmed mirror in her room.

Having spent an hour painstakingly dressing and applying her makeup, she now looked like a woman who from birth had known only the luxuries of life. On her head she wore a white silk turban, under which her oiled and scented hair curled appealingly. She knew from long experience that her bronze skin was more attractive to the Allies, and so she left it its natural color. She applied violet-tinted shadow to her eyelids and carefully waxed and separated her lashes, their silky ends curling upward. Two graceful arches were drawn in place of her eyebrows. Her lips were painted a lush scarlet that accented her dazzling white teeth. Large lotus-shaped pearls dangled on chains from her ears. She wore a gold wristwatch, and a diamond-studded crescent brooch was pinned to her turban. The low neck of her white dress revealed a pink undergarment, and her short skirt drew attention to well-shaped legs. She wore flesh-colored silk stockings for no reason except that they were expensive. Perfume wafted from her palms, neck, and armpits. Things had indeed changed for Hamida!

From the very beginning Hamida chose her path of her own free will. Experience had shown her that her future life would be gaiety and pleasure mixed with pain and bitter disappointment. Hamida realized she had arrived at a critical point in her life. Now she stood perplexed and not sure where to turn.

She knew from the first day what was expected of her. Her instinctive reaction was to rebel. This she had done, not in the hope of breaking her lover's iron will, but simply for the love of the consequent battle. When eventually she gave way to the eloquence of Ibrahim Faraj, it was because she wished to do so. Hamida had entered into her new life with no regrets. She had justified her lover's comment that she was a "whore by instinct." Her natural talents made a stunning display; indeed, in a short time she had thoroughly mastered the principles of makeup and dress, even though at first everyone made fun of her vulgar taste. She had now learned Oriental and Western dancing, and she also showed a quick ear for learning the sexual principles of the English language. It was not surprising that she had become so successful. She was a favorite of the soldiers and her savings were proof of her popularity.

Hamida had never known the life of a simple respectable girl. She had no happy memories of the past and was now quite engrossed in the enjoyable present. Her case was different from that of the majority of the other girls, who had been forced by necessity or circumstances into their present life and were often tormented by remorse. Hamida's dreams of clothes, jewelry, money, and men were now fulfilled and she enjoyed all the power and authority they gave her.

One day she recalled how miserable she had been the first time when Ibrahim Faraj said he did not want to marry her. She had asked herself if she really wanted to marry him. The answer, in the negative, had come immediately. Marriage would have confined her to the home, exhausting her with the duties of a wife, housekeeper, and mother; all those tasks she knew she was not created for. She now saw how farsighted he had been.

Despite this, Hamida still felt strangely restless and dissatisfied. Not entirely ruled by her sexual instincts, she longed for emotional power. It was perhaps because she knew she had not achieved control over her lover that her attachment to him increased, along with her feeling of resentment and disillusion.

This, then, was her state of mind as she stood before the mirror. Suddenly she saw his reflection as he hurried toward her; his face wore the look of a merchant who was just about to engage in a profitable transaction. He no longer bore the tender look of a man pleased with his new conquest. It was true he had encountered no resistance to the seduction. Many times since then she recalled that for a full fortnight she was saturated in what she believed to be his full capacity for love. Then his commercial instincts overcame her lover and he gradually revealed himself as the sex merchant he was.

He himself had never known love, and it seemed strange to the romantically inclined girl that his whole life should be built on this sentiment. Whenever a new girl fell into his net, he played the part of the ardent lover— until she succumbed; after that he continued to court her for a short time. From then on he had made sure of his influence by making her dependent upon him emotionally and financially; often he even threatened to expose her to the police. When his mission was accomplished he dropped his role of lover for that of the flesh merchant.

Hamida concluded that his sudden indifference to her was the result of his constantly being surrounded by girls eager for his attention. She was obsessed with mixed feelings of love, hostility, and suspicion as she stood looking at his reflection in the mirror.

To give the impression that he was in a hurry, Ibrahim Faraj said quickly, "Have you finished, my darling?"

She determined to show her disapproval of his preoccupation with her trade by ignoring him. She sadly recalled those days and nights when he spoke only of his love and admiration for her. Now he spoke only of the work and profit. It was this work, together with the tyranny of her own emotions, which now prevented her emancipation. She no longer had that freedom for which she had risked her whole life.

Hamida only felt a sense of powerful independence when she was soliciting on the streets or in a tavern. The rest of the time she was tortured by a sense of imprisonment and humiliation. If only she were sure of his affection, if only he knew the humiliation of loving her, then she could feel victorious. Hostility toward him was her only escape from her predicament.

Faraj was aware of her animosity, but he hoped she would become accustomed to his coldness, so that she would offer a minimum of resistance to the separation he planned. He thought it best to move slowly before delivering the decisive blow.

"Come, my darling, time is money." His tone was gentle but businesslike.

"When will you stop using those vulgar terms?" she asked, turning suddenly toward him.

"When will you, my darling, stop talking nonsense?"

"So now you think you can talk to me that way?" she shrieked.

Putting on a bored expression, he answered, "That's right. . . . Are we off on that old subject again? Must I say 'I love you' every time we meet? Can't what we feel be love without interfering with our work by talking about it constantly? I wish your brains were as sharp as your tongue and that you would dedicate your life, as I do mine, to our work and put it before everything else."

She stood listening, her face pale, to his ice-cold words, without a trace of feeling. This was merely a repetition of what she had now heard countless times from him. She recalled how cleverly he had planned all this by first criticizing her. One day he had examined her hands and said, "Why don't you take better care of your hands; let your nails grow and put polish on them. Your hands are a weak point, you know."

On another occasion he said after a stormy quarrel, "Be careful. You have a serious flaw I've not noticed before—your voice, my darling. Scream from your mouth, not from your larynx. It's a most ugly sound. It must be worked on. Those traces of Midaq Alley must be removed. Remember, your clients now come to see you in the best section of Cairo."

These words had hurt and humiliated her more than any she had ever heard in her life. Whenever she brought up the matter of her love for him he would avoid a discussion and soothe her with flattery about her work. Recently he had even dropped his false show of affection, and once he told her, "Get to work, my dear, 'love' is only a silly word."

Damn him! Indignantly she commented, "You have no right to talk like that to me. You know perfectly well that I work hard and make more money for you than all the other girls put together. So just remember that! I'm fed up with all your cunning. Just tell me honestly whether you still love me or not."

Now, he told himself, was the time to tell her. His almond-shaped eyes looked intently into her face as his mind worked furiously. He decided to choose peace for the time being. Doing his best to humor her, he said, "We're on that same old subject, as usual. . . ."

"Tell me," exploded Hamida. "Do you think I'll die of grief if you deny me your love?"

The time was not right. If she asked him that question when she returned from work in the early morning, he would have more room to maneuver. Now if he told her the truth, he would risk losing the entire profits for the day.

"I love you, darling . . ." he said softly, moving toward her.

How filthy it sounded coming from him now. Utter mortification swept over her and she felt she would never be able to stop despising herself, even if he were to guarantee to come back to her arms. For a fleeting moment she felt that his love was something worth sacrificing the world for, but a feeling of spitefulness welled up quickly within her and she stepped a few paces nearer to him, her eyes glinting like the diamond brooch pinned to her turban. Determined to carry on the argument to its ultimate end, Hamida went on: "So you really love me? Then let's get married!"

His eyes revealed his astonishment, and he looked at her only half believing what he had heard. "Would marriage change our situation?" he asked in reply.

"Yes, it would. Let's get married and get out of this kind of life."

His patience quite exhausted, he made a firm decision. He would deal with this matter with the candor and severity it deserved and so carry out what had long been running through his mind, even though it would probably mean the loss of the night's profits. He broke into loud, sarcastic laughter and said:

"A brilliant idea, my darling! We'll get married and live like lords. Ibrahim Faraj and His Wife and Children, Incorporated! But really, what is marriage? I seem to have forgotten all about it, just like the other social graces. Let me think for a moment. . . . Marriage . . . is a very serious thing, I seem to remember. It unites a man and a woman. There is a marriage official, a religious contract, and all kinds of rites. . . . When did you learn that, Faraj? In the Quran or in school? I've forgotten where. Tell me, my darling, are people still getting married?"

Hamida was now trembling from head to foot. Suddenly she could restrain herself no longer. In one swift leap she reached for his throat. He anticipated her sudden action and met her attack with complete calm. Seizing her arms, he forced them apart and then released her, the mocking smile still on his lips. Hamida raised her arm and slapped his face with all her strength. His smile faded, and an evil, threatening look came into his eyes. She stared back at him challengingly, impatiently waiting for the battle to begin. He was well aware that to engage in physical combat with her would only mean a strengthening of the ties he wished to sever and so he withdrew without defending himself. He retreated a step, turned his back on her, and walked off, saying, "Please come to work, my darling."

Hamida refused to believe her eyes as she stood there looking at the door through which he had disappeared. She knew what his retreat meant. She was suddenly consumed with an irresistible urge to kill this man.

Hamida felt she must leave that house at once. Walking heavily toward the door, she realized that she was leaving that room, their room, for the last time. She turned around as though to say farewell to it.

Suddenly she felt as though she would faint. Oh God! How had everything come to an end so quickly? This mirror, how often she had looked
into it so full of happiness. And the bed, which harbored so much love-
making and so many dreams. That settee where she had often been in his
arms, listening to his advice amidst caresses. There was the dressing table
with a picture of them both in evening dress. In one swift dash she fled
from the room.

The hot air of the street almost scorched her and she could scarcely
breathe. She walked along saying to herself, "I'll murder him!" That would
be a consolation, if she didn't have to pay for his life with her own. She
knew that her love would always remain a scar deep within her, but she was
not the sort of woman love could actually destroy. This thought cheered her
a little and she waved to the driver of a carriage she saw approaching. She
climbed in, feeling an urgent need for more air and a rest.

She told the driver, "Drive first to Opera Square and then come back
along Fuad I Street. And drive carefully, please."

She sat in the middle of the seat, leaning back comfortably with her legs
crossed. Her short silk dress revealed a portion of leg above her knees. She
lit a cigarette and puffed it nervously, unaware of passersby staring at the
flesh she revealed.

Hamida sat completely engrossed in her thoughts. A variety of future
hopes and dreams came to comfort her, but it never occurred to her that she
might discover a new love to make her forget this old one.

After some time she turned her attention to the road. The open carriage
was now circling around in front of the Opera House and in the distance she
caught sight of Queen Farida Square. Her thoughts flew from there up to the
Mousky, New Street, Sanadiqiya Street, and Midaq Alley, and shadowy figures of men and women from the past flitted before her eyes. She wondered
whether any of them would recognize her if they were to see her now. Would
they see Hamida underneath Titi? Why should she care anyway? After all,
she had no father or mother of her own. She finished the cigarette and threw
it from the carriage.

Settling back, she enjoyed the ride until the carriage returned to Sharif
Street and made its way toward the tavern where she worked. Just then she

heard a shrill cry rend the air: "Hamida!" She turned in terror and saw Abbas, the barber, only an arm's length away from her.

Translated by Trevor Le Gassick

from *The Beginning and the End*, 1949

The novel is set in Cairo of the 1930s and tells a grim tale of the fate of the members of a family living in poverty, with crime and drugs an integral part of it.

It was midnight. There were only a few customers at the Al Gamal café, which was now almost empty. Hassan's companions had left and he was sitting alone at a table. The piasters he had managed to gain from them were safely tucked in his pocket. As though deep in thought, he cast a languid look about the café with his tired eyes. The owner of the café began to check his daily accounts, heaping the metal counters on a large tin plate, while the waiter stood leaning against one of the door panels, his hand in the pocket of his apron, temptingly jingling the coins inside it. Hassan's thoughts rambled off. *My father, may the mercy of God be on you. How much I have suffered since your death! We never ceased to quarrel and sometimes I felt I hated you. But your days are gone! Since your death, I haven't taken a meal at home except on the feast days. And what do they eat at home? I eat nothing but beans. Beans. Always beans. Even donkeys get a change in diet. Maybe I really should seriously search for a job.*

He remembered that he had tried his luck twice and that each time had ended in a quarrel that almost sent him to jail. No. Such trivial jobs were not his aim. He still preferred the life of a vagabond and mean gambler. In fact, he lived by stealing. He and his coterie knew this perfectly well. They would ensnare the new customers at the café and give them the illusion that they were playing a fair game of cards. But the truth was that they were stealing from them. It was a hard, risky life for the sake of a few piasters. How could he be satisfied with this kind of life? He was neither happy nor contented.

He seemed to be waiting for a miracle to save him from the depths his life had reached and take him to a land of dreams. On the whole, his life was as violent and as savage as the murderous drug he was taking. Jobless though he was, he remained a leader among his company, because he could strike awe and fear in their hearts. Thus, he found it unbearable to start a new life as a simple and obedient worker, even though he was fully aware of how much his mother needed him to develop a serious attitude toward life. He still heard her afflicted and complaining voice humming in his ears, never ceasing to chase him whenever he came out of the stupor of drugs. He loved his mother and family. But he did not exert the slightest effort; he kept waiting inertly for something to happen, and remained at the bottom of the ladder, doing this donkey work for the sake of a few piasters. To him, this seemed a folly even worse than . . .

"Good evening, Mr. Hassan," came a voice in greeting.

Emerging from the mist of his thoughts, he raised his head to see Master Ali Sabri sitting in front of him, calm and proud.

"Good evening, Master," Hassan cried, his heart full of delight.

The so-called master summoned the waiter and ordered a narghile. Then he turned to Hassan.

"I have decided that we should work together. I want you to join my band," he said at once.

Hassan's eyes, opening wide, suddenly glistened. Working for the master's music band was the only thing he liked, not because he was aesthetically disposed to this kind of work, but because it was light, pleasurable, and usually associated with the fragrance of liquor, drugs, and women's perfume. Though he never expected much from Ali Sabri, he thought the offer was better than nothing. Perhaps it would lead to other things. Who could tell?

"Do you mean it, Master?" Hassan said.

"Sure."

"Will we be working in a music hall or a café?"

"Maybe one day soon we'll have a place at the broadcasting station. But for the time being, we'll be playing at weddings," the master said, passing his long, lean fingers through his unruly hair.

Hassan's enthusiasm died. Had he been dealing with anybody other than Ali Sabri, on whom he still pinned some hope, he would have given him a stunning blow and sent him flying head over heels. He had actually worked with him at a few family parties in return for supper and a twenty-piaster piece, but only a few times a year. There was nothing new in this. Yet he felt a hidden motive behind this offer, and new hope stirred in his breast. He feigned delight.

"There is no doubt," he said, "that you will one day occupy the place you deserve. Your voice is superior to that of Abdul Wahab himself."

Ali Sabri grinned. "Which of the instruments of the band do you want to play?" he asked. "You told me that your late father was an excellent lute player."

"I haven't learned to play any instrument at all."

"Not even the tambourine?"

"You tried me out as a Sannid, chanting refrains for you, and I think I'm the right man for the job."

The master shook his head as he said, "As you like. Do you know many songs?"

"Yes. Mawawil, songs, and takatiqs."

"How about a solo right now?"

At bottom, Hassan felt disdain for the pomposity of his companion, but he was determined to go along with him to the end. He was dreaming of one day becoming an independent singer, even in low popular coffeehouses. He waited until the waiter came back with the narghile and the master enjoyed his first puffs.

"What would you say to my singing the mawal 'My Eyes, Why Are You Weeping?' for you?" Hassan asked with a cough.

"Excellent."

As best as he could, Hassan began to chant the mawal in a low voice, while the other man kept moving his head forward and backward, pretending to be absorbed in the song. When Hassan finished he said, "For a Sannid, that's more than enough, but I should like to hear you singing Hank, too. Do you know the song 'How I Waited When I Lost Your Love'?"

Hassan coughed again, clearing his throat, his enthusiasm grew, and he began to sing with more zest. He sang without a pause to the end.

"Excellent. Excellent. Do you know the basic tunes, Sica, Biati, Hijaz, and so on?" the master asked.

Sure of the master's ignorance of those tunes, Hassan answered, with extraordinary daring that others rarely exhibited. "Of course."

"Chant the Laiali 'Rast' for me."

He chanted the first Laiali that came to his mind.

"Bravo. Chant another—a Nahawound," Ali Sabri said, shaking his head.

Hassan continued to sing, suppressing a feeling of inward sarcasm. The other man was following him, feigning attention. Suddenly, he looked meditative and seemed to have something important to say. Instinctively, Hassan was waiting for this moment. Perplexed, he wondered whether Ali Sabri wanted to appoint him to lead a fight. What did he want precisely?

"Your voice is good enough. But working for the band requires other talents and skills. Here we must be in complete agreement. For instance, you should know all about propaganda methods, too," the master said.

"Propaganda!"

"Yes. You should, for example, speak highly of my art whenever an occasion arises. You should also persuade people to ask me to sing at their marriage ceremonies. You will get your reward, of course. When you are at a songfest held by another singer, you should criticize his voice and tell everyone around you how wonderful Ali Sabri would have been if he had been singing instead, and so on."

"That's easy. You can expect even more," Hassan said with a smile on his face.

Ali Sabri paused for a moment, and then said, "You are a strong and daring young man, and you should exploit your talents to the utmost. But let me ask you one more question. Which narcotic most appeals to you?"

Hassan wondered what made him ask such a question. Did he want to offer him a present? Impossible. He was always ready to accept presents, and generosity was certainly not part of his personality. Or was he seeking his collaboration on an important task? His heart fluttered at such a thought. He had long dreamt of trafficking in narcotics. Yet, he decided to be wary and on his guard.

"I think narcotics harm the throat," he said slyly.

Ali Sabri laughed. With a thunderous and powerful voice, he started to sing a Laiali.

"What do you think of that singing?" he asked when he finished.

"Peerless."

Ali Sabri went on to say, "This is what comes of fifteen years of addiction to hashish, opium, and manzoul, and five years of taking cocaine as well."

"You don't say!"

"Narcotics are the very lifeblood of vocalizing. Any singer worthy of the name is as much addicted to drugs as he is to such basic foods as molokhiya and fool mudammis."

Hassan laughed. "Only if those drugs are available," he said, surrendering.

"You are right. And it is as I thought. You don't hate narcotics, but you have no access to them. Let me tell you, it is easy to turn rivers of water into rivers of wine, and mountains into mountains of hashish. You are both daring and strong. But I will be frank with you; I was very much afraid!"

"Of what?"

Ali Sabri gave a short laugh that revealed his yellow teeth. "Of all people," he said, "I hate most those who say, 'My morals won't allow me to do this' or 'I have fear of God' or those who fearfully ask, 'What about the police?' Now, are you one of them?"

Hassan smiled, feeling that he would be well rewarded for his long patience.

"I live in this world, assuming that there is no morality, God, or police," he said.

Ali Sabri erupted in a powerful laugh that shook the café as much as his singing, and said, "Let's spend the rest of the night at my place and continue our talk."

Hassan agreed, hoping some profitable scheme would come of all this. His confidence never failed him for a single moment, but he had little faith in his interlocutor. However, he had not quite given up hope in him. Deep down, he felt that he would have to wait a long time before the earth, shaking underneath his feet, became stable once more.

At the sound of the word "policeman," their souls burst apart like shrapnel. Hassanein leapt to his feet, staring at the servant. Hassan flung one of his feet from the bed to the floor. With a gruesome glance at the window, he muttered, "Escape!" Their mother looked dazedly from one son to the other, her throat so dry that she was unable to utter a word. Hassanein remained momentarily immobile. Realizing how stupid it was just to stand there doing nothing, he shrugged his shoulders in despair and went to the policeman at the door. They exchanged salutes.

"Yes?" Hassanein inquired.

"Am I addressing the respected officer Hassanein Kamel Ali?" the man asked gruffly.

"You are."

"The respected officer of Al Sakakini police station wants to see you at once."

Looking beyond the policeman as far as the road, Hassanein was reassured when he saw none of the faces he might have expected. Uncertain, he inquired, "What does he want me for?"

"He ordered me only to inform you that he wanted to see you."

Hassanein hesitated a little. Then he went to the room to put on his clothes. He found his brother eavesdropping behind the door. At once Hassan asked anxiously, "Have they come?" In a sickly, feeble voice his mother repeated the question. As he dressed, Hassanein recounted the conversation with the policeman.

"Perhaps," Hassan spoke up immediately, "this officer is one of your acquaintances. Maybe he wants to alert you before they ambush the house. This is clear enough. Listen to me. If he asks you about me, tell him you haven't seen me for ages. Don't hesitate and don't be afraid about lying to them, for they'll never be able to trace me. As soon as you leave, I'll disappear. So have no scruples about what you tell them. May God protect you!"

Hassanein hid his eyes from his brother lest they reveal the gleam of an emerging hope. "Are you strong enough to make your escape?" he asked.

Hassan snatched his suit from the peg. "I'm all right," he said. "Goodbye!"

Hassanein went off with the policeman. The first thing to occur to him was to ask the officer's name. Maybe he actually was one of his acquaintances. But he was once more in the dark when the policeman gave him a name he had never heard before. Now matters were complicated indeed. However, Hassanein was relieved and reassured at Hassan's decision to disappear. They reached the police station a little before sunset, and the policeman led him to the officer, stopped, and saluted.

"Lieutenant Hassanein Kamel Ali," he said.

At arm's length from the officer as he sat at his desk stood two lower-class men and a woman, the marks of a recent fight on their faces. The officer rose, stretched out his hand.

"Welcome!" he said. He ordered the policeman to leave the room and close the door. He waved the young man to a chair in front of the desk.

What does it all mean? Hassanein thought as he sat down. *Welcome and compliments. What next?*

The officer rose, and leaning with his right hand on the edge of the desk, stood facing Hassanein, carefully studying his face; a curious, perplexed sort of glance, as if he didn't quite know how to begin the conversation. Hassanein found this short interval of silence coarse and intolerable. An abhorrent feeling of awe, worry, and annoyance had come over him from the very moment he stepped into the station.

Maybe he's a refined officer and is too embarrassed to fling the charge in my face, he thought. *This is curious in itself. Speak out and take the burden off my chest. How much I've dreaded this nightmarish moment. I already know what you want to say. Speak.*

"The policeman said you wanted to see me," he said, losing his patience.

"Sorry to bother you," the officer apologized. "I'd have preferred to meet you under better circumstances. But you know what duty dictates sometimes!"

Breathing out his last hope of safety, Hassanein replied gloomily, "Thank you for your kindness. I'm listening."

"I hope you'll take what I have to say with courage," the officer said earnestly and gently, "and behave in a manner that suits an officer who respects the law."

Hassanein was wan and almost fainting. "Naturally," he said.

The officer clenched his teeth, his cheeks contracting. "This," he said curtly, "has to do with your sister."

Hassanein raised his eyebrows in surprise. "You mean my brother?" he said.

"I mean Madam, your sister. But excuse me. First I should like to ask you: Do you have a sister by the name of Nefisa?"

"Yes. Has she had an accident?" Hassanein asked.

"I'm sorry to tell you this," the man said, lowering his eyes, "but she was arrested in a certain house in Al Sakakini."

Hassanein rose to his feet. Frightened, rigid, and pale, he stared at the officer. "What are you saying?" he asked, out of breath.

The officer patted his shoulder sympathetically. "Get hold of yourself," he said. "This has to be handled with reason and calm judgment. I hope you'll help me do my duty without making me regret the measures I've taken to protect your reputation."

Staggered, Hassanein stared at the officer, listened vaguely to his voice. As if in a dream, the voice would vanish, the face remain; the face vanished, the voice remained, sometimes only two lips spewing forth a stream of frightful, disconnected, incomprehensible words. Despairing, Hassanein glanced nervously around the room, his eyes blinking: a gun fixed on the wall here, a row of rifles there, an inkstand, and the strange odors, the dead smell of old tobacco, the strange scent of leather. In a kind of receding consciousness, his mind harked back to memories which had no connection with the present. The old alley floated in his mind's eye; now he was again a boy playing with marbles with his brother Hussein.

She was arrested in a certain house, he thought. *What house? Surely one of us has lost his mind! But which one of us? First, I've got to be sure that I've not gone crazy.*

Resigned, Hassanein sighed weakly. "What did you say, sir?" he asked the officer.

"A Greek woman has a house in this quarter," the officer continued. "She rents rooms to lovers at so much per hour. This afternoon, we raided the house, and found Madam . . . with a young man. We arrested her, of course, and I proceeded with the customary cold-blooded formalities, of which, of course, she was frightened, you know, and in the hope that I would release her, she confided that her brother was an officer."

"My own sister? Are you sure? Let me see her."

"Please control yourself. Had I been sure she was your sister, I'd have released her. But I was afraid she was lying. So I referred the matter to my boss, the Mamur. He approved of suspending legal action on condition that we could prove the truth of what she was saying."

Curiously enough, Hassanein entertained no doubt about the identity of the arrested girl. Yes, his pessimistic heart told him, it's got to be Nefisa. Was this the end of his journey in life? In his state of shock, he felt like some ancient relic of the past, of no relevance to the present. He was eager to get it all over with.

"Where is she?" he said in a lifeless voice. "Please let me see her."

The officer pointed to a closed door. "She fainted when she knew I'd sent for you instead of setting her free, so we left her in this room. Conduct yourself like a man with respect for law and remember I'm responsible for security. You're a decent, respectable man. So use your head. Nobody in this police station needs to know anything about it. But don't forget, everything depends on you."

"Please let me see her," Hassanein repeated in the same lifeless voice.

With heavy steps, the officer walked to the door and opened it. Like a sleepwalker Hassanein approached, casting a glance over the officer's shoulder like a man entering a morgue to identify a corpse. Close to the wall facing the door, a girl huddled against a sofa, her head flung back, her eyes half closed, dim, unseeing. She was either unconscious or had just recovered. Her face was as pale as death, and a few wet strands of hair stuck to her forehead. It was unmistakably Nefisa.

When it comes to disaster, he thought, *my heart never lies to me. If she was dead, I'd disown her without hesitation.* Unaware of their presence, she remained motionless, perhaps too exhausted to move. The officer looked inquiringly at him. But Hassanein's eyes became glazed as he stared at his sister. Surprisingly, in the deathlike silence, he found a temporary escape from his agony. Oblivious of the passage of time, he seemed to hear a terrible inner voice shattering the silence: *Everything is finished!* it proclaimed. He recalled the scene at home before he had left, an hour earlier, his mother desperate and perplexed, standing between him and Hassan, who was then preparing to escape. His mind filled with blasphemous imprecations, Hassanein wished he might die.

What does the officer expect me to do? he thought. *What should I do? Oh, God! How can I leave this place?* He heard the man address him. "I've done my duty. The rest is up to you."

"Where is the other?" Hassanein asked, avoiding the officer's eyes.

Understanding his meaning at once, the officer replied rather sternly, "After the usual legal routine, I released him."

"Thanks," Hassanein murmured. "Let's get out of here."

Translated by Ramses Awad

from *The Cairo Trilogy*, 1956–57

If one had to choose a single work by which Mahfouz will be remembered, the choice would inevitably be *The Cairo Trilogy*.

He has said that it took him no less than seven years to perfect this novel, before it was completed in 1952. Originally he had given it the title "Palace Walk." To Mahfouz's dismay, his publisher first rejected the book as being too long. It was then serialized in the literary magazine of his day, *al-Risala al-jadida*. Later the publisher changed his mind, but demanded that the book be divided into three books, each with a different title. And so the trilogy was born, coming out under the titles *Palace Walk*, *Palace of Desire*, and *Sugar Street*.

The events of the novel start in the middle of the First World War and end toward the end of the Second World War. In between, it tells the story of the change that Egypt goes through, as reflected in the family of Abd al-Jawwad.

Rasheed El-Enany, in his book about Naguib Mahfouz, sums up its contents as follows: "There is no other source, literary or otherwise, that records with such detail and liveliness the habits, sentiments, and living environment of Cairene Egyptians at the beginning of the century." It was no doubt this literary masterpiece that made of the author the first writer in Arabic to be awarded the Nobel Prize in Literature.

from *Palace Walk*

A feeling spread through the household that they would have a day's reprieve from their oppressively prim life. Safe from their guardian's eye, they would be able, if they so desired, to get an innocent breath of fresh air. Kamal was of the opinion that he could do as he wished and spend the whole day playing, inside the house and out. Khadija and Aisha wondered if they might slip over to Maryam's house in the evening to spend an hour there having fun and amusing themselves.

This break did not come as a result of the passing of the gloomy winter months and the arrival of the first signs of spring with intimations of warmth and good cheer. It was not occasioned by spring granting this family liberty they had been deprived of by winter. This respite came as a natural consequence of a business trip, lasting a day or more, that al-Sayyid Ahmad made to Port Said every few years. It so happened that he set out on a Friday morning when the weekly holiday brought the family together. They all responded eagerly to the freedom and the peaceful, relaxed atmosphere the father's departure from Cairo had unexpectedly created.

The mother hesitantly dashed the girls' hopes and the young boy's high spirits. She wanted to make sure the family persisted with its customary schedule and adhered, even when the father was absent, to the same rules it observed when he was present. She was more concerned to keep from vexing him than she was convinced that he was right to be so severe and stern.

Before she knew what was happening, though, here was Yasin saying, "Don't oppose God's plan. . . . Nobody else lives like us. In fact, I want to say something novel. . . . Why don't you have some fun too? What do you all think about this suggestion?"

Their eyes looked at him in astonishment, but no one said a word. Perhaps, like their mother, who gave him a critical look, they did not take what he was saying seriously. All the same, he continued: "Why are you looking at me like this? I haven't contravened any of the directives of the Prophet recorded in the revered collection of al-Bukhari. Praise God, no crime has been committed. All it would amount to is a brief excursion to have a look at a little of the district you've lived in for forty years but never seen."

The woman sighed and murmured, "May God be merciful to you."

The young man laughed out loud. He said, "Why should you ask God to be merciful to me? Have I committed some unforgivable sin? By God, if I were you, I'd go as far as the mosque of our master al-Husayn. . . . Our master al-Husayn, don't you hear? . . . Your beloved saint whom you adore from afar when he's so near. Go to him. He's calling you."

Her heart pounded and the effect could be seen in her blush. She lowered her head to hide how deeply she was affected. Her heart responded to the call with a force that exploded suddenly in her soul. She was taken by surprise. No one around her could have anticipated this, not even Yasin himself. It was as though an earthquake had shaken a land that had never experienced one before. She did not understand how her heart could answer this appeal, how her eyes could look beyond the limits of what was allowed, or how she could consider the adventure possible and even tempting, no—irresistible. Of course, since it was such a sacred pilgrimage, a visit to the shrine of al-Husayn appeared a powerful excuse for the radical leap her will was making, but that was not the only factor influencing her soul. Deep inside her, imprisoned currents yearning for release responded to this call in the same way that eager, aggressive instincts answer the call for a war proclaimed to be in defense of freedom and peace.

She did not know how to announce her fateful surrender. She looked at Yasin and said in a trembling voice, "A visit to the shrine of al-Husayn is something my heart has wished for all my life . . . but . . . your father?"

Yasin laughed and answered, "My father's on his way to Port Said. He won't be back until tomorrow morning. As an extra precaution you can borrow Umm Hanafi's wrap, so anyone who sees you leaving the house or returning will think you're a visitor."

She looked back and forth between her children with embarrassment and dread, as though seeking more encouragement. Khadija and Aisha were enthusiastic about the suggestion. In their enthusiasm they seemed to be expressing both their own imprisoned desire to break free and their joy at the visit to Maryam, which had become, after this revolution, a certainty.

Expressing his heartfelt approval, Kamal shouted, "I'll go with you, Mother, and show you the way."

Fahmy gazed at her affectionately when he saw the expression of anxious pleasure on her face, like that of a child hoping to get a new toy. To encourage her and play down the importance of the adventure, he said, "Have a look at the world. There's nothing wrong with that. I'm afraid you'll forget how to walk after staying home so much."

In an outburst of enthusiasm Khadija ran to Umm Hanafi to get the black cloth she wrapped around herself when she went out. Everyone was laughing and offering their comments. The day turned into a more joyous festival than any they had experienced. They all participated, unwittingly, in the revolution against their absent father's will. Mrs. Amina wrapped the cloth around her and pulled the black veil down over her face. She looked in the mirror and laughed until her torso shook. Kamal put on his suit and fez and got to the courtyard before her, but she did not follow him. She was afflicted by the kind of fear people feel at crucial turning points. She raised her eyes to Fahmy and asked, "What do you think? Should I really go?"

Yasin yelled at her, "Trust God."

Khadija went up to her. Placing her hands on her shoulders, she gave her a gentle push, saying, "Reciting the opening prayer of the Quran will protect you." Khadija propelled her all the way to the stairs. Then she withdrew her hands. The woman descended, with everyone following her. She found Umm Hanafi waiting for her. The servant cast a searching look at her mistress, or rather at the cloth encompassing her. She shook her head disapprovingly, went to her, and wrapped the cloth around her again. She taught her how to hold the edge in the right place. Her mistress, who was wearing this wrap for the first time, followed the servant's directions. Then the angles and curves of her figure, ordinarily concealed by her flowing housedresses, were visible in all their details. Smiling, Khadija gave her an admiring look and winked at Aisha. They burst into laughter.

As she crossed the threshold of the outer door and entered the street, she experienced a moment of panic. Her mouth felt dry and her pleasure was dispelled by a fit of anxiety. She had an oppressive feeling of doing something wrong. She moved slowly and grasped Kamal's hand nervously. Her gait seemed disturbed and unsteady, as though she had not mastered the first principles of walking. She was gripped by intense embarrassment as she showed herself to the eyes of people she had known for ages but only through the peephole of the enclosed balcony. Uncle Hasanayn, the barber, Darwish, who sold beans, al-Fuli, the milkman, Bayumi, the drinks vendor, and Abu Sari', who sold snacks—she imagined that they all recognized her just as she did them. She had difficulty convincing herself of the obvious fact that none of them had ever seen her before in their lives.

They crossed the street to Qirmiz Alley. It was not the shortest route to the mosque of al-Husayn, but unlike al-Nahhasin Street, it did not pass by al-Sayyid Ahmad's store or any other shops and was little frequented. She stopped for a moment before plunging into the alley. She turned to look at her latticed balcony. She could make out the shadows of her two daughters behind one panel. Another panel was raised to reveal the smiling faces of Fahmy and Yasin. The sight of them gave her some courage for her project.

Then she hurried along with her son down the desolate alley, feeling almost calm. Her anxiety and sense of doing something wrong did not leave her, but they retreated to the edges of her conscious emotions. Center stage was occupied by an eager interest in exploring the world as it revealed one of its alleys, a square, novel buildings, and lots of people. She found an innocent pleasure in sharing the motion and freedom of other living creatures. It was the pleasure of someone who had spent a quarter of a century imprisoned by the walls of her home, except for a limited number of visits to her mother in al-Khurunfush, where she would go a few times a year but in a carriage and chaperoned by her husband. Then she would not even have the courage to steal a look at the street.

She began to ask Kamal about the sights, buildings, and places they encountered on their way. The boy was proud to serve as her guide and volunteered lengthy explanations. Here was the famous vaulted ceiling of Qirmiz Alley. Before walking beneath it one needed to recite the opening prayer of the Quran as a defense against the jinn living there. This was Bayt al-Qadi Square with its tall trees. She might have heard him refer to the square as Pasha's Beard Square, from the popular name for its flowering lebbek trees, or at times also as Shangarly Square, giving it the name of the Turkish owner of a chocolate shop. This large building was the Gamaliya police station. Although the boy found little there to merit his attention, except the sword dangling from the sentry's waist, the mother looked at it with curiosity, since it was the place of employment of a man who had sought Aisha's hand. They went on until they reached Khan Ja'far Primary School, where Kamal had spent a year before enrolling at Khalil Agha Elementary School. He pointed to its historic balcony and remarked, "On this balcony Sheikh Mahdi made us put our faces to the wall for the least offense. Then he would kick us five, six, or ten times. Whatever he felt like."

Gesturing toward a store situated directly under the balcony, he stopped walking and said in a tone she could not mistake, "This is Uncle Sadiq, who sells sweets." He refused to budge until he had extracted a coin from her and bought himself a gummy red candy.

After that they turned into Khan Ja'far Alley. Then in the distance they could see part of the exterior of the mosque of al-Husayn. In the center was an expansive window decorated with arabesques. The façade was topped by a parapet with merlons like spear points bunched tightly together.

With joy singing in her breast, she asked, "Our master al-Husayn?" He confirmed her guess. Her pace quickened for the first time since she left the house. She began to compare what she saw with the picture created by her imagination and based on what she had seen from her home of mosques like Qala'un and Barquq. She found the reality to be less grand than she had imagined. In her imagination she had made its size correspond to the veneration in which she held its holy occupant. This difference between imagination and reality, however, in no way affected the pervasive intoxication of her joy at being there.

They walked around the outside of the mosque until they reached the green door. They entered, surrounded by a crowd of women visitors. When the woman's feet touched the floor of the shrine, she felt that her body was dissolving into tenderness, affection, and love and that she was being transformed into a spirit fluttering in the sky, radiant with the glow of prophetic inspiration. Her eyes swam with tears that helped relieve the agitation of her breast, the warmth of her love and belief, and the flood of her benevolent joy. She proceeded to devour the place with greedy, curious eyes: the walls, ceiling, pillars, carpets, chandeliers, pulpit, and the mihrab niches indicating the direction of Mecca.

Kamal, by her side, looked at these things from his own special point of view, assuming that the mosque served as a shrine for people during the day and the early evening but afterward was the home for his martyred master al-Husayn. The Prophet's grandson would come and go there, making use of the furnishings in much the same way any owner uses his possessions. Al-Husayn would walk around inside and pray facing a prayer niche. He would climb into the pulpit and ascend to the windows to look out at his district surrounding the mosque. How dearly Kamal wished, in a dreamy kind of way, that they would forget him in the mosque when they locked the doors so he would be able to meet al-Husayn face to face and pass a whole night in his presence until morning. He imagined the manifestations of love and submission appropriate for him to present to al-Husayn when they met and the hopes and requests suitable for him to lay at his feet. In addition to all that, he looked forward to the affection and blessing he would find with al-Husayn. He pictured himself with his head bowed, approaching the martyr, who would ask him gently, "Who are you?"

He would answer, before kissing his hand, "Kamal Ahmad Abd al-Jawad." Al-Husayn would ask what his profession was. He would reply, "A pupil in Khalil Agha School," and not forget to hint that he was doing well. Al-Husayn would ask what brought him at that hour of the night. Kamal would reply that it was love for all the Prophet's family and especially for him.

Al-Husayn would smile affectionately and invite him to accompany him on his nightly rounds. At that, Kamal would reveal all his requests at once: "Please grant me these things. I want to play as much as I like, inside the house and out. I want Aisha and Khadija to stay in our house always. Please change my father's temper and prolong my mother's life forever. I would like to have as much spending money as I can use and for us all to enter paradise without having to be judged."

The slowly moving flow of women carried them along until they found themselves near the tomb itself. How often she had longed to visit this site, as though yearning for a dream that could never be achieved on this earth. Here she was standing within the shrine. Indeed, here she was touching the walls of the tomb itself, looking at it through her tears. She wished she could linger to savor this taste of happiness, but the pressure of the crowd was too great. She stretched out her hands to the wooden walls and Kamal imitated her. Then they recited the opening prayer of the Quran. She stroked the walls and kissed them, never tiring of her prayers and entreaties. She would have liked to stand there a long time or sit in a corner to gaze at it and then circle around again, but the mosque attendant was watching everyone closely. He would not allow any of the women to tarry. He urged on women who slowed down and waved his long stick at them threateningly. He entreated them all to finish their visit before the Friday prayer service.

She had sipped from the sweet spiritual waters of the shrine but had not drunk her fill. There was no way to quench her thirst. Visiting the shrine had so stirred up her yearnings that they gushed forth from their springs, flowed out, and burst over their banks. She would never stop wanting more of this intimacy and delight. When she found herself obliged to leave the mosque, she had to tear herself away, her heart bidding it farewell. She left very regretfully, tormented by the feeling that she was saying farewell to it forever, but her characteristic temperance and resignation intervened to chide her for giving in to her sorrow. Thus she was able to enjoy the happiness she had gained and use it to banish the anxieties aroused by leaving the shrine.

Kamal invited her to look at his school and they went to see it at the end of al-Husayn Street. They paused there for a long time. When she wanted to return the way they had come, the mention of returning signaled the conclusion of this happy excursion with his mother, which he had never before dreamed would be possible. He refused to abandon it so quickly and fought desperately to prolong it. He proposed a walk along New Street to al-Ghuriya.

In order to put an end to the opposition suggested by the smiling frown visible through her veil, he made her swear by al-Husayn. She sighed and surrendered herself to his young hand.

They made their way through the thick crowd and in and out of the clashing currents of pedestrians flowing in every direction. She would not have encountered even a hundredth of this traffic on the quiet route by which she had come. She began to be uneasy and almost beside herself with anxiety. She soon complained of discomfort and fatigue, but his desperation to complete this happy excursion made him turn a deaf ear to her complaints. He encouraged her to continue the journey. He tried to distract her by directing her attention to the shops, vehicles, and passersby. They were very slowly approaching the corner of al-Ghuriya. When they reached it, his eyes fell on a pastry shop, and his mouth watered. His eyes were fixed intently on the shop. He began to think of a way to persuade his mother to enter the store and purchase a pastry. He was still thinking about it when they reached the shop, but before he knew what was happening his mother had slipped from his hand. He turned toward her questioningly and saw her fall flat on her face, after a deep moan escaped her.

His eyes grew wide with astonishment and terror. He was unable to move. At approximately the same time, despite his dismay and alarm, he saw an automobile out of the corner of his eye. The driver was applying the brakes with a screeching sound, while the vehicle spewed a trail of dust and smoke. It came within a few inches of running over the prostrate woman, swerving just in time.

Everyone started shouting and a great clamor arose. People dashed to the spot from every direction like children following a magician's whistle. They formed a deep ring around her that seemed to consist of eyes peering, heads craning, and mouths shouting words, as questions got mixed up with answers.

Kamal recovered a little from the shock. He looked back and forth from his prostrate mother at his feet to the people around them, expressing his fear and need for help. Then he threw himself down on his knees beside her. He put his hand on her shoulder and called to her in a voice that was heartrending, but she did not respond. He raised his head and stared at the surrounding faces. Then he screamed out a fervent, sobbing lament that rose above the din around him and almost silenced it. Some people volunteered meaningless words of consolation. Others bent over his mother, examining her curiously, moved by two contrary impulses. Although they hoped the victim was all right, in case there was no hope for recovery they were grateful to see that death, that final conclusion which can only be delayed, had knocked on someone else's door and spirited away someone else's soul. They seemed to want a rehearsal free of any risks of that most perilous role each of them was destined to end his life playing.

One of them shouted, "The left door of the vehicle hit her in the back."

The driver had gotten out of the car and stood there half blinded by the glare of the accusations leveled at him. He protested, "She suddenly swerved off the sidewalk. I couldn't keep from hitting her. I quickly put on my brakes, so I just grazed her. But for the grace of God I would have run her down."

One of the men staring at her said, "She's still breathing. . . . She's just unconscious."

Seeing a policeman approaching, with the sword he carried on his left side swinging back and forth, the driver began speaking again: "It was only a little bump. . . . It couldn't have done anything to her. . . . She's fine . . . fine, everybody, by God."

The first man to examine her stood up straight and as though delivering a sermon said, "Get back. Let her have air. . . . She's opened her eyes. She's all right . . . fine, praise God." He spoke with a joy not devoid of pride, as though he was the one who had brought her back to life. Then he turned to Kamal, who was weeping so hysterically that the consolation of the bystanders had been without effect. He patted Kamal on the cheek sympathetically and told him, "That's enough, son. . . . Your mother's fine. . . . Look. . . . Come help me get her to her feet."

Even so, Kamal did not stop crying until he saw his mother move. He bent toward her and put her left hand on his shoulder. He helped the man lift her up. With great difficulty she was able to stand between them, exhausted and faint. Her wrap had fallen off her and some people helped put it back in place as best they could, wrapping it around her shoulders. Then the pastry merchant, in front of whose store the accident had taken place, brought her a chair. They helped her sit down, and he brought a glass of water. She swallowed some, but half of it spilled down her neck and chest. She wiped off her chest with a reflex motion and groaned. She was breathing with difficulty and looked in bewilderment at the faces staring at her. She asked, "What happened? . . . What happened? . . . Oh Lord, why are you crying, Kamal?"

At that point the policeman came forward. He asked her, "Are you injured, lady? Can you walk to the police station?"

The words "police station" came as a blow to her and shook her to the core. She shouted in alarm, "Why should I go to the police station? I'll never go there."

The policeman replied, "The car hit you and knocked you down. If you're injured, you and the driver must go to the police station to fill out a report."

Gasping for breath, she protested, "No . . . certainly not. I won't go. . . . I'm fine."

The policeman told her, "Prove it to me. Get up and walk so we can see if you're injured."

Driven by the alarm that the mention of the police station aroused in her, she got up at once. Surrounded by inquisitive eyes, she adjusted her wrap and began to walk. Kamal was by her side, brushing away the dust that clung to her. Hoping this painful situation would come to an end, no matter what it cost her, she told the policeman, "I'm fine." Then she gestured toward the driver and continued: "Let him go. . . . There's nothing the matter with me." She was so afraid that she no longer felt faint. The sight of the men staring at her horrified her, especially the policeman, who was in front of the others. She trembled from the impact of these looks directed at her from everywhere. They were a clear challenge and affront to a long life spent in seclusion and concealment from strangers. She imagined she saw the image of al-Sayyid Ahmad rising above all the other men. He seemed to be studying her face with cold, stony eyes, threatening her with more evil than she could bear to imagine.

She lost no time in grabbing the boy's hand and heading off with him toward the Goldsmiths Bazaar. No one tried to stop her. No sooner had they turned the corner and escaped from sight than she moaned. Speaking to Kamal as though addressing herself, she said, "My Lord, how did this happen? What have I seen, Kamal? It was like a terrifying dream. I imagined I was falling into a dark pit from high up. The earth was revolving under my feet. Then I didn't know anything at all until I opened my eyes on that frightening scene. My Lord . . . did he really want to take me to the police station? O Gracious One, O Lord . . . my Savior, my Lord. How soon will we reach home? You cried a lot, Kamal. May you never lose your eyes. Dry your eyes with this handkerchief. You can wash your face at home. . . . Oh."

She stopped when they were almost at the end of the Goldsmiths Bazaar. She rested her hand on the boy's shoulder. Her face was contorted.

Kamal looked up with alarm and asked her, "What's the matter?"

She closed her eyes and said in a weak voice, "I'm tired, very tired. My feet can barely support me. Get the first vehicle you can find, Kamal."

Kamal looked around. All he could see was a donkey cart standing by the doorway of the ancient hospital of Qala'un. He summoned the driver, who quickly brought the cart to them. Leaning on Kamal's shoulder, the mother made her way to it. She clambered on board with his help, supporting herself on the driver's shoulder. He held steady until she was seated cross-legged in the cart. She sighed from her extreme exhaustion and Kamal sat down beside her. Then the driver leaped onto the front of the cart and prodded the donkey with the handle of his whip. The donkey walked off slowly, with the cart swaying and clattering behind him.

The woman moaned. She complained, "My pain's severe. The bones of my shoulder must be smashed." Meanwhile Kamal watched her with alarm and anxiety.

The vehicle passed by al-Sayyid Ahmad's store without either of them paying any attention. Kamal watched the road ahead until he saw the latticed balconies of their house. All he could remember of the happy expedition was its miserable conclusion.

When Umm Hanafi opened the door she was startled to see her mistress sitting cross-legged on a donkey cart. Her first thought was that Mrs. Amina had decided to conclude her excursion with a cart ride just for the fun of it.

So she smiled but only briefly, for she saw that Kamal's eyes were red from crying. She looked back at her mistress with alarm. This time she was able to fathom the exhaustion and pain the lady was suffering. She moaned and rushed to the cart, crying out, "My lady, what's the matter? May evil stay far away from you."

The driver replied, "God willing, it's nothing serious. Help me get her down."

Umm Hanafi grasped the woman in her arms and carried her inside. Kamal followed them, sad and dejected. Khadija and Aisha had left the kitchen to wait for them in the courtyard, thinking about some joke they could make when the two returned from their excursion. They were terribly surprised when Umm Hanafi appeared, struggling to carry their mother in from the outer hall. They both screamed and ran to her. Terrified, they were shouting, "Mother . . . Mother . . . what's wrong?"

They all helped carry her. At the same time Khadija kept asking Kamal what had happened. Finally the boy was forced to mutter with profound fear, "A car!"

"A car!"

The two girls shouted it together, repeating the word, which sounded incredibly alarming to them. Khadija wailed and screamed, "What terrible news! . . . May evil stay far away from you, Mother."

Aisha could not speak. She burst into tears. Their mother was not unconscious but extremely weak. Despite her fatigue she whispered to calm them, "I'm all right. No harm's done. I'm just tired."

The clamor reached Yasin and Fahmy. They came to the head of the stairs and looked down over the railing. Alarmed, they immediately hurried down, asking what had happened. From fear of repeating the dreadful word, Khadija gestured to Kamal to answer for himself. The two young men went over to the boy, who once again muttered sadly and anxiously, "A car!"

Then he started sobbing. The young men turned away from him, postponing for a time the questions that were troubling them. Together they carried the mother to the girls' room and sat her down on the sofa. Then Fahmy asked her anxiously and fearfully, "Tell me what's the matter, Mother. I want to know everything."

She leaned her head back and did not say anything while she tried to catch her breath. Meanwhile Khadija, Aisha, Umm Hanafi, and Kamal were weeping so loudly that they got on Fahmy's nerves. He scolded them till they stopped. Then he caught hold of Kamal to ask, "How did the accident come about? What did the people there do to the driver? Did they take you to the police station?" Without any hesitation Kamal answered his questions in full, giving most of the details.

The mother followed the conversation, despite her feeble condition. When the boy finished, she summoned all the strength she had and said, "I'm fine, Fahmy. Don't alarm yourself. They wanted me to go to the police station, but I refused. Then I came along as far as the end of the Goldsmiths Bazaar, where my strength suddenly gave out. Don't be upset. I'll get my strength back with a little rest."

In addition to his alarm over the accident Yasin was extremely upset, since he was responsible for suggesting what they would later term the ill-omened excursion. He said they should get a doctor. Without waiting to hear what anyone else thought of his idea, he left the room to carry it out. The mother shuddered at the mention of the doctor just as she had earlier at the reference to the police station. She asked Fahmy to catch his brother and dissuade him from going. She asserted that she would recover without any need for a doctor, but her son refused to give in to her request. He explained to her the need for one.

Meanwhile the two girls assisted each other in removing the wrap. Umm Hanafi brought a glass of water. Then they all crowded around her, anxiously examining her pale face and asking over and over how she felt. So far as she was able, she pretended to be calm. When the pain got bad, the most she said was: "There's a slight pain in my right shoulder." Then she added, "But there's no need for a doctor." The truth was that she did not like the idea of sending for a doctor. She had never had a doctor before, not merely because her health had been good but also because she had always succeeded in treating whatever ailed her with her own special medicine. She did not believe in modern medicine and associated it with major catastrophes and serious events. Furthermore, she felt that summoning a doctor would have the effect of highlighting a matter she wanted to hush up and conceal before her husband returned. She did her best to explain her fears to her children, but at that delicate moment they were only concerned about her well-being.

Yasin was not gone more than a quarter of an hour, since the doctor's clinic was in Bayt al-Qadi Square. He returned ahead of the doctor, whom he took to his mother the moment he arrived. They emptied the room of everyone except Yasin and Fahmy. The doctor asked the mother where she hurt and she pointed to her right shoulder. He throat was dry with fear, but she swallowed and said, "I feel pain here."

Guided by what she said and what Yasin had told him before in general terms, he set about examining her. The examination seemed to take a long time, both to the young men waiting inside and to the women with throbbing hearts who were listening from the other side of the door. The doctor turned from his patient to Yasin and said, "There's a fracture of the right collarbone. That's all there is to it."

The word 'fracture' caused dismay both inside and outside the room. They were all astonished that he had said, "That's all there is to it." It sounded as though there was something about a fracture that made it bearable. All the same, they found the phrase and the tone in which it was delivered reassuring. Torn between fear and hope, Fahmy asked, "Is that serious?"

"Not at all. I'll move the bone back where it belongs and fix it there, but she'll have to sleep a few nights sitting up with her back supported by a pillow. It'll be hard for her to sleep on her back or side. The fracture will set within two or three weeks at the most. There's no cause for alarm at all. . . . Now let me get to work."

They all breathed a sigh of relief after having been worried sick, especially those outside the door. Khadija murmured, "May the blessing of our master al-Husayn rest with her. The only reason she went out was to visit him."

Kamal asked in astonishment, as though her words had reminded him of something important he had forgotten for too long, "How could this accident happen after she was blessed with a visit to our master al-Husayn?"

Umm Hanafi replied with great simplicity, "Who knows what might have befallen her, we take refuge in God, had she not been blessed by visiting her master and ours?"

Aisha had not recovered from the shock. All the talk was getting on her nerves. She cried out fervently, "Oh, my Lord, when will everything be over, as though it had never happened?"

With sorrow and regret Khadija spoke again: "What was she doing in al-Ghuriya? If she had returned home directly, immediately after the visit, nothing would have happened to her."

Kamal's heart pounded with fear and alarm. In his eyes his offense appeared an abominable crime. Even so, he tried to evade their suspicions. In a disapproving tone he said, "She wanted to walk along the road and I tried in vain to talk her out of it."

Khadija gave him an accusing look. She started to reply, but she stopped out of sympathy and concern for his pale face. She told herself, "We've got enough troubles for the time being."

The door opened and the doctor left the room. He told the two young men, who followed him, "I'll have to see her every day until the fracture sets, but as I told you, there's absolutely no cause for alarm."

They all rushed into the room. They saw their mother sitting on the bed with her back supported by a pillow folded behind her. The only difference was a bulge in her dress over her right shoulder that betrayed the existence of a bandage beneath it. They rushed over to her and called out, "Praise to God."

When the doctor had been treating her fracture, the pain had been intense. She had moaned continually. Had it not been for her natural reserve, she would have screamed aloud. The pain was gone now, or so it appeared. She felt relatively comfortable and peaceful. The diminution of her sharp pain, though, allowed her mind to resume its energetic activity and she was able to think about the situation from different points of view. She was soon consumed by fear. With her eyes wandering back and forth between them she asked, "What can I say to your father when he returns?"

This question, like a protruding boulder blocking the safe passage of a ship, mockingly challenged the wisps of reassurance they had grasped. It did not take their minds by surprise. It had perhaps insinuated itself into the crowd of painful emotions their hearts had harbored since they were first confronted by the news, but it had been lost sight of in the confusion.

Consideration of it had been postponed for a time. Now it had returned to occupy the place of honor in their souls. They found no alternative to confronting it. They considered it to be more threatening to them and their mother than the fracture from which she would soon recover. When her question was greeted by silence, the mother felt isolated, like a guilty person whose comrades desert him when an accusation is lodged against him. She complained softly, "He'll certainly learn about the accident. Moreover, he'll discover I went outside, because that's what led up to it."

Although Umm Hanafi was no less worried than the family members and understood the seriousness of the situation just as well as the others, she still wanted to say something reassuring to lighten the atmosphere. She also felt it her duty as a longtime and devoted servant of the family not to keep quiet when calamity struck. She was afraid they might think she did not care. Even though she was well aware that her words were remote from reality, she observed, "When my master learns what happened to you, he'll have to overlook your mistake and praise God for your safe recovery."

Her comment was received with the neglect it deserved from people who could see the reality of the situation quite clearly. All the same, Kamal believed it. As though completing Umm Hanafi's statement, Kamal said enthusiastically, "Especially if we tell him we only went out to visit our master al-Husayn."

The woman looked back and forth from Yasin to Fahmy with her half-closed eyes, and asked, "What can I say to him?"

Yasin, who was overwhelmed by the weight of his responsibility, said, "What demon led me astray so that I advised you to go out? A word slipped from my tongue. I wish it never had. But the fates wanted to cast us into this painful predicament. Even so, I assure you that we'll think of something to tell him. In any case, you shouldn't trouble your mind about what might happen. Leave the matter to God. The pains and fears you've endured today are enough for you now."

Yasin spoke with intensity and affection. He was pouring out his indignation against himself and his affection for their mother. He was commiserating with her situation. Although his words did not help or hinder anything, they provided some relief for his oppressive feeling of anguish. At the same time he was probably expressing what was going through the minds of those standing there with him. He spared them from having to express it themselves.

He had learned from experience that sometimes the best way to defend one's actions it to attack them. A confession of guilt would promote good-will as much as an attempt to defend himself would have aroused anger. What he had most to fear was that Khadija would seize this golden opportunity to attack him openly about his responsibility for the consequences of his advice. She could use it to assail him. He had anticipated her plan and pulled the rug out from under her.

He was right about his hunch, for Khadija was just about to demand that he, as the person with primary responsibility for what had happened, should find them some solution. After he had made his little speech, she was ashamed to attack him, especially since she did not usually assail him in anger but only when they were bickering. Thus Yasin's situation was slightly improved, but the overall situation remained bad. Nothing improved it, until Khadija volunteered, "Why don't we claim she fell on the stairs?"

Her mother looked at her with a face that yearned for salvation by any means. She looked at Fahmy and Yasin too. There was a glimmer of hope showing in her eyes. All the same, Fahmy asked anxiously, "What about the doctor? He'll be checking on her day after day. Father will certainly bump into him."

Yasin refused to close the door through which a breath of hope had slipped to hint he might be rescued from his pains and fears. He said, "We can reach an agreement with the doctor about what Father should be told."

They looked back and forth at each other, trying to decide whether to accept or reject this idea. Then the gloomy atmosphere became festive, and a mutual feeling of salvation was evident in their faces. It was like a blue streak appearing unexpectedly in the middle of dark clouds. By an amazing miracle, the blue streak spread in just a few minutes until it covered the entire celestial dome and the sun came out.

Yasin said, "We've been saved, praise God."

After Khadija recovered her normal vivacity in the new climate, she told Yasin, "No, you've been saved. You're the one who thought it all up."

Yasin laughed until his huge body shook. He replied, "Yes, I've been saved from the scorpion sting of your tongue. I've been expecting it would reach out and bite me."

"But it's my tongue that saved you. For the sake of the rose, the thorns get watered."

In their happiness at being saved they had almost forgotten that their mother was confined to bed with a broken collarbone, but she herself had almost forgotten it too.

She opened her eyes and found Khadija and Aisha sitting on the bed by her feet. They were gazing at her with expressions wavering between hope and fear. She sighed and turned toward the window. She saw bright daylight steaming through the gaps in the shutters. She murmured in disbelief, "I slept a long time."

Then Aisha said, "Just a few hours. It was dawn before you closed your eyelids. What a night! I'll never forget it, no matter how long I live."

The mother was visited once again by memories of the past night dominated by sleeplessness and pain. Her eyes expressed her sorrow for herself and the two girls who had sat up with her all night, sharing her pain and insomnia. She moved her lips as she inaudibly sought God's protection. Then she whispered, almost in embarrassment, "I've really worn you out. . . ."

In a playful tone Khadija answered. "Wearing ourselves out for you is relaxing, but you had better not scare us again." Then she continued in a voice that showed emotion was getting the better of her: "How could that dreadful pain pick on you? . . . I'd think you were sound asleep and in good shape and lie down to get some sleep myself, only to wake up hearing you moan. You kept going 'Oh . . . oh' till dawn."

Aisha's face shone with optimism as she said, "In any case, here's good news. This morning I told Fahmy how you were doing when he asked about your health. He told me the pain troubling you was a sign the broken bone was starting to mend."

Fahmy's name brought Amina back from the depths of her thoughts. She asked, "Did they all get off safely?"

Khadija replied, "Of course. They wanted to speak to you and reassure themselves about you, but I wouldn't let anyone wake you after we'd gotten white hair waiting for you to doze off."

Their mother sighed with resignation, "Praise to God in any case. May our Lord make everything turn out for the best. . . . What time is it now?"

Khadija said, "It's an hour till the noon call to prayer."

The lateness of the hour prompted her to lower her eyes thoughtfully. When she raised them again, her anxiety was reflected in her look. She murmured, "He may be on his way home now. . . ."

They understood what she meant. Although they could feel fear creeping through their hearts, Aisha said confidently, "He's most welcome. There's no reason to be anxious. We've agreed on what has to be said, and that ends the matter."

All the same, his impending arrival spread anxiety through Amina's feeble soul. She asked, "Do you think it will be possible to conceal what happened?"

In a voice that became noticeably sharper as her anxiety increased, Khadija answered, "Why not? We'll tell him what we agreed on, and the matter will pass peacefully."

Their mother wished that Yasin and Fahmy could have stayed by her side at that hour to give her courage. Khadija had said, "We'll tell him what we agreed on, and the matter will pass peacefully," but could what had happened remained a closed secret forever? Would the truth not find some opening through which it could reach the man? She feared lying just as much as she feared the truth. She did not know what destiny lay in wait for her. She looked affectionately at one girl and then the other. She had opened her mouth to speak when Umm Hanafi rushed in. She whispered, as though afraid someone outside the room might hear, "My master has come, my lady."

Their hearts beat wildly. The girls got off the bed in a single bound. They stood facing their mother. They all exchanged glances silently. Then the mother mumbled, "Don't you two say anything. I'm afraid of what might happen to you if you deceive him. Leave the talking to me, may God provide assistance."

A tense silence reigned like that of children in the dark who hear footsteps they think are those of jinn prowling around outside. Then they could hear al-Sayyid Ahmad's footsteps coming up the stairs. As they drew nearer, the mother struggled to break the nightmare silence. She mumbled, "Should we let him climb up to his room and not find anyone?"

She turned to Umm Hanafi and said, "Tell him I'm here, sick. Don't say anything more."

She swallowed to wet her dry throat. The two girls shot out of the room, each trying to escape first. They left her alone. Finding herself cut off from the entire world, she resigned herself to her destiny. Frequently this resignation on her part, since she was deprived of any weapon, seemed a passive kind of courage. She collected her thoughts in order to remember what she was supposed to say, although her doubt that she was doing the right thing never left her. It hid at the bottom of her emotions and announced its presence whenever she was anxious and tense or her confidence dwindled.

She heard the tip of his stick striking the floor of the sitting room. She mumbled, "Your mercy, Lord, and assistance."

Her eyes watched the doorway until he blocked it with his tall and broad body. She saw him come in and approach her. He gave her a searching look with his wide eyes. When he reached the center of the room he stopped and asked in a voice she imagined was more tender than usual, "What's the matter with you?"

Lowering her eyes, she said, "Praise to God for your safe return, sir. I'm well so long as you are."

"But Umm Hanafi told me you're sick. . . ."

With her left hand she pointed to her right shoulder and said, "My shoulder has been injured, sir. May God not expose you to any evil."

Examining her shoulder with concern and anxiety, the man asked, "What injured it?"

It was destined to happen. The crucial moment had arrived. She had only to speak, to utter the saving lie. Then the crisis would be safely concluded. She would receive even more than her share of sympathy. She raised her eyes in preparation for it. Then her eyes met his, or, more precisely, were consumed by his. Her heart beat faster, pounding mercilessly. At that moment all the ideas she had collected in her mind evaporated. The determination she had accumulated in her will was dispersed. Her eyes blinked from dismay and consternation. Then she gazed at him with a bewildered expression and said nothing.

Al-Sayyid Ahmad was amazed to see her confusion. He was quick to ask her, "What happened, Amina?"

She did not know what to say. She did not seem to have anything to say, but she was now certain she would not be able to lie. The opportunity had escaped without her knowing how. If she renewed the attempt, the words would come out in a disjointed and damning way. She was like a person who after having walked over a tightrope in a hypnotic trance is asked to repeat the trick in a conscious state. As the seconds passed she felt increasingly nervous and defeated. She was on the brink of despair.

"Why don't you speak?" His tone seemed to suggest he was growing impatient and would soon start shouting angrily. By God, she certainly needed some assistance. What demon had tempted her to go on that ill-omened excursion?

"Strange. Don't you want to speak?"

The silence then was more than she could bear. Driven by despair and defeat, she murmured in a shaking voice, "I have committed a grave error, sir. . . . I was struck by an automobile."

His eyes widened with astonishment. A look of alarm coupled with disbelief could be seen in them. It seemed he had begun to doubt her sanity. The woman could no longer bear to hesitate. She resolved to give a complete confession, no matter what the consequences. She was like a person who risks his life in a dangerous surgical operation to get relief from a painful disease he can no longer endure. Her feeling of the seriousness of her offense and the danger of her confession doubled. Tears welled up in her eyes. In a voice she did not attempt to keep free from sobs, either because she could not help it or because she wanted to make a desperate appeal to his sympathy, she said, "I thought I heard our master al-Husayn calling me to visit him. So I obeyed the call. . . . I went to visit his shrine. . . . On the way home an automobile ran into me. . . . It's God's decree, sir. I got up without anyone needing to help me." She spoke this last sentence very distinctly. Then she continued: "At first I didn't feel any pain. So I thought I was fine. I walked on until I reached the house. Here the pain started. They brought me a doctor, who examined my shoulder. He decided it was broken. He promised to return every day until the fracture is healed. I have committed a grave error, sir. I have been punished for it as I deserve. . . . . God is forgiving and compassionate."

Al-Sayyid Ahmad listened to her without commenting or moving. He did not turn his eyes away from her. His face revealed nothing of his internal agitation. Meanwhile she bowed her head humbly like a defendant waiting for the verdict to be pronounced. The silence was prolonged and intense. The oppressive atmosphere was shot through with intimations of fearful threats. She was nervous about it and did not know what decree was being worked up or what fate would be allotted her.

Then she heard his strangely calm voice ask, "What did the doctor say? . . . How serious is the fracture?"

She turned her head toward him in bewilderment. She had been ready for anything except this gracious response. If the situation had not been so terrifying, she would have asked him to repeat it so she could be sure she had heard him correctly. She was overcome by emotion. Two large tears sprang from her eyes. She pressed her lips tightly together to keep from being choked up by weeping. Then she mumbled contritely and humbly, "The doctor said there's absolutely no reason to worry. May God spare you any evil, sir."

The man stood there for a time, struggling with his desire to ask more questions. He got control of himself and then turned to leave the room, saying, "Stay in bed till God heals you."

Khadija and Aisha rushed into the room after their father left. They stopped in front of their mother and looked at her inquisitively. Their expression revealed their concern and anxiety. When they noticed that their mother's eyes were red from crying they were disturbed. Although her heart was fearful and pessimistic, Khadija asked, "Good news, God willing?"

Blinking her eyes nervously, the mother limited herself to replying tersely, "I confessed the truth to him."

"The truth!"

With resignation she said, "I wasn't able to do anything but confess. There was no way the affair could have been kept from him forever. I did the best thing."

Khadija thumped her chest with her hand and cried out, "What an unlucky day for us!"

Aisha was struck dumb. She stared at her mother's face without uttering a word. The mother smiled with a mixture of pride and embarrassment. Her pale face blushed when she remembered the affection he had showered on her when she had been expecting nothing but his overwhelming anger that would blow her and her future away. Yes, she felt both pride and embarrassment when she started to talk about their father's sympathy for her in her time of need and how he had forgotten his anger because of the affection and pity that had seized hold of him.

Then Amina murmured in a soft voice that was barely audible, "He was merciful to me, may God prolong his life. He listened silently to my story. Then he asked me what the doctor had said about the seriousness of the fracture and left. He directed me to stay in bed till God would take me by the hand."

The two girls exchanged astonished and incredulous glances. Then their fear quickly left them. They both sighed deeply with relief, and their faces became bright with joy. Khadija shouted, "Don't you see? It's the blessing of al-Husayn."

Her prediction having come true, Aisha commented proudly, "Everything has its limits, even Papa's anger. There was no way he could be angry with her once he saw her in this state. Now we know how much she means to him." Then she teased her mother, "What a lucky mother you are! Congratulations to you for the honor and affection shown you."

The blush returned to the mother's face and she stammered modestly, "May God prolong his life. . . ." She sighed and continued, "Praise to God for this salvation."

She remembered something and turned to Khadija. She told her with concern, "You've got to go to him. He'll certainly need your help."

The girl was nervous and uncomfortable in her father's presence. She felt she had fallen into a trap. She replied angrily, "Why can't Aisha go?"

Her mother said critically, "You're better able to serve him. Don't waste time, young lady. He may be needing you this very moment."

Khadija knew it would be pointless to protest, since it always was when her mother asked her to undertake a task for which she thought Khadija better suited than her sister. All the same, she was determined to voice her objection as she always did at such times, driven by her fiery temper as well as her aggressive nature that made her tongue its most willing and incisive weapon. She wanted to force her mother to say once more that she was more proficient at this or that than Aisha. That would be an admission from her mother, a warning to her sister, and a consolation for her.

The fact was that if one of these important tasks had been awarded to Aisha instead of her, she would have been even more furious and would have intervened. In her heart she still felt that performing these duties was one of her rights. They set her apart as a woman worthy of her status as second-in-command to her mother in the household. Yet she refused to acknowledge openly that she was exercising one of her rights when she undertook the task. It was, rather, a heavy burden that she accepted only under duress. Thus anyone summoning her to do something would feel uncomfortable about it. If she objected, she would be able to protest with an anger that would provide her some relief. She could make whatever commentary she wished about the situation. Finally, she would be reckoned to be doing the person a favor meriting his thanks.

Therefore as she left the room, she said, "In every crisis you call on Khadija, as though there was no one else at hand. What would you do if I weren't here?"

The moment she left, her pride abandoned her. Its place was taken by terror and agitation. How could she present herself to him? How would she go about serving him? How would he treat her if she stuttered or was slow or made a mistake?

Al-Sayyid Ahmad had removed his street clothes by himself and put on his house shirt. When she stood at the door to ask what he needed, he ordered her to make a cup of coffee. She hastened to fetch it. Then she presented it to him, walking softly with her eyes lowered, feeling shy and afraid. She retreated to the sitting room just outside his door to wait there for any signal from him. Her sense of terror never left her. She wondered how she would be able to continue serving him through all the hours he spent at home, day after day, until the three weeks were over. The matter seemed nerve-racking to her. She perceived for the first time the importance of the niche her mother filled in the household. She prayed for her speedy recovery out of both love for her mother and pity for herself.

Unluckily for her, al-Sayyid Ahmad was of a mind to rest up after the fatigue of his journey and did not go to the store as she hoped. Accordingly, she was obliged to remain in the sitting room like a prisoner. Aisha came up to the top floor and crept silently into the room where her sister was sitting. She came to parade herself before Khadija. She winked at her to ridicule her situation. Then she returned to her mother, leaving her sister boiling with rage. The thing that infuriated Khadija most was for someone to tease her, even though she happily teased everyone else. Khadija regained her freedom, and then just provisionally, only when her father fell asleep. Then she flew to her mother and began to tell her about all the real and imaginary services she had rendered her father. She described to her the signs of affection and appreciation for her services that she had noticed in his eyes. She did not forget to turn on Aisha and rain abuse and reprimands on her for her childish conduct.

She went back to her father when he woke up and served him lunch. After the man finished eating, he sat reading over some papers for a long time. Then he summoned her and asked her to send Yasin and Fahmy to him the moment they got home.

The mother was upset about his request. She was afraid that the man's soul had some concealed anger trapped inside and that he now wished to find a target for his anger—namely, the two young men.

When Yasin and Fahmy came home and learned what had happened and that their father had ordered them to appear before him, their minds entertained the same thought. They went to his room with fearful forebodings, but the man surprised them by greeting them more calmly than usual. He asked them about the accident, the circumstances surrounding it, and the doctor's report. They recounted at length what they knew while he listened with interest. Finally he asked, "Were you at home when she went out?"

Although they had expected this question from the outset, when it came after this unexpected and unusual calm, it alarmed them. They feared it was a prelude to change from the harmony they had enjoyed with relief, thinking they were safe. They were unable to speak and chose to remain silent. All the same, al-Sayyid Ahmad did not insist on his question. He seemed to attach little importance to hearing the answer he had guessed in advance. Perhaps he wanted to point out their error, without caring whether they confessed. After that he did nothing but show them the door, allowing them to depart. As they were walking out, they heard him say to himself, "Since God has not provided me with any sons, let Him grant me patience."

Although the incident appeared to have shaken al-Sayyid Ahmad enough that he was altering his conduct to an extent that amazed everyone, it could not dissuade him from enjoying his traditional nightly outing. When evening came he dressed and left his room, diffusing a fragrance of perfume. On his way out he passed by his wife's room to inquire about her. She prayed for him at length, gratefully and thankfully. She did not see anything rude in his going out when she was confined to bed. She may have felt that for him to stop to see her and ask after her was more recognition than she had expected. Indeed, if he refrained from pouring out his anger on her, was that not a boon she had not even dreamt of?

Before their father had left his room, the brothers had asked, "Do you suppose he'll forsake his evening's entertainment tonight?"

The mother had replied, "Why should he stay home when he's learned there's nothing to be worried about?" Privately she might have wished he would complete his kind treatment of her by renouncing his night out, as was appropriate for a husband whose wife had suffered what she had. Since she knew his temperament well, though, she fabricated an excuse for him in advance, so that if he did rush off to his party, as she expected, she could put a pleasant face on her situation. She would justify his departure with the excuse she had already invented and not let it seem to be caused by his indifference.

All the same, Khadija had asked, "How can he bear to be at a party when he sees you in this condition?"

Yasin had answered, "There's nothing wrong with his doing that once he's satisfied himself that she's all right. Men and women don't react to sorrow the same way. There's no contradiction between a man going out to a party and feeling sad. It may actually be his way of consoling himself so he'll be able to carry on with his difficult life." Yasin was not defending his father so much as his own desire to step out that was beginning to stir deep inside him.

His cunning did not work on Khadija. She asked him, "Could you stand spending the evening in your coffee shop?"

Although he cursed her secretly, he quickly replied, "Of course not. But I'm one thing and Papa's something else."

When al-Sayyid Ahmad left the room, Amina felt again the relief that follows a rescue from genuine danger. Her face lit up with a smile. She observed, "Perhaps he thought I'd already been punished enough for my offense. So he forgave me. May God forgive him and all of us."

Yasin struck his hands together and objected, "There are men as jealous as he is, some of them friends of his, who see no harm in permitting their women to go out when it's necessary or appropriate. What can he be thinking of to keep you imprisoned in the house all the time?"

Khadija glanced at him scornfully and asked, "Why didn't you deliver this appeal for us when you were with him?"

The young man began laughing so hard his belly shook. He replied, "Before I can do that I need a nose like yours to defend myself with."

Her days in bed passed without a recurrence of the pain that had devastated her the first night, although the slightest movement would make her shoulder and torso hurt. She convalesced quickly because of her sturdy constitution and superabundant vitality. She had a natural dislike of being still and sitting around and that made obedience to the doctor's orders a difficult ordeal. The torment it caused her overshadowed the pains of the fracture at their worst. Perhaps she would have violated the doctor's commands and gotten up prematurely to look after things if her children had not watched her so relentlessly.

Yet her confinement did not prevent her from supervising household affairs from her bed. She would review everything assigned to the girls with a tiresome precision, especially the details of tasks she was afraid they might neglect or forget. She would ask persistently, "Did you dust the tops of the curtains? . . . The shutters? . . . Did you burn incense in the bathroom for your father? . . . Have you watered the hyacinth beans and jasmine?"

Khadija got annoyed by this once and told her. "Listen, if you took care of the house one carat, I'm taking care of it twenty-four."

In addition to all this, her compulsory abandonment of her important position brought with it some ambivalent feelings that troubled her a great deal. She asked herself whether it was true that the house and its inhabitants had not lost anything, in terms of either order or comfort, by her relinquishing her post. Which of the two alternatives would be preferable: for everything to remain just the way it ought to be, thanks to her two girls who had been nurtured by her hands, or that there should be sufficient disturbance of the household's equilibrium to remind everyone of the void she had left behind her? What if it was al-Sayyid Ahmad himself who sensed this void? Would that be a reason for him to appreciate her importance or a reason to become angry at her offense that had caused all this? The woman wavered for a long time between her abashed fondness for herself and her open affection for her daughters. It became clear that any shortcoming in the management of the house disturbed her immensely. On the other hand, if it had retained its perfection as though nothing had happened, she would not have been totally at ease.

In fact, no one did fill her place. Despite the earnest and energetic activity of the two girls, the house showed evidence of being too large for them. The mother was not happy about that, but she kept her feelings to herself. She defended Khadija and Aisha sincerely and vehemently. Even so, she suffered from alarm and pain and could not endure her seclusion patiently.

At dawn on the promised day, the day for which she had waited so long, she hopped out of bed with a youthful nimbleness derived from her joy. She felt like a king reclaiming his throne after being exiled. She went down to the oven room to resume her routine that had been interrupted for three weeks. She called Umm Hanafi. The woman woke up and could not believe her ears. She rose to greet her mistress, embracing her and praying for her. Then they set about the morning's work with an indescribable happiness.

When the first rays of the rising sun could be seen, she went upstairs. The children greeted her with congratulations and kisses. Then she went over to where Kamal was sleeping and woke him. The moment the boy opened his eyes he was overcome by astonishment and joy. He clung to her neck, but she was quick to free herself gently from his arms. She asked him, "Aren't you afraid my shoulder will get hurt again?"

He smothered her with kisses. Then he laughed and asked mischievously, "Darling, when can we go out together again?"

She replied in a tone that had a ring of friendly criticism, "When God has guided you enough so you don't lead me against my will to a street where I almost perish."

He understood she was referring to his stubbornness that had been the immediate cause of what befell her. He laughed until he could laugh no more. He laughed like a sinner who has been reprieved after having his offense hang over his head for three weeks. Yes, he had been terribly afraid that the investigation his brothers were conducting would reveal the secret culprit. The suspicions entertained by Khadija at one time and Yasin at another had come close to uncovering him in his redoubt. He had been spared only because his mother had defended him firmly and had resolved to bear responsibility for the accident all by herself. When the investigation had been transferred to his father, Kamal's fears had reached their climax. He had expected from one moment to the next to be summoned before his father. In addition to this fear, he had been tormented during the past three weeks by seeing his beloved mother confined to bed, suffering bitterly, unable either to lie down or to stand up. Now the accident was past history. Gone with it was its bad taste. The investigation was terminated. Once again his mother had come to wake him in the morning. She would put him to bed at night. Everything had returned to normal. Peace had unfurled its banners. He had a right to laugh his heart out and congratulate his conscience on its reprieve.

The mother left the boys' room to go to the top floor. When she approached the door of al-Sayyid Ahmad's room she could hear him saying in his prayers, "Glory to my Lord, the Magnificent." Her heart pounded and she stood hesitating, a step away from the door. She found herself wondering

whether to go in to wish him good morning or prepare the breakfast tray
first. She was less interested in the actual question than in fleeing from the
fear and shame rampant in her soul, or perhaps she was interested in both.
At times a person may create an imaginary problem to escape from an actual
problem he finds difficult to resolve.

She went to the dining room and set to work with redoubled care. Even
so, her anxiety increased. The period of delay she had granted herself was
worthless. She did not find the relief she had hoped for. The ordeal of waiting was more painful than the situation she had shrunk from confronting. She
was amazed that she had been scared to enter her own room, as though she
were preparing to enter it for the first time. All the more so because al-Sayyid
Ahmad had continued to visit her, day after day, during her convalescence.
The fact was that her recovery had removed the protection afforded her by
ill health. She sensed that she would be meeting him without anything to
hide behind for the first time since her error had been disclosed.

When the boys arrived for breakfast one after the other, she felt a little
less desolate. Their father soon entered the room in his flowing gown. His
face revealed no emotion on seeing her. He asked calmly as he headed for
his place at the table, "You've come?" Then, taking his seat, he told his sons,
"Sit down."

They began to consume their breakfast while she stood in her customary
place. Her fear had peaked when he came in, but she started to catch her
breath after that. The first encounter after her recovery had taken place and
passed peacefully. She sensed that she would find no problem in being alone
with him shortly in his room.

The breakfast ended, al-Sayyid Ahmad returned to his room. She joined
him a few minutes later carrying a tray with coffee. She placed it on the low
table and stepped aside to wait until he had finished. Then she would help
him get dressed. Her husband drank the coffee in profound silence, not the
silence that comes naturally either as a rest, when people are tired, or as a
cloak for someone with nothing to say. It was a deliberate silence. She had
not given up her hope, however faint, that he was fond enough of her to grant
her a kind word or at least discuss the subjects he usually did at this hour of
the morning. His deliberate silence unsettled her. She began asking herself

again whether he still harbored some anger. Anxiety was pricking her heart once more. Yet the heavy silence did not last long.

The man was thinking with such speed and concentration that he had no taste for anything else. It was not the kind of thought that arises on the spur of the moment. It was a type of stubborn, long-lasting thought that had stayed with him throughout the past days. Finally, without raising his head from his empty coffee cup, he asked, "Have you recovered?"

Amina replied in a subdued voice, "Yes, sir, praise God."

The man resumed speaking and said bitterly, "I'm amazed, and never cease to be amazed, that you did what you did."

Her heart pounded violently, and she bowed her head dejectedly. She could not bear his anger when defending a mistake someone else had made. What could she do now that she was the guilty person? . . . Fear froze her tongue, although he was waiting for an answer.

He continued his comments by asking her disapprovingly, "Have I been mistaken about you all these years and not known it?"

At that she held out her hands in alarm and pain. She whispered in troubled gasps, "I take refuge with God, sir. My error was really a big one, but I don't deserve talk like this."

Nevertheless, the man continued to talk with his terrifying calm, compared to which screaming would have been easy to bear. He said, "How could you have committed such a grave error? . . . Was it because I left town for a single day?"

In a trembling voice, its tones swayed by the convulsions of her body, she replied, "I have committed an error, sir. It is up to you to forgive me. My soul yearned to visit our master al-Husayn. I thought that for such a blessed pilgrimage it was possible for me to go out just once."

He shook his head fiercely as though saying, "There's no point trying to argue." Then he raised his eyes to give her an angry, sullen look. In a voice that made it clear he would tolerate no discussion, he said, "I just have one thing to say: Leave my house immediately."

His command fell on her head like a fatal blow. She was dumbfounded and did not utter a word. She could not move. During the worst moments of her ordeal, when she was waiting for him to return from his trip to Port Said, she had entertained many kinds of fears: that he might pour out his anger on her and deafen her with his shouts and curses. She had not even ruled out physical violence, but the idea of being evicted had never troubled her. She had lived with him for twenty-five years and could not imagine that anything could separate them or pluck her from this house of which she had become an inseparable part.

With this final statement, al-Sayyid Ahmad freed himself from the burden of a thought that had dominated his brain during the past three weeks. His mental struggle had begun the moment the woman tearfully confessed her offense when confined to her bed. At the first instant he had not believed his ears. As he started to recover from the shock, he had become aware of the loathsome truth that was an affront to his pride and dignity but had postponed his wrath when he saw her condition. In fact, it would be correct to say that he was unable to reflect then on the challenge to his pride and dignity because of his deep anxiety for this woman, verging on fear and alarm. He had grown used to her and admired her good qualities. He was even fond enough of her to forget her error and ask God to keep her safe. Confronted by this imminent threat to her, his tyranny had shrunk back. The abundant tenderness lying dormant within his soul had been awakened. He had gone back to his room that day sad and dispirited, although his face had remained expressionless.

When he saw her make rapid and steady progress toward recovery, his composure returned. Consequently he began to review the whole incident, along with its cause and results, with a new eye, or, more accurately, the old one he was accustomed to using at home. It was unfortunate, unfortunate for his wife, that he reviewed the matter when he was calm and all alone. He convinced himself that if he forgave her and yielded to the appeal of affection, which he longed to do, then his prestige, honor, personal standards, and set of values would all be compromised. He would lose control of his family, and the bonds holding it together would dissolve. He could not lead them unless he did so with firmness and rigor. In short, if he forgave her, he would no longer be Ahmad Abd al-Jawad but some other person he could never agree to become.

Yes, it was unfortunate that he reviewed the situation when he was calm and all alone. If he had been able to give vent to his anger when she confessed, his rage would have been satisfied. The accident would have passed without trailing behind it any serious consequences. The problem was that he had not been able to get angry at the suitable moment and his vanity would not let him announce his anger after she had recovered, when he had been calm for three weeks. That kind of anger would have been more like a premeditated reprimand. When his anger flared up, normally it was because of a combination of premeditation and natural emotion. Since the latter element had not found an outlet at the appropriate time, premeditation, which had been provided with plenty of quiet time to review its options, was left to discover an effective method of expressing itself in a form corresponding to the seriousness of the offense. Thus the danger that threatened her life for a time, which protected her from his anger by stirring up his affection, turned into a cause of far-reaching punishment, because the scheming side of his anger had been given so much time to plan and think.

He rose with a frown and turned his back on her. He reached for his garments on the sofa and said, "I'll put my clothes on myself."

She had stayed put, oblivious to everything. His voice roused her. She quickly grasped from his words and stance that he was ordering her to leave. She headed for the door, making no sound as she walked.

Before she got through it she heard him say, "I don't want to find you here when I come back this noon."

from *Palace of Desire*

An hour before his departure for the Friday prayer service, Ahmad Abd al-Jawad summoned Kamal to his room. He never called a member of his family to see him unless the subject was important, and something was indeed troubling him. He was impatient to interrogate his son about a matter that had disturbed him. The previous evening some friends had directed his attention to an article in *al-Balagh* attributed to "the young writer Kamal Ahmad Abd al-Jawad," The men had not read any of the article except its title, "The Origin of Man," and the credit, but they took advantage of it to congratulate and tease al-Sayyid Ahmad, offering various comments. Concerned that such praise might attract the evil eye, he had

seriously considered commissioning Sheikh Mutawalli Abd al-Samad to prepare a special talisman for the young man.

Muhammad Iffat had said, "Your son's name is printed in the same magazine with those of important authors. Take heart! Pray that God will prepare
a career for him as dazzling as theirs."

Ali Abd al-Rahim had told him, "I heard from a reliable source that the
late writer al-Manfaluti bought a country estate with the profits of his pen.
So hope for the best."

Others had mentioned how writing had opened the way for many to find
favor with the ruling elite, citing the authors Shawqi, Hafiz, and al-Manfaluti.

Ibrahim al-Far had used his turn to kid him: "Glory to the One who created a scholar from the loins of a fool."

Al-Sayyid Ahmad had cast one glance at the title and another at the reference to the "young writer" before placing the magazine on his cloak,
which he had removed because of the June heat and a warm feeling derived
from whiskey. He had postponed reading the article until he was alone—at
home or in his store—and had continued to feel happy, boastful, and proud
throughout the evening's festivities. In fact, for the first time he had begun
to reconsider his hostility toward Kamal's choice of the Teachers College,
telling himself it seemed "the boy" would amount to "something," in spite
of that unfortunate choice. He started to fantasize about "the pen," gaining
favor with the elite, and al-Manfaluti's country estate. Yes, who could say?
Perhaps Kamal would not be just a teacher. He might really make a better
life for himself than al-Sayyid Ahmad had dreamed possible.

The following morning, after prayers and breakfast, al-Sayyid Ahmad
made himself comfortable on the sofa and opened the magazine with interest.
He began to read it out loud to get the sense of it. But what did he find? He
could read political articles and understand them without difficulty. But this
essay made his head turn and agitated his heart. He read it aloud again carefully. He came across a reference to a scientist named Darwin and his work on
some distant islands. This man had made tedious comparisons between various different animals until he was astonished to reach the strange conclusion
that man was descended from animals; in fact, that he had evolved from a kind
of ape. Al-Sayyid Ahmad read the offensive paragraph yet another time with

increasing alarm. He was stunned by the sad reality that his son, his own flesh and blood, was asserting, without objection or discussion, that man was descended from animals. He was extremely upset and wondered in bewilderment whether boys were really taught such dangerous ideas in government schools. Then he sent for Kamal.

Kamal arrived, not having the least idea of what was on his father's mind. Since he had been summoned a few days before so his father could congratulate him on his promotion to the third year of the Teachers College, he did not suspect that this new invitation implied anything unpleasant. He had grown pale and emaciated of late. His family attributed this to the exceptional effort he put out before an examination. The real secret was hidden from them. It was the pain and torment he had suffered for the last five months as a prisoner of hellishly tyrannical emotion, which had almost killed him.

Al-Sayyid Ahmad gestured for him to sit down. Kamal sat at the end of the sofa, facing his father politely. He noticed that his mother was seated near the wardrobe, busy folding and mending clothes. Then his father threw the copy of *al-Balagh* down in the space between them on the sofa and said with feigned composure, "You've got an article in this magazine. Isn't that so?"

The cover caught Kamal's eye. His look of astonishment made it clear that he had certainly not been expecting this surprise. Where had his father acquired this new familiarity with literary journals? In a magazine called *al-Sabah*, Kamal had previously published some "reflections," or innocent philosophical speculations and emotional laments in both regular and rhymed prose. He was quite sure his father did not know about them. The only member of the family who did was Yasin. Kamal himself had read them to his brother. Yasin's comment had been: "This is the fruit of my early guidance. I'm the one who taught you about poetry and stories. It's beautiful, Professor. But this philosophy's really deep. Where'd you pick that up?" Yasin had teased him: "What pretty girl inspired this delicate complaint? Professor, one day you'll learn that nothing works with women except beating them with a shoe."

But now his father had read the most dangerous thing he had written— this essay that had stirred up the devil of a battle in his breast when he was thinking about it. His mind had almost been incinerated in that furnace. How had this happened? What explanation could there be unless some of his father's friends who were Wafd party loyalists made a point of buying all the papers and journals affiliated with the party? Could he hope to escape safely from this predicament? He looked up from the magazine. In a tone that did not even begin to convey his inner turmoil, he answered, "Yes. I thought I'd write something to bolster what I was learning and to encourage myself to continue my studies. . . ."

With spurious calm, al-Sayyid Ahmad commented, "There's nothing wrong with that. Writing for the papers has been and still is a way to gain prestige and recognition from the elite. What's important is the topic a person writes about. What did you intend by this article? Read it and explain it to me. It's not clear what you were getting at."

What a disaster this was! The essay had not been intended for the general public and especially not for his father. "It's a long article, Papa. Didn't you read it, sir? I explain a scientific theory in it. . . ."

His father stared at him with an impatient, glinting look. "Is this what they claim is science nowadays?" al-Sayyid Ahmad asked himself. "God's curse on science and scientists."

"What do you say about this theory? I noticed some strange phrases that seem to imply that man is descended from animals, or something along those lines. Is this true?"

Kamal had recently struggled violently with his soul, his beliefs, and his Lord, exhausting his spirit and body. Today he had to contend with his father. In the first battle he had felt tortured and feverish, but this time he was even more frightened and alarmed. God might delay punishment, but his father's practice was to mete out retribution immediately.

"That's what the theory states."

Al-Sayyid Ahmad's voice rose as he asked in dismay, "And Adam, the father of mankind, whom God created from clay, blowing His spirit into him—what does this scientific theory say about him?"

Kamal had repeatedly asked himself this same question, finding it just as dismaying as his father did. The night he had worried about it, he had not been able to get any sleep. He had thrashed about in bed wondering about

Adam, the Creator, and the Quran. If he had said it once he had said ten times: "Either the Quran is totally true, or it's not the Quran." Now he thought, "You're attacking me because you don't know how I've suffered. If I hadn't already grown accustomed to torture, I would have died that night."

In a faint voice he replied, "Darwin, the author of this theory, did not mention our master Adam. . . ."

The man yelled angrily, "Then Darwin's certainly an atheist trapped by Satan's snares. If man's origin was an ape or any other animal, Adam was not the father of mankind. This is nothing but blatant atheism. It's an outrageous attack on the exalted status of God. I know Coptic Christians and Jews in the Goldsmiths Bazaar. They believe in Adam. All religions believe in Adam. What sect does this Darwin belong to? He's an atheist, his words are blasphemous, and reporting his theory's a reckless act. Tell me: Is he one of your professors at the college?"

"How ridiculous this comment would seem if my heart were free to laugh," Kamal mused. "But it's crammed with the pains of disappointed love, doubt, and dying belief. The dreadful encounter of religion and science has scorched you. But how can an intelligent person set his mind against science?"

In a humble voice, Kamal said, "Darwin was an English scientist who lived a long time ago."

At this point, the mother's voice piped up shakily: "God's curse on all the English."

They turned to look at her briefly and found that she had put down her needle and the clothes in order to follow their conversation. They soon forgot her, and the father said, "Tell me: Do you study this theory in school?"

Kamal grabbed for this safety rope suddenly thrown to him. Hiding behind a lie, he said, "Yes."

"That's strange! Will you eventually teach this theory to your pupils?"

"Certainly not! I'll teach literature, and there's no connection between that and scientific theories."

Al-Sayyid Ahmad struck his hands together. At that moment he wished he had as much control over science as he did over his family. He yelled furiously, "Then why do they teach it to you? Is the goal to turn you into atheists?"

Kamal protested, "God forbid that it should have any influence on our religious beliefs."

His father studied him suspiciously and said, "But your essay spreads atheism."

Kamal replied gingerly, "I ask God's forgiveness. I'm explaining the theory so the reader will be familiar with it, not so he'll believe it. It's out of the question that an atheistic notion should influence the heart of a Believer."

"Couldn't you find some other subject besides this criminal theory to write about?"

Why had he written this article? He had hesitated a long time before sending it to the journal. He must have wanted to announce the demise of his religious beliefs. His faith had held firm over the past two years even when buffeted by gales coming from two of the great poets and skeptics of Islam: Abu al-Ala al-Ma'arri and Umar al-Khayyam. But then science's iron fist had destroyed it once and for all.

"At least I'm not an atheist," Kamal told himself. "I still believe in God. But religion? . . . Where's religion? . . . It's gone! I lost it, just as I lost the head of the holy martyr al-Husayn when I was told it's not in his tomb in Cairo . . . and I've lost Aïda and my self-confidence too."

Then in a sorrowful voice he said, "Maybe I made a mistake. My excuse is that I was studying the theory."

"That's no excuse. You must correct your error."

What a good man his father was—wanting to get Kamal to attack science in order to defend a legend. He really had suffered a lot, but he would not open his heart again to legends and superstitions now that he had cleansed it of them.

"I've experienced enough torment and deception," Kamal reflected. "From now on I won't be taken in by fantasies. Light's light. Our father Adam! He wasn't my father. Let my father be an ape, if that's what truth wants. It's better than being one of countless descendants of Adam. If I really were descended from a prophet like Adam, reality wouldn't have made such a fool of me."

"How can I correct my error?"

Al-Sayyid Ahmad said with equal measures of simplicity and sharpness, "You can rely on a fact that's beyond doubt: God created Adam from dust, and Adam's the father of mankind. This fact is mentioned in the Quran. Just explain the erroneous aspects of the theory. That'll be easy for you. If it isn't, what's the use of your education?"

Here the mother's voice said, "What could be easier than showing the error of someone who contradicts the word of God the Merciful? Tell this English atheist that Adam was the father of mankind. Your grandfather was blessed by knowing the Book of God by heart. It's up to you to follow his example. I'm delighted that you wish to be a scholar like him."

Al-Sayyid Ahmad's displeasure was apparent in his expression. He scolded her, "What do you understand about the Book of God or scholarship? Spare us his grandfather and pay attention to what you're doing."

She said shyly, "Sir, I want him to be a scholar like his grandfather, illuminating the world with God's light."

Her husband shouted angrily, "And here he's begun to spread darkness."

The woman replied apprehensively, "God forbid, sir. Perhaps you didn't understand."

Al-Sayyid Ahmad glared at her harshly. He had relaxed his grip on them, and what had been the result? Here was Kamal disseminating the theory that man's origin was an ape. Amina was arguing with him and suggesting he did not understand. He yelled at his wife, "Let me speak! Don't interrupt me. Don't interfere in things you can't comprehend. Pay attention to your work. May God strike you down."

Turning to Kamal with a frowning face, he said, "Tell me: Will you do what I said?"

"You're living with a censor who's more relentless than any afflicting free thought elsewhere in the world," Kamal told himself. "But you love him as much as you fear him. Your heart will never allow you to harm him. Swallow the pain, for you've chosen a life of disputation."

"How can I answer this theory? If I limit my debate to citing Quran references, I won't be adding anything new. Everyone knows them as well as I do and believes them. To discuss it scientifically is a matter for specialists in that area."

"So why did you write about something outside your area?"

Taken at face value, this objection was valid. Unfortunately Kamal lacked the courage to tell his father that he believed in the theory as scientific truth and for this reason had felt he could rely on it to create a general philosophy for existence reaching far beyond science. Al-Sayyid Ahmad considered his silence an admission of error and so felt even more resentful and sad. To be misled on a topic like this was an extremely grave matter with serious consequences, but it was a field where al-Sayyid Ahmad could exercise no authority. He felt that his hands were as tied with this young freethinker as they had been previously with Yasin when he had escaped from paternal custody. Was he to share the experience of other fathers in these strange times? He had heard incredible things about the younger generation. Some schoolboys were smoking. Others openly questioned their teachers' integrity. Still others had rebelled against their fathers. His own prestige had not been diminished, but what had his long history of resolute and stern guidance achieved? Yasin was stumbling and practically doomed. Here was Kamal arguing, debating, and attempting to slip from his grasp.

"Listen carefully to me. I don't want to be harsh with you, for you're polite and obedient. On this subject, I can only offer you my advice. You should remember that no one who has neglected my advice has prospered." Then after a brief silence he continued: "Yasin's an example for you of what I'm saying, and I once advised your late brother not to throw himself to destruction. Had he lived, he would be a distinguished man today."

At this point the mother said in a voice like a moan, "The English killed him. When they're not killing people, they're spreading atheism."

Al-Sayyid Ahmad went on with his remarks: "If you find things in your lessons that contradict religion and are forced to memorize them to succeed in the examination, don't believe them. And it's equally important not to publish them in the papers. Otherwise you'll bear the responsibility. Let your stance with regard to English science be the same as yours toward their occupation of Egypt. Do not admit the legality of either, even when imposed on us by force."

The shy, gentle voice interposed once more: "From now on, dedicate your life to exposing the lies of this science and spreading the light of God."

Al-Sayyid Ahmad shouted at her, "I've said enough without any need for your views."

She returned to her work, while her husband stared at her in a threatening way until sure she would be quiet. Then he looked at Kamal and asked, "Understand?"

"Most certainly," Kamal answered in a voice that inspired confidence.

From that time on, if he wanted to write he would have to publish in *al-Siyasa*. Because of its political affiliation it would never fall into the hands of a Wafdist. And he secretly promised his mother he would consecrate his life to spreading God's light. Were not light and truth identical? Certainly! By freeing himself from religion he would be nearer to God than he was when he believed. For what was true religion except science? It was the key to the secrets of existence and to everything really exalted. If the prophets were sent back today, they would surely choose science as their divine message. Thus Kamal would awake from the dream of legends to confront the naked truth, leaving behind him this storm in which ignorance had fought to the death. It would be a dividing point between his past, dominated by legend, and his future, dedicated to light. In this manner the paths leading to God would open before him—paths of learning, benevolence, and beauty. He would say goodbye to the past with its deceitful dreams, false hopes, and profound pains.

Ahmad Abd al-Jawad was able to leave the house after two more weeks. The first thing he did was to take Yasin and Kamal on a visit to the tomb and mosque of al-Husayn to perform their prayers and give thanks to God.

At the time, news of the death of the politician Ali Fahmy Kamil was in the papers. After pondering this event at length, on the way out of the house al-Sayyid Ahmad told his sons, "He dropped dead after addressing a great gathering. I'm walking on my own two legs after a stay in bed when I almost saw death face to face. Who can know the mysteries the future holds? Truly our lives are in God's hands."

He had to wait patiently for days and even weeks to regain his lost weight, but despite that fact, his dignified appearance and good looks seemed not to have been affected. He walked ahead, followed by Yasin and Kamal. This weekly parade had been abandoned after Fahmy's death. On the way from Palace Walk to the mosque, the two young men observed the prestige their father enjoyed throughout the district. Every merchant with a shop on the street greeted him with open arms and shook hands while applauding his recovery.

Yasin and Kamal responded to these warm demonstrations of mutual affection with joyful pride and smiles that lasted the whole way. All the same, Yasin asked himself innocently why he did not enjoy the same standing as his father, since they were equal both in their dignified and handsome exterior and in their shortcomings. Kamal, although momentarily touched, reexamined his perceptions of his father's remarkable prestige in a new light. In the past, to his small eyes his father's status had seemed the epitome of distinction and greatness. Now he saw it as nothing special, at least not in comparison with his own high ideals. It was merely the prestige enjoyed by a good-hearted, affable, and chivalrous man. True greatness was something totally unlike that, for its thunder shook sluggish hearts and drove sleep from dozing eyes. It was capable of arousing hatred not love, anger rather than satisfaction, and enmity instead of affection. Before it rebuilt, it forced disclosure and destruction. But was it not happiness for a man to be blessed with such love and respect? Yes . . . and the proof was that at times the greatness of important figures was measured by the amount of love and tranquility they sacrificed for lofty goals. In any case, his father was a happy man who was to be congratulated on that.

"See how handsome he is," Kamal told himself. "And how charming Yasin is too! What a strange sight I make between the two of them—like a distorted, trick photograph at a carnival. Claim to your heart's content that good looks are the domain of women not men, but that will never erase from your memory that alarming scene at the gazebo. My father's recovered from his high blood pressure. When will I recover from love? Love's an illness, even though it resembles cancer in having kept its secrets from medical science. In his last letter Husayn Shaddad says, 'Paris is the capital of beauty and love.' Is it also the capital of suffering? My dear friend is growing as stingy with his letters as if they were drops of his precious blood. I want a world where hearts are not deceived and do not deceive others."

At the corner of Khan Ja'far, they could see the great mosque. He heard his father say, "O Husayn!" in a heartfelt way, which combined the charm of a greeting with the fervor of a plea for help. Then al-Sayyid Ahmad quickened his steps. Looking into the mosque with an enigmatic smile, Kamal trailed after him and Yasin. Did he suspect for a moment that Kamal was only accompanying him on this blessed visit to please him or that his son no longer shared any of his religious beliefs? To Kamal, this mosque was now nothing more than one of the many symbols of the disappointment his heart had suffered. In the old days when he had stood beneath its minaret, his heart had pounded, tears had come to his eyes, and his breast had throbbed with ardor, belief, and hope. As he approached it today, all he saw was a vast collection of stone, steel, wood, and paint covering a great tract of land for no clear reason.

"Although forced by obedience to my father's authority, respect for the other people present, and fear of what they might do," Kamal reflected, "to play the role of a Believer until the visit to the shrine's concluded, I find my hypocritical conduct an affront to honor and truth. I want a world where men live free from fear and coercion."

They removed their shoes and entered one after the other. The father headed for the prayer niche and invited his sons to perform a prayer in front of it as a way of saluting the mosque. He raised his hands to his head to begin the prayer ritual, and they followed his example. As usual, the father lost himself in his prayers, and his eyelids drooped as he yielded his will to God's. Yasin too forgot everything except that he was in the presence of God the Merciful and Forgiving. Kamal began to move his lips without reciting anything. He bowed, straightened up, knelt, and prostrated himself as if performing insipid athletic exercises.

He told himself, "The most ancient remaining human structures, on the face of the earth or carved inside it, are temples. Even today, no area is free of them. When will man grow up and depend on himself? That loud voice coming from the far corner of the mosque reminds people of the end. When has there ever been an end to time? How beautiful it would be to see man wrestle with his illusions and vanquish them. But when will the struggle cease and the fighter announce that he's happy and that the world looks so different that it might have been created the day before? These two men are my father and brother. Why shouldn't all men be my fathers and brothers?

How could this heart I carry within me let itself torment me in so many different ways? How frequently throughout the day I'm confronted by people I don't like. . . . Why should the friend I love have departed to the ends of the earth?"

When they finished praying, the father said, "Let's rest here a little before circling the tomb."

They sat there silently, their legs folded beneath them, until the father said gently, "We haven't been here together since that day."

Yasin replied emotionally, "Let's recite the 'Fatiha' for Fahmy's spirit."

They recited the opening prayer of the Quran, and then the father asked Yasin somewhat suspiciously, "I wonder whether worldly affairs have not kept you from visiting al-Husayn."

Yasin, who had not set foot in the mosque all those years except a handful of times, answered, "I don't let a week go by without visiting my master al-Husayn."

The father turned toward Kamal and cast him a glance as if to ask, "And you?"

Feeling embarrassed, Kamal replied, "Me too!"

The father said humbly, "He's our loved one and our intercessor with his grandfather Muhammad on a day when no mother or father can be of any assistance."

He had recovered from his illness this time, but only after it had taught him a lesson he would not forget. He had found its violence convincing and feared a recurrence. His intention to repent was sincere. He had always believed he would repent, no matter how long he waited. He was now certain that postponing it after this sickness would be stupidity and a blasphemous rejection of God's blessings. Whenever he happened to think of forbidden amusements, he consoled himself with the innocent pleasures awaiting him in life, like friendship, music, and jests. Therefore he entreated God to preserve him from the whispered temptations of Satan and to strengthen his resolve to repent. He proceeded to recite some of the Quran's simpler, shorter suras that he knew by heart.

When he rose, his sons did too. Then they went to the sepulcher, where they were greeted by the sweet fragrance pervading the place and a murmur of whispered recitations. They walked around the tomb with the throngs of visitors. Kamal's eyes looked up at the great green turban and then rested for a time on the wooden door, which he had kissed so often. He compared the present with the past and his former state of mind with his current one. He remembered how revelation of this tomb's secret had been the first tragedy in his life and then how the succession of tragedies following it had carried off love, belief, and friendship. Despite all that, he was still standing on his own two feet as he gazed worshipfully at truth, so heedless of the jabs of pain that even his bitterness caused him to smile. He had no regrets over his rejection of the blind happiness illuminating the faces of the men circumambulating the tomb. How could he buy happiness at the price of light when he had vowed to live with his eyes open? He preferred to be anxious and alive rather than comfortable and sleepy. He chose wakeful insomnia over restful sleep.

When they had finished walking around the sepulcher, the father invited them to rest for a while in the shelter of the shrine. They went to a corner and sat down next to each other. Some acquaintances noticed al-Sayyid Ahmad and approached to shake hands and congratulate him on his recovery. Some stayed to sit with them. Most of them knew Yasin either from his father's store or from al-Nahhasin School, but hardly anyone knew Kamal. Some of them noticed how thin the boy was and one jokingly asked al-Sayyid Ahmad, "What's wrong with this son of yours? He's skinny as a ramrod."

As if returning the man's compliment with an even nicer one, al-Sayyid Ahmad shot back, "No, you're the ram!"

Yasin smiled. Kamal did too, for this was the first chance he had had to observe his father's secret personality of which he had heard so much. His father was obviously a man who would not miss a chance for a little joke even when he was beside the tomb of al-Husayn in a sacred place devoted to praise of God and repentance. Yasin was inspired to reflect on his father's future, wondering whether al-Sayyid Ahmad would return to his previous joys even after this serious illness.

Yasin told himself, "Knowing this is extremely important to me."

from *Sugar Street*

K amal had barely reached the stairway door after showing out the last visitors of the evening when an alarming din reached his ears from above. His nerves were still on edge, and he feared the worst as he bounded up the steps. The sitting room was empty, but through the closed door of his father's chamber he could hear the loud voices of several people, who were all speaking at once. Rushing to the door, he opened it and entered, expecting something unpleasant but refusing to think what it might be.

His mother's hoarse voice was exclaiming, "Master!"

Aisha was calling curtly for "Papa!"

Mumbling to herself, Umm Hanafi stood riveted to her spot by the head of the bed. When Kamal looked in that direction, he was overcome by desperate alarm and mournful resignation, for he saw that the bottom half of his father's body lay on the bed while the upper half rested on Amina's breast. The man's chest was heaving up and down up and down mechanically as he emitted a strange rattling sound not of this world. His eyes had a new blind look, which suggested that they could not see anything or express the man's internal struggle. Kamal, near the end of the bed, felt that his feet were glued to the floor, that he had lost the ability to speak, and that his eyes had turned to glass. He could think of nothing to say or to do and had an overwhelming sense of being utterly impotent, forlorn, and insignificant. Although aware that his father was bidding farewell to life, Kamal was in all other respects as good as unconscious.

Glancing away from her father's face long enough to look at Kamal, Aisha cried out, "Father! Here's Kamal. He wants to talk to you."

Umm Hanafi abandoned her murmured refrain to say in a chocking voice, "Get the doctor."

With angry sorrow, the mother groaned, "What doctor, you fool?"

The father moved as if trying to sit up, and the convulsions of his chest increased. He stretched out the forefinger of his right hand and then that of the left. When Amina saw this, her face contracted with pain. She bent down toward his ear and recited in an audible voice, "There is no god but God, and Muhammad is the Messenger of God." She kept repeating these words until his hand became still. Kamal understood that his father, no longer able to speak, had asked Amina to recite the Muslim credo on his behalf and that the inner meaning of this final hour would never be revealed. To describe it as pain, terror, or a swoon would have been a pointless conjecture. At any rate it could not last long, for it was too momentous and significant to be part of ordinary life. Although his nerves were devastated by this scene, Kamal was ashamed to find himself snatching a few moments to analyze and study it, as if his father's death was a subject for his reflections and a source of information for him. This doubled his grief and his pain.

The contractions of the man's chest intensified and the rattling sound grew louder. "What is this?" Kamal wondered. "Is he trying to get up? Or attempting to speak? Or addressing something we can't see? Is he in pain? Or terrified? . . . Oh. . . ." The father emitted a deep groan, and then his head fell on his breast.

With every ounce of her being Aisha screamed, "Father! . . . Na'ima! . . . Uthman! . . . Muhammad!" Umm Hanafi rushed to her and gently shoved her out of the room. The mother raised a pale face to look at Kamal and gestured for him to leave, but he did not budge.

She whispered to him desperately, "Let me perform my last duty to your father."

He turned and exited to the sitting room, where Aisha, who had flung herself across the sofa, was howling. He took a seat on the sofa opposite hers, while Umm Hanafi went back into the bedroom to assist her mistress, closing the door behind her. But Aisha's weeping was unbearable, and rising again, Kamal began to pace back and forth, without addressing any comment to her. From time to time he would glance at the closed door and then press his lips together.

"Why does death seem so alien to us?" he wondered. Once his thoughts were collected enough for him to reflect on the situation, he immediately lost his concentration again, as emotion got the better of him. Even when no longer able to leave the bedroom, al-Sayyid Ahmad had defined the life of the household. It would come as no surprise if on the morrow Kamal found the house to be quite a different place and its life transformed. Indeed, from this moment on, he would have to accustom himself to a new role. Aisha's wails made him feel all the more distraught. He considered trying to silence her but then refrained. He was amazed to see her give vent to her emotions after she had appeared for so long to be impassive and oblivious to everything. Kamal thought again of his father's disappearance from their lives. It seemed almost inconceivable. Remembering his father's condition in the final days, he felt sorrow tear at his heartstrings. When he reviewed the image of their father at the height of his powers and glory, Kamal felt a profound pity for all living creatures. But when would Aisha ever stop wailing? Why could she not weep tearlessly like her brother?

The door of the bedroom opened, and Umm Hanafi emerged. During the moment before it was shut again, he could hear his mother's lamentations. He gathered that she had finished performing her final duty to his father and was now free to cry. Umm Hanafi approached Aisha and told her brusquely, "That's enough weeping, my lady." Turning toward Kamal, she remarked, "Dawn is breaking, master. Sleep, if only a little, for you have a hard day ahead of you."

Then she suddenly started crying. As she left the room, she said in a sobbing voice, "I'll go to Sugar Street and Palace of Desire Alley to announce the dreadful news."

Yasin rushed in, followed by Zanuba and Ridwan. Then the silence of the street was rent by the cries of Khadija, whose arrival caused the household's fires of grief to burn at fever pitch, as wails mixed with screams and sobs. It would not have been appropriate for the men to mourn on the first floor, and they went up to the study on the top floor. They sat there despondently, overwhelmed by a gloomy silence, until Ibrahim Shawkat remarked, "The only power and strength is God's. The raid finished him off. May God be most compassionate to him. He was an extraordinary man."

Unable to control himself, Yasin started crying. Then Kamal burst into tears too. Ibrahim Shawkat said, "Proclaim that there is only one God. He did not leave you until you were grown men."

With morose sorrow and some astonishment Ridwan, Abd al-Muni'm, and Ahmad gazed at the weeping men, who quickly dried their tears and fell silent.

Ibrahim Shawkat said, "It will be morning soon. Let's consider what has to be done."

Yasin answered sadly and tersely, "There's nothing novel about this. We've gone through it repeatedly."

Ibrahim Shawkat responded, "The funeral must suit his rank."

Yasin replied with conviction, "That's the least we can do."

Then Ridwan commented, "The street in front of the house isn't wide enough for a funeral tent that can hold all the mourners. Let's put it in Bayt al-Qadi Square instead."

Ibrahim Shawkat remarked, "But it's customary to install the tent in front of the home of the deceased."

Ridwan replied, "That isn't so important, especially since cabinet ministers, senators, and deputies will be among the mourners."

They realized that he was referring to his own acquaintances. Yasin commented indifferently, "So let's erect it there."

Thinking about the part he was to play, Ahmad said, "We won't be able to get the obituary in the morning papers. . . ."

Kamal said, "The evening papers come out at about three P.M. Let's have the funeral at five."

"So be it. The cemetery's not far, at any rate. There'll be time to have the burial before sunset."

Kamal considered what they were saying with some amazement. At five o'clock the previous day his father had been in bed, listening to the radio. At that time the following day . . . next to Yasin's two young children and Fahmy. What was left of Fahmy? Life had done nothing to diminish Kamal's childhood desire to look inside his brother's coffin. Had his father really been preparing to say something? What had he wanted to say?

Yasin turned toward Kamal to ask, "Were you there when he died?"

"Yes. It was shortly after you left."

"Did he suffer much?"

"I don't know. Who could say, brother? But it didn't last more than five minutes."

Yasin sighed and then asked, "Didn't he say anything?"

"No. He probably wasn't able to speak."

"Didn't he recite the credo?"

Looking down to hide his tearful expression, Kamal replied, "My mother did that for him."

"May God be compassionate to him."

"Amen."

They were silent for a time until finally Ridwan remarked, "The funeral pavilion must be large, if there's to be room for all the mourners to sit."

Yasin said, "Naturally. We have many friends." Then, looking at Abd al-Muni'm, he added, "And there are all the Muslim Brethren." He sighed and continued: "If his friends had been alive, they would have carried his coffin on their shoulders."

The funeral went off according to their expectations. Abd al-Muni'm had the most friends in attendance, but Ridwan's were higher in rank. Some of them attracted attention because they were well known to readers of newspapers or magazines. Ridwan was so proud they were there that his pride almost obscured his grief. The people of the district, even those who had not known al-Sayyid Ahmad personally, came to bid farewell to their lifelong neighbor. The only thing missing from the funeral was the deceased man's friends, who had all preceded him to the other world.

At Bab al-Nasr, as the funeral cortege made its way to the cemetery, Sheikh Mutawalli Abd al-Samad materialized. Staggering from advanced age, he looked up at the coffin, squinted his eyes, and asked, "Who is that?"

One of the men from the district told him, "Al-Sayyid Ahmad Abd al-Jawad, God rest his soul."

The man's face trembled unsteadily back and forth as a questioning look of bewilderment spread across it. Then he inquired, "Where was he from?"

Shaking his head rather sadly, the other man replied, "From this district. How could you not have known him? Don't you remember al-Sayyid Ahmad Abd al-Jawad?"

But the sheikh gave no sign of remembering anything and after casting a final glance at the casket proceeded on his way.

Translated by William M. Hutchins, Olive E. Kenny,
Lorne M. Kenny, and Angele Botros Samaan

from *Children of the Alley,* 1959

Considered one of Mahfouz's masterpieces, when the novel first appeared in serialized form in 1959 it created an uproar in Islamic circles and was to become responsible, years later, for an attempt on his life in which he was seriously wounded.

The novel takes place in a typical Cairene quarter. The main characters are Gabalawi, who represents God; other characters who stand for Moses, Jesus, and Muhammad; and last but not least, a character named Arafa who represents knowledge and science—the Arabic root 'arafa' means 'to know.'

The novel is divided into five parts, of which we have reproduced a portion of the part dealing with the character representing Jesus.

This is the story of our alley—its stories, rather. I have witnessed only the most recent events, those of my own time, but I have recorded all of them the way our storytellers told them. Everyone in our alley tells these stories, just as they heard them in coffeehouses or as they were handed down for generations—these sources are my only basis for what I'm writing. Most of our social occasions call for storytelling. Whenever someone is depressed, suffering, or humiliated, he points to the mansion at the top of the alley at the end opening out to the desert, and says sadly, "That is our ancestor's house, we are all his children, and we have a right to his property. Why are we starving? What have we done?" Then he will tell the stories and cite the lives of Adham and Gabal, of Rifaa and Qassem—some of our alley's great men.

But this ancestor of ours is a puzzle! He has lived longer than any man dreams of living—his long life is the stuff of proverbs. He has dwelled aloof in his house for long ages, and no one has seen him since he isolated himself up there. The stories of his old age and isolation are bewildering, and perhaps fantasy and rumor have helped to make them so. Anyway, he was called Gabalawi, and our alley was named for him. He owns everything and everyone in it, and everything in the desert around it. Once I heard a man say about him, "He created our alley and from our alley grew Egypt, the most important place in the world. He lived here alone when the place was empty and desolate, and became master of it by force and his standing with the ruler. There will never again be anyone like him. He was tough; the wild beasts dreaded his very name." And I heard someone else say, "He was truly noble. He was unlike other leaders. He didn't collect protection money or behave arrogantly; he was kind to humble people." Then came a time when some people talked about him in a way unsuited to his rank and dignity— you know how people can be. I always found talk about him fascinating, never boring. How often that moved me to stroll around his tall mansion trying to catch a glimpse of him—always in vain. How often I stood before his massive gate, gazing at the stuffed crocodile mounted above it. How often I sat in the Muqattam Desert, not far from his high walls, able to see no more than the tops of the mulberry, sycamore, and palm trees enclosing the house, and the closed windows that disclosed no sign of life. Is it not sad to have a grandfather that we never see, and who never sees us? Is it not strange of him to disappear inside that locked mansion, while we live in the dirt? If you are curious about what brought us to this, here are the stories; you will hear all about Adham, Gabal, Rifaa, and Qassem—though none of it will soothe or comfort you.

I said that no one had seen him since he secluded himself. That did not bother most people, as all they ever cared about was his estate, and his much-talked-about Ten Conditions. This was how the dispute started before I was born, whose ferocity has only grown with the passing of generations, up until today—and tomorrow. So I do not want any bitter ridicule when I speak of the close family ties that bind the people in our alley. We were and still are one family, which no stranger has penetrated. Everyone in our alley knows everyone else, men and women alike; and yet no alley has ever known the terrible quarrels ours has, nor have any people even been as divided by controversy as we, and for every decent man you will find ten gangsters brandishing clubs and ready to pick a fight. The people are even used to buying their safety with bribes, and their security with obedience and abasement, and were severely punished for the smallest thing they said or did wrong—or even for thinking something wrong. The strangest thing is that the people in nearby alleys, in Atuf, Kafr al-Zaghari, in al-Darasa and al-Husseiniya, envy us because of our alley's property and our tough men. They say property and a well-protected alley mean wealth and invincible protectors. All that is true, but they don't know that we are crushed by misery, that we live in squalor, with flies and lice, that we are content with crumbs, that we are half naked. They see our protectors strut around on top of us and are struck with admiration, and our only comfort is to look up at the mansion, and say, in sorrow and pain, "There is Gabalawi, the owner. He is our ancestor and we are his grandchildren."

I have witnessed the recent period in the life of our alley, and lived through the events that came about through the coming of Arafa, a dutiful son of our alley. It is thanks to one of Arafa's friends that I am able to record some of the stories of our alley. One day he said to me, "You're one of the few who know how to write, so why don't you write down the stories of our alley? They've never been told in the right order, and even then always at the mercy of the storytellers' whims and prejudices; it would be wonderful if you wrote them carefully, all together so that people could benefit from them, and I'll help you out with what you don't know, with inside information." I acted on his advice, both because it struck me as a good idea and because I loved the person who suggested it. I was the first in our alley to make a career out of writing, though it has brought me much contempt and mockery. It was my job to write the petitions and complaints of the oppressed and needy. Although many wretched people seek me out, I am barely better off than our alley's beggars, though I am privy to so many of the people's secrets and sorrows that I have become a sad and brokenhearted man.

But, but—I am not writing about myself or my troubles, which amount to nothing compared with those of our alley—our strange alley with its strange stories! How did it happen? What was it all about? And who were the children of our alley?

After leaving Bayoumi's house, Rifaa headed for his own house. The skies were swathed in autumn mist, and a mild breeze was in the air. The whole alley was crowded around the lemon stalls; it was pickling season, and there was a roar of storytelling and laughter. Some boys had got into a fight and were pelting each other with dirt. Several people greeted Rifaa, but he was also spattered with dirt, so he went on to his house, dusting off his shoulders and his turban. He found Zaki, Ali, Hussein, and Karim waiting for him, and they embraced as they did whenever they met, and he told them—and his wife, who joined them—what had gone on between him and Bayoumi and Khunfis. They listened carefully and worriedly, and by the time he finished his story all their faces were grim. Yasmina asked herself: So what would be the outcome of this trying situation? Was there a solution that would save this good man from ruin without threatening her happiness? All their eyes were curious. Rifaa rested his head somewhat wearily against the wall.

"An order from Bayoumi is not something to take lightly," said Yasmina.

"Rifaa has friends," said Ali, the most impetuous of them all. "They defeated Batikha, and he vanished from the alley!"

"Bayoumi is not Batikha!" Yasmina scowled. "If you challenge Bayoumi, you've spoken your last words!"

"Let's listen to our master first!" said Hussein, turning to Rifaa.

"Don't even think of fighting," said Rifaa, his eyes nearly closed. "Anyone who struggles for people's happiness cannot take lightly the shedding of their blood."

Yasmina's face was radiant. She hated the idea of widowhood, fearing that she would be watched again, and thus unable to get away to her wonderful other man.

"The best thing you can do is to spare yourself that mess," she assured him.

"We will never stop our work," Zaki protested. "We'll leave the alley."

Yasmina's heart pounded with fear as she imagined living far from her lover's alley, and she spoke up. "We are not going to live like lost strangers, far from our alley."

Every gaze hung on Rifaa's face. Slowly he moved his head to face them and said, "I don't want to leave our alley.

There was a sudden long, impatient knocking on the door, and Yasmina opened it. The seated men heard the voices of Shafi'i and Abda asking for their son. Rifaa got up and greeted his parents with hugs. They all sat down, and Shafi'i and his wife were out of breath; their faces expressed the unpleasant news they brought.

"My boy," the father was saying before they knew it, "Khunfis has given you up. Your life is in danger. My friends tell me that the gangster's men are surrounding your house."

"Our house," said Abda, drying her bloodshot eyes. "If only we'd never come back to this alley that sells lives for nothing!"

"Don't be afraid, ma'am," said Ali. "All our neighbors are our friends, and they love us."

"What have we done to deserve punishment?" sighed Rifaa.

"You're from the Al Gabal, whom they hate," said Shafi'i anxiously. "How my heart has suffered fear ever since you first mentioned Gabalawi!"

"Only yesterday they fought Gabal because he claimed the estate," marveled Rifaa, "and now they're fighting me because I disdain the estate!"

Shafi'i made a despairing gesture with his hand. "Say whatever you like about them, but it won't change them one bit. All know is that you are lost if you leave your house, and I doubt whether you're safe even if you stay in it."

For the first time, fear stole into Karim's heart, but he hid it with a firm will and spoke to Rifaa. "They are lying in wait for you outside. If you stay here they will come for you, if they're the gangsters of our alley that I know. Let's escape to my house over the rooftops, and think there about what to do next.

"From there you can escape from the alley in the dark," shouted Shafi'i.

"And let everything I've built up be demolished?"

"Do what he says," his mother begged him, crying. "Please, for your mother!"

"Resume your work across the desert somewhere, if you want," said his father sharply.

Karim got up, looking concerned. "Let's make a plan. Shafi'i and his wife will stay a little longer, then go to the House of Triumph as if they were coming home after a normal visit. The lady Yasmina will go out to Gamaliya as if to go shopping, and when she comes back you will slip out to my house. That's easier than escaping over the rooftops.

Shafi'i liked the plan.

"We must not waste a single minute," said Karim. "I'll go and check out the roofs."

He left the room, and Shafi'i rose and took Rifaa by the hand. Abda ordered Yasmina to pack some clothes in a bundle.

Yasmina began to pack a few clothes, with a constricted chest and wounded heart, a tempest of hatred gathering inside her. Abda kissed her son, hugged him and tearfully murmured a few incantations to protect him from the evil eye. Rifaa left, pondering his situation with a sorrowing heart. How he loved people with his heart; how he had labored for their contentment; how he had suffered their hatred. Would Gabalawi condone failure?

"Follow me," Karim, now back again, was saying to Rifaa and his companions.

"We'll follow you," said Abda, overcome with weeping, "maybe in a little bit."

"God bless you and protect you, Rifaa," said Shafi'i, trying hard not to cry.

Rifaa hugged his parents, and then turned to Yasmina.

"Pull your cloak and veil around you tightly so that no one will recognize you." He leaned closer to her ear. "I can't stand to think of any hand harming you."

Yasmina left the house swathed in black, Abda's parting words ringing in her ears: "Goodbye, daughter, may God keep you and protect you. Rifaa is in your hands. I will pray for both of you day and night." Night was beginning to fall; the coffeehouse lamps were being lit, and boys were playing in the light shed by the handcart lanterns. At the same time, cats and dogs were fighting—as they always did at that time of day—around the heaps of garbage. Yasmina walked toward Gamaliya with no room for mercy in her passionate heart. She did not hesitate, but was filled with fear, and imagined that many eyes were watching her. She had no sense of composure until she had left al-Darasa for the desert, and felt truly safe only when she was in the reception hall, in Bayoumi's arms.

When she pulled the veil away from her face, he looked at her attentively. "Are you afraid?"

"Yes," she answered, panting.

"No, you're a lot of things but not a coward. Tell me, what's wrong?"

"They fled over the rooftops to Karim's house, and they'll leave the alley at dawn."

"At dawn, sons of bitches!" muttered Bayoumi scornfully.

"They talked him into going away. Why don't you let him go?"

"Long ago, Gabal went away, then came back," he said with a smile of mockery. "These vermin don't deserve to live."

"He renounces life," she said distractedly, "but he does not deserve death."

"The alley has enough madmen," he said, his mouth distorted in disgust.

She looked at him earnestly, then lowered her gaze, and whispered, as if to herself. "He saved my life once."

"And here you are handing him over to his death," said Bayoumi with a coarse laugh. "An eye for an eye, and the one who started it loses!"

She felt an alarm as painful as a sickness, and glanced at him rebukingly. "I did what I did because I love you more than my life."

He stroked her cheek tenderly. "We'll be free. And if things get hard for you, you have a place in this house."

She felt a little better. "If they offered me Gabalawi's mansion without you, I wouldn't take it."

"You are a loyal girl."

The word "loyal" pierced her, and the sickening sense of alarm came back to her. She wondered if the man was mocking her. There was no more time for talk, and she got up. He stood to say goodbye to her, and she stole out the back door. She found her husband and his friends waiting for her, and sat beside Rifaa.

"Our house is being watched. It was wise of your mother to leave the lamp lit in the window. It will be easy to get away at dawn."

"But he's so sad," Zaki said to her, looking sorrowfully at Rifaa. "Aren't there sick people everywhere? Don't they need healing too?"

"There is a greater need for healing where the disease is out of control."

Yasmina looked at him pityingly. She said to herself that it would be a crime to kill him. She wished that there was one thing about him that deserved punishment. She remembered that he was the one person in this world who had been kind to her, and that his reward for that would be death. She cursed these thoughts to herself, and thought, *Let those who have good lives do good.* When she saw him returning her look, she spoke up as if commiserating with him. "Your life is worth so much more than this damned alley of ours."

"That's what you *say*," Rifaa said, smiling, "but I read sadness in your eyes!"

She trembled, and said to herself: God help me if he reads minds as well as he casts out demons!

"I'm not sad, I'm just afraid for you!" she said.

"I'll get supper ready," said Karim, getting up.

He came back with a tray and invited them to sit down, and they seated themselves around it. It was a supper of bread, cheese, whey, cucumbers, and radishes, and there was a jug of barley beer. Karim filled their cups. "Tonight we'll need warmth and morale."

They drank, and Rifaa smiled. "Liquor arouses demons, but it revives people who have got rid of their demons." He looked at Yasmina beside him, and she knew the meaning of his look.

"You'll free me of my demon tomorrow, if God spares you," she said.

Rifaa's face shone with delight, and his friends exchanged congratulatory looks and began to eat their supper. They broke the bread, and their hands came together over the dishes. It was as if they had forgotten the death that surrounded them.

"The owner of the estate wanted his children to be like him," said Rifaa. "But they insisted on being like demons. They were foolish, and he has no love for foolishness, as he told me."

Karim shook his head regretfully, and swallowed. "If only I had some of the power he used to have, things would be the way he wants them to be."

"If, if, if, what good does 'if' do us!" said Ali crossly. "We must *act*."

"We have never failed," said Rifaa firmly. "We have fought the demons ruthlessly, and whenever a demon departs, love takes its place. There is no other goal."

Zaki sighed. "If only they had let us do our work, we would have filled the alley with health, love, and peace."

"It's incredible that we're thinking of fleeing when we have so many friends!" Ali objected.

"Your demon still has roots deep inside you." Rifaa smiled. "Don't forget that our aim is healing, not killing. It is better for a person to be killed than to kill."

Rifaa turned abruptly to Yasmina and said, "You're not eating or paying attention!"

Her heart contracted with fear, but she fought down her agitation. "I'm just marveling at how cheerfully you all talk, as if you were at a wedding!"

"You'll get used to being cheerful when you're cleansed of your demon tomorrow." He looked at his brothers. "Some of you are ashamed of conciliation—we are the sons of a nation that respects only power, but power is not confined to terrorizing others. Wrestling with demons is hundreds of times harder than attacking the weak, or fighting the gangsters."

Ali wagged his head sadly. "The reward of good deeds is the terrible situation we find ourselves in now."

"The battle will not end as they expect," said Rifaa decisively. "And we are not as weak as they imagine! All we have done is shift the battle from one field to a different one, only our battlefield now calls for more courage and tougher force.

They resumed their dinner, thinking over what they had heard. He seemed to them just as calm, reassured, and strong as he was handsome and meek. In the long lull came the voice of the local poet, reciting: "One noon Adham sat in Watawit Alley to rest, and fell asleep. A movement woke him, and he saw boys stealing his cart. He got up and threatened them, and one boy who saw him warned his friends with a whistle; they overturned the cart to distract him from going after them. The cucumbers tumbled all over the ground while the boys dispersed like locusts. Adham was so enraged that he forgot his decent upbringing and screamed obscenities at them, then bent down to retrieve his cucumbers from the mud. His anger redoubled with no outlet, so he asked emotionally, *Why was your anger like fire, burning without mercy? Why was your pride dearer to you than your own flesh and blood? How can you enjoy an easy life when you know we are being stepped on like insects? Forgiveness, gentleness, tolerance have no place in your mansion, you oppressor!* He seized the handles of the cart and set out to push it as far as he could get from this accursed alley, when he heard a taunting voice. 'How much are the cucumbers, uncle?' Idris stood there with a mocking grin." Then there was a woman's shout, over the poet's voice, crying, "Little boy lost, good people!"

Time passed, with the men in conversation and Yasmina in torment. Hussein wanted to look around out in the alley, but Karim opposed the idea; someone might see him and get suspicious. Zaki wondered whether Rifaa's house had been attacked, and Rifaa pointed out that all they could hear was the lament of the rebec and the cheering of the street boys. The alley was leading its usual life, and there was no sign that any crime was being planned. Yasmina's mind was such a whirlpool of worry that she was afraid her eyes would give her away. She wanted her torment to end any way possible and at any cost; she wanted to fill her belly with wine until she no longer knew what was happening around her. She said to herself that she was not the first woman in Bayoumi's life and she would not be the last; that stray dogs always collected around piles of garbage; only let this torment end at any cost. With the passage of time, silence slowly overcame the racket, and the voice of the children and cries of the peddlers died down, leaving only the lament of the rebec. A sudden revulsion at these men seized her, for no other reason than that, in a way, it was they who tormented her.

"Should I prepare the pipe?" asked Karim.

"We need clear heads!" said Rifaa firmly.

"I thought it would help us pass the time."

"You're too afraid."

"It looks like there's no need to be afraid at all," Karim protested.

Yes, there had been no incidents, and Rifaa's house had not been attacked. The melodies had fallen silent and the poets had gone home. They could hear the sounds of doors slamming, the conversations of people going back to their houses, laughter and coughing, and then nothing. They continued to wait and watch until the first cock crowed. Zaki got up and went to the window to see the street, then turned to them.

"Quiet and emptiness. The alley is just the way it was the day Idris was kicked out."

"We should go," said Karim.

Yasmina was overcome with anguish, wondering what would become of her if Bayoumi was late for the appointment, or had changed his mind. The men got up, each carrying a bundle.

"Farewell, hellish alley," said Hussein, leading the way out. Rifaa gently guided Yasmina ahead of him, and followed with his hand on her shoulder, as if afraid of losing her in the darkness. Then came Karim, Hussein, and Zaki. They slipped out of the apartment door one by one, and ascended the stairs, using the railing as a guide in the total blackness. The darkness on the roof seemed less intense, though not a single star could be seen. A cloud absorbed all the light of the moon concealed behind it, and its surface reflected the scudding clouds.

"The walls of the roofs almost touch," said Ali. "We can give the lady help if she needs it."

They followed, and as Zaki—coming last—arrived, he felt a movement behind him and turned to the door of the roof, where he detected four phantoms. "Who is there?" he asked in alarm.

They all halted and turned around.

"Stop, you bastards," said Bayoumi's voice.

Gaber, Khalid, and Handusa fanned out from his right and left, and Yasmina gasped. She slipped away from Rifaa's hand and moved toward the door of the roof. None of the gangsters stopped her.

"The woman has betrayed you," said Ali dazedly to Rifaa.

In a moment they were surrounded. Bayoumi began to examine them at close range, one by one, asking, "Who's the exorcist?"

When he found him, he grabbed him by the shoulder with an iron hand and sneered. "The demon's companion! Where did you think you were going?"

"You don't want us here," said Rifaa indignantly. "We're leaving."

After a brief sarcastic laugh, Bayoumi turned to Karim. "You—what good did it do, hiding them in your house?"

Karim gulped with a dry mouth, and his muscles trembled. "I didn't know of any trouble between you and them!"

Bayoumi struck him in the face with his free hand, and he fell to the ground, but quickly jumped up again and ran, terrified, toward the adjacent roof. Suddenly Hussein and Ali ran after him, but Handusa pounced on Ali and kicked him in the stomach. He fell down, groaning from his depths. At the same time, Gaber and Khalid went after the others, but Bayoumi said contemptuously, "There's nothing to fear from them. Neither of them will say a single word, and if they do they're dead."

Rifaa, whose head was bent toward Bayoumi's fist by the terrible grip, said, "They have done nothing to deserve punishment."

Bayoumi slapped him and taunted, "Tell me, didn't they hear from Gabalawi the way you did?" He pushed Rifaa in front of him and said, "Walk in front of me and don't open your mouth."

He walked, resigned to his fate. He descended the dark stairs carefully, and the heavy footfalls followed him. He was so overcome by the darkness, confusion, and evil that threatened him that he could scarcely think of those who had fled or betrayed him. A profound and absolute sadness seized him, eclipsing even his fears. It seemed to him the darkness would prevail over the earth. They came out into the alley and crossed the neighborhood, in which, thanks to him, no sickness remained. Handusa went before them to the Al Gabal neighborhood, and they passed under the closed-up House of Triumph, until he imagined that he could hear his parents' hesitant breaths. He wondered for a moment about them, and imagined that he heard Abda crying in the quiet night, but he was speedily brought back to the darkness, confusion, and evil that threatened him. The Al Gabal neighborhood seemed like a collection of colossal phantom hulks shrouded in darkness; how intense the darkness was, how deep its sleep. The footfalls of the executioners in the pitch-blackness and the creaking of their sandals were like the laughter of devils playing in the night. Handusa turned toward the desert, opposite the mansion wall, and Rifaa raised his eyes to the mansion, but it was as dark as the sky. There was a figure at the end of the wall.

"Khunfis?" asked Handusa

"Yes," said the man.

He joined the men wordlessly. Rifaa's eyes were still raised to the mansion. Didn't his ancestor know his situation? One word from him could save him from the claws of these monsters and spare him from their plot. He was capable of making them hear his voice, just as he had made Rifaa hear it in this place. Gabal had been in a predicament like this, and he had been delivered, and triumphed. But Rifaa passed the wall and heard nothing but the footfalls of these evil men, and their regular breathing. They pressed on into the desert, where the sand made their steps heavy. Rifaa had a feeling of banishment in this desert as he thought back on how the woman had betrayed him and how his friends had sought refuge in flight. He wanted to turn back to the mansion, but abruptly Bayoumi's hand shoved at his back and he fell on his face.

"Khunfis?" called Bayoumi, lifting his club.

"With you to the end, sir," said Khunfis, also lifting his club.

"Why do you want to kill me?" Rifaa asked despairingly.

Bayoumi slammed his club down on his head, and Rifaa cried out, then called out from the depths of his soul, "Gabalawi!"

In the next instant, Khunfis' club came down on his neck, and then the clubs took turns.

Then there was silence, broken only by his death rattle.

Their hands began to dig furiously in the sand in the dark.

The killers left the desert, heading for the alley, and quickly vanished in the darkness. Four human shapes rose to stand at a spot near the scene of the crime, and could be heard sighing and weeping quietly.

"Cowards!" one of them shouted. "You held me back and wore me out, so he died undefended."

"If we had obeyed you, we would all have been lost, without saving him," another told him.

"Cowards!" Ali repeated. "You are nothing but cowards."

"Don't waste time talking," sobbed Karim. "We have a terrible job to finish before morning."

Hussein raised his head and trained his tearful eyes on the sky, and muttered anxiously, "It will be dawn soon. Let's be quick."

"A man whose life was as short as a dream—but in him we lost the most precious thing we knew in life!" wept Zaki.

"Cowards," muttered Ali through his clenched teeth as he headed toward the scene of the crime.

They followed him, and all knelt in a half circle to examine the ground searchingly.

"Here!" shouted Karim abruptly, like a man stung. He sniffed his hand. "This is his blood!"

"And this fresh area is where he's buried," shouted Zaki at the same moment.

They crowded around him and began to scoop the sand away with their hands. No one in the world was more wretched than they, because of the loss of their cherished one, and their helplessness at his death. Karim experienced a moment of madness and said simplemindedly, "Maybe we'll find him alive!"

"Listen to the delusions of cowards," snapped Ali, his hands still working.

Their noses were full of the smell of dirt and blood. A dog howled from the direction of the mountain.

"Slow down," called Ali softly. "This is his body."

Their hearts pounded, and their hands relented slightly as they heartbrokenly felt the edges of his clothing, then they began to weep loudly. They all helped to draw the corpse out of the sand, and gently lifted it up as the cocks in the alleys and lanes began to crow. Some of them said to hurry, but Ali reminded them that they would need to fill up the hole. Karim took off his cloak and spread it on the ground, and they laid the body on it. They all helped to refill the hole. Hussein removed his cloak and covered the body with it, then they took it up and marched toward Bab al-Nasr. The darkness was lifting over the mountain, revealing clouds, and the dew fell on their tearful faces. Hussein led them along the way to his tomb until they arrived there, and they preoccupied themselves silently with opening the tomb. The light of day spread gradually, until they could see the shrouded body, their bloodstained hands, and eyes red from weeping; then they lifted up the body and descended with it into the tomb's interior. They stood humbly around it, pressing their eyes to stop the unseen tears that flowed.

"Your life was a brief dream," said Karim in a voice choked with tears. "But it filled our hearts with love and purity. We did not imagine that you would leave us so quickly, let alone that you would be murdered by a member of our infidel alley, which you healed and loved; our alley, which wanted only to murder the love, mercy, and healing that you represented. It has brought a curse upon itself until the end of time."

"Why do the good die?" sobbed Zaki. "Why do the criminals live?"

"If it had not been for your love that lives on in our hearts," moaned Hussein, "we would have hated people forever!"

"We will never know peace until we expiate our cowardice," added Ali.

As they left the tomb, heading back into the desert, the light was dyeing the horizons with the melting hue of a red rose.

None of his four companions appeared in Gabalawi Alley again. People thought they had left the alley secretly, after Rifaa, out of fear of the gangsters' retribution. But the friends lived at the edge of the desert in a state of frayed nerves, wrestling with all their might against the oppression of their pain and sharp regret. Rifaa's passing pained their hearts more than death, and being deprived of his company was a lethal torment; none of them had any further hope in life than to mourn Rifaa's death properly by keeping his message alive and seeing to the punishment of his killers, as Ali insisted they must. While it was true that they could not return to the alley, they hoped to accomplish what they wished outside it. One morning the House of Triumph awoke to Abda's cries, and the neighbors hurried to her to hear the news.

"They killed my son Rifaa," she shouted hoarsely.

The neighbors were shocked into silence, and looked to Shafi'i, who was drying his eyes.

"The gangsters killed him in the desert," he said.

"My son, who never hurt anyone in the world," wept Abda.

"Does our protector Khunfis know about this?" some of them asked.

"Khunfis was one of the killers," said Shafi'i angrily.

"Yasmina betrayed him—she led Bayoumi to him," wept Abda.

Horror was plain in their faces.

"So that's why she's been staying in his house after his wife left," someone said.

The news spread through the Al Gabal neighborhood, and Khunfis came to Shafi'i's house.

"Are you crazy?" he shouted. "What have you been saying about me?"

Shafi'i stood before him unafraid, and said sternly, "That you took part in killing him, when you were his protector!"

Khunfis pretended to be angry. "Shafi'i, you are crazy!" he shouted. "You don't know what you're saying. I won't stay here, so I won't be forced to punish you!"

He left the house frothing at the mouth. The news spread to Rifaa's neighborhood, where he had lived after leaving the Al Gabal's. The people were shocked, and raised their voices, raging and weeping, but the gangsters went out into the alley and patrolled it up and down, clubs in their hands and trouble blazing in their eyes. Then the news spread that sands west of Hind's Rock had been found blotched with Rifaa's blood. Shafi'i and his best friends went to look for the corpse there. They searched and excavated but found nothing. The people were frenzied and anxious at the news, and many of them expected trouble in the alley. The people of Rifaa's neighborhood wondered what he could have done to have been killed. The Al Gabal said, *Rifaa was killed, and Yasmina is living in Bayoumi's house.* The gangsters infiltrated by night the place of Rifaa's murder and dug up his grave by torchlight, but they found no trace of the corpse.

"Did Shafi'i take it?" Bayoumi asked.

"No," said Khunfis. "My spies have told me he found nothing."

"It's his friends," shouted Bayoumi, stamping his foot. "It was a mistake to let them escape. Now they're fighting us behind our backs."

When they returned, Khunfis leaned close to Bayoumi's ear and whispered, "Your keeping Yasmina is giving us problems."

"Admit that you're a weak leader in your territory," said Bayoumi, exasperated.

Khunfis bid him an exasperated farewell. The tension had mounted in the Al Gabal and Rifaa neighborhoods, and the gangsters continued to attack any complainers. The alley was so thoroughly terrorized that its people hated going out unless it was unavoidable. One night—when Bayoumi was in Shaldum's coffeehouse—some of his wife's relatives sneaked into his house with the intention of attacking Yasmina, but she became aware of them and fled in her nightgown into the desert. They chased her, and she ran like a crazed thing through the darkness even after her pursuers had given up the chase, and kept running until she could scarcely breathe, and had to stop. She panted violently, threw her head back and closed her eyes, until she had regained her breath, then looked behind her and, though she saw nothing, shied at the idea of going back to the alley by night. She looked ahead and saw a faint, faraway light that might be from a hut, and made for it, hoping to find there a place to stay until morning. It took her a long time to get there, but it did seem like a hut, so she went up to the door and called out to the people inside. Suddenly she found herself facing her husband's most intimate friends: Ali, Zaki, Hussein, and Karim.

Yasmina froze where she stood and looked from one face to another; they seemed to her like a wall blocking her escape in a nightmare. They stared at her with aversion, and the aversion in Ali's eyes had an iron severity.

"I'm innocent," she shouted instinctively. "By the Lord of Heaven, I'm innocent. I went with you until they attacked us, and ran away the same as you did!"

They scowled.

"And who told you we ran away?" asked Ali hatefully.

"If you hadn't run away," she quavered, "you wouldn't be alive now. But I am innocent. I didn't do anything. All I did was run away!"

"You ran to your master, Bayoumi," said Ali through clenched teeth.

"Never. Let me go. I am innocent."

"You'll go into the belly of the earth!" shouted Ali.

She tried to escape, but he jumped at her and grabbed her shoulders tightly.

"Let me go, for his sake—he never loved killing or killers!"

His hands closed around her neck.

"Wait until we've thought about this," said Karim uneasily.

"Be quiet, cowards!" he shouted, grasping her neck with all of the rage, hatred, pain, and remorse at war inside him. She tried in vain to free herself from his grip; she clutched his arms, kicked him, and shook her head, but all her effort was lost and in vain. Her strength gave out, her eyes bugged out, and then she began to spit blood. Her body convulsed violently, and then was still for good. He let go of her, and she fell at his feet, a corpse.

The next morning, Yasmina's body was found dumped in front of Bayoumi's house. The news spread like the dust of a hot sandstorm and everyone, men and women alike, ran toward the gangster's house. There was a huge din of competing comments, but everyone kept his true feelings secret. The gate of Bayoumi's house flew open, and the man rushed out like a raging bull and began to club everyone he could. Everyone ran away terrified and took shelter in homes and coffeehouses while the man stood in the empty alley cursing and threatening, and striking the dirt, the walls, and the empty air.

The same day, Shafi'i and his wife abandoned the alley. It seemed that every trace of Rifaa had vanished.

But there were things that spoke of him constantly, such as Shafi'i's home in the House of Triumph, the carpentry shop, Rifaa's house in the neighborhood that was called "the hospice," the site of his death west of Hind's Rock, and most of all his loyal companions, who stayed in contact with his admirers and taught them the mysteries of his way of cleansing souls of demons to treat the sick; thus, they were certain, they were restoring Rifaa to life. Ali, however, could not rest unless he was punishing criminals.

"You have nothing to do with Rifaa!" Hussein once scolded him.

"I know Rifaa better than any of you do," said Ali sternly. "He spent his short life in a violent struggle against demons."

"You want to go back to gangsterism—the most hateful thing in the world to him."

"He was a leader, bigger than any gangster, but his gentleness fooled you," cried Ali fervently.

Each of them went on to promote his own view, in total sincerity. The alley retold Rifaa's story, with all the facts, which most people had not known. It was reported that his body had lain in the desert until Gabalawi himself came and got it; now it was concealed in the soil of his own fabulous garden. The perilous events were just trailing off there, when the gangster Handusa vanished mysteriously. His mutilated corpse was discovered dumped in front of the house of Ihab the overseer. The overseer's house was just as convulsed as Bayoumi's had been, and the alley went through a terrible period of fear. Violence fell like rain on anyone who had had any relation, or imagined relation, with Rifaa or any of his men. Clubs crushed heads and feet trampled bellies, words pierced hearts and hands inflamed necks. Some people locked themselves in their houses, and some abandoned the alley altogether; some, contemptuous of the danger, were executed in the desert. The alley, covered in blackness and gloom, was loud in its screams and wails, and smelled of blood, but strangely, this did not impede further actions. Khalid was killed as he left Bayoumi's house before dawn, and the rage of the terror mounted to madness, but our alley was awakened from its last sleep one night by a tremendous fire that destroyed the house of the gangster Gaber and killed his family.

"Rifaa's crazy people are everywhere, like bedbugs!" shrieked Bayoumi. "I swear to God, they are going to be killed, even in their houses!"

Word got around the alley that their houses were to be attacked at night, and people were practically insane with fear. They ran out of their houses in a frantic mob, carrying sticks, chairs, cooking-pot lids, knives, clogs, and bricks. Bayoumi planned to strike before things got completely out of control; he lifted his club and came out of his house surrounded by a ring of his followers.

Ali appeared for the first time, leading the rioters with some other strong men. As soon as he saw Bayoumi coming, he ordered bricks to be thrown, and a swarm of bricks as thick as locusts landed on Bayoumi and his men, and the blood began to spout. Bayoumi pounced like a madman, screaming like a savage, but a rock struck the top of his head, and he stopped, and in spite of his rage, his strength, and his boldness, he staggered, and then fell down, his face a mask of blood. His followers were quick to flee, and waves of angry rioters swept into the gangster's house; the sounds of smashing and breaking could be heard by the overseer in his house. Mischief reigned as punishment was meted out to the remaining gangsters and their followers and their houses were laid waste. The danger mounted, and total chaos was near when the overseer summoned Ali, and Ali came to meet him. Ali's men held off from further revenge and destruction, awaiting the results of this meeting, and things calmed down and people cooled off.

The meeting produced a new covenant in the alley. The followers of Rifaa were recognized as a new community, just like Gabal's, with its own rights and prerogatives, and Ali was appointed overseer of their estate, and their protector. He would receive their share of the revenues, and distribute them on the basis of total equality. All those who had fled the alley during times of trouble now returned to the new community, led by Shafi'i and his wife, Zaki, Hussein, and Karim. Rifaa enjoyed respect, veneration, and love in death that he had never dreamed of during his lifetime. There was even a wonderful story, retold by every tongue and recited to rebec tunes, particularly of how Gabalawi lifted up his body and buried it in his fabulous garden. All Rifaa's followers agreed on that and they were unanimously loyal and reverent to his parents, but they differed on everything else. Karim, Hussein, and Zaki insisted that Rifaa's mission had been limited to healing the sick and despising power and majesty; they and their sympathizers in the alley did as he had done. Some went further and refrained from marriage, to imitate him and live their lives his way. Ali, however, retained his rights to the estate, married, and called for the renewal of their community. Rifaa had not hated the estate itself, but only to prove that true happiness was achievable without it, and to condemn the vices inspired by covetousness. If the revenue was distributed justly, and put toward building and charity, then it was the greatest good.

In any case, the people were delighted with their good lives, and welcomed life with radiant faces; they said with confident security that today was better than yesterday, and that tomorrow would be better than today.

Why is forgetfulness the plague of our alley?

"Welcome, Zuqla." Qassem embraced him.

"I was never against you," said the shepherd fervently. "My heart was always with you, and if I hadn't been afraid, I would have been one of the first people to join you. As soon as I heard that Sawaris had been killed—God send him to Hell!—I hurried to you, and I drove all your enemies' sheep ahead of me!"

Qassem looked at the mass of sheep in the clearing between the huts, where the women were watching and chatting delightedly, then laughed. "It is legitimate to take them, considering the property of ours they have stolen in the alley."

In the course of that day, an unprecedented number of people joined Qassem, strengthening the general resolve and bolstering morale. But Qassem woke up early the next morning to a strange uproar. He immediately went outside and saw his men coming toward his hut, quickly and with worried looks on their faces.

"The alley has come for revenge. They are massed below the passage."

"I was the first to go out to work," said Khurda. "I saw them when I was just a few steps away, and I ran back. Some of them chased me and hit me in the back with rocks. I began to shout for Sadeq and Hassan, until a group of our brothers came to the top of the passage. They saw the danger, and threw rocks at the attackers until they withdrew."

Qassem looked over at the opening of the passage and saw Hassan and some of the men standing there, clutching rocks. "We can hold them off there with ten men," he said.

"Coming up there will mean suicide for them," said Hamroush. "Let them come up if they want."

The men and women crowded around Qassem until all the huts were empty. The men brought their clubs, and the women had baskets of bricks that had been kept ready for a day like this. The first rays of light shone from the clear sky.

"Is there any other road to the city?" asked Qassem.

"There is a road to the south, two days' walk from the mountain," said Sadeq grimly.

"I don't think we have more than two days' worth of water," said Agrama.

An uneasy murmur ran through the crowd, especially from the women.

"They have come for revenge, not a siege," said Qassem. "If they surround us, we'll head for the other road to break the siege."

He began to think, keeping his face serene, for every eye was upon it. If they were besieged, they would have the greatest trouble bringing water by the southern road. If his men attacked them, could they be sure of success against such men as Lahita, Galta, and Hagag? What destiny did this day have in store for them? He went back to his hut, and returned holding his club. He walked over to Hassan and his men at the opening of the passage.

"None of them will dare to come any closer," said Hassan.

Qassem stepped to the mountain ledge and saw his enemies gathered in a crescent-shaped formation in the desert, far out of rock-throwing range. Their sheer numbers were frightening, but he was unable to make out any gangsters among them. His gaze moved over the empty space to the mansion, Gabalawi's house, immersed in silence, as if oblivious to his children's struggle for his sake. How desperately they needed his supernatural strength, to which this place had submitted in the past. Perhaps he would not be assailed by anxiety, had it not been for Rifaa's murder so near his ancestor's house. He felt an urge, deep inside him, to shout "Gabalawi!" at the top of his voice, as the people of his alley did all the time, but he heard the voices of the women nearby, and turned to look around. He saw the men spreading out over the mountain ledge and watching their enemies, and the women heading for the same spots. He shouted for them to come back, and shouted again when they hesitated. He ordered them to prepare food and do their usual chores, and they obeyed him.

Sadeq came over to Qassem. "That was the right thing to do. The most worrisome thing for me is the power of Lahita's name over us."

"The only thing we can do is strike," said Hassan, shaking his club. "It will be impossible for us to go out and earn livings now that they know our hiding place. The only thing we can do is attack."

Qassem turned his head to look out toward the mansion. "What you say is true. What do you say, Sadeq?"

"Let's wait until nightfall."

"Waiting will only hurt us," said Hassan. "And darkness won't help us in battle."

"So what's their plan?"

"To force us to go down to them."

Qassem thought that over. "If Lahita is killed, victory is assured," he said, looking from one man to the other. "If he falls, Galta and Hagag will battle it out to succeed him."

As the sun rose higher, the gravelly ground blazed with the heat that radiated everywhere.

"Tell me, what will we do?" said Hassan. He meant: about the siege; but before anyone could answer, there was a shout from a woman in the square, immediately followed by other shouts.

"We're being attacked from the other side!" someone shouted.

The men abandoned the ledge and ran toward the southern side of the square. Qassem commanded the defenders at the passage to be even more alert, ordered Khurda to have capable women join the defenders of the passage, then ran, with Sadeq and Hassan on either side of him, to the center of his men in the square. Lahita was visible to all of them, leading a large gang of men coming from south of the mountain.

"He distracted us with his men, so that he could make his way around the mountain, to attack us by the southern road," raged Qassem.

"He is walking into his own death!" shouted Hassan, his massive body swelled up with enthusiasm.

"We must win, and we will win," said Qassem.

His men spread around him like two strong arms as the advancing force came closer, clubs in the air, looking like a patch of thorns. As they came nearer into view, Sadeq said, "Galta isn't with them. Neither is Hagag!"

Qassem realized that Galta and Hagag were leading the siege below the mountain, and guessed that they would attack the passage no matter what it cost them, though he confided his suspicions to no one. He took a few steps forward, brandishing his club, and his men gripped theirs.

Lahita's crude voice rang out. "You'll never get a burial service, you sons of whores!" he shouted.

Qassem and his men sped forward to attack, and the others flung themselves forward like a hail of stones, until their clubs clashed together, and raging and clamor grew loud. At the same time, bricks were launched at attacks below by the women defending the opening of the passage, but every one of Qassem's men was locked in battle with an enemy attacker. Qassem and Dingil fought hard and artfully. Lathita's club landed on Hamroush's collarbone, breaking it. Sadeq and Zainhum fought long and hard, but Hassan lashed out with his furious club, and Zainhum dropped. Lahita struck Zuqla, knocking him over. Qassem was able to wound Dingil on the ear, and the man screamed and retreated, then slumped over. Zainhum made a fierce lunge at Sadeq, but Sadeq speedily made a thrust at his belly that stopped his hands, then made a second thrust that dropped him. Khurda fought off Hafnawi, but Lahita crippled his arm before he could savor his victory. Hassan aimed a blow at Lahita, but he dodged it nimbly and raised his club to strike back. Before he could, Qassem swung his club, and their clubs clashed; like the wind, Abu Fisada came in to deliver a third blow, but Lahita butted him with his head and broke his nose; Lahita looked like a force that could not be resisted. The fighting grew fiercer, with the clubs batting one another relentlessly, a flood of curses and obscenities, and blood spurted in the fiery sun. Each side in turn lost men who dropped to the ground. Lahita burned with rage at this heroic resistance, which he had never expected, and redoubled his forays, his blows, and his cruelty. On the other side, Qassem ordered Hassan and Agrama to seize the opportunity to join him attacking Lahita, to destroy the backbone that gave the attackers strength.

One of the women defending the opening of the passage suddenly came to shout, "They're coming up with dough boards for shields!"

The mountain men's hearts froze.

"You'll never get a burial service, you sons of whores!" shouted Lahita.

"Win before the criminals come up!" Qassem shouted to his men.

He went for Lahita, flanked by Hassan and Agrama. The gangster met him with a terrible blow he deflected with his club. Agrama wanted to anticipate him with a blow, but the gangster hit him on the chin, and he sprawled out on his face. Hassan jumped in front of him and they exchanged two blows; Hassan threw himself on him, and they were locked in a deadly struggle. The women at the passage began to scream, and some of them started to flee, endangering the position. Qassem quickly sent Sadeq and several men to the mountain ledge, then charged at Lahita, but Zihlifa blocked his way, and they engaged in violent combat. Hassan pushed Lahita back with all his strength, and he took one step back. He spat in Lahita's eye, roared, and kicked him, crippling one of his knees. With lightning speed, Hassan attacked him, hunched low, and butted him in the stomach like a raging bull; the tyrant lost his balance and fell backward. Hassan knelt over him and slammed his club over his neck with both hands, pushing it down with all his strength. Men hurried over to defend their gangster, but Qassem and some of his men fought them off. Lahita kicked his feet, his eyes bulged, and his face was bright with blood. He began to choke. Suddenly Hassan leaped up to stand over his powerless adversary, and swung his club in a wild, furious blow, smashing Lahita's skull, killing him.

"Lahita is dead!" he thundered. "Your protector is dead! Look at his corpse!"

Lahita's unexpected death had a violent effect, as the fighters' resolution either flared up or waned, and hope and despair drove the bitter fighting. Hassan joined Qassem in his struggle, and not one of his blows failed. Men sprang out and stood firm, and clubs were swung and then brought down. The dust rose and blew away, and combatants were seized by a bloody daze. Their lungs spewed curses, screams, obscenities, moans, and menacing yells. Every few moments a man staggered and fell, or retreated and fled. The field was covered with the fallen, and blood glistened in the sunlight. Qassem turned aside to look over at the opening of the passage, which preyed on his mind, and saw Sadeq and his men passing down stones in baskets with a fervid tension that indicated the approach of mounting danger. He heard the women, his wife among them, as they screamed for help. He saw some of Sadeq's men hefting their clubs in preparation for meeting the enemies who would ascend through the downpour of stones. He assessed the danger, at once started toward Lahita's body, for the battle had moved away from it as the men from the alley had pulled back, and dragged it behind him toward the opening of the passage. He shouted for Sadeq, who hurried to him, and they both took up the corpse and carried it to the beginning of the passage. They heaved it together and threw it, and it landed, then rolled down and stopped at the feet of the climbers holding the boards, throwing them into confusion.

Hagga's voice reverberated as he shouted in rage. "Forward! Climb! Death to the criminals!"

"Forward!" shouted Qassem scornfully, with strange self-control. "This is your protector's corpse, and your other men's corpses are behind me. Forward! We are waiting for you!"

He gave the men and women a sign, and rocks flew like rain until the attackers' vanguard halted and then began to retreat slowly, despite the urging of Hagag and Galta. Qassem could hear the babble of argument, protest, and complaint.

"Galta!" Qassem called. "Hagag! Come forward—don't run!"

"Come down, if you are men!" Galta bawled hatefully. "Come down, you women, you bastards!"

Hagag, standing amidst a wave of retreating men, shouted, "I won't live any longer without drinking your blood, you stinking shepherd!"

Qassem picked up a stone and threw it with all his might. The rain of stones continued, and the retreating wave moved more quickly, until almost everyone was carried along. Hassan came up and wiped the streaming blood from his forehead.

"The battle's over," he said. "The survivors have fled south."

"Call the men to follow them!" said Qassem.

"You're bleeding from the teeth and chin!" Sadeq pointed out.

He wiped his mouth and chin with his palm, spread it out and saw that it was bright red.

"They killed eight of us," said Hassan sadly. "Our survivors are badly wounded and won't be able to move."

He looked down through the hail of stones to see his enemies racing through the end of the passage.

"If they had kept coming, they wouldn't have found anyone to resist them here," said Sadeq. He kissed Qassem's bloody chin and said gratefully, "Your brain saved us!"

Qassem ordered two men to stand guard at the top of the passage, and sent others to pursue the retreating force and to reconnoiter, then walked back, between Sadeq and Hassan, as they limped wearily and heavily to the square, on whose surface nothing was left but corpses. It had been a massacre, and what a massacre! Eight of his men had been killed, and ten of his enemies, not counting Lahita. None of his living men had been spared a broken bone or wound. They had made their way back to their huts, where the women began to bandage their wounds, while the huts of the dead were loud with shouts and sobs. Badriya came, grief-stricken, and had them come into the hut so that she could wash their wounds, then Sakina came carrying Ihsan, who was shrieking with tears. The sun, at its zenith, flung its fire below as the kites and crows circled and dipped in the hot air, which reeked of blood and earth. Ihsan did not stop crying, but not one paid attention to her. Even the giant Hassan seemed to be tottering.

"God have mercy on our dead," murmured Sadeq.

"God have mercy on the dead and the living too," said Qassem.

Suddenly awakening to a kind of rapture, Hassan said, "Soon we will have victory, and our alley will say farewell to its age of blood and terror."

"Down with terror and blood," said Qassem.

The alley had never known a catastrophe like this. The men returned silent, dazed and feeble, their eyes cast down, as if studying the surface of the ground. They found that news of the defeat had preceded them to the alley, and that their homes resounded with wailing and the smacking of cheeks in mourning. The news spread through every lane and alley, making the alley's imposing reputation the gloating gossip of every vengeful tongue. It came to light that the Desert Rats had entirely evacuated their neighborhood from fear of revenge: the houses and shops were empty, and no one doubted that they had all joined their victorious compatriot, increasing his numbers and strength. Sorrow descended over the whole mourning-dulled alley, but its hot breath dripped with resentment, loathing, and lust for revenge. The men of Gabal wondered who would be the next protector of the alley, and everyone in Rifaa wondered the same thing. Distrust spread like dust in a gale. The overseer, Rifaat, learned what mutters were circulating, and summoned Galta and Hagag to a meeting. They came, each surrounded by his toughest men, so that the overseer's reception hall was overcrowded. Each group occupied one side of the hall, as if neither felt safe mixing with the other any longer. The overseer was not slow to see the significance of this, and it made him even more worried.

"You know that we have suffered a catastrophe, but we have survived," he said. "It has not stopped us. We are still capable of achieving victory with our own hands, as long as we maintain our unity. Otherwise we are finished."

"We will strike the last blow," said one of the men of Gabal, "and then we will never have this problem again."

"If they had not taken refuge on the mountain, they would all be dead," said Hagag.

"Lahita engaged them after a long, terrible journey that would have brought a camel to its knees," said a third man.

"Tell me about your unity—how united are you?" asked the overseer irritably.

"We are brothers, by God's grace, and always will be," Galta said.

"That's what you say, but the way you came here in these numbers is a sign of the distrust that divides you."

"That's because of the revenge that we all want," Hagag said.

The overseer stood tensely, and gazed at the rows of somber faces.

"Be frank. You are all watching each other with one eye, and have the other on Lahita's empty position. The alley will never be safe as long as this is the case. The worst thing would be for the thing to be settled with clubs. You would all be ruined, and Qassem would eat you for breakfast."

"God forbid—never!" many of them shouted.

"The alley has only two neighborhoods now, Gabal and Rifaa. We can have two protectors. There is no need to have just one. Let us commit ourselves to that, so that we can act as one against the rebels."

Dreadful moments of silence passed, then several voices spoke in tepid agreement.

"Yes . . . yes."

"We will go along with that," said Galta, "even though we have been the elect of this alley since earliest history."

"We will accept, but no one is doing us a favor," protested Hagag. "There are no masters or servants here, especially since the Desert Rats are gone. Who could deny, after all, that Rifaa was the noblest man this alley ever saw?"

"Hagag!" objected Galta resentfully. "I know what you're getting at."

One of the Al Rifaa was about to say something, but the overseer began to shout angrily. "Tell me! Have you made up your minds to act like men, or not? If any word of your weakness gets out, the Desert Rats will march down the mountain like wolves. Tell me, are you able to agree and stand together, or should I make other plans?"

The answer was scattered.

"Shhhhhh!"

"Shame!"

"The alley is going to lose everything!"

Eventually they all looked at him resignedly.

"You still have better numbers and greater strength, but don't attack the mountain again." Their faces were questioning. "We will imprison them up there on the mountain. We will occupy the two roads that lead to the mountain, and they will either starve to death or be forced to come down to you, and you will kill them."

"Good idea," said Galta. "I pointed that out to Lahita, God rest his soul, but he considered sieges cowardly and insisted on attacking."

"That's the idea," said Hagag. "But we have to delay doing it until the men are rested."

The overseer asked them to commit themselves to brotherhood and cooperation, and they all shook hands and swore they would. In the days that followed, it became clear to anyone who could see that Galta and Hagag were much harder on their followers, to hide the effect of the defeat they had suffered. They spread the word in the alley that if it had not been for Lahita's stupidity, they could have destroyed Qassem easily; his insistence on going up the mountain had exhausted the men and strained their strength and courage—they had met the enemy in terrible shape. The people believed what they were told, and anyone who showed skepticism was cursed, insulted, and beaten. No one was allowed to get into discussions about the leading position in the alley, at least publicly, but many people—of both Gabal and Rifaa—debated, in the drug dens, who would replace Lahita after the victory. Despite the agreement and all the oaths, an atmosphere of secret suspicion had taken root in the alley. Every gangster kept himself surrounded, and never went far from his base without a crowd of his men. But preparations for the day of revenge never stopped for a moment. They agreed among themselves that Galta and his men would camp at the Muqattam Road, at the marketplace, Hagag and his men would camp at the Citadel Road, and neither group would leave their positions at all, even if it meant spending the rest of their lives there. Their womenfolk would take over the buying and selling, and would bring them food. In the evening of the day before they were supposed to head out, they gathered in all the drug dens. They brought flasks of wine and liquor, and drank and smoked hashish until late that night. Hagag's men said goodbye to him in front of his building in Rifaa; he was in a state of superb pleasure and relaxation. He pushed open the door and walked down the hallway, humming "First we—" but he never finished. A figure seized him from behind, clapped a hand over his mouth, and with the other hand drove a knife into his heart. The body shuddered powerfully in his arms, but, not wanting to let it drop and make a sound, he laid it down gently on the floor, where it did not move in the gloomy shadows.

The alley awoke early the next morning to a startling outburst of screams. Windows flew open and heads popped out, and people ran toward the building where Hagag, the protector of the Rifaa community, lived, where a numerous crowd had gathered. Wails of mourning were interrupted by shouts, and the hall of the building was filled with men and women making comments and asking questions; eyes red with weeping warned of truly perilous mischief. The people of Rifaa ran from every building, every house and basement, and before long Galta and his men came. People made way for them until they reached the hall.

"This is the most horrible thing!" Galta shouted. "If only it could have been me instead, Hagag!"

People who were crying stopped crying, the shouters stopped shouting, and the morbidly curious stopped asking questions, but he did not hear one kindly word.

"Despicable plots!" he resumed. "Gangsters don't betray one another, but Qassem is a shepherd, a beggar, not a gangster, and I will never rest until I've thrown his corpse to the dogs."

"Congratulations, Galta, you're the new gangster of the alley!" shouted a grief-stricken woman.

His features contracted angrily, and the people near him fell silent, but farther back there was a wave of grumbling.

"Let women keep their mouths shut on this tragic day!"

"Let everyone who's got a mind understand!" the woman said.

The grumbling rose into a lively babble, and Galta waited for this storm to die down before speaking again. "This is a sly conspiracy, carried out at night, to sow dissension among us!"

"Conspiracy!" said another woman. "Qassem and his Desert Rats are on the mountain, and Hagag was killed in his house, among his own people and his neighbors, who want to take over!"

"Crazy bitch! All of you are crazy if you think like that, and if you do, we'll all be killing one another the way Qassem plotted we should!"

A jug landed and shattered at Galta's feet, and he and his men stepped back.

"The son of a whore knew how to sow dissension among us," he said.

He left for the overseer's house, but the clamor only grew after he was gone. Two men—one of Rifaa, the other of Gabal—got into a violent argument, and were immediately imitated by two women. Boys from both neighborhoods started fighting, people began swearing matches from the windows, and riot spread through the alley until each neighborhood's men massed with their clubs. The overseer came out of his house, surrounded by his men and servants, and strode out to the dividing line between the two districts.

"Come to your senses!" he shouted. "Anger will blind you to your real enemy, Hagag's killer!"

"Who told you that?" shouted one of the men of Rifaa. "What Desert Rat would dare enter this alley?"

"How could they kill Hagag today, when they needed him so much?" Rifaat shouted.

"Ask the criminals, don't ask us."

"The people of Rifaa will not obey a gangster of Gabal."

"They will pay dearly for his blood."

"Don't serve the conspiracy," said the overseer, "or you'll be seeing Qassem come in here like a plague!"

"Let him come if he wants, but Galta will not rule us as protector."

The overseer wrung his hands. "We are finished! We will be ruined."

"Ruin is better than Galta!" they yelled.

A brick was thrown from Rifaa and landed among the assembled men of Gabal. Someone from Gabal responded in kind, and the overseer quickly withdrew. Bricks began to fly in both directions, and in no time a bloody battle had broken out between the two neighborhoods. Cruel blows were struck, and fighting spread to some roofs, where women pelted each other with bricks, stones, dirt, and pieces of wood. The clash lasted a long time, despite the fact that the people of Rifaa were fighting without their gangster; but they lost many casualties to Galta's lethal blows. Women's voices now shrieked from windows, a noise that could not be heard above the chaos of the battle, though they could be seen pointing in terror, now to the east end of the alley, now to the other end. The people turned to see what the women were pointing at, and saw Qassem in front of the mansion, leading a band of men with clubs. At the other end was Hassan, leading more men; the place rang with screams of warning, and then everything happened very quickly. As if paralyzed, people stopped throwing punches. On a spontaneous impulse, they intermingled and re-formed, the fighters and the fought, and divided up into two detachments to confront the newcomers.

"I said it was a plot, and you didn't believe me!" shouted Galta furiously.

They prepared for battle, though they were now in the worst state of strain and hopelessness. But Qassem suddenly halted, and so did Hassan, as if they were executing a single plan.

"We do not want to harm anyone," cried Qassem as loudly as he could. "We want no winner and no loser. We are all a people with one alley and one ancestor, and the estate belongs to all."

"It's a new plot!" shouted Galta.

"Don't push them to fight to defend your gang rule. Defend it yourself, if you want to."

"Attack!" bellowed Galta.

He charged at Qassem's men, and his men followed. Others attacked Hassan and his men, but many held back. Some who were wounded or exhausted slipped into their houses, and were followed by the hesitant others. Only Galta and his band of men were left, but even so they plunged into a ferocious battle and fought a desperate defensive fight, battering one another with clubs, heads, feet, and hands. Galta concentrated his attack on Qassem with blind hatred. They exchanged violent blows, but Qassem met his adversary's blows with his club, nimbly and cautiously. With their superior numbers, his men surrounded Galta's gang, who fell under dozens of clubs. Hassan and Sadeq set upon Galta as he fought with Qassem; Sadeq struck his club, and Hassan landed his club on Galta's head, then a second time, and a third. The club dropped from his hand, and he bounded up like a slaughtered bull, then collapsed on his face like a gate slamming shut. The battle was over. The crack of clubs and shouts of men fell silent. The victors stood up, out of breath, wiping the blood from their heads, faces, and hands, but their mouths were bright with smiles of victory and peace. Wailing could be heard from the windows, Galta's men were scattered on the ground, and the brilliant sun shed its fierce rays.

"You have won," Sadeq told Qassem, confident and assured. "God gave you victory; our ancestor does not err when he chooses. Our alley will never mourn again after today."

Qassem smiled serenely and turned resolutely to look at the overseer's house, but all their heads were turned to him.

Translated by Peter Theroux

from *The Thief and the Dogs*, 1961

> Said Mahran, the hero of this short and highly readable novel,
> fails in his attempt to be avenged, defeated by "the dogs" of
> the title, those who serve the interests of the state.

By the time Said had returned to the flat, dressed in his officer's uniform, and left, it was well after one o'clock. He turned toward Abbasiyya Street, avoiding the lights and forcing himself to walk very naturally, then took a taxi to Gala' Bridge, passing an unpleasant number of policemen en route.

At the dock near the bridge he rented a small rowboat for two hours and promptly set off in it south, toward Rauf Ilwan's house. It was a fine starry night, a cool breeze blowing, the quarter-moon still visible in the clear sky above the trees along the riverbank. Excited, full of energy, Said felt ready to spring into vigorous action. Ilish Sidra's escape was not a defeat, not as long as punishment was about to descend on Rauf Ilwan. For Rauf, after all, personified the highest standard of treachery, from which people like Ilish and Nabawiyya and all the other traitors on earth sought inspiration.

"It's time to settle accounts, Rauf," he said, pulling hard on the oars. "And if anyone but the police stood as judges between us, I'd teach you a lesson in front of everyone. They, the people, everyone—all the people except the real robbers—are on my side, and that's what will console me in my everlasting perdition. I am, in fact, your soul. You've sacrificed me. I lack organization, as you would put it. I now understand many of the things you used to say that I couldn't comprehend then. And the worst of it is that despite this support from millions of people I find myself driven away into dismal isolation, with no one to help. It's senseless, all of it, a waste. No bullet could clear away its absurdity. But at least a bullet will be right, a bloody protest, something to comfort the living and the dead, to let them hold on to their last shred of hope."

At a point opposite the big house, he turned shoreward, rowed in to the bank, jumped out, pulled the boat up after him until its bow was well up on dry land, then climbed the bank up to the road, where, feeling calm and secure in his officer's uniform, he walked away. The road seemed empty and when he got to the house he saw no sign of guards, which both pleased and angered him. The house itself was shrouded in darkness except for a single light at the entrance, convincing him that the owner was not yet back, that forced entry was unnecessary, and that a number of other difficulties had been removed.

Walking quite casually, he turned down the street along the left side of the house and followed it to its end at Sharia Giza, then he turned along Sharia Giza and proceeded to the other street, passing along the right side of the house, until he regained the riverside, examining everything along the way most carefully. Then he made his way over to a patch of ground shaded from the streetlights by a tree, and stood waiting, his eyes fixed on the house, relaxing them only by gazing out from time to time at the dark surface of the river; his thoughts fled to Rauf's treachery, the deception that had crushed his life, the ruin that was facing him, the death blocking his path, all the things that made Rauf's death an absolute necessity. He watched each car with bated breath as it approached.

Finally one of them stopped before the gate of the house, which was promptly opened by the doorkeeper, and Said darted into the street to the left of the house, keeping close to the wall, stopping at a point opposite the entrance, while the car moved slowly down the drive. It came to a halt in front of the entrance, where the light that had been left on illuminated the whole entranceway. Said took out his revolver now and aimed it carefully as the car door opened and Rauf Ilwan got out.

"Rauf!" Said bellowed. As the man turned in shock toward the source of this shout, Said yelled again: "This is Said Mahran! Take that!"

But before he could fire, a shot from within the garden, whistling past him very close, disturbed his aim. He fired and ducked to escape the next shot, then raised his head in desperate determination, took aim, and fired again.

All this happened in an instant. After one more wild, hasty shot, he sped away as fast as he could run toward the river, pushed the boat out into the water, and leapt into it, rowing toward the opposite bank. Unknown sources deep within him released immediate reserves of physical strength, but his thoughts and emotions swirled as though caught in a whirlpool. He seemed to sense shots being fired, voices of people gathering, and a sudden loss of power in some part of his body, but the distance between the riverbanks was small at that point and he reached the other side, quickly leapt ashore, leaving the boat to drift in the water, and climbed up to the street, clutching the gun in his pocket.

Despite his confused emotions, he proceeded carefully and calmly, looking neither to the right nor to the left. Aware of people rushing down to the water's edge behind him, of confused shouts from the direction of a bridge, and a shrill whistle piercing the night air, he expected a pursuer to accost him at any moment, and he was ready to put all his efforts into either bluffing his way out or entering one last battle. Before anything else could happen, however, a taxi cruised by. He hailed it and climbed in; the piercing pain he felt as soon as he sat back on the seat was nothing compared to the relief of being safe again.

He crept up to Nur's flat in complete darkness and stretched out on one of the sofas, still in his uniform. The pain returned now, and he identified its source, a little above his knee, where he put his hand and felt a sticky liquid, with sharper pain. Had he knocked against something? Or was it a bullet, when he'd been behind the wall perhaps, or running? Pressing fingers all around the wound, he determined that it was only a scratch; if it had been a bullet, it must have grazed him without penetrating.

He got up, took off his uniform, felt for his nightshirt on the sofa, and put it on. The he walked around the flat testing out the leg, remembering how once he'd run down Sharia Muhammad Ali with a bullet lodged in the leg. "Why, you're capable of miracles," he told himself. "You'll get away all right. With a little coffee powder this wound will bind up nicely."

But had he managed to kill Rauf Ilwan? And who had shot at him from inside the garden? *Let's hope you didn't hit some other poor innocent fellow like before. And Rauf must surely have been killed—you never miss, as you used to demonstrate in target practice out in the desert beyond the hill. Yes, now you can write a letter to the papers: "Why I Killed Rauf Ilwan." That will give back the meaning your life has lost: the bullet that killed Rauf Ilwan will at the same time have destroyed your sense of loss, of waste. A world without morals is like a universe without gravity. I want nothing, long for nothing more than to die a death that has some meaning to it.*

Nur came home worn out, carrying food and drink. She kissed him as usual and smiled a greeting, but her eyes suddenly fastened on his uniform trousers. She put her parcel on the sofa, picked them up, and held them out to him.

"There's blood!" she said.

Said noticed it for the first time. "It's just a minor wound," he said, showing her his leg. "I hit it on the door of a taxi."

"You've been out in that uniform for some specific reason! There's no limit to your madness. You'll kill me with worry!"

"A little bit of coffee powder will cure this wound even before the sun rises."

"My soul rises, you mean! You are simply murdering me! Oh, when will this nightmare end?"

In a burst of nervous energy Nur dressed the wound with powdered coffee, then bound it up with a cutting from fabric she was using to make a dress, complaining about her ill-fortune all the time she worked.

"Why don't you take a shower?" said Said. "It'll make you feel good."

"You don't know good from bad," she said, leaving the room.

By the time she came back to the bedroom, he had already drunk a third of a bottle of wine and his mood and nerves felt much improved.

"Drink up!" he said as she sat down. "After all, I'm here, all right, in a nice safe place, way out of sight of the police."

"I'm really very depressed," Nur whimpered, combing her wet hair.

"Who can determine the future anyway?" he said, taking a swallow.

"Only our own actions can."

"Nothing, absolutely nothing is certain. Except your being with me, and that's something I can't do without."

"So you say now!"

"And I've got more to say. Being with you, after being out there with bullets tearing after me, is like being in Paradise." Her long sigh in response was deep, as if in self-communion at night; and he went on: "You really are very good to me. I want you to know I'm grateful."

"But I'm so worried. All I want is for you to be safe."

"We'll still have our opportunity."

"Escape! Put your mind to how we can escape."

"Yes, I will. But let's wait for the dogs to close their eyes a while."

"But you go outside so carelessly. You're obsessed with killing your wife and this other man. You won't kill them. But you will bring about your own destruction."

"What did you hear in town?"

"The taxi driver who brought me home was on your side. But he said you'd killed some poor innocent fellow."

Said grunted irritably and forestalled any expression of regret by taking another big swallow, gesturing at Nur to drink, too. She raised the glass to her lips.

"What else did you hear?" he said.

"On the houseboat where I spent the evening one man said you act as a stimulant, a diversion to relieve people's boredom."

"And what did you reply?"

"Nothing at all," Nur said, pouting. "But I do defend you, and you don't look after yourself at all. You don't love me either. But to me you're more precious than my life itself; I've never in my whole life known happiness except in your arms. But you'd rather destroy yourself than love me." She was crying now, the glass still in her hand.

Said put his arm around her. "You'll find me true to my promise," he whispered. "We will escape and live together forever."

Translated by Trevor Le Gassick and M.M. Badawi
Revised by John Rodenbeck

from *Adrift on the Nile,* 1966

The novel describes a group of people on a houseboat on the Nile, living in an atmosphere of hashish, alcohol, and sex. In the scene reproduced here, the group takes a crazy drive in a car, with catastrophic consequences.

It is interesting to note that the commander of the armed forces at the time of the novel's publication suggested to Nasser that the writer had "gone over the top and must be taught a lesson." Nasser consulted his minister of culture, Tharwat 'Ukasha, who reportedly responded: "Mr. President, in all honesty I tell you that if art could not enjoy this margin of freedom, it would cease to be art." To this, Nasser is said to have replied: "Point taken; consider the matter closed!"

The car set off, Ragab, Samara, and Ahmad sat in front, and the rest were squashed together in the back like one flattened body with six heads. They made for Pyramids Road, crossing the almost deserted city. Ragab suggested that the road to Saqqara would make a nice trip and everybody concurred, whether they knew the road or not. Anis sat hunched and silent in his white robe, pressed against the right-hand side of the car.

They covered Pyramids Road in minutes, and then turned left toward Saqqara. They began to travel at speed down the dark and deserted road, the headlights picking out the landmarks ahead. The road stretched infinitely out into the darkness, bordered on either side by great evergreens whose branches met overhead. On both sides lay the open spaces, the landscape and the air of the country. To their left the scenery was cut across by a canal running alongside the road. The water's surface stood out here and there under the faint starlight, iron gray against the black. The car went faster; the air rushed in, dry and refreshing and smelling of greenery. "Slow down," said Saniya to Ragab.

"Don't break the smokers' speed limit," said Khalid.

"Are you a speed freak?" Samara asked him.

We are on the way to the site of an ancient Pharaonic tomb. A good moment to recite the opening verse of the Quran. . . .

Ragab soon slowed down again. Khalid suggested that they stop for a while and go for a stroll in the dark. Everybody agreed, so Ragab turned off onto a dusty patch of ground between two trees, and stopped the car. Doors were opened. Ahmad, Khalid, Saniya, Layla, Mustafa, and Ali got out. Anis shifted himself away from the car door and sat comfortably for the first time. He shook out his tunic and stretched his legs. He searched with one foot for the slipper he had lost in the crush. When they called him to go with them, he replied tersely: "No."

Ragab caught hold of Samara's hand as she was about to get out. "We can't leave the master of ceremonies alone," he said.

The expedition moved off. They were going toward the canal, laughing and talking. They turned into phantoms in the starlight, and then disappeared altogether, leaving only disembodied voices.

"What is the meaning of this journey?" asked Anis thickly.

"It's the journey that is important," Ragab teased, "not the meaning."

Samara said: "Hmm!"—in protest at his allusion to her; but Anis was complaining now. "The darkness makes me sleepy," he grumbled.

"Enjoy it, master of ceremonies," said Ragab eagerly. Then he turned to Samara. "We must talk about us," he said. "Honestly. Like the honesty of the nature surrounding us."

It is difficult to sleep when you are witnessing a romantic comedy. Very fitting, honesty, in the middle of the night on the road to Saqqara! Now his arm is creeping along the back of her seat. Anything can happen on the road to Saqqara.

"Yes," he continued. "Let us talk about our love."

"*Our* love?"

"Yes, ours! That is exactly what I meant!"

 "It is not possible for me to have anything to do with a god."

"It is not possible that our lips have not yet become acquainted."

She turned her head away toward the fields as if to listen to the crickets and frogs. How beautiful the stars were over the fields, she murmured. I wonder if any new ideas have been recorded in the notebook. Could we still perhaps see ourselves one night on the theater stage, and guffaw along with the audience?

"I know what you would like to say," Ragab went on.

"What?"

"That you are not like the other girls."

"Is that what you think?"

"But love . . ."

"But love?"

"You don't believe me!"

Where is honesty in this darkness? What do our voices mean to the insects? You are in your forties, Ragab. You'll have to start playing different roles soon. Do you not know how the great Casanova hid in the Duke's library?

"Please don't say 'bourgeois mentality' again," she said now.

"But how else can I interpret your fear?"

"I'm not afraid."

"Then it's a problem of trust?"

"I heard you say that in a film."

"Perhaps I don't believe in seriousness yet, but I believe in you."

"That's the Don Juan mentality!" she replied.

Ghosts, walking abroad in the fields—or in my head. Like the village in days gone by. Marriage, fatherhood, ambitions, death. The stars have lived for billions of years, but they have not yet heard of the stars of the earth. No ghosts out there; just lone trees, forgotten in the midst of the fields.

"I could perhaps remain chaste until we get married," Ragab was saying now.

"Get married?"

"But I have a devil in me that rebels against routine."

"Routine!"

"One hint, and you understand everything! But I do not understand you. . . ."

Where is the balcony, and the lapping of the waves? The water pipe, and the smell of the river? Where is Amm Abduh? And those thoughts that gleam like lightning striking the shades of the evergreens and then vanish, but where?

"Why did you refuse to marry your important suitor?"

"I was not satisfied with him."

"You mean, you did not love him."

"If you like."

"He was in his forties, like me."

"It wasn't that."

"Satisfaction is only important in free choice. Not in love."

"I don't know."

"And sex?"

"That's a question that should properly be ignored!"

With a voice that broke the spell of the night, Anis shouted: "Rulings and classifications of age and love and sex? You damn grammarians!"

They turned around uncomfortably—and then both laughed. "We thought you were asleep," said Ragab.

"How long will we stay in this prison?"

"We've only been here an hour."

"Why haven't we committed suicide?"

"We were trying to talk about love!"

Across the abyss of the night came the voices of the expedition. Then their scattered shapes could be made out. They approached the car to stand together around the hood. Yes, my dear, we could easily have been killed out there. . . . Where are they now, the days of knights and troubadours? Khalid said that he had been about to commit the primary sin, had the "fraudulent pioneer" not been so prudish.

"And then in the dark," Mustafa added, "we decided to find out how modern we really are, and see who could admit to the most misdeeds!"

Ragab thought it was a clever idea. "And so everyone confessed to their sins," continued Mustafa.

"Sins!"

"I mean, what are considered such in public opinion."

"And what was the outcome?"

"Wonderful!"

"How many could be called crimes?"

"Dozens."

"And how many were misdemeanors?"

"Hundreds!"

"Have none of you committed a virtue?"

"He who goes by the name of Ahmad Nasr!"

"Perhaps you mean his fidelity to his wife."

"And to financial directives and stocktaking and regulations for the acquisition of goods!"

"And what was your opinion of yourselves?"

"Our consensus was that we are in a state of nature, immaculate; and that the morals which we lack are the dead morals of a dead age; and that we are the pioneers of a new and honest ethic as yet unsanctioned by legislation!"

"Bravo!"

Anis gave himself over to the view of the trees that bordered the road. They had been planted with extraordinary regularity. If they moved out of their fixed order, the known world would come tumbling down. There was a snake coiled around a branch; it wanted to say something. Very well, say something worth listening to. But what a cursed row. "Let me hear it!" he cried aloud.

At his bellow, they all laughed.

"What do you want to hear?" asked Mustafa.

They piled back into the car, and Anis was once more pressed against the door. The snake had completely disappeared.

"You will be driven by a thoroughly modern driver!" Ragab said. The car moved onto the road, engine roaring, and then they set off, faster and faster, until they were traveling at an insane speed.

People laughed hysterically; then their voices shook; and then they began to protest and shout for help. The trees flew by. They felt as if they were plummeting into a deep gulf, and waited in dread to hit the bottom.

"Madness—this is madness!"

"He'll kill us in cold blood!"

"Stop! We have to get our breath back!"

"No! No! Even madness has to stop somewhere!"

But Ragab put his head back in a terrifying frenzy, and drove as fast as the car would go, whooping like a Red Indian. Samara was forced to put a hand on his arm, and whisper: "Please!"

"Layla's crying," Khalid snapped. "Will you return to your senses!"

My mind is dead. All that is left in my head is the pulse of my blood. My heart is sinking as in the worst depressions of kif—close your eyes—that way you will not see death. . . .

Suddenly a horrifying scream rang out. He opened his eyes, shaking, to see a black shape flying through the air. The car was jolted with the shock and nearly turned over, and they were thrown against the seats and doors by Ragab's violent braking. Sobs and cries of "God forbid!" broke out.

"Somebody was hit!"

"Killed ten times over."

"We should have seen this coming!"

"God, what an appalling night!"

"Get a grip on yourselves!" Ragab shouted. He pushed himself up in his seat and turned to look out through the back window. Then he sat down again and started to drive off. Ahmad leaned toward him, a question on his lips. "We must get out of here!" Ragab said decisively.

There was a sick silence. "It's the only solution!" he continued.

Nobody uttered a word. Then Samara whispered: "Perhaps he needs help?"

"He's already finished."

She said, this time more loudly: "You can't just . . . lay down the law like this!"

"What can we do, anyway! We are not doctors!"

"Well, what do you all think?" said Samara, turning to the others. And when not a word was said, she began: "I think. . . ."

Ragab furiously slammed on the brakes. The car stopped in the middle of the road. Then he turned to the others. "Let no one say tomorrow that I took this decision into my own hands. I leave it up to you. What do you think we should do?" And then, when there was silence, he shouted: "Answer me! I promise you that I will do whatever you tell me!"

"We must get out of here!" said Khalid. "It's the only solution. If anyone disagrees, let them say so now."

"Get moving," Mustafa said anxiously. "Otherwise there's no hope."

Layla was still crying, which made Saniya start as well. At that point, Ragab turned to Samara. "As you see," he said, "we have a consensus."

And when she said nothing, he started off.

"We're living in the world," he said. "Not in a play."

They set off at a slow and steady pace. He drove woodenly, tense and thunderous. A funereal silence reigned. Anis closed his eyes, only to see the black shape flying through the air. Was he still perhaps in pain? Or did he not know why, and how, he had been killed? Or why he existed? Or was he finished forever? Did life just pass away, as if it had never been?

They drove without stopping until they reached the houseboat. They got out of the car without speaking. Ragab stayed behind to look at the hood of the car. Amm Abduh rose to greet them, but no one paid him any attention. Their faces looked pallid and devastated in the light of the blue lamp. It was not long before Ragab joined them, his features set hard in a way that they had not seen before.

When the silence became intolerable, Ali said: "It could perhaps have been an animal. . . ."

"That scream was human," replied Ahmad.

"Do you think the investigation will lead to us?"

"We'll only lose sleep over that idea."

"And it was accidental," muttered Ragab.

"But to run away is a crime," said Samara.

"We had no option!" he said harshly. "And the decision was unanimous!" And he began to pace back and forth between the balcony and the door. Then he said: "I am desolate . . . but it is best that we forget the whole thing."

"If only we could!"

"We must forget; any other action would ruin the reputation of three ladies, and confound the rest of us—and send me straight to court."

Amm Abduh came. They looked at him in irritation, but he did not notice anything unusual. "Do you need anything?" he asked.

Ragab signaled him to go. He left the room, saying that he was going to the mosque.

After he had gone, Ragab asked: "Do you think the old man understood anything?"

"He understands nothing," Anis replied.

"We should all leave now," said Ragab nervously.

Khalid agreed. "Dawn is about to break."

Khalid, Layla, Ali, Saniya, Mustafa, and Ahmad left.

Ragab turned to Samara. "I am sorry to have caused you such distress," he said, "but come with me now, so that I can take you home."

She shook her head in revulsion. "Not in that car."

"You don't believe in ghosts, surely!"

"No—but it was me it ran over. . . ."

"Don't let your imagination run away with you!"

"It's true. I'm . . . shattered."

"All the same, I won't leave you. We can walk together until you find a taxi." And he stood in front of her, waiting for her to rise to her feet.

Translated by Frances Liardet

from *Miramar*, 1967

Miramar deals with a pension in Alexandria, the city in which Naguib Mahfouz used to spend the summer months. It was translated by Fatma Moussa Mahmoud, mother of the novelist Ahdaf Soueif, and was—as was the custom at that time—edited and revised jointly by an Egyptian and an Englishman who was teaching at the American University in Cairo, with copious notes provided by another Egyptian. What is particularly interesting about this novel is that the original edition also included an introduction by the English writer

John Fowles, who writes in highly complimentary tones about the novel and states his belief that the writer of *Miramar* is "a considerable novelist"—this at a time several years before Mahfouz was awarded the Nobel Prize, when he was virtually unknown in the West.

O utside the wind roars. Inside, even though it's still only early afternoon, my room exudes evening. My mind pictures the dense clouds outside and the mounting waves of the sea. Zohra comes in and switches on the light. I haven't seen her since yesterday and I've been in torment waiting for her.

"Let's go away, Zohra." I plead. She sets the cup on the table and looks at me with biting reproach. "We'll live together forever. Forever."

"And there won't be any problems then?" she asks sarcastically.

I answer with shameful frankness. "The problems I was referring to are created by marriage."

She mutters, "I should be sorry I ever fell in love with you."

"Please don't say that. Please try to understand. I love you—I can't live without you. But marriage would cause difficulties for me, with my family and at work too. It would ruin my career and that would inevitably threaten the home we make together. What can I do?"

She says even more angrily, "I didn't realize I could bring you so much calamity."

"It's not you! It's people's stupidity. These rigid barriers, these stinking facts! What can I do?"

"What can you do indeed?" she says, her eyes narrow with rage. "Turn me into a woman like the one from yesterday?"

"Zohra!" I say desperately. "If you loved me as much as I love you, you'd understand me better."

"I do love you," she says acidly. "It's a mistake I can't help."

"Love is stronger than everything. Everything."

"Everything except your problems," she says contemptuously.

We look at each other, feverish and desperate, furious and inflexible. If it wasn't for my fear and my strength of will, I might give in. I think quickly, in a flash. "Zohra, there are compromises. There's the Islamic marriage in its pure original form." Curiosity replaces anger in her eyes. I really know very little about the subject, but I go on. "We marry as the first Muslims used to marry."

"How was that?"

"I solemnly declare in the company of us two that I take you for my wife, according to the commandments of God and the doctrines of His Prophet."

"With no witnesses?"

"God is our witness."

"Everyone else around us behaves as if they didn't believe in His existence." She shakes her head stubbornly. "No."

She's really mulish. It hasn't been as easy as I expected. There's no persuading her. If she consents to live with me, I'm ready to give up the prospect of marriage, including my plans for advancement through a suitable match. I've thought of leaving the pension as a first step to getting her out of my mind, but I can't. We haven't quarreled; she still brings in my tea as usual, and lets me kiss her or take her in my arms.

One afternoon I am stunned to see her sitting in the hall bent over a primary reader, deciphering the letters. I look at her incredulously. Madame is at her place under the statue of the Virgin. Amer Wagdi is in the armchair.

"Look at our scholar, Monsieur Sarhan," exclaims Madame smiling. "She's made an arrangement for private lessons with a neighbor, a teacher. What do you think of that?"

I am about to laugh at Madame's teasing irony when suddenly I feel genuinely impressed. "Bravo, Zohra! Good for you."

The old man watches me with clouded eyes. I am all at once afraid of him. I don't know why. I go out.

I am deeply moved. Some inner voice tells me that I have been taking the girl's feelings too lightly and that God will not look kindly on me. But I can't come to terms with the idea of marrying her. Love is only an emotion and you can cope with it one way or another, but marriage is an institution, a corporation not unlike the company I work for, with its own accepted laws and regulations. What's the good of going into it if it doesn't give me a push up the social ladder? And if the bride has no career, how can we compete in the rat race, socially or otherwise? My problem is that I've fallen in love with a girl whose credentials are insufficient for that sort of thing. But if she'd accept my love without conditions I'd give up the ideal I've always had of marriage altogether.

"You've got a lot of willpower, Zohra," I say later, to give her her due. "But it's a pity you're tiring yourself out and wasting all your wages."

"I won't stay illiterate all my life," she says proudly, standing on the other side of the table.

"What good will it do you?"

"I'll learn some profession. And I won't be a servant anymore."

That stabs me to the heart. I sit there tongue-tied.

"Some of my people came to take me back home today," she says in a new voice.

I look at her, smiling to hide my anxiety, but she ignores my expression. "What did you tell them?"

"We settled it. I'll go back next month."

I cry out in extreme anxiety. "Seriously! You're going back to the old man!"

"No. He's married now." She drops her voice. "There's someone else."

I catch her by the hand. "Let's go away together. Tomorrow," I beg. "Today if you like . . ."

"I said I was going home next month."

"Zohra! Have a heart."

"That's one solution, without problems."

"But you love me!"

"Love and marriage are two different things," she answers angrily. "Isn't that what you said?"

But her lips soon give her away; I detect the shadow of a smile. "Zohra, you devil, you've been joking." I am tremendously relieved.

Madame comes in, drinking tea out of a cup in her hand. She sits on the bed and tells me the story of Zohra's refusing to go back home with her relations.

"Don't you think it would have been better for her to go back home?" I suggest slyly.

Madame smiles that knowing smile of a procuress. "Her true relations are here, Monsieur Sarhan."

I avoid her eyes, completely ignoring the implication of her remark, but guessing that a little bird has carried gossip about us from one room to another. She probably thinks worse of us than we deserve, but I'm pleased at the idea of my imaginary conquest. Zohra's obstinacy will not give an inch, though, and I ask myself when I shall have the courage to get out of the pension.

Translated by Fatma Moussa Mahmoud
Edited and revised by Maged el-Kommos and John Rodenbeck

from *Mirrors*, 1972

This unusual work consists of 55 character sketches of people living during the writer's lifetime, with portraits by the Alexandrian artist Seif Wanli.

Durriya Salim

"Allow me to say hello . . ."

The shadow of a smile appeared on her lips. Encouraged, I said, "It's impossible not to exchange greetings after what happened . . ."

She broke her silence. "After what happened?"

"After what happened between our eyes."

She laughed innocently. "I accept the greeting," she said.

"That's the first step."

"Are there others?"

She came with three children to Montaza, they swam in the sea while she sat alone in the casino, watching them from the window. My attention was attracted to a smiling face and a body bursting with feminine maturity. I was enamored by an affectionate look in her eyes, made to receive and welcome. I soon felt a gentle invitation like a delicate flower; ignoring it was beyond human power. We exchanged passing words, agreeing to meet in the Swan Garden. On my way there, I was convinced she was a special type of woman, a widow or divorced.

But she simply said, "I'm married!"

Taken aback, I said, "But I always see you alone."

"He's on a short scholarship abroad that ends this year."

I was dumbfounded.

"Are you afraid of married women?" she asked with a laugh.

"I'm thinking . . ."

"Think about preparing a safe place to meet in Cairo," she interrupted.

"Agreed," I replied enthusiastically.

"And don't misunderstand me."

"How, and why?"

"Maybe you wonder what's behind a woman who responded to your first gesture?"

Those were my thoughts, but I said, "I was no less responsive and I was the initiator."

"We have a right to be candid," she replied gently.

I contemplated the affair with the sobriety of one who hadn't fallen under a mad urge. I told myself that I liked this woman and desired her but would not love her. A place was found on the Saqqara road. I had imagined a flaming episode, but when I had closed the door, I found myself in the presence of a new woman. Relaxed on the sofa, not even removing the silk scarf around her neck, she was calm, surrendering, peering at me with affectionate eyes. I caressed her and kissed her lips. She responded to my emotions with a contented, loving smile. When I offered her a drink, she refused; when I invited her to bed, she whispered in my ear, "I wish we could spend our time in quiet, innocent happiness."

"I don't believe it."

She rose. "Don't consider it an end in itself."

Despite the attraction, I believe it was quite possible for her to spend the time in "quiet, innocent happiness"—a great contradiction between the easy woman responding to the first gesture and this gentle, ascetic woman.

"You're a strange character," I said.

"Really. Why?"

When I hesitated, she asked, "Do you value my company?"

"Certainly."

"That's what interests me."

The weekly meetings continued—with no real love on my side and no infidelity on hers. When the curtain of formality was removed, I said, "I confess I thought you playful, in Montaza."

"What do you mean?" she asked with interest.

"An innocent meaning."

"God forgive you."

I held her hand. "I wonder what drives you to another man's arms?"

"Another?!"

"I mean other than your husband?"

A tear fluttered in her lashes. "People hate being cross-examined."

After consistent meetings, and tamed by habit, she surrendered her memories.

"I was married after a profound love story."

She was a nurse and he an intern.

"We shared a beautiful love. Frankly I submitted to him on our first meeting."

"And he married you?"

"He was gallant, a true lover."

"How beautiful!"

"We lived for a long time as happy as could be, and I bore him three children."

She stopped. "Then what?" I asked.

"Nothing," she replied, as one awakening from a sweet dream.

"How are things today?"

"As usual."

"What do you mean?"

"All this time lost at the expense of our love," she said laughing.

"Can we continue to meet when he returns?"

"Why not?"

My attachment was courtesy, then habit. Her gentleness, care, and affection grew, until one day she said, "I can't imagine my life without you."

I found the safest answer was a long kiss but she demanded stubbornly, "And you?"

"Like you and more."

"You never told me that you loved me."

"But I really do love you, and that's more important," I replied.

Doctor Sadiq Abd al-Hamid returned from his scholarship. She talked about him objectively, as if he were a phenomenon that she was not strongly related to, but with a respect that could not be surpassed. At that time, I had started visiting Gad Abu al-Ela's salon, and there I met Doctor Sadiq Abd al-Hamid! Gad Abu al-Ela told us how he had visited the doctor for a medical consultation and how their relationship had become close. A rare spiritual friendship developed between us, and in turn, I introduced him to the Salim Gabr and Zuhayr Kamil meetings and to Doctor Mahir Abd al-Karim's salon. I was amazed to see a man of Durriya's age, perhaps a few years younger, handsome, intelligent, with unlimited spiritual aspiration. And so our friendship began four months after my affair with his wife! It upset me to the point of torture. Durriya, not expecting it, was shocked. She noticed my agitation and the gloom that hung over our meetings, strangling them—it seemed the current of life was flowing toward a blocked corner to pronounce its death.

"Forget he's my husband. I need never have mentioned a word about his identity or name," she pleaded.

"It's useless to imagine unrealistic possibilities," I replied in confusion.

"We must preserve our relationship—it's more important than every-thing else."

"I'm in torment," I said, truly sad.

"Maybe if he knew about our relationship, he wouldn't care," she said with unusual passion. I looked at her shocked, not believing what she was saying.

"He doesn't love me—hasn't loved me for three years or more, believe me."

"I believe you and I'm sorry."

"He's seeing another woman. If he weren't so devoted to his children, he'd have left us and married her!"

"Durriya, I'm sorry."

"What do you mean, sorry?"

"Sorry about your situation. And mine is not enviable."

"If you loved me, you wouldn't feel sorry at all!"

"The fact is, I can't bear this situation."

She turned her red-eyed face away. "You hardly know him. Does friendship grow from nothing? Love is stronger than friendship. But the truth is that you don't love me."

I had nothing to say, so I remained silent. And with silence, the curtain came down on our sad, contrived affair. When we left our nest, I observed her mature person, suffering life's most difficult stage under the weight of abandonment and disappointment. My heart shriveled in pain and sorrow. Outside, a cold wind lashed at us like a whip in the dark night.

Abd al-Wahab Ismail

Today he is a legend, and as a legend, interpretations vary. Although he always showed me generous fraternity, I was never comfortable with his face or the look in his bulging, serious eyes. We met at Doctor Mahir Abd al-Karim's salon during the Second World War; he was in his thirties, an Arabic teacher in a secondary school, occasionally publishing pieces of criticism or traditional poetry in literary magazines. An Azhar graduate with no knowledge of foreign languages, still he earned my respect and interest with his powerful logic debating with people known for broad culture and extensive readings in foreign languages—like Doctor Ibrahim Aql, Salim Gabr, and Zuhayr Kamil. He was a calm, polite conversationalist who never lost his temper, digressed from objectivity, or appeared below their refined levels, their peer in every sense. I was convinced of his sharp intelligence, debating ability, and broad reading despite his complete dependence on heritage and translations, not doubting that he was brighter than them. Even his criticism of contemporary works was not marred by wit or superficiality as in the case of the specialists with degrees from Paris and London, except for a subtle difference revealed only to the eyes of meticulous cognoscenti.

"He's a talented young man, it's a pity he wasn't sent on a scholarship abroad," Doctor Mahir Abd al-Karim, who always weighed his words carefully, told me.

Although Abd al-Wahab Ismail never spoke about religion, pretended modernity in his ideas and dress, and adopted European habits in food and going to the cinema, yet the effect religion had on him, his belief, even fanaticism, were not a secret to me.

A young Coptic writer had offered him his book of articles on criticism and sociology. He talked about him one day at Fishawi's.

"He's intelligent, well-informed, sensitive, original in style and ideas."

"When will you write about him?" I asked innocently, as I was fond of the writer.

He smiled mysteriously. "Wait, and it'll be a long wait!" he said.

"What do you mean?"

"I will not help build a pen that tomorrow will slander our Islamic heritage in every twisted way," he replied decisively.

"Do I understand then that you're a fanatic?" I asked angrily.

"Don't threaten me with clichés, they don't move me," he jeered.

"Your position saddens me."

"There's no point arguing about this with a Wafdist, I was a Wafdist once. Frankly I don't trust people of other religions."

He had been a Wafdist, but broke away with Ahmad Mahir whom he greatly admired. When the Saadists were in power, he was promoted to inspector. But his dream was lost with Ahmad Mahir's assassination, as though he had been hit by the bullet that killed the man.

"The nation's greatest man is lost," he told me in despair.

He complained about his health at every opportunity, using it as an excuse not to fast in Ramadan, but he never told anyone the nature of his malady. He was not interested in women and never married—in that regard, he was upright. Yet despite his serious morality and sincere crusades against corruption, an aspect was disclosed that I would not have believed had I not seen it. Abd al-Wahab despised a writer who owned a magazine and printing press that published a monthly series of books.

"If it weren't for his magazine, he'd never find a place to publish a word of his," he said.

I was stunned to read an article by him in *al-Risala*, praising the magazine owner to seventh heaven. I had difficulty explaining it until I learned they had agreed to publish one of Abd al-Wahab's books in the monthly series for an extraordinary fee no other author had yet received! Recalling his blind attitude toward the Coptic writer, I was disturbed by this opportunistic side, doubting his integrity. A permanent revulsion, despite our friendship, settled in my heart.

He continued as an inspector and writer until the Wafd formed the government in 1950. Uncomfortable with the Wafdist minister's treatment, he resigned and devoted himself to the press. He was known at that time for his relentless attacks on the Wafdist government, simultaneously publishing contemporary books on Islam that were extremely successful. The 1952 revolution found him immersed in fighting the Wafd and defending Islam.

Some two years had passed without our meeting, and I had lost track of his news. On a visit to Salim Gabr, he told me, "It seems Abd al-Wahab Ismail's star will shine soon."

"What do you mean?" I asked with interest.

"He's in the inner circle," he replied.

"As a political writer or a religious writer?" I asked.

"As a member of the Muslim Brothers."

"The Brothers?" I asked in amazement. "But I knew him as a fanatical Saadist."

"Praise be to Him Who causes change but never changes!" he replied sarcastically.

A year later, we met in front of the Anglo Bar; shaking hands warmly, we strolled and chatted until the revolution came up.

"A blessed revolution, but it's difficult to know what they're after," he said with reserve.

I sensed a bitterness—I could not fathom its secret, nor did he reveal it. He had the ability, rare in Egyptians, to keep his secrets.

"I heard that you've joined the Muslim Brothers," I said.

"Any Muslim is liable to that," he replied with a cryptic smile.

"It's a pity you've abandoned literary criticism."

He laughed. "What a pagan wish!"

As we parted, I felt that henceforth we'd meet only by chance in the street.

At the first clash between the revolution and the Brothers, he was arrested, tried, and sentenced to ten years in prison. He was released in 1956. Carrying my good wishes, I went to his house on Khayrat Street. He had not changed much—his hair had grayed, as expected for a man of fifty-seven or fifty-eight, and he had put on weight. I thought his health had improved. We exchanged questions about our lives. With his usual sedateness and remarkable cool nerve, he plunged straight into public affairs, expounding his views with confidence.

"The Quran must replace all imported laws. . . . The woman must return to the home. It's all right to be educated—for the home, not for a job. The state may guarantee her a pension in case of divorce or absence of the provider. . . . Socialism, nationalism, and European civilization are a malice we must uproot from our souls," he said with force.

He launched such a tirade against science that I was shocked.

"Even science?!" I asked.

"Yes. It will not give us an edge. We're behind there, and will stay behind no matter how hard we try. We have no scientific message to offer the world, but we have the message of Islam and the worship of God alone, not capitalism or dialectic materialism."

I listened, politely controlling myself. Rising to leave, I asked, "What about the future?"

"Do you have a suggestion?"

"Yes, but I'm afraid it might be pagan. Go back to literary criticism."

"I've received an invitation to work abroad," he said calmly.

"What have you decided?"

"I'm thinking."

A year later, newspapers greeted us with news of another Brothers' conspiracy. I knew nothing about Abd al-Wahab Ismail, assuming he had left the country to work abroad. But my friend Qadri Rizq confirmed that he had been part of the conspiracy and had resisted the force that had gone to arrest him until he was shot dead.

Yusriya Bashir

Return to childhood, to Bait al-Qadi Square and walnut trees with sparrows' nests. From a side window, as a little boy, I looked out on Qurmuz alley, a narrow, paved street that sloped downhill. On one corner stood the Bashir house. I was seven or eight, and I liked the sight of

Sheikh Bashir, sitting in front of his house every afternoon with his prayer beads, his white skin, gray beard, and the bright colors of his turban, jubba, and caftan illuminating the place.

When he walked toward Bait al-Qadi Square on his way to the Egyptian Club, Yusriya would appear in the window. She might have been sixteen, her face like the moon—white, cheerful, comfortable, and shining—crowned with black hair. She'd call my name in a soft voice and joke with me. I started at her, happy, satisfied, amorous—if a boy of seven can be amorous. My attachment can only be love: she was neither a relative nor my age, and she never gave me a toy or a piece of candy, or extolled her beautiful face.

She sometimes tempted me to go to her. I'd sneak from the house into the alley, but the servant always caught me just at the right moment and carried me back inside, as I kicked and screamed to no avail. One day it rained. I stood by the window, watching the rain pour down the alley and flow like a river into the old drain. Soon the water level rose, and the street was awash. Qurmuz became a stagnant pond impossible to traverse except by porters or a cart. Through the pouring rain I saw Yusriya in the window beckoning me. I had an idea and decided to try it out immediately. I secretly climbed to the roof and carried a copper washing basin and a broom with a long wooden handle down to the street. I set the basin on the water, jumped in, and started punting with the broom toward the Bashir house. The servant realized, but it was too late: this time she couldn't brave the water, and she stood at the corner yelling but getting no reply. I disembarked from the basin at the door of the Bashir house (a stuffed crocodile hung over it) and went inside barefoot, my gallabiya soaking wet.

Yusriya met me at the top of the stairs. She led me into the room and sat me on a Turkish sofa in front of her, then played gently with my hair, as I glued my eyes to her luminous face. Despite the effort and wetness, I felt accomplishment and exultation in her hands.

She wanted to entertain me, so she took my palm and spread it.

"I'll read your fortune," she said.

She followed the lines on my palm and read the unknown, but I was absorbed in her beautiful face.

Translated by Roger Allen

from *Karnak Café*, 1974

The novel deals with the harsh times that followed Egypt's defeat in the 1967 War. In the passage chosen, a woman who frequents the café talks of her unpleasant experiences at the hands of those in power.

A few weeks later I was summoned to Khalid Safwan's office again. He looked as calm as usual, even more so perhaps. It was just as though nothing had ever happened.

" 'You've been proved innocent,' he said tersely.

"For a long time I simply looked straight at him. For his part, he gave me a fixed, lackadaisical stare.

" 'Were you watching?' I screamed at him.

" 'I simply see what there is to be seen,' he replied quietly.

" 'But now I've lost everything,' I shouted angrily.

" 'Oh no! Everything can be put right. We can see to that.'

" 'I don't believe,' I yelled madly, 'that the revolution would be happy to hear what went on in this room!'

" 'We're here to protect the revolution, and that's much more important than the few isolated mistakes we may happen to make. We always make sure to put right whatever needs to be put right. You'll be leaving here now with a brand new boon—our friendship.'

"With that I burst into tears, a prolonged fit of nervous weeping that I was totally unable to stop. He waited silently until I'd finished.

" 'You're going to see one of my assistants now,' he said. 'He's going to make you an offer beyond price.' For a few moments, he said nothing, then he went on, 'I would strongly advise you not to turn it down. It's the chance of a lifetime.' "

So Zaynab had become an informer as well. She was offered special privileges, and it was decided that Isma'il was to be the pawn in the whole thing. It was made very clear to her that she had to maintain total silence; she was told that the people she was working for had absolute control of everything.

"When I went home," Zaynab told me, "and had some time to myself, I was utterly horrified by what I'd lost, something for which there could be no compensation. For the first time in my entire life I really despised myself."

"But . . . ," I began trying to console her.

"No, don't try to defend me," she interrupted. "Defending something that is despicable places you in the same category." She continued angrily, "I kept telling myself that I'd become a spy and a prostitute. That was the state I was in when I met Isma'il again."

"I assume you kept your secret to yourself."

"Yes."

"You were wrong to do that, my dear!"

"My secret job was far too dangerous to reveal to anyone else."

"I'm talking about the other matter."

"I was too afraid and ashamed to tell him about it. I was keeping my hopes up as well. I told myself that, if I had things put right by surgery, then I might be able to think about a happy life in the future."

"But that hasn't happened so far, has it?"

"Small chance!"

"Maybe I can do something for you," I offered hopefully.

"Forget it," she replied sarcastically. "Just wait till I've finished my story. I may have made a mistake, but in any case I proceeded to take the only course open to me, torturing my own self and submitting to the very worst punishments I could possibly imagine. By taking such action I was relying on an unusual kind of logic. I'm a daughter of the revolution, I convinced myself. In spite of everything that's happened, I refuse to disavow everything it stands for. Therefore I am still responsible for its welfare and must fulfill that obligation. As such, I am implicitly to blame for the things that have happened to me. On that basis I decided to stop pretending to live an honorable life and instead to behave like a dishonorable woman."

"You did yourself a grievous wrong."

"I could tolerate everything about it except the idea that Isma'il might come to despise me. At the same time I didn't want to betray him. While I was going through all this, I couldn't even think straight and went completely astray." She shook her head sadly. "A number of things happened which made it impossible for me to put things right again or to return to the straight and narrow. It was at precisely that point that old Hasaballah, the chicken seller, saw me again."

I stared at her in alarm.

"This time he found the path wide open."

"No!"

"Why not? I told myself that this was the way to lead a debauched life. You couldn't do that without there being a price to pay."

"I don't believe you!"

"I took the money."

With that I felt a sense of revulsion toward the entire world.

"And Zayn al-'Abidin 'Abdallah as well!" she continued, giving me a sarcastic and defiant stare.

I didn't say a word.

"He used Imam al-Fawwal and Gum'a, the bootblack, as go-betweens," she added.

"But I always thought they were both decent, loyal people," I blurted out in amazement.

"So they were," she replied sadly. "But just like me, they were both devastated. What's happened to everyone? We seem to have turned into a nation of deviants. All the costs in terms of life—the defeat and anxiety—they have managed to demolish our sense of values. The two of them kept hearing about corruption all over the place, so what was to stop them having a turn too? I can tell you that both of them are acting as pimps as we speak and without the slightest sense of shame."

"But Zaynab," I asked, "should we despair about everything?" After a moment's pause I proceeded to answer my own question, "No! This particular phase we're going through is just like the plague, but afterwards life will be renewed once again."

Zaynab paid no attention to what I was saying. "I decided to tell Isma'il everything," she said.

"But you said you wouldn't," I said in amazement.

"I decided to do it in a very original way, so I just gave myself to him."

"I must confess that at this point I can't work out what kind of relationship there is between you and Isma'il."

"After the storm that we've been through, there's no point in trying to find some fixed logical process to apply."

"But do you still love Isma'il?"

"I've never been in love with anyone else."

"What about now?"

"All I can feel now is death, not love."

"But Zaynab, you're a young girl right at the beginning of her life. Everything will change."

"Will it be for better or worse, do you think?"

"It can't possibly get any worse than it is now. So change must be for the better."

"Let's go back to my story. The only consolation I was getting out of what I was doing was that I could feel the pain involved in the self-punishment. But then I did something that can never be expiated, no matter what the price."

"Really?"

"Yes. Are you starting to feel disgusted with me?"

"No, Zaynab," I replied. "I'm actually feeling very sorry for you."

"One evening Isma'il and I went to Hilmi Hamada's home. We found he was planning revolution. He confided in us that he was distributing secret pamphlets. . . ."

The sheer force of the memory was so great that she had to stop talking for a while. For my part, I welcomed this break that had arrived like some kind of truce-period in the midst of a prolonged saga of torture.

"His frank admission came as a total surprise to me. I dearly wished that I'd not gone to his home."

"I can well understand your feelings."

"I immediately thought of the force that was in control of everything. I was overwhelmed by panic and started worrying about Isma'il."

Aha! So there was Isma'il assuming they had used special methods to find out that he had failed to communicate with them, when all the time it had never even occurred to him that it was Zaynab who had given Hilmi away. So she was the one who had revealed his secret, assuming that by so doing she would be sparing him even greater agonies.

We stared sadly at each other.

"So I'm the one who killed Hilmi Hamada," she said.

"No, you're not," I replied. "He was killed by whoever it was made the decision to torture all of you."

"I'm the one who killed him. And they arrested Isma'il even so. Why? I don't understand. This time he spent even longer in prison than the two previous times. When he came out, he was even more crushed than before. Why? I don't know. In my report I'd put down that he'd argued with his friend and advised him to abandon the project. But any appeal to logic in these circumstances is obviously futile."

"At the time you were out of prison, weren't you?"

"Oh yes. I was free to enjoy my liberty to the full, along with all the suffering and loneliness that went with it. And then, along came the precursors of war, bringing their threats to our very existence. Like everyone else, I had a limitless trust in our armed forces. Everything would go on and on, I told myself, both good and bad. But then came the disaster and . . ."

She fell silent; her expression was one of total dismay.

"There's no need to explain," I assured her. "We all went through it. But did you support the demonstrations on the ninth and tenth of June?"

"Yes, I certainly did, and to the maximum extent possible."

"So your basic faith has not been shaken then?"

"Quite the contrary, it has been completely uprooted from its foundations. I've come to believe that it's a castle built on sand."

"I have to tell you that I don't understand your attitude."

"It's all very simple. All of a sudden, I found I could no longer tolerate having to shoulder responsibility. After relying on a laissez-faire attitude for so long, I found that I was actually afraid of genuine freedom. How about you? Were you for or against the demonstrators at the time?"

"I was with them all the way, clinging desperately to a last spark of national pride."

"When I heard that Isma'il was going to be set free," she went on angrily, "I told myself that I had the defeat to thank for letting me see him again."

As I thought about what she had just said, the entire idea made me feel utterly sad and miserable.

Then she told me about her first meeting with Isma'il after his release, and the confused babble of their conversation.

"You know, when we first graduated and got jobs, we talked all the time about getting married, that being a requirement enjoined by traditional notions of modesty. We talked about it over and over again. It's not so strange for me to have changed and abandoned the dreams of the past, but what has caused such a change in Isma'il? What really happened inside that prison, I wonder?"

So, at this point, each one of them acknowledges that they have changed, but keeps asking himself or herself about the other one. They're both convinced that they can't live a normal life now; on that score I tend to agree with them— at least, with regard to this wretched period we're now living through. All of us need time so we can bandage our wounds and purify the collective national soul. In fact, the process may even involve a recovery of self-confidence and self-respect as well. But by the very nature of things matters like that could not be discussed in this particular context.

"If humanity simply gives up or waits," I commented, using generalities as a smoke screen, "it will never change—for the better, I mean."

"It's so easy to philosophize, isn't it!" she retorted angrily.

"Maybe so," I said, "but these days Isma'il seems to be edging toward the fedayeen."

"I know."

"And what about you?" I asked after another pause. "What are your thoughts?"

She said nothing for a while. "Before I give you a reply," she said, "I must first correct something that I said about Imam al-Fawwal and Gum'a. Actually they knew nothing about the details of the arrangement they made between Zayn al-'Abidin 'Abdallah and me after our second period in prison; they had no idea what was going on."

"Do you mean they're innocent of what you accused them of doing?"

"No, I don't. But they've only given in to temptation recently, not before. Things are still really confused in my own mind, and I want you to keep in mind that I'm telling you my own story from memory. I can't guarantee that all the details are accurate."

I nodded my head sadly. "What are your thoughts now?" I repeated.

"Do you really want to know?"

"I assume you're not still. . . ." I stopped in spite of myself.

"Being a prostitute, you mean?" she said, completing my sentence for me. I said nothing.

"Thank you for thinking so well of me," she said.

Again I did not comment.

"At the moment," she said, "I'm living a very puritan existence."

"Really?" I asked happily.

"Certainly."

"And how did that come about?"

"Quickly, through a counter-revolution, but also because I still feel a sense of utter revulsion."

"Where, oh where have those former days of innocence and enthusiasm gone?" I asked affectionately.

Translated by Roger Allen

from *Fountain and Tomb*, 1975

This work, published three years after *Mirrors*, is made up of seventy-eight tales, many of them reflecting incidents from the author's own childhood. Mahfouz called it the most autobiographical of his novels.

I enjoy playing in the small square between the archway and the takiya where the Sufis live. Like all the other children, I admire the mulberry trees in the takiya garden, the only bit of green in the whole neighborhood. Our tender hearts yearn for their dark berries. But it stands like a fortress, this takiya, circled by its garden wall. Its stern gate is broken and always, like the windows, shut. Aloof isolation drenches the whole compound. Our hands stretch toward this wall—reaching for the moon.

Once in a while one of the longbeards appears in the garden in a bright, patterned skullcap and a huge rippling cape, and then we all yell, "If God wills, you dervish, you might get your wish."

But he just gazes at the grass and goes on, pausing, perhaps, beside the garden's small stream before vanishing behind the inner gate.

"Father, who are those men?"

"They are the men of God." And then in a very meaningful tone, "Damned be anyone who disturbs their peace."

But I still burn for those mulberries.

One day, tired of playing, I sit down to rest and immediately begin dozing. I wake to an empty square; even the sun has gone into hiding behind the ancient wall. The spring scene fades, heavy with the breath of sunset. I have to get away from the archway and back to our alley before it's pitch dark, so I jump up, ready to go. But then comes the uncanny feeling that I'm not alone, that I'm roaming in some pleasant magnetic field. When a warm breeze flows over me, I peer toward the takiya.

There, under the central mulberry tree, stands a man, a dervish unlike those I've seen before. He is great with age but extremely tall, his face a pool of glowing light. His cape is green, his long turban white. Everything about him is munificent beyond imagining. I look at him so intently that I become intoxicated, the sight of him filling the whole universe. It comes to me that he must be the owner and overseer of the place, and I see that he is loving, not like those others. I go up to the wall and say most respectfully, "I love mulberries."

Since he doesn't answer, doesn't even move, I assume he hasn't heard me, so I say it louder. "I love mulberries."

I believe that his single glance takes in everything and that his deep, melodious voice says, "My nightingale, *khoon deli khord wakuli hasel kared.*"

Then I think I see him tossing me a berry. I bend down to pick it up. I find nothing. When I stand up again, the place is empty. Darkness veils the inner gate.

Of course I tell my father the whole thing. He glares at me doubtfully. I tell it all over again. He says, "Your description doesn't fit anyone but the High Sheikh himself, but he never leaves his retreat."

On all the names of God, I swear I'm telling the truth; I even repeat the words of the sheikh. My father says, "I wonder what this gibberish you've memorized could mean."

"I've heard it before in the chanting from the takiya."

My father broods for a while before saying, "Don't tell a soul about this." He spreads his hands and recites the sura of the Oneness of the Eternal.

I dash back across the square and wait about till all the other children are gone. I expect the sheikh to appear, but he doesn't. In my thin voice, I call out, "My nightingale, *khoon deli khord wakuli hasel kared.*"

No answer. I ache with expectation, but he takes no pity on my desire to see him. Mulling over the event much later, I wonder about its reality. Did I really see the sheikh or just pretend I did to get attention—and then end up believing my own fantasy? Did I merely see a drowsy mirage and then make the daydream real from stories about the High Sheikh I'd heard around the house? It seems it must have been something like that since the sheikh never appeared again and since everyone agreed that he never came outside.

That's how I created a myth and then destroyed it—except that this supposed vision of the sheikh burrowed deep down into my very marrow, a memory of great purity. And except that I'm still crazy about mulberries. In mosque school, boys and girls sit together on the same mat and recite the verses in one voice. The leather lash of our teacher the sheikh doesn't see any difference between a boy's shin and a girl's. We all sit cross-legged for lunch, faces to the wall; each unknots his bundle and spreads it out. Everybody has a flat round bread, cheese, and some halawa.

I steal glimpses of Darwisha while she recites or eats.

I follow her down the street till she turns into her dead-end lane. Then I go on to my house, carrying my slate and her image.

When the proper time for it comes, we visit the cemetery, and I get left sitting in the courtyard at the entrance. Bored, I run out into the grounds. There, by accident, we meet, Darwisha and I, among the roofless tombs of the poor.

I give her half my pastry, and we exchange glances as we eat.

"Where do you play?"

"In the lane."

Though her lane branches off our street, I don't dare sneak into it in broad daylight. The feeling that stops me is unclear, but I know it isn't innocent. We now make silent promises with our eyes. When evening comes, I go into her lane and find her standing on her doorstep.

We stand there, two silent phantoms shrouded in darkness and guilt.

"Shouldn't we sit down?"

She doesn't answer.

I sit on the step and tug at her hand to make her join me, then slide over till we are side by side. A strange and mysterious joy flows over me. Taking her chin in my hand, I turn her face to mine, lean toward her and kiss her. I put my arm around her. I am silent, spellbound, melting into a mist of rushing sensations; I know drunkenness before touching liquor.

We forget time and fear.

We forget our families and the alley.

Even the phantoms cannot part us.

Nipples engorged and swollen, the cat lies on her side while the little ones blindly jostle each other in her bosom. Alone in the room, I study this scene closely. All of a sudden, I hear breathing and look around. It's Senaya, our postman's oldest daughter, some years older than I. Her fine features and feathery spirit brim over with vitality and joy. Entranced, she gazes at the cat and whispers, "Nothing could be more beautiful."

When I answer with a nod, she says, "I love cats, don't you?"

Unable to think of anything but how close we are, I say, "Yes, I . . ."

Then she presses even closer to see better and I feel her breasts against my shoulder. She goes on talking but I don't hear her. I'm on fire, the flames lick up my shyness, and I spin around and crush her to my chest. And so begins a close relationship filled, on my side, with both joy and regret.

I come to know her better, beautiful and bold as she is wary. Though she becomes wonderfully, melodiously drunk with passion, there are still uncrossable barriers between us. I obey her signals, rush into her shelter—but she doesn't understand innocence or dreams or even secret conspiracies and so lures me into the rose garden where she kindles all the fires of hell. We know neither peace nor safety and pluck buds while we tremble in fear of the guardians. We run in a fever of love, two madly snatching pickpockets hovering between conflict and open-eyed drowsiness. Life is a crazy song overflowing with sweetness and pain.

After two years of our love, Senaya gets married.

We meet again years and years later.

She has grown stupendously fat and has a sleepy look, but she's sensible, too, very dignified, balanced, and stable. We shake hands and hold an ordinary gossipy conversation without one meaningful smile, remark, or gesture. She's a respectable lady, a living symbol of motherhood, devotion, and piety.

I flash back to the time of her ripening youth when she was a butterfly of many hues, a fresh apple, a sweet flower, a flowing stream.

Those were happy days.

I got to know Sheikh Omar Fikri, a retired law clerk, through his visits to my father. As soon as his pension began, he opened a business to help the residents of our alley, for the connections between us and the big city were becoming stronger and more complex every day. From his office between the small mosque and the school he provided such services as renting houses, moving furniture, arranging funerals, and advising on commercial ventures as well as matters of marriage and divorce.

I heard him tell my father with proud self-confidence, "With my vast experience, I can offer services for any sphere of life.!"

A craving long concealed boiled deep inside me and I asked, "Would you do a service for me?"

"What can I do to help you, my lad?" he beamed down at me.

"I want to see the High Sheikh of the takiya!"

Sheikh Omar laughed out loud and my father joined him. Then he said: "The concerns I manage are serious, related to the very essence of practical affairs."

"But you said you could do anything in any sphere of life."

"Don't you think the takiya lies outside the walls of life?"

"Well, no, actually, it's not like that. . . ."

"Recite some Sufi poetry for us," my father said.

"My nightingale, *khoon deli khord wakuli hasel kared*," I recited with joy.

Sheikh Omar Fikri said to my father, "Nothing is worse than repeating verses like this without understanding them." Then he looked down at me and asked if I understood a word of it. I shook my head. "They're strange folks speaking a weird language," he said, "but our quarter is all gaga over them."

Then I said to him, "You can do anything."

"Forgive him, almighty God," my father murmured.

"Why is it so important to see the High Sheikh of the dervishes?" the sheikh asked.

My father told him my old story. Sheikh Omar laughed and said: "Well, I guess I ought to confess that I once wanted to see the High Sheikh myself."

"Really?"

"Yes. I told myself, 'Here's a whole neighborhood repeating his name in spite of the fact that almost no one claims to have seen him.' I burned with desire to see him, craved it with the craving of a little kid. 'What stands between me and this wish?' So I marched boldly up to the takiya and demanded to see whoever was in charge. But from behind their wall they met me with grim, anxious looks and seemed very unwilling to understand what I was saying. When I tried to talk with gestures, they jumped back so startled and afraid I was sorry I'd bothered them. I saw I'd been stupid and went away in despair of fulfilling my wish by direct means. Legal penetration of the takiya was difficult or downright impossible and sneaking in was clearly against the law, hence not an option for a man whose life's work is based on respect for the judicial system."

"So you gave up your wish?"

"No, not exactly. I tried something else. I mixed with residents of our quarter great with age and famous in piety. A few said they'd seen him, but no two of them ever agreed on an accurate description. In fact, they differed to the point of outright contradiction, implying, in my opinion, that none of them had seen him."

"But I did," I put in eagerly.

"You aren't lying, but you *are* imagining."

"Why is it impossible to see him? Wouldn't he want to take an occasional stroll in the garden, for example?"

"But how do you know the one you saw was the High Sheikh and not just one of the dervishes?"

"That's a question you could ask any time. Is that how you washed your hands of the problem?"

"Not at all. I was crazier than you might think. I went defiantly to the Bureau of the Waqf and gathered a fair amount of information about the takiya's endowment, the particular order of Sufism they adhere to, and the dervish in charge of collecting the income. But I didn't hear one word about the High Sheikh except that he has miraculous powers, something our whole alley already believes."

I wilted in disappointment, glared at him, and said, "There must be some way."

With a smile, he answered, "Well, there's logic, which is what freed me from my feverish obsession. It told me that we see the takiya and the dervishes, but we don't see the High Sheikh."

"Can that be taken as a proof of his non-existence?" my father asked.

"No, it doesn't prove that, it just states what we all know: we see the takiya and the dervishes, we don't see the High Sheikh."

"But there must be a way to prove his existence and see him," I insisted.

"I don't believe it will be accomplished by legal means, and, as you know, I never stray from the law."

My father laughed and said, "So, Sheikh Omar, you have to admit there's at least one service you can't perform."

"So be it. But what's the use of seeing the High Sheikh? Wasn't it a silly wish?"

Then I asked him heatedly, "Why do they slam the gate in our faces?"

"The takiya was originally built in the open because this order sings of seclusion, isolation from people and the world, but as time passed the city overtook and surrounded them with the living and the dead. As a last resort, they closed their doors to attain solitude."

He smiled a lukewarm smile. "I've given you all the information you could possibly want. It may be useless for the fulfillment of your wish, but at least it makes it clear that you can't fulfill it without breaking the law."

This is an unforgettable memory.

To this very day I've never been able to muster enough courage to break the law, but, at the same time, I can't imagine a takiya without a High Sheikh.

As days go by, I stop looking at the takiya except when we pass it to visit the tombs. Then I throw it a smiling glance and let a few memories come back. I try to remember the figure of the Sheikh—or whoever it was I once upon a time thought was the Sheikh—and then I just go on along the narrow path leading to the cemetery.

Translated by Soad Sobhy

from *The Harafish*, 1977

The word 'harafish' is used to indicate the poor and oppressed, those whose rights have been trampled on by those in power. The story takes place in the same hara (quarter) of Cairo that is the locale for a number of other novels by the author. The novel is made up of ten separate stories, telling the history of a single family over several centuries. Its author has called it one of his favorite works, together with *Children of the Alley* and *The Cairo Trilogy*.

"I never dreamed you'd become clan chief, in spite of your great strength," said his father, beaming with joy.

"Nor did I," smiled Galal.

"I was strong like you, but to be chief you need the stomach and the ambition," said Abd Rabbihi proudly.

"You're right, father. I was planning to be a respected member of the community, then I had a sudden notion . . ."

"You could be Ashur himself, you're so strong," laughed his father. "So be happy, and make the people of your alley happy."

"Let's not talk about happiness yet," he said in measured tones.

He began to act, inspired by his strength and visions of immortality. He planned out a route for himself. He challenged the chiefs of neighboring alleys to put his excess strength to use, and won Atuf, Darasa, Kafr al-Zaghari, Husayniyya, and Bulaq. Every day a piper paraded down the alley, announcing a new victory. He became chief of chiefs, all-powerful, like Ashur and Shams al-Din.

The harafish rejoiced, pinning their hopes on his reputed generosity and benevolence. The notables were uneasy, anticipating lives poisoned by restrictions and hardship.

Abd Rabbihi swaggered about, proud and dignified. In the bar he announced that a new era had begun. These days he was received with admiration and respect. The drunks hung around him, sniffing out news.

"Ashur al-Nagi has returned," he announced. He emptied the calabash down his throat. "Let the harafish rejoice. Let all who love justice rejoice. The poor will have plenty to eat. The notables will learn that God is truth!"

"Did Galal promise that?" asked Sanqar.

"It was his sole aim in wanting to become chief," declared Abd Rabbihi confidently.

Friends and enemies alike owed Galal allegiance. No power challenged him, nothing worried him. He had supremacy, status, and wealth. Feelings of boredom and inertia crept up on him. He thought seriously about himself. His life appeared to him in sharp relief, the features and colors clearly visible, right down to its ludicrous, definitive ending. His mother's shattered head, his childhood trials and humiliations, Qamr's ironic death, his unlimited power and dominance, and Shams al-Din's tomb awaiting one funeral procession after another. What was the point of being sad or happy? What did strength mean, or death? Why did the impossible exist?

"People are wondering when justice will be done," said his father one morning.

Galal smiled with some irritation. "What does it matter?"

"It's everything, son," cried his father in astonishment.

"They're dying like flies all the time, and they don't complain," he said scathingly.

"Death has rights over us, but you have it in your power to eradicate poverty and indignity."

"Damn these stupid ideas!" shouted Galal.

"Don't you want to follow al-Nagi's example?" asked Abd Rabbihi sorrowfully.

"Where is he now?"

"In Paradise, my son."

"That's meaningless."

"God preserve us from losing our faith!"

"God preserve us from nothing at all," he said savagely.

"I never imagined my son would go the same way as Samaka al-Allaj."

"Samaka al-Allaj is finished, the same as Ashur."

"Not at all. They took power and lost it in completely different ways."

Galal sighed angrily. "Don't make things worse for me, father. Don't make demands on me. Don't be deceived by my achievements. Just understand that I'm not happy."

Abd Rabbihi despaired and stopped talking about the promised utopia.

"God's will is supreme," he declared, completely drunk, "and we just have to accept it."

"If we'd been more cagey about him in the past, we'd be content now," lamented the harafish.

The notables were reassured by the relative tranquility, paid the protection money, and showered him with gifts.

Galal went about with the winds of despondency and anguish blowing through his empty heart, although he continued to exude power, strength, and voracious ambition from his dazzling exterior. He gave the overwhelming impression of someone dominated, almost against his will, by a passion to make more money and acquire more possessions. Not only was he in partnership with his brother Radi in the cereal business, but also with the timber merchant, the coffee merchant, the spice merchant, and others. He could never have too many ventures on the go, and the other merchants were only too happy to make him one of them, to bind him firmly to their world of respectability and power. He became the most powerful clan chief, the most successful merchant, the wealthiest of the wealthy, and still did not think it was beneath him to collect protection money and accept presents. Apart from his gang members, the only people to prosper were those who were unconditionally and abjectly loyal to him. He had many tenement buildings constructed, and a dream house to the right of the fountain, aptly known as The Citadel, because it was so large and imposing. He filled it with magnificent furniture, adorned it with curios and objets d'art like a fantasy of the immortals, sailed around in rich silks, and always traveled in a carriage. Gold flashed from his teeth and gleamed on every finger.

He was uninterested in the state of the harafish or the Nagi covenant, not from egotism or weakness in the face of life's temptations, but because he despised their concerns and found their problems trivial. The strange thing was that he was naturally inclined to asceticism, and scorned the demands of the flesh. Some blind, faceless power was behind his desire for status, money, and possessions, at the heart of which was anxiety and fear. It was as if he was fortifying himself against death, or strengthening his ties with the world, fearful it would betray him. Although he was submerged in the vast ocean of material existence, he never overlooked its capacity for treachery, was not lulled into oblivion by its smiles, nor captivated by its sweet talking. He was acutely aware of its preplanned game, the end it had in store for him. He did not drink, take drugs, have love affairs, or become addicted to the chanting from the monastery. When he was alone sometimes, he would sigh and say, "My heart, how you suffer!"

"Why don't you get married?" asked his brother Radi, who was perhaps the only friend he had.

Galal laughed and did not reply, so Radi went on, "A bachelor's always the subject of speculation."

"What's the point of marriage, Radi?" he asked scathingly.

"Pleasure, fatherhood, perpetuating your name."

Galal laughed noisily. "What a lot of lies people talk, brother."

"Who are you gathering all this wealth for?" demanded Radi.

A good question. Would a man like him not be better off as a dervish?

Death chased him all the time. Zahira's crushed head and Qamr's waxy face loomed before his eyes again. Neither The Citadel nor an army of clubs would be any use. The splendor would fade. The edifice of strength and pride would crumble. Other people would inherit the wealth, and make sarcastic remarks about him. The magnificent victories would be followed by everlasting defeat.

He sat cross-legged on the chief's traditional wooden sofa in the café. An image of beauty and power, dazzling eyes, inspiring hearts. No one was aware of the deepening shadows inside his skull. A ray of light penetrated this darkness in the shape of a brilliant, seductive smile of greeting, and left its glowing traces. Who was the woman? A prostitute living in a small flat above the moneylender's, with many eminent customers. She always greeted him deferentially as she passed, and he neither turned away nor responded. He did not deny the soothing effect she had on him in his tormented state. Medium build, luscious body, attractive face. Zaynat. And because she dyed her hair gold, they called her Zaynat the Blonde. He did not deny her soothing effect but was reluctant to respond to her advances. His desires were constantly held in check by his preoccupation with fighting, putting up buildings, amassing wealth, and embracing boredom.

One evening, Zaynat the Blonde asked to see him. He received her in the guest hall and let her marvel at the furniture, the objets d'art, the ornamented lamps. She removed her wrap and veil and sat on the divan, armed with all her weapons of seduction.

"How should I justify my presence here?" she asked adroitly. "Shall I say that I was trying to rent a flat in one of your new buildings?"

He found himself being pleasant, trying to put her at her ease. "No one's going to ask you to justify yourself."

She laughed contentedly. "I said to myself, I'll go and visit him, since he can't decide to come and see me!"

He sensed he had taken a step down into the abyss of temptation, but did not let it concern him. "That's as good a reason as any. Welcome!"

"I was encouraged by the nice way you received me each afternoon."

He smiled. Behind the smile he was wondering as he so often did what

Qamr looked like now.

"Don't you like me?" she asked with unusual boldness.

"You're exquisite," he replied truthfully.

"And is a man like you content to have this feeling and not act on it?"

"You're forgetting certain things," he said in embarrassment.

"You're the most powerful man around. How can you sleep like the poor people?"

"The poor sleep deeply," he said sarcastically.

"What about you?"

"Maybe I don't sleep at all!"

She laughed sweetly. "I've heard from people who know that you've never drunk or smoked in your life, and never touched a woman. Is it true?"

He was at a loss to know how to reply, but had the feeling she would find out what she wanted.

"Love and pleasure—they're what life's about," she continued, undaunted.

"Really?" he replied, feigning surprise.

"The rest we leave to others when we go!"

"We leave love and pleasure too," he said angrily.

"No! They're absorbed by the body and soul, so no one else can have them!"

"What a farce!"

"I haven't lived a single day without some loving or enjoyment," she said passionately.

"You're an astonishing woman!"

"I'm a woman, that's all."

"Aren't you worried about death?"

"We all have to die, but I don't like how it happens."

Have to? Have to? "Do you know anything about the life of Shams al-Din?" he asked her abruptly.

"Of course," she answered proudly. "He's the one who fought old age."

"He resisted it for all he was worth."

"The lucky ones are really the people who enjoy a quiet old age," she said softly.

"The lucky ones are those who never grow old."

She was taken aback at the change in him. "This moment's all you've got for sure," she said provocatively.

He laughed. "That sounds like an appropriate homily when night's approaching."

She closed her eyes, listening to the wind whistling and the rain beating on the shuttered windows.

Zaynat the Blonde became Galal's lover. People were shocked but said in any case it was better than what happened to Wahid. Her former lovers stayed away from her, and he had her to himself. She taught him everything, and added a gilded calabash and ornately embellished water pipe to the other luxurious objects in the house. He had no regrets, and thought this way of life had a certain appeal. Zaynat loved him with a love that possessed her heart and soul, and was tantalized by a strange dream that one day she would be his lawful wife. To his surprise his old love for Qamr was reborn too, like an unchanging memory filled with sweetness. He realized he would never escape it. Nothing would cease to exist. Not even his love for his mother. He would remain indebted to Zahira's shattered head and Qamr's face for his knowledge of the tragedy of existence, the faint, recurrent melody of sorrow beneath the façade of bright lights and brilliant victories. He had no idea of Zaynat's age. She could have been the same age as him, or older. It would remain a secret. He grew attached to her. Was he in love again? He grew attached to the calabash and the water pipe. To them he owed this inner ecstasy which gave rise to both joy and anguish, and he had no qualms about abandoning himself to the current.

His father cornered him alone, looking concerned.

"Why don't you marry her? Surely it's better to make it legal?"

He didn't answer.

"If you married Zaynat," went on his father, "you'd be following Ashur's example."

He shook his head.

"In any case, I've definitely decided to marry again."

"You!" exclaimed Galal in amazement, "but you're in your sixties, father!"

"So what?" laughed Abd Rabbihi. "I'm in excellent health, in spite of everything, and I've got high hopes—God willing—of the herbalist's potions."

"Who's the lucky girl?"

"Zuwayla al-Faskhani's daughter," he boasted. "A nice, respectable girl in her twenties."

"Wouldn't it be better to choose a lady nearer your own age?" smiled Galal.

"No. I need someone young to make me feel young again."

"I hope you'll be happy," murmured Galal.

Abd Rabbihi began singing the praises of the herbalist and his magic powers, and how he could restore a man's youth.

Farida al-Faskhani married Abd Rabbihi, and the couple set up house in a wing of The Citadel. Galal thought constantly about the magic powers of the herbalist, Abd al-Khaliq. One night he invited him and they got stoned together and ate fruit and sweetmeats.

"What passes between us here must be kept secret," said Galal earnestly.

Abd al-Khaliq promised that it would, pleased with the new status bestowed on him by the chief.

"I've heard you give mature men back their youth," began Galal tentatively.

The herbalist smiled confidently. "With the help of the Al-mighty."

"Perhaps it's easier for you to stop people aging?"

"That goes without saying."

Galal's face brightened. He looked visibly relieved. "You see why I sent for you?" he murmured.

The man thought for a moment, awed by the burden of trust. "The herbalist's potions aren't everything," he said finally. "They must be used in conjunction with the will to act sensibly."

"What do you mean?"

"You must be honest," said Abd al-Khaliq cautiously. "Have you experienced any kind of weakness?"

"I'm in perfect health."

"Splendid. Then you must stick devotedly to a regime."

"Don't talk in riddles."

"You have to eat, but excessive eating is harmful."

"Anyone in my position should be able to understand that," said Galal, relieved.

"A little alcohol is a pleasant stimulus but too much is bad for you."

"Obviously."

"You shouldn't try to exceed your capabilities when it comes to sex."

"Not a problem."

"A sound faith is highly beneficial."

"Fine."

"When all that's taken care of, the herbalist's prescription can work wonders."

"Has it been tried before?"

"By many of the notables. Some of them have preserved their youth so well that people who know them have started to get scared and wonder what's going on!"

Galal's eyes gleamed delightedly.

"If someone follows my advice, God willing, he should be able to live to a hundred," continued Abd al-Khaliq. "And there's nothing to stop him going on beyond that, until he actually wants his time to be up!"

Galal gave a gloomy smile. "Then what?"

"Death comes to us all," shrugged the herbalist.

Galal cursed to himself at this general conspiracy to venerate death.

One evening as he and Zaynat were sitting together, relaxed and at ease with one another, she asked suddenly, "Why don't you do something to fulfill the expectations of the harafish?"

He looked at her, startled. "What does it matter to you?"

She kissed him and said frankly, "To stop people being jealous. That's fatal."

He shrugged his shoulders indifferently. "To tell you the truth, I despise them."

"But they're poor and miserable."

"That's why I despise them!"

A spasm of disgust distorted her pretty face.

"All they think about is getting enough to eat."

"Your ideas frighten me," she said pityingly.

"Why don't they resign themselves to hunger, like they do to death?"

Memories of her youth swept over her like a choking dust storm.

"Hunger's more terrible than death."

He smiled, half closing his eyes to hide the cold scorn in them.

The days went by and Galal grew more powerful, more beautiful, more glorious. Time slid over him leaving no trace, like a trickle of water on a polished mirror. Zaynat herself changed, like everything else, despite the great care she took of her beauty. Galal realized that he had begun his sacred struggle of resistance against the passage of time. How sad that it was bound to end! He might delay it for a while, but there was no escaping destiny.

The ties of friendship grew firmer between him and Abd al-Khaliq. The herbalist claimed that if his potions did not cost so much, the alley would be full of centenarians. Galal thought often of sharing the magic potion with Zaynat, but always abandoned the idea. Perhaps he had begun to fear her power over him and her charm, and was loath to immunize her against the tyranny of age. He loved her most of the time, but every now and then he felt like getting his own back and ejecting her on to the nearest rubbish heap. His relationship with her was not simple or clear-cut. It spread and merged into a complex web of relationships, indivisible from his memories of his mother and Qamr, his hostility toward death, his self-respect, his dependence on her which held him captive. What annoyed him most of all about her was her deep-seated assurance, her seemingly boundless confidence. And yet she was worn out by drink and sleepless nights, her cheeks aflame with makeup. Could he detect sly glances of envy in his direction?

"I suppose you've heard the tale of Ashur al-Nagi?" he asked Abd al-Khaliq one day.

"Everyone knows it by heart."

"I believe he's still alive," said Galal after a pause.

Abd al-Khaliq was shocked and didn't know how to reply. He knew that

Ashur was a saint for some, a crook for others, but they all accepted that he was dead.

"That he didn't die," persisted Galal.

"Ashur was a good man. Death doesn't spare good men."

"Does a person have to be evil to live forever?" protested Galal.

"We all have to die. A believer shouldn't try and live forever."

"Are you certain of that?"

"So they say. God knows," said Abd al-Khaliq, taking fright.

"Why?"

"I think people can only live forever if they associate with jinns."

"Tell me what you mean," demanded Galal, ablaze with a sudden fierce interest.

"Associating with jinns means you become immortal, and damned forever. You sign an everlasting pact with the devil."

"Do you think that's drivel, or is there some truth in it?" asked Galal, his interest mounting.

Abd al-Khaliq hesitated. "It may be true," he said eventually.

"Let's hear more details."

"Why? Are you really thinking of taking such a risk?"

Galal laughed edgily. "I just like to know everything."

"It's said that . . . Shawar . . . " began Abd al-Khaliq slowly.

"The mysterious sheikh who claims to read the future?" asked Galal.

"That's what he does on the face of it. But he knows some terrible secrets."

"It's the first I've heard of it."

"He's scared of believers."

"Do you think there's anything in it?"

"I don't know, but the whole business is cursed."

"Immortality?"

"Mixing with jinns!"

"You're scared of immortality!"

"That's not surprising. Imagine if I survived long enough to witness the world I know ceasing to exist, all my friends and family gone, leaving me surrounded by strangers, permanently on the move, rejected. I'd go mad and long to be dead."

"You'd preserve your youth forever!"

"You'd have children you had to avoid. With each generation you'd have to start all over again, lose a wife and children all over again. You'd be classified as a permanent alien, have no true links of any kind."

"That's enough!" cried Galal.

They laughed uproariously.

"But what a dream," murmured Galal.

Shawar lived in a large basement directly opposite the animals' drinking trough. It had several rooms, including one reserved for women and another for men. He himself was a mysterious character whom no one had ever seen. He received his clients in a dark room at night. They heard his voice, but saw no sign of him. Most of them were women, but a few may have been men driven to consult him on the advice of knowledgeable women. After the consultation the client was expected to leave an offering with an Ethiopian maid called Hawa.

Galal sent for the sheikh, but was told he lost his magic powers if he left his room, so he had to make his way there under cover of darkness, late enough to ensure that he was the only customer.

Hawa showed him into the room, sat him down on a soft cushion, and vanished. He was in pitch-darkness. He peered around him but could see nothing. It was as if he had lost all sense of time and space. He had been warned to keep quiet, not to initiate conversation, and answer all questions briefly and to the point. The time dragged by oppressively. They seemed to have forgotten all about him. It was ridiculous. He had not been slighted in this way since he had become chief. What had happened to Galal the giant? Could he really be this resigned creature, patiently waiting? It would be the worse for mankind and the spirit world if this escapade came to nothing.

"What's your name?" asked a calm, sonorous voice from the darkness.

Galal gave a sigh of relief. "Galal, the clan chief," he answered.

"Answer the question," repeated the voice.

He stuck his chest out. "Galal Abd Rabbihi al-Nagi."

"Answer the question."

"Galal," he said dryly.

"And your mother's name?"

His anger flared dangerously. Lurid demons danced in the darkness.

"Your mother's name?" asked the voice, mechanical yet threatening.

He swallowed, suppressing his rage. "Zahira."

"What do you want?"

He hesitated, but the voice did not allow him this respite. "What do you want?"

"To know about associating with jinns."

"What do you want?"

"I've just told you."

"What do you want?"

Anger seized him. "Don't you know who I am?" he said menacingly.

"Galal, son of Zahira."

"I could flatten you with a single blow."

"I think not." This was said with absolute confidence.

"Shall we try?" shouted Galal.

"What do you want?" asked the voice, cold and indifferent.

"Immortality," answered Galal, surrendering on all fronts.

"Why?"

"That's my business."

"The believer does not challenge God's will."

"I'm a believer, and I want to be immortal."

"It's risky."

"Too bad."

"You'll long to die and be unable to."

"Too bad," he said again, his heart pounding.

The voice fell silent. Had he gone away? Once again Galal lost all his bearings, and waited impatiently, his nerves on edge. He peered desperately around him, but could see nothing.

After a period of agony, the voice returned. "Are you ready to do whatever is required of you?"

"Of course," he replied with alacrity.

"Give my maid Hawa the largest building you own so that I can atone for my sin by providing her with a good source of income."

"I agree," he said after a brief pause.

"Build a minaret ten stories high."

"Onto the present mosque?"

"No."

"A new mosque?"

"No. A freestanding minaret."

"But . . ."

"No arguments."

"I agree."

"Spend a whole year in your private apartments seeing no one and being seen by no one except your manservant. Avoid all distractions."

"I agree," he said, feeling his heart contract.

"On the last day of your seclusion your pact with the Evil One will be sealed and you will never know death."

Galal made his largest building over to the Ethiopian maid, Hawa. He hired a contractor to erect a giant minaret on a piece of waste ground. The man agreed to this strange commission out of a mixture of greed and fear. Galal put Mu'nis al-Al in charge of his men, leaving him numerous instructions, and announced that he was withdrawing from public life for a year to fulfill a holy vow. He entrenched himself in his rooms, recording each passing day as Samaha had done in exile, and stayed away from the calabash, the narghile, and Zaynat the Blonde in the firm hope that he would triumph in the greatest struggle known to man.

His decision hit Zaynat the Blonde like a death blow. A painful severance, with no preliminaries, no satisfactory reason given for it. It evoked bitterness, fear, desperation. Hadn't they been like butter and honey, blending sweetly? She had been sure he was hers forever, and now he was shutting the door in her face like the dervishes in the monastery, leaving those who loved him hurt and confused. She wept inconsolably when the servants prevented her entering his room. She went to visit Radi, but found him equally perplexed. She sat with Abd Rabbihi in his room. The old man had changed. These days he seldom visited the bar and had become proper and modest. He too was troubled about his son.

"I'm not allowed to see him, even though we're living under the same roof," he said.

Zaynat lived a tormented existence. She was not short of money but had lost her lord and master. Her self-confidence was shaken, and the future loomed threatening and mysterious.

The clan was thrown into disarray. No one was content with Mu'nis al-Al, but they were obliged to obey him. They wondered what vow Galal had made, why he had handed over the leadership of the clan, and entrusted his business and property to his brother.

The dangerous news leaked out to rival chiefs. As time passed, they announced the resumption of hostilities. Mu'nis al-Al suffered his first defeat at the hands of the men of the Atuf clan, followed closely by the gangs from Kafr al-Zaghari, Husayniyya, and other neighborhoods. Eventually he was forced to pay out protection money to safeguard the alley's peace and security. The men wanted to tell Galal of the disastrous turn of events, but they were prevented as surely as if death had snatched him from them and buried him in a sealed tomb.

The people watched the strange minaret going up in astonishment. It rose higher and higher toward infinity, straight from its firm foundations in the ground. There was no mosque beneath it. No one knew its function or purpose. Even the man responsible for building it knew nothing about it.

"Has he gone mad?" people asked one another.

The harafish said a curse had fallen on him for betraying his great ancestor's covenant and ignoring his true people in pursuit of his insatiable greed.

As time went by, he sank deeper into isolation. Gradually he pulled up the roots attaching him to the outside world—his power in the clan, money, his beautiful lover—and abandoned himself to silence, to patience, to his conscience. He was worn out by the hope of being the first human being to achieve the impossible dream. Every day he stared time in the face, alone with no diversions, no drugs or alcohol. He confronted its inertia, its torpor, its solid weight. An obstinate, unyielding, impenetrable mass, where he floundered like someone in a nightmare. A thick wall, oppressive and gloomy. Time was unendurable without the aid of work or companionship. As if we only work, make friends, fall in love, seek amusement to escape from it. Seeing time pass too quickly is less painful than seeing it grind to a halt. When he achieved immortality, he would try everything, unhindered by fear or laziness. He would rush into battle without stopping to think. Scorn reason as much as folly. One day he would be at the forefront of the human race. Now he crawled over the seconds and begged for mercy, palms outstretched. He wondered when the devil would come, how he would form a bond with him. Would he see him in the flesh, hear his voice, or be joined with him like the air he breathed? He was exhausted, bored. But he would not succumb to weakness. He was not going to fail. It didn't matter if he suffered, or gave in to tears. He believed in what he was doing. He could not turn back. Eternity did not scare him. He would never know death. The rest of the world would be subject to the changing seasons, but for him it would be eternal spring. He would be the vanguard of a new form of existence, the one to discover life without death, the first to reject eternal repose. A secret power made manifest. Only the weak are afraid to live. However, living face-to-face with time is an unimaginable torment.

On the last day of the appointed year, Galal stood naked in front of an open window. The sun's rays, cleansed in the moist air of winter, struck him full in the face, and the cool wind played gently over his body. The time had come for him to reap the fruits of his patience. The weary, lonely night was over. Galal Abd Rabbihi was no longer an ephemeral creature. A new spirit breathed in him, intoxicating him, inspiring him with strength and confidence. He would talk to himself and to others too, and listen to the voice of his conscience with no misgivings. He had triumphed over time by holding out against it, unaided. He was no longer afraid of it. It could threaten others with its ominous passing. He would never be afflicted with wrinkles, gray hair, or impotence. His soul would not betray him. No coffin would ever carry him, no tomb shelter him. This firm body would never disintegrate and become dust. He would never know the grief of parting.

He strolled naked around the room, repeating serenely, "This life is blessed indeed."

The door opened agitatedly and Zaynat the Blonde rushed into the room. She flew at him in a frenzy of longing and they melted in a long, passionate embrace. She began to sob convulsively. "What did you do?" she asked him reproachfully.

He kissed her on the cheeks and lips.

"How did you pass the time?"

He was overcome by a rush of yearning for her. A precious, transient feeling. He saw her young and beautiful, old and ugly in turn. A sweet deception. As if fidelity had become impossible.

"Let's forget what's happened," he said.

"But I want to know."

"Think of it as an illness that's over now."

"You're so deceitful."

"You're so nice."

"Do you know what happened while you were away?"

"Let's talk about that later."

She took a step back. "How beautiful you look," she said admiringly.

He felt a pang of guilt and looked at her regretfully. "I'm sorry for making you suffer."

"I'll be fine again in a few hours. But I want to know your secret," she said stubbornly.

He hesitated, then said firmly, "I was ill and now I'm cured."

"I should have stayed with you."

"Isolation was the cure!"

She held him close and whispered amorously, "Show me if love's still the same. I'll tell you my troubles later."

He received Abd Rabbihi and Radi in the salon and embraced them warmly. They were followed by Mu'nis al-Al and men from the gang. They kissed him respectfully.

"It's all gone. We were powerless to stop it," said Mu'nis pitifully.

Escorted by his men, Galal emerged into the alley and made for the café. The whole alley turned out to greet him, friends, enemies, admirers, detractors. He leaned toward Mu'nis. "Do some people think I'm crazy?" he asked.

"God forbid, chief," murmured Mu'nis.

"Let them get back to work. Tell them we're grateful," said Galal, gazing at the crowd contemptuously. Then he muttered, "How much hatred there is. How little affection!"

He visited the minaret, accompanied by Abd Rabbihi and Radi. It was firmly planted in the waste ground, with the rubble and litter cleared from around about it. It had a square base the size of a large room with an arched door of polished wood. Its sturdy bulk rose endlessly toward an invisible summit, towering above the surrounding buildings. It sharp sides evoked power, its red color strangeness and terror.

"If we accept that this is a minaret," asked Abd Rabbihi, "then where's the mosque?"

Galal did not answer.

"It cost us an inordinate sum of money," said Radi.

"What's it for, son?" persisted Abd Rabbihi.

"God knows," laughed Galal.

"Since it was finished, people talk of nothing else."

"Don't pay them any attention," said Galal disdainfully. "It's part of my vow. A man may do a lot of stupid things in the course of becoming unusually wise."

His father was about to repeat his question, but he interrupted him in a decisive tone. "Look, you see this minaret? It will still be here when everything else in the alley is in ruins. Interrogate it. It'll answer your questions if it pleases."

Taking the herbalist aside, he asked him with terrifying solemnity, "What did you think of my year's retreat?"

"I took what you told me at face value," said the man sincerely, his heart beating with fright.

"What about the minaret?"

"I suppose it's part of your vow," he said hesitantly.

"I thought you were a man of sound judgment, Abd al-Khaliq," scowled Galal.

"I'm damned if I've breathed a word of our secret," he said hurriedly.

At dead of night he crept along to the minaret and climbed the stairs, floor by floor, until he reached the balcony at the very top. He braved the winter cold, armored in his absolute power over existence. He craned up at the festival of bright stars spread like a canopy above his head. Thousands of eyes sparkling down at him, while beneath him everything was immersed in gloom. Perhaps he had not climbed up to the top of the minaret, but simply grown to the height he ought to be. He had to grow higher, ever higher, for there was no other way to achieve purity. At the top the language of the stars was audible, the whisperings of space, the prayers for power and immortality, far from the exaggerated complaints, the lassitude, the stink of decay. Now the poems from the monastery sang of eternity. The truth revealed many of its hidden faces. Destinies were laid bare. From this balcony he could follow successive generations, play a role in each, join the family of the celestial bodies for all eternity.

He led his men out to teach his enemies a lesson and restore the alley to its former status. In a short space of time he had won brilliant victories over Atuf, Husayniyya, Bulaq, Kafr al-Zaghari, and Darasa. He hurled himself at his adversaries and they scattered before him, crushed by the humiliation of defeat. He was known to be invincible. No amount of strength or courage could work against him.

He changed his style of life. He began to eat, drink, and smoke to excess. Whenever a whore flirted with him, he responded discreetly. Zaynat soon lost her hold over him and became no more than a pretty rose in a garden full of roses. Reports of his escapades reached her ears and she was consumed by a frenzy of jealousy and loss. In the mirror of the future she saw her face fading away in the murky gloom of oblivion. She had always seen him as an innocent child with some unorthodox beliefs. His innocence had opened the doors for her to a faraway hope: she was sure of love and hoped for marriage. Perhaps it would be easier to give up life itself than to lose him, the embodiment to her of strength, beauty, youth, and boundless glory. But his year's isolation had made a different person of him: a creature smitten with power and beauty, and terrified of change, of madness, of being treated with contempt, of having to acquire wisdom the hard way. She felt herself growing small, thin, feeble, almost ceasing to exist in the face of his dreadful, mysterious domination. She could only confront him with weakness, pleading, and a sense of failure. But he met her with haughty gentleness, exulting in his arrogance, clothed in cold tenderness, fortified by a bottomless sense of superiority.

"Be content with your lot," he told her. "Many would envy you."

She saw him blossoming as she withered, and realized they were going opposite ways. Her heart swelled with love and despair.

Abd Rabbihi had a son, Khalid, and tore himself away from the bar once and for all. He found happiness in prayer and meditation, and Sheikh Khalil al-Dahshan became his friend and confidant.

He was desperately anxious about Galal, and even more so about the terrible minaret. It seemed to him that his relationship with his son was destroyed, that he had become a stranger unconnected to him. He was an alien presence among the people of the alley, like the minaret among its buildings: strong, beautiful, sterile, and incomprehensible.

"I shan't rest easy until you marry and have a family," he told him.

"There's plenty of time, father."

"And until you revive the glorious covenant of the Nagis," he entreated.

Galal smiled without answering.

"And repent and follow God."

Remembering his father's distant and not so distant past, Galal let out a guffaw like a drum roll.

The passing days and changing seasons held no fears for him. His inflexible will dominated the aggressive forces of nature. The unknown no longer scared him.

In the pit of despair and sorrow, Zaynat the Blonde received a summons to love. She had been waiting for it, yearning for it all along, preparing for it in her battered heart.

Now he was granting her one of his precious nights. She made her way to his house, outwardly pleased at the way she was being treated. She removed the drapes, flung open all the windows in her old rooms to allow the May breezes to circulate, and met him cheerfully, hiding her sorrows. She had learned to treat him with caution, apprehensive of his reactions. She prepared a tray with drinks and glasses.

"Drink up, my love," she whispered in his ear.

"How kind you are!" he said, gulping down the wine.

She observed to herself that he had lost his heart along with his innocence and that, like winter, he gloried in his power, oblivious to his cruelty. She also acknowledged that she was willfully destroying herself.

He stared at her, already fairly drunk. "You're not your usual self," he murmured.

"It's the solemnity of love," she said gently.

He laughed. "Nothing is solemn." Playing idly with a lock of her golden hair, he went on, "You're still in a very powerful position. But you're such an ambitious woman!"

"I'm just a sad woman," she cried impetuously.

"Remember what you said about seizing life's pleasures while you can . . ."

"That was in the days when you loved me."

"I'm following your advice, and I'm grateful for it."

He did not know what he was saying, she thought. She was much better acquainted with the mystery of life than him and knew that evil raised a man against his will to the ranks of the angels. She gazed at him passionately, restraining a desire to cry. Lulled by the breeze, she thought what a treacherous month this was. Soon the khamsin winds would blow, transforming it into a demon which would wreck the spring. He took her in his arms and she clasped him to her with frantic strength.

He freed himself from her arms and began stripping off his clothes until he stood naked, like a statue of light. He walked around the bedroom, laughing at his unsteady progress.

"You've drunk a whole sea," she said.

"I'm still thirsty."

"Our love's over," she murmured, as if to herself.

He staggered a few more steps, before collapsing onto a divan, shaking with laughter.

"You're drunk."

He frowned. "No. It's more than that. It's as if I'm sleepy." He tried to rise to his feet, without success. "I'm falling asleep just when I don't want to," he muttered.

She bit her lip. The world would end like this one day. The most pitiful people were those who sang victory songs in their hour of defeat.

"Try to stand up," she said hoarsely.

"There's no need," he answered, languorous yet dignified.

"Are you sure you can't, my love?"

"Quite sure. There's a burning like the fires of hell, and I'm sleepy."

She leapt to her feet and stepped back into the center of the room, staring wildly at him, all the softness gone. She was a mass of taut muscle, ready to spring, but there was an air of bitterness and sorrow about her. He looked at her dully, then his eyes swam out of focus.

"Why am I falling asleep?" he said thickly.

She spoke in the tones of someone making a sacred confession. "It's not sleep, my love."

"So it must be the bull that carries the world on its horns."

"It's not the bull either, my love."

"You're acting the fool, Zaynat. Why?"

"I've never been more serious. I'm killing myself."

"Huh?"

"It's death, my love."

"Death?"

"You've swallowed enough poison to kill an elephant."

"You mean, you have?"

"No, you, my love."

He burst out laughing, but quickly fell silent, too weak to continue.

"I killed you to put an end to my torment," she said, starting to cry.

He attempted another laugh. "Galal is immortal," he muttered.

"I can see death in your beautiful eyes."

"Death has died, stupid woman."

Gathering all his strength, he rose to his feet, dominating the room. She drew back, terrified, and rushed out of the room like someone possessed.

It was as if he was carrying the dreadful minaret on his shoulders. Death charged at him like a bull, blind with fury, charging solid rock.

"What terrible pain!" he cried, still without fear.

He staggered outside, stark naked.

"Galal can feel pain, but he cannot die," he muttered as he emerged into the dark alley.

He inched forward in the pitch-darkness, mumbling inaudibly, "I'm on fire. I want some water."

He began to move slowly in the gloom, groaning faintly, believing he was filling the alley with his cries. Where was everybody? Where were his men? Why didn't they bring him water? Where was Zaynat, the criminal? This must be a terrible nightmare, weighing down on him with all its odious force, but it wasn't death. The mysterious powers would be working at full strength now to restore him to his mocking, immortal self. But what terrible pain! What unbearable thirst!

As he stumbled along, he bumped against a cold, unmoving mass. The animals' drinking trough! A wave of joy and relief swept over him. He bent over the edge of the trough, overbalanced, stretched out his arms. The water closed over them. His lips touched water full of animal fodder. He drank greedily, dementedly, then let out a cry which rang out around the alley, a sound distorted by the savage pain. The top half of his body vanished in the murky water. His knees sagged and his lower half sank down into the mud and droppings. The dark shadows of that terrible, eventful spring night closed around him.

Translated by Catherine Cobham

from *Arabian Nights and Days*, 1979

This novel is recognized as one of the author's major works. As the title suggests, the author takes much of his material from *The Arabian Nights* by weaving together thirteen different stories from the Arabic classic into a single narrative. The novel starts where the Arabian Nights ends—that is, with Shahrazad having finished her final story and being spared the ruler's wrath against women.

Sindbad

I

Ma'rouf the governor of the quarter suggested with all modesty to the sultan that he transfer Sami Shukri the private secretary and Khalil Faris the chief of police to another quarter, and that he should be gracious enough to appoint Nur al-Din as personal secretary and the madman as chief of police under a new name—Abdullah al-Aqil, which is to say, "Abdullah the Sane." It was extraordinary that the sultan should grant his request, although he did ask him, "Are you really happy about the madman being your chief of police?"

"Absolutely so," answered Ma'rouf confidently.

He wished him all success, then asked, "What about your policy, Ma'rouf?"

"I have spent my life, Your Majesty," the man said humbly, "mending shoes until mending has become lodged in my blood."

The vizier Dandan was disturbed by this and said to the sultan after Ma'rouf's departure, "Do you not think, Your Majesty, that the quarter has fallen into the hands of a group of people with no experience?"

"Let us venture," said the sultan gently, "upon a new experience."

II

The habitués of the Café of the Emirs were whiling away the evening in merry conversation in keeping with the change that had happened in their quarter, when a stranger appeared at the entrance to the café. Of slender build, rather tall, with a black and elegant beard, he was dressed in a Baghdad cloak, a Damascene turban, and Moroccan sandals, while in his hand he held a Persian string of prayer beads made of precious pearls. The people were tongue-tied and all eyes gravitated toward him. In spite of the fact that he was a stranger, he let his smiling eyes roam familiarly among the people there. Then suddenly Ragab the porter leapt to his feet, shouting "Praise the Lord, it is none other than Sindbad!"

The newcomer guffawed loudly and took his old comrade in his arms. The two embraced warmly, and soon hands were being grasped in friendly handshakes. Then he went to an empty place beside Master Sahloul, drawing Ragab with him, who protested in whispered embarrassment, "That's the place for the gentlemen!"

"As of now, you're my business agent," said Sindbad.

"How many years have you been away, Sindbad?" Shamloul the hunchback asked him.

"In truth, I've forgotten time!" he said in confusion.

"It seems like ten centuries," said Ugr the barber.

"You have seen many worlds," said the doctor Abdul Qadir al-Maheeni. "What did you see, Sindbad?"

He savored the great interest being taken in him, then said, "I have delightful and edifying tales, but everything in its due time. Have patience until I settle down."

"We will tell you our own tales," said Ugr.

"What has God done with you?"

"Many have died and have had their fill of death," answered Hasan al-Attar, "and many have been born and have not had their fill of life. People have fallen down from the heights, and other people have risen up from the depths; some have grown rich after being hungry, while others are begging after having been of high rank. Some of the finest and the worst of jinn have arrived in our city, and the latest news is that Ma'rouf the cobbler has been appointed to govern our quarter."

"I had reckoned that wonders would be restricted to my travels. Now I am truly amazed!"

"It is clear," said Ibrahim the water-carrier, "that you have become rich, Sindbad."

"God bestows fortune upon whom He will without limit."

"Tell us," said Galil the draper, "about the most extraordinary things you encountered."

"There is a time for everything," he said, swinging his string of Persian prayer beads. "I must buy a palace and I must open an agency for putting up for sale the rare and precious objects I have brought from the mountains and from the depths of the seas and unknown islands, and I shall shortly invite you to a dinner at which I shall present to you strange foods and drinks, after which I shall recount my extraordinary journeys."

III

Immediately his choice fell on a palace in Cavalry Square. He entrusted to Sahloul the task of furnishing and decorating it, while he opened a new agency in the market, over which Ragab the porter was put in charge from the first day. Meanwhile he visited the governor. They were no sooner alone that they embraced like old friends. Ma'rouf told him his story, while Sindbad related what had happened to him during his seven voyages.

"You are deserving of your position," Sindbad told him.

"I am the servant of the poor under God's care," answered Ma'rouf with conviction.

He visited Sheikh Abdullah al-Balkhi, his teacher when he was a young boy. Kissing his hands, he said to him, "I was under your tutelage only so long as was necessary for my primary schooling, but I gained from it some words that lit up the darkness for me when I was faced by misfortune."

"It is useless to have good seed unless it is in good earth," said the sheik amiably.

"Perhaps, master, you would like to hear my adventures?"

"Knowledge is not gained by numerous narratives but through following knowledge and using it."

"Master, you will find in them things to please you."

"Blessed is he who has but one thing to worry about," answered the sheikh with little enthusiasm, "and whose heart is not preoccupied by what his eyes have seen and his ears heard. He who has known God is abstemious about everything that distracts from Him."

Having made his arrangements to settle down, Sindbad invited his friends to a feast. There he recounted what had happened to him on his seven voyages. From them the stories spread to the quarter and then to the city, and hearts were stirred and imaginations kindled.

IV

One day Ma'rouf the governor of the quarter asked him to pay a visit.

"Rejoice, Sindbad, for His Majesty the Sultan Shahriyar wishes to see you."

Sindbad was delighted and went off immediately to the palace in the company of the chief of police, Abdullah al-Aqil. As he presented himself before the sultan only at the beginning of the night, they took him to the garden. There he was shown to a seat in profound darkness, while the breaths of spring brought to the depths of his being a blending of the perfumes of flowers under a ceiling that sparkled with stars. The sultan talked gently, so he was put at ease and his sense of awe was replaced by feelings of love and intimacy. Shahriyar asked him about his original occupation, about sciences he had acquired, and about what it was that had caused him to resolve to travel. Sindbad answered with appropriate brevity, frankly and truthfully.

"People have told me of your travels," said Shahriyar, "and I would like to hear from you what you learned from them, whether you have gained from them any useful knowledge—but don't repeat anything unless it is necessary."

Sindbad thought for a time, then said, "It is of God that one seeks help, Your Majesty."

"I am listening to you, Sindbad."

He filled his lungs with the delightful fragrance, then began:

"The first thing I have learned, Your Majesty, is that man may be deceived by illusion so that he thinks it is the truth, and that there is no safety for us unless we dwell on solid land. Thus when our ship sank on our first journey, I swam, clinging to a piece of wood until I reached a black island.

I and those with me thanked God and we set off wandering about all over it searching for fruit. When we found none, we gathered together on the shore, with our hopes set upon a ship that might be passing by. All of a sudden someone shouted, 'The earth is moving.'

"We looked and found that we were being shaken by the ground. We were overcome with terror. Then another man called out, 'The earth is sinking!'

"It was indeed submerging into the water. So I threw myself into the sea. It then became apparent to us that what we had thought was land was in fact nothing but the back of a large whale which had been disturbed by our moving about on top of it and was taking itself off to its own world in stately fashion.

"I swam off, giving myself up to fate until my hands struck against some rocks and from these I crawled to a real island on which there was water and much fruit. I lived there for a time until a ship passed by and rescued me."

"And how do you make a distinction between illusion and truth?" inquired the sultan.

"We must use such senses and intelligence as God has given us," he answered after some hesitation.

"Continue, Sindbad."

"I also learned, Your Majesty, that sleep is not permissible if wakefulness is necessary, and that while there is life, there is no reason to despair. The ship crashed against some projecting rocks and was wrecked, and those on it moved onto an island, a bare island that had no water and no trees, but we carried with us food and waterskins. I saw a large rock not so far away and I told myself that I could sleep in its shade for a while. I slept and when I awoke I could find no trace of my companions. I called out but heard no answer. I ran toward the shore and saw a ship slipping beyond the horizon; I also saw waves surging and giving out an anthem of despair and death. I realized that the ship had picked up my comrades, who, in the ecstasy of being saved, had forgotten about their friend sleeping behind the rock. Not a sound issued from a living soul, not a thing was to be seen on the surface of the desolate land except for the rock. But what a rock! I looked, my eyes sharpened by terror, and I realized that it was not a rock, as it had seemed to my exhausted sight, but an egg—an egg the size of a large house. The egg of what possible bird? Terror seized hold of me at that unknown enemy, as I plunged into the void of a slow death. Then the light of the sun was extinguished and a dusk-like gloom descended. Raising my eyes, I saw a creature like an eagle, though hundreds of times bigger. I saw it coming slowly down until it settled over the egg. I realized that it was taking it up to fly off with it. A crazy idea occurred to me and I tied myself to the end of one of its legs, which was as big as a mast. The bird soared off with me, flying along above the ground. To my eyes everything looked so small and insignificant, as though neither hope nor pain pulsated there, until the bird came down on a mountain peak. I untied myself and crawled behind a towering tree, the like of which I had never seen before. The bird rested for a while, then continued its journey toward the unknown, while I was vanquished by sleep. When I awoke the noon sun was shining. I chewed some grasses to assuage my hunger, while I quenched my thirst from a hollow that was full of clear water. Then I noticed that the earth was giving out beams that dazzled my eyes. When I investigated, the surface of the ground revealed uncut diamonds. Despite my wretchedness, my avidity was aroused and I tore out as many as I could and tied them up in my trousers. Then I went down from the mountain till I ended up on the shore, from where I was rescued by a passing ship."

"It was the roc, which we have heard of but not seen," said Shahriyar quietly. "You are the first human to exploit it to his own ends, Sindbad—you should know that too."

"It is the will of Almighty God," said Sindbad modestly. Then he went on with what he had to say.

"I also learned, Your Majesty, that food is nourishment when taken in moderation but is a danger when taken gluttonously—and this is also true of the carnal appetites. Like the one before, the ship was wrecked and we found ourselves on an island which was governed by a giant king. He was nevertheless a generous and hospitable man and gave us a welcome that surpassed all out hopes, and under his roof we did nothing but relax and spend our evenings in conversation. He produced for us every kind of food and we set about it like madmen. However, some words that I had learned of old in my childhood from my master Sheikh Abdullah al-Balkhi prevented me from eating to excess. Much time was afforded me for worship, while my companions spent their time in gobbling up food and in heavy sleep after filling themselves so that their weight increased enormously and they became barrel-shaped, full of flabby flesh and fat. One day the king came and looked us over man by man. He then invited my companions to his palace, while to me he turned in scorn.

" 'You're like rocky ground that doesn't give fruit,' he said.

"I was displeased by this and it occurred to me that I might slip out at night and see what my companions were doing. So it was that I saw the king's men slaughtering the captain and serving him up to their ruler. He gobbled him down with savage relish and the secret of his generosity was immediately borne upon me. I made my escape to the shore, where I was rescued by a ship."

"May He maintain you in your piety, Sindbad," murmured the sultan. Then, as though talking to himself, he said, "But the ruler too is in need of piety."

Sindbad retained the echo of the sultan's comment for a minute, then continued with what he had to say:

"I learned too, Your Majesty, that to continue with worn-out traditions is foolishly dangerous. The ship sank on its way to China. I and a group of those traveling with me took refuge on an island that was rich in vegetation and had a moderate climate. Peace prevailed there and it was ruled over by a good king, who said to us, 'I shall regard you as my subjects—you shall have the same rights and the same obligations.'

"We were happy about this and gave up prayers for him. As a further show of hospitality to us he presented us with some of his beautiful slave-girls as wives. Life thus became easy and enjoyable. It then happened that one of the wives died and the king had her prepared for burial and said to our comrade who was the woman's widower, 'I am sorry to part from you but our traditions demand that the husband be buried alive with his dead wife; this also goes for the wife if the husband happens to die before her.'

"Our friend was terror-struck and said to the king, 'But our religion does not require this of us.'

" 'We are not concerned with your religion,' the king said, 'and our traditions are sacrosanct.'

"The man was buried alive with the corpse of his wife. Our peace of mind was disturbed by this and we looked to the future with horror. I began to observe my wife apprehensively. Whenever she complained of some minor indisposition my whole being was shaken. When she became pregnant and was in labor pains, her state of health deteriorated and I quickly fled into the forest, where I stayed. Then, one day, a ship passed by close to the shore, so I threw myself into the water and swam toward it, calling out for help. When I was almost on the point of drowning they picked me out of the water."

As though addressing himself, the sultan muttered, "Traditions are the past and of the past there are things that must become outdated."

It seemed to Sindbad that the sultan had something more to say, so he kept silent. However, Shahriyar said, "Continue, Sindbad."

"I also learned, Your Majesty, that freedom is the life of the spirit and that Paradise itself is of no avail to man if he has lost his freedom. Our ship met with a storm which destroyed it, not one of its men escaping apart from myself. The waves hurled me onto a fragrant island, rich with fruits and streams and with a moderate climate. I quenched my hunger and thirst and washed, then went off into the interior to seek out what I could find. I came across an old man lying under a tree utterly at the end of his resources.

" 'I am decrepit, as you see, so will you carry me to my hut?' he said, pointing with his chin. I did not hesitate about picking him up. I raised him onto my shoulders and took him to where he had pointed. Finding no trace of his hut, I said, 'Where's your dwelling, uncle?'

"In a strong voice, unlike that with which he had first addressed me, he said, 'This island is my dwelling, my island, but I need someone to carry me.'

"I wanted to lower him from my shoulders, but I couldn't tear his legs away from my neck and ribs; they were like a building held in place by iron.

" 'Let me go,' I pleaded, 'and you will find that I am at your service when you need me.'

"He laughed mockingly at me, ignoring my pleas. He thus condemned me to live as his slave so that neither waking nor sleeping was enjoyable, and I took pleasure in neither food nor drink, until an idea occurred to me. I began to squeeze some grapes into a hollow and left the juice to ferment. Then I gave it to him to drink until he became intoxicated and his steel-like muscles relaxed and I threw him from my shoulders. I took up a stone and smashed in his head, thus saving the world from his evil. I then spent a happy period of time—I don't know how long—until I was rescued by a ship."

Shahriyar sighed and said, "What many things we are in thrall to in this world! What else did you learn?"

"I learned too, Your Majesty," said Sindbad, "that man may be afforded a miracle, but it is not sufficient that he should use it and appropriate it; he must also approach it with guidance from the light of God that shines in his heart. As before, my ship sank and I took refuge on an island that deserves the name 'island of dreams': an island rich with beautiful women of every kind. My heart was taken by one of them and I married her and was happy with her. When the people felt they trusted me they fastened feathers under my arms and told me that I could fly any time I wanted. I was overjoyed and rushed to embark upon an experience that no other man had tried before me. But my wife said to me secretly, 'Be careful to mention God's name when you are in the air or else you will be burnt up.'

"I immediately realized that the Devil was in their blood and, shunning them, I flew off, determined to escape. I floated in the air for a long time with no other objective but to reach my city. I went on until I reached it, having despaired of doing so, so praise be to God, Lord of the Worlds."

The ruler was silent for a while, then said, "You have seen such wonders of the world as no human eye has seen, and you have learned many lessons, so rejoice in what God has bestowed upon you in the way of wealth and wisdom."

V

Shahriyar rose to his feet, his heart surging with overpowering emotions. He plunged into the garden above the royal walkway as a faint specter amid the forms of giant trees under countless stars. Voices of the past pressed in on his ears, erasing the melodies of the garden; the cheers of victory, the roars of anger, the groans of virgins, the raging of believers, the singing of hypocrites, and the calling of God's name from atop the minarets. The falseness of specious glory was made clear to him, like a mask of tattered paper that does not conceal the snakes of cruelty, tyranny, pillage, and blood that lie behind it. He cursed his father and his mother, the givers of pernicious legal judgments, and the poets, the cavaliers of deception, the robbers of the treasury, the whores from noble families, and the gold that was plundered and squandered on glasses of wine, elaborate turbans, fancy walls and furniture, empty hearts, and the suicidal soul, and the derisive laughter of the universe.

He returned from his wanderings at midnight. He summoned Shahrzad, sat her down beside him, and said, "How similar are the stories of Sindbad to your own, Shahrzad!"

"All originate from a single source, Your Majesty," said Shahrzad.

He fell silent as though to listen to the whispering of the branches and the chirping of the sparrows.

"Does Your Majesty intend to go out on one of his nightly excursions?"

"No," he said listlessly. Then in a lowered voice, "I am on the point of being bored with everything."

"A wise man does not become bored, Your Majesty," she said with concern.

"I?" he asked with annoyance. "Wisdom is a difficult requirement—it is not inherited as a throne is."

"The city today enjoys your upright wisdom."

"And the past, Shahrzad?"

"True repentance wipes away the past."

"Even if the ruler concerned himself with killing innocent young girls and the cream of the men of judgment?"

"True repentance . . ." she said in a trembling voice.

"Don't try to deceive me, Shahrzad," he interrupted her.

"But, Majesty, I am telling the truth."

"The truth," he said with resolute roughness, "is that your body approaches while your heart turns away."

She was alarmed—it was as if she had been stripped naked in the darkness.

"Your Majesty!" she called out in protest.

"I am not wise but also I am not stupid. How often have I been aware of your contempt and aversion!"

"God knows . . ." she said, her voice torn with emotion, but he interrupted her. "Don't lie, and don't be afraid. You have lived with a man who was steeped in the blood of martyrs."

"We all extol your merits."

Without heeding her words, he said, "Do you know why I kept you close by me? Because I found in your aversion a continued torment that I deserved. What saddens me is that I believe that I deserve punishment."

She could not stop herself from crying, and he said gently, "Weep, Shahrzad, for weeping is better than lying."

"I cannot," she exclaimed, "lead a life of ease and comfort after tonight."

"The palace is yours," he said in protest, "and that of your son who will be ruling the city tomorrow. It is I who must go, bearing my bloody past."

"Majesty!"

"For the space of ten years I have lived torn between temptation and duty: I remember and I pretend to have forgotten; I show myself as refined and I lead a dissolute life; I proceed and I regret; I advance and I retreat; and in all circumstances I am tormented. The time has come for me to listen to the call of salvation, the call of wisdom."

"You are spurning me as my heart opens to you," she said in a tone of avowal.

"I no longer look to the hearts of humankind," he said sternly.

"It is an opposing destiny that is mocking us."

"We must be satisfied with what has been fated for us."

"My natural place is as your shadow," she said bitterly.

"The sultan," he said with a calm unaffected by emotions, "must depart once he has lost competence; as for the ordinary man, he must find his salvation."

"You are exposing the city to horrors."

"Rather am I opening to it the door of purity, while I wander about aimlessly seeking my salvation."

She stretched out her hand toward his in the darkness, but he withdrew his own with the words "Get up and proceed to your task. You have disciplined the father and you must prepare the son for a better outcome."

VI

Sindbad thought he would be able to enjoy the pleasures of work and evening conversation until the end of his life, but there came to him a dream. When he awoke he could not forget it and its effect did not disappear. What was this yearning? Was he fated to spend his life being tossed about by sea waves? Who was it who was calling to him from beyond the horizon? Did he want from the world more than it had already given him? He closed his warehouse in the evening and set off for the house of Abdullah al-Balkhi, telling himself that the sheikh would have the solution. On the way to the sheikh's room he caught a glimpse of Zubeida his daughter, and the ground shook under him. His visit took on a new perspective, one that had not previously occurred to him. He found that the sheikh had with him the doctor Abdul Qadir al-Maheeni. He sat down, hesitant and confused, then said, "Master, I have come to ask for the hand of your daughter."

The sheikh pierced him with a smile and said, "Not at all—you came for another reason."

Sindbad was taken aback and said nothing.

"My daughter, since her husband Aladdin was killed, has devoted herself to the Path."

"Marriage does not divert one from the Path."

"She has said her final word on this."

Sindbad gave a sad sigh and the sheikh asked him, "Why did you really come to me, Sindbad?"

There was a long silence, which seemed to divide pretension and truth. Then he whispered, "Anxiety, master."

"Has your business been hit by a slump?" asked Abdul Qadir al-Maheeni.

"He who finds no tangible reason for anxiety is nonetheless anxious," said Sindbad.

"Speak out, Sindbad," said the sheikh.

"It is as though I have received a call from beyond the seas."

"Travel," said Abdul Qadir al-Maheeni simply. "For in journeys there are numberless benefits."

"I saw in a dream the roc fluttering its wings," said Sindbad.

"Perhaps it is an invitation to the skies," said the sheikh.

"I am a man of seas and islands," said Sindbad submissively.

"Know," said the sheikh, "that you will not attain the rank of the devout until you pass through six obstacles. The first of these is that you should close the door of comfort and open that of hardship. The second is that you should close the door of renown and open that of insignificance. The third is that you should close the door of rest and open that of exertion. The fourth is that you should close the door of sleep and open that of wakefulness. The fifth is that you should close the door of riches and open that of poverty. The sixth is that you should close the door of hope and open the door of readiness for death."

"I am not of that elite," Sindbad said courteously. "The door of devoutness is wide open for others."

"What you have uttered is the truth," said the doctor Abdul Qadir al-Maheeni.

"If you want to be at ease," the sheikh said to Sindbad, "then eat what falls to your lot, dress in what you find at hand, and be satisfied with what God has decreed for you."

"It suffices me that I worship God, master," said Sindbad.

"God has looked into the hearts of his saints and some of them are not suited to bearing a single letter of gnosis, so He has kept them busy with worship," said the sheikh.

"He has seen and he has heard," said the doctor, addressing the sheikh. "I am happy for him."

"Blessed is he who has but one worry and whose heart is not occupied with what his eyes have seen and his ears heard," said the sheikh.

"Calls have poured down from a thousand and one wondrous places."

The sheikh recited:

I in exile weep.
May not the eye of a stranger weep!
The day I left my country
I was not of right mind,
How odd for me and my leaving
a homeland in which is my beloved!

Al-Maheeni looked at the sheikh for some time, then said, "He is traveling, master, so bid him farewell with a kind word."

The sheikh smiled gently and said to Sindbad, "If your soul is safe from you, then you have discharged its right; and if people are safe from you, then you have discharged their rights."

Sindbad bent over his hand and kissed it, then looked at the doctor in gratitude. He was about to get to his feet when the doctor placed his hand on his shoulder and said, "Go in peace, then return laden with diamonds and wisdom, but do not repeat the mistake."

A confused look appeared in Sindbad's eyes and al-Maheeni said to him, "The roc had not previously flown with a man, and what did you do? You left it at the first opportunity, drawn by the sparkle of diamonds."

"I hardly believed I would make my escape."

"The roc flies from an unknown world to an unknown world, and it leaps from the peak of Waq to the peak of Qaf, so be not content with anything for it is the wish of the Sublime."

And it was as if Sindbad had drunk ten drafts of wine.

Translated by Denys Johnson-Davies

from *The Journey of Ibn Fattouma*, 1983

This work was obviously inspired by the writings of the fourteenth-century traveller Ibn Battuta, who started his journey from Tangier and returned twenty-five years later, having journeyed through the greater part of the known world. The hero of Mahfouz's novel travels in search of an ideal world. He makes six separate journeys to countries of the author's invention. One of these journeys is reproduced here.

The Land of Halba

As in days past the caravan moved off with unhurried majesty. We plunged into the gentle darkness of dawn, not this time to drink deeply of poetry but to relive the blows from memories of prison, the sorrows of a wasted life. When I saw the shapes of my companions, it was a new generation of traders that I was viewing, but energy still persisted, wealth increased, and honor and glory still stalked the adventurous. As for the dreamers, perplexity was for them. My former failures passed before me: the moment I had quit my homeland, mourning Halima, the moment I had been turned out of Mashriq, weeping for Arousa, and the moment I had said farewell to Haira, bemoaning the loss of happiness and youth. I became aware of the east and saw it surging with red rosewater, while the face of the sun, as had been its habit throughout these past twenty years, swelled forth. The desert revealed itself as endless, and summer unloaded its heat. We continued our journey for about a month. At one of the rest stops I asked the owner of the caravan about al-Qani ibn Hamdis, and he said, "God rest his soul." I then asked about Sheikh Maghagha al-Gibeili, but he had not heard of him, not had any of the traders in the caravan.

We made camp at Shama, preparatory to entering Halba. My hair and beard had begun to grow and healthy blood was again running in my veins. We continued on out way until we saw the great walls in the lunar light.

The director of customs advanced towards us. He wore a light jacket suited to the mild summer weather. "Welcome to Halba," he said joyfully, "the capital of the land of Halba, the land of freedom."

I was amazed to hear the accursed word wherever I went; I was amazed too that his words were devoid of any warning note, declared or hidden.

"The first land to welcome the newcomer without a warning," I said to the owner of the caravan.

"It's the land of freedom," he answered, laughing, "but as a foreigner your security lies in being on your guard."

They took me off to the inn for guests. On the way, under the light of the moon, the city's landmarks were scattered in a grandeur that suggested a new panorama. So too did the great number of sedan chairs coming and going in the light of flares at such a late hour. The entrance to the inn stood erect, broad, and tall under a roofed gallery from which hung candelabra that dazzled the eyes. The building itself looked high and vast, beautifully and richly constructed. My room gave me another surprise, with its blue walls, sumptuous carpet, raised brass bedstead with its embroidered coverings, and other things usually to be found only in upper-class houses in my homeland.

It disclosed to me eloquently a civilization without doubt very many degrees superior to that of Haira. I found myself wondering where and how Arousa was now living. Before I had immersed myself in my memories, I was paid a visit by a middle-aged man wearing a blue jacket and short white trousers. "Qalsham," he said to me, smiling, "the manager of the inn."

I introduced myself to him and he inquired politely if there was anything he could do for me.

"Nothing before I go to sleep now," I said frankly, "except to let me know the rates for staying here."

"Three dinars the night," he said, smiling.

I was horrified at the figure and told myself that everything in Halba appeared to enjoy freedom, including the prices. As usual, I paid for ten nights in advance.

I went to bed, and not since leaving my homeland did I enjoy so welcoming a one. I rose early and breakfast was brought to me in my room; it consisted of bread, milk, cheese, butter, honey, and eggs. I was astonished by both the quality and the quantity of the food and was ever more convinced that I was visiting a new and exciting world. Leaving the room, I was stirred by heartfelt longings and by the hope that I might also come across Arousa, so that destiny's game might be completed. Qalsham met me at the entrance to the inn. "Sedan chairs are available to the traveler for seeing the important sights," he said.

I thought a while, then said, "I'd like to start on my own and take it as it comes."

From the first instant I felt I was in a city so large that the individual melted into anonymity. In front of the inn was a vast square, on the surrounds of which stood buildings and shops; at the far end, in the middle, there was a bridge across a river leading to a small square from which large streets branched out, stretching away endlessly, their sides bordered by buildings and trees. Where was I bound for? Where was Arousa to be found? How could I proceed without a guide? I allowed my feet to lead me freely in this city of freedom, and I was enchanted by all that met my gaze at every step. A network of streets without beginning or end, rank upon rank of buildings: houses, palaces, shops as numerous as the desert sands exhibiting countless varieties of goods, factories, places of business, and places of entertainment. There were numerous parks of every kind and description, and endless streams of men and women and sedan chairs: the rich and the great, and the poor too, though these were several degrees better off than the poor of Haira and Mashriq; and not a street without a mounted policeman. The clothes of the men and the women were varied, and beauty and elegance were much in evidence. Modesty was to be found alongside emancipation that was close to nakedness, while seriousness and gravity went hand in hand with gaiety and simplicity. It was as if I were meeting for the first time human beings who had their own existence, their significance, their pride in themselves. But how could a person hope to come across Arousa in this raging sea without shores? I walked, grew tired, and rested in the parks, feeling all the time that I had not yet started. I regretted that I had not taken one of the sedan chairs for travelers that Qalsham had mentioned.

However, I saw two interesting incidents. The first was an isolated incident in a public park, when I saw policemen questioning some people; I then learned that the gardener had come across the body of a murdered woman in a corner of the park. Similar things often occur everywhere. The second thing I saw, though, aroused my disconcerted astonishment: the passing of a demonstration of men and women shouting their demands, while the police followed them without interfering in any way. I recollected a similar demonstration I had witnessed in my homeland, which was on its way to the Sultan to complain about increased taxes and the straitened material situation. But this demonstration was demanding legal recognition of homosexual relations. I could believe neither my eyes nor my ears. I was convinced I was going around in a strange world and that a vast chasm separated me from it, and I was overcome by fear of the unknown. Noontime approached and the temperature rose to its highest. Nonetheless, Halba's summer was bearable. I was asking the way back to the inn when a voice rang out with the words "God is greatest!"

My heart jumped violently, kindling a fire in my senses. Good Lord, this was a muezzin giving the call to prayers! Did this mean that Halba was a Muslim country? Guided by the direction of the voice, I rushed off until I found a mosque at the entrance to a street. I had not heard such a sound or seen such a sight for a quarter of a century. I was being born anew, and it was as though I were discovering God for the first time. I entered the mosque, made my ablutions, and, taking my place in the ranks of those praying, I performed the noon prayer with a glowing joy, a tearful eye, and a happy heart. When the prayers were over the people left, but I stood pinned to the ground till there was no one left in the mosque but the imam and I. I hurried towards him and clasped him in my arms, kissing him on both cheeks warmly. He submitted to my enthusiasm, quietly smiling, then muttered, "Welcome, stranger."

We sat down not far from the mihrab and introduced ourselves. He was Sheikh Hamada al-Sabki, a true native inhabitant of Halba. Breathlessly, my voice shaking, I said, "I didn't imagine that Halba was a Muslim country."

"Halba is not a Muslim country," he said gently. Having read my astonishment, he added, "Halba is a free country. All religions are to be found in it. It has Muslims, Jews, Christians, and Buddhists; in fact it also has atheists and pagans."

"How has this come about, Master?" I asked, my astonishment increased.

"Halba was originally heathen," he said simply, "and its state of freedom gave to all who wanted it the opportunity of propagating their religion. The various religions spread among its people, so that today there is only a minority of heathens in some of the oases."

"What religion does the state observe?" I asked with increasing interest.

"The state has nothing to do with religion."

"How, then, are the different creeds and sects reconciled?"

"All are treated on the basis of complete equality," he said simply.

"And are they content with that?" I asked him, as though remonstrating against it.

"Every faith preserves within itself its own traditions, and mutual respect rules social relations, no distinction being given to any one faith, even if the head of state is of it. Talking of which, I would inform you that our present head is heathen."

An astonishing and thought-provoking country!

"A freedom of which I have never previously heard," I said thoughtfully.

"Are you aware, Master, of the demonstration demanding legal recognition of homosexual relations?"

"It also contained Muslims," he said, smiling.

"They are no doubt penalized by their coreligionists."

The sheikh removed his turban and rubbed his hand across his head, then put it back and said, "Freedom is the sacred value accepted by everyone."

I protested. "This freedom has overstepped the boundaries of Islam."

"But it is also sacred in the Islam of Halba."

Frustrated, I said, "If our Prophet were to be resurrected today he would reject this side of your Islam."

"And were he, may the blessings and peace of God be upon him, to be resurrected," he in turn inquired, "would he not reject the whole of your Islam?"

Ah, the man had spoken the truth and had humbled me by his question.

"I have traveled much through the lands of Islam," the imam said.

"It was for this purpose," I said sadly, "that I undertook my journey, Sheikh Hamada. I wanted to see my homeland from afar, and to see it in the light of other lands, that I might perhaps be able to say something of benefit to it."

"You have done well," said Sheikh Hamada approvingly. "May God grant you success. You will be taking from our land more than one lesson."

"If you will permit, we shall have other opportunities of exchanging views," I said, taken up again by a traveler's curiosity. "But for now, could you tell me about the system of government in this extraordinary land?"

"It's a unique system," said Sheikh Hamada. "You have not met it in anything you've seen, and you will not meet it in what you will yet see."

"Not even in the land of Gebel?"

"I know nothing about the land of Gebel to be able to make the comparison. What you should know is that the head of our state is elected in accordance with political, moral, and scientific specifications. He rules for a period of ten years, after which he retires and is replaced by the chief judge. New elections are then held between the retired head of state and the new nominees."

"A good system," I exclaimed enthusiastically.

"It would have been more appropriate for the Muslims to have propagated it before others. The head of state has an assembly of experts in all fields, whose opinion is of assistance to him."

"And is this is opinion binding?"

"If there is some difference of opinion they all are retired and elections are held again."

"What an excellent system!" I exclaimed.

"As for agriculture, industry, and trade," continued the sheikh, "they are carried out by those citizens most capable."

"And so it is that there are both rich and poor," I said, remembering some of the scenes I had seen.

"There are also unemployed people, robbers, and murderers," said the sheikh.

"Perfection is with God alone," I said meaningfully with a smile.

"But we have made great headway on that path," he said seriously.

"If only you were to apply the canonical law of Islam!"

"But *you* apply it!"

"The fact is that it is not applied," I insisted.

"Here commitment is to the Authority, applied both in the letter and in the spirit."

"But the state is committed solely to maintaining order and to defense, so it seems to me."

"And public projects which individuals are unable to undertake, such as parks, bridges, and museums. It runs schools which are free to outstanding students who are poor, as well as free hospitals, but most activities are carried on by individuals."

I thought for a while, then asked, "Perhaps you consider yourselves the happiest of people?"

He nodded his head seriously. "It's a relative judgment, Sheikh Qindil, but one cannot generalize with complete confidence so long as there are rich and poor and criminals. Apart from which our life is not devoid of anxiety: there are conflicting interests between us and Haira in the north and Aman in the south. Thus this unique civilization is threatened and could be wiped out in a single battle; even with victory we could go into a decline if we were to suffer great losses. Also, the religious differences are not always resolved peacefully."

He asked me about my journey and I summarized for him what I had encountered since leaving my homeland. The man was saddened for me and wished me success. "I would advise you," he said, "to hire a sedan chair because the sights of the capital are too numerous for you to see by yourself. We also have many other cities that are worth seeing. As for finding Arousa in our land, it would be easier to reach the land of Gebel."

"I know that perfectly well," I said sorrowfully, "but I have another request: I wish to visit the sage of Halba."

"What do you mean?" he said in astonishment. "Mashriq has its sage and Haira its sage, but here the centers of learning are teeming with sages. With any one of them you will find the knowledge you wish to have, and more."

Thanking him for his conversation and his friendship, I rose to my feet saying, "The time has come for me to go."

"But you will lunch with us at my house," he said, taking hold of me.

I welcomed the invitation as an opportunity to immerse myself in the life of Halba. We walked together for about a quarter of an hour to a quiet street bordered by acacia trees on both sides. We made our way to a handsome building, on the second floor of which lived the imam. I did not doubt that the imam was from the middle class, but the beauty of the reception room gave an indication of the high standard of living in Halba.

I was faced by strange traditions which in my homeland would have been considered inconsistent with Islam, for I was welcomed by both the imam's wife and his daughter, as well as by his two sons. We all sat down at the one table. Even glasses of wine were served. It was a new world and a new Islam. I was disconcerted by the presence of his wife and daughter, for since attaining adolescence I had not shared a dining table with any woman, not even with my own mother. I was uncomfortable and overcome by shyness, and I did not touch the glass of wine.

"Let him do as suits him," the imam said, smiling.

"I see that you follow Abu Hanifa's opinion," I said.

"With us there is no necessity for that," he said, "as individual judgments continue to be made, and we drink according to the weather and traditions, but we do not become dunk."

His wife ran the household, but Samia, his daughter, was a pediatrician at a large hospital, while the two sons were preparing themselves to be teachers. Even more than at the nudity I had encountered in Mashriq,

I was amazed at the unrestrained way in which the mother and her daughter took part in the conversation. They talked with a bold and spontaneous frankness just like men. Samia asked me about life in the land of Islam and about the role of women there, and when I had explained the situation she was extremely critical. She made comparisons with women at the time of the Prophet, and the role that they had played then. Then she said, "Islam is wilting away at your hands and you are just standing back and contemplating."

I was also much impressed by her youthful beauty, my admiration the greater for the long time I had been deprived of female company and for my advancing years. The imam related to them something of my life, as well as of my journey and of what I sought to achieve from it.

"He is not, in any event," he said, "one of those who give up."

"You deserve acclaim," said Samia to me.

I was greatly touched by this. Then, in the afternoon, we all performed the prayers behind the imam, and this caused me yet more thoughtful consideration.

The imam's family occupied the depths of my soul even after I had physically left them. On the way back I was overtaken by a yearning for stability and for the warmth of love. Where was Arousa? Where the land of Gebel? Youth had been lost under the ground, so when would I settle down and forge a family and have children? Until when would I remain torn between two conflicting calls?

On the following day I hired a sedan chair, in which I was taken around the important sites of the capital, the centers of teaching, the citadels, the largest factories, the museums, the old quarters. The guide informed me that the people of the different religions acted out the lives of their prophets in the mosques, churches, and temples. I announced my desire to witness the life of our Prophet, may the blessings and peace of God be upon him, so he took me to the biggest of the capital's mosques. I seated myself among the audience and his life was acted out from beginning to end in the courtyard of the mosque. I saw the Prophet, his Companions, and the polytheists: a boldness that approached blasphemy, but I felt I should see everything that deserved to be recorded. The person who performed the role of the Prophet so impressed me that I believed in him, and he affected me more than any vision I had had in my dreams. "What truly astonishes me," I thought, "is that the faith of these people is so sincere and genuine."

I invited the imam and his family to lunch at the inn, thus consolidating my attachment to them still further.

"I shall arrange a meeting for you with a sage of stature named Marham al-Halabi," said the sheikh. I thanked him for his solicitude and we spent a pleasant time together, my heart beating all the while with joy and delight.

On the morning of the following day I left my room at the inn to visit the sage. However, I found many of the guests gathered at the entrance, engaged in animated conversations.

"There is news that one of Haira's leaders has revolted against the king, but that he has failed and has fled to Halba."

"Do you mean that he's now living in Halba?"

"It is said that he is living in one of the oases of Halba."

"The important thing is that the king of Haira is demanding that he be arrested and handed over."

"But that is contrary to the principles of the Authority."

"And his request has been turned down."

"Will the matter end there?"

"There are whispers of war."

"What if the land of Aman seizes the opportunity and attacks Halba?"

"That is the real problem."

Anxiety crept deep into me, feeling I was being chased from one land to another by wars. I wanted to go to the sage but I was frightened when I found the square filled with various demonstrations, meeting up there as though it had been prearranged. I was forced to stay on in the entrance to the inn, looking and listening in a state of extreme astonishment: one demonstration was demanding the handing over of the commander who had fled, another giving dire warning to anyone who handed him over, another demanding that war be declared on Haira, and yet another demanding that peace be maintained at any price. I was overwhelmed by confusion and wondered what a ruler could do faced with such contradictory opinions. I waited until the square had cleared and then hurried to the house of the sage Marham, reaching it an hour late for my appointment. He met me in an elegant room that contained couches and chairs as well as cushions arranged on the floor. I found him to be a tall, thin man in his sixties, with white hair and beard, wrapped round in a lightweight blue cloak. Accepting my apologies for being late, he welcomed me, then inquired, "Would you prefer to sit on chairs or cushions?"

"I like cushions better," I said, smiling.

"That's the way with Arabs: I know you, I visited your countries and studied your cultural background."

"I am not one of the scholars or philosophers of my country," I said shyly, "but I like to acquire knowledge and it is for this that I undertook this journey."

"That alone is sufficient," he said with encouraging quietness. "And what is the goal of your journey?"

I thought for a time, then said, "To visit the land of Gebel."

"I have not known anyone who has visited it or written about it."

"Have you not thought of visiting it one day?"

"He who believes with his mind can dispense with everything."

"The land of Gebel is not my final goal," I added. "I would hope to return from there to my homeland with something that might benefit it."

"I wish you success."

"The fact is that I came here to listen, not to talk," I said apologetically.

"Is there some question that worries you?"

"The life of every people is generally revealed through some basic idea," I said with interest.

Sitting up straight, he said, "Thus lovers of knowledge such as yourself ask us how it is that we have fashioned our life."

"And your life is worthy of provoking such a question."

"The answer is very simple: we have fashioned it ourselves." In concentrated silence I followed what he was saying. "There is no credit for this to any god. Our first thinker believed that the aim of life is freedom, and so from him there issued the first call for freedom, and this has continued generation after generation." He smiled and was silent until his words became firmly embedded in my soul. Then he went on, "Thus I regard everything that liberates as good and everything that fetters as evil. We have set up a system of government that has freed us from despotism. We have dedicated our work to freeing ourselves from poverty. We have achieved outstanding advances in knowledge so that it may free us from ignorance. And so on and so on. It is a long road without an end."

I very carefully committed to memory every word he said.

"The road to freedom was not an easy one," he continued, "and we have paid the price for it in sweat and blood. We were prisoners of superstition and despotism. Pioneers came to the fore, heads fell, revolutions flared, civil wars broke out, until freedom and knowledge triumphed."

I inclined my head in a gesture of admiration for what he was saying. He went on to criticize and make fun of the systems of government in Mashriq and Haira. He also made fun of the system in the land of Aman, which I had not yet visited. Even the land of Islam did not escape censure from his tongue. He must have seen a change on my face, for he grew silent, then said in an apologetic tone, "You are not used to freedom of opinion?"

"Within defined limits," I said gently.

"Excuse me, but one should reconsider everything."

"Your land is not without its poor people and deviants," I said defensively.

"Freedom," he said fervently, "is a responsibility which only the competent can be conversant with. Not everyone who belongs to Halba is equal to it. There is no place for the weak among us."

"Does not mercy have a value in the same way as freedom?" I inquired hotly.

"This is what the people of the various religions are always saying, and it is they who encourage the weak to remain so. As for me, I find no meaning for such words as mercy or justice—we must first of all agree as to who deserves mercy and who deserves justice."

"I disagree with you completely."

"I know."

"Perhaps you welcome war."

"Yes, if you promise an increase in freedom," he said clearly. "I have not the slightest doubt that a victory by us over Haira and Aman would be the best guarantee for the happiness of their two peoples. Speaking of which, I am for the principle of holy war in Islam."

He went on to give an aggressive interpretation of it, so I applied myself to correcting his theory, but he gave a contemptuous wave of his hand and said, "You have a splendid principle, but you do not possess sufficient courage to acknowledge it."

"To what religion do you belong, sage Marham?" I asked him.

"To a religion whose god is reason and whose prophet is freedom," he answered, smiling.

"And all sages are like you?"

"I wish I were able to state that," he said, laughing.

He brought me two books: the first was *The Authority*, or the principal law in Halba, while the second had been written by him and was entitled *Storming the Impossible*. "Read these two books," he said, "and you will know Halba as it really is."

I thanked him for his generosity and for his kind hospitality, then I bade him farewell and left. I had my lunch at the inn, where all tongues were eagerly speaking of the war. In the afternoon I went to the mosque and prayed behind Sheikh Hamada al-Sabki. He then invited me to sit with him and I accepted with pleasure. Then, smiling, he asked me, "Have you found Arousa?"

"Continuing to be attached to Arousa is a meaningless self-delusion," I said seriously.

"That's the truth," he said, confirming my words. Then, after a short silence, he asked, "Will you continue on your journey with the first caravan?"

Feeling slightly embarrassed, I answered, "No, I want to stay on a while longer."

"A good decision. And right in the circumstances, for the king of Haira has prohibited the passage of caravans between Haira and Halba in response to our refusal to hand over the escaped commander."

I was astonished and perturbed.

"The big landowners and the men of industry and business are angry and held an important meeting with the ruler at which they demanded that war be declared," said the sheikh.

"And what is the position of the land of Aman?" I inquired uneasily.

"It's as though you had become an inhabitant of Halba!" said the sheikh, smiling. "The quarrel between Halba and Aman revolves round the ownership of certain wells in the desert between our two lands. The dispute will be settled in favor of Aman right away so that they will not think of treachery."

"I am a stranger," I said uneasily, "and warnings of war are flying all around me."

"The best thing you can do is to remain in Halba. If your stay is extended, you have sufficient funds to allow you to engage in some lucrative business."

I gave up the idea of joining the caravan despite my worry that it could be the last caravan for Aman. I was strongly drawn to Halba by the cleanliness of its atmosphere and by hopes of enjoying myself in the company of some of its inhabitants. I divided my time between sightseeing and the family of Sheikh Hamada al-Sabki. As for Arousa, she hovered as distantly from me as the stars of the night.

Daily life was saturated with thoughts of war. Many were upset at the concessions obtained by Aman without having shed a single drop of blood. The manager of the inn said sullenly, "Despite our sacrifice of the wells, Aman may still double-cross us."

Nerves were strained to the utmost and I was infected by the same feelings as the people around me. I was terrified during the limited hours I spent on my own in the inn, when not sightseeing or with the al-Sabki family. My nerves rebelled and demanded that I find satisfaction in stability. And when Halba declared war and sent its army to Haira my nerves rebelled even more and I began to search around in the violent storm for some safe cave in which to take refuge. People talked of the war, comparing the forces of the two sides and their capabilities, while I strictly confined myself to looking for the means by which to obtain satisfaction in stability. I forgot everything but the objective close at hand, as if I were engaged in a race or being chased. I was encouraged in this by the atmosphere of the family and Samia's sincere friendship, her admiration for me as a traveler, and her sympathy for my never-ending sorrows. "She is a girl of genuine worth," I thought, "and there is no life for me without her."

"I have put my trust in God and have decided to marry," I said to the imam.

"Have you found Arousa?" he inquired.

"Arousa, in any event, is over and done with," I said shyly.

"Have you chosen anyone?"

"What I seek lies with you," I said quietly.

He gave an encouraging smile and asked, "Are you going to marry as someone who is traveling or as someone who stays in one place?"

"I do not think that the dream will vanish," I said truthfully.

"Everything depends upon what she wants. Why don't you yourself speak to her?"

"It is better for you to act on my behalf," I said in embarrassment.

"So be it," he said affectionately. "I appreciate your situation."

I received her agreement the following day. I was impatient to proceed and they complied with my wishes. I rented a flat in the same street and we both furnished it together. The marriage contract was concluded in a quiet atmosphere befitting the circumstances of the war, and so we were brought together in the matrimonial home. My heart was gladdened and I recovered my balance. Encouraging news of the fighting came to us, but sadness forced its way into many hearts, and the prices of innumerable goods rose. Sheikh Hamada al-Sabki suggested I should go into partnership in a shop selling works of art and jewelry, and I agreed with enthusiasm. My partners were two Christian brothers, and their shop was located in the square where the inn was. The work required me to stay in the shop with them all day long, so—for the first time in my life—I devoted myself to work with commendable zeal. Samia would spend the same hours at the hospital.

"You must make Halba your permanent residence," she said to me. "If you wish, complete your journey, but return here."

"I may think of returning to my homeland," I said frankly, "as I had planned to write my book, but there is nothing wrong in taking up residence here."

"In that event," she said joyfully, "I shall accompany you to your homeland and return with you. As for permanent residence, you will not find such a civilized place as Halba."

I hesitated a while, then said, "It seems to me that my new work will bring us a good income. Wouldn't it be a good idea to think about resigning from your work at the hospital?"

"In our land, work, for man and woman alike, is something sacred," she said with a sweet laugh. "From now on you must think like a man of Halba."

I gazed tenderly at her. "You are all but a mother, Samia."

"That's my affair," she said gaily.

As summer rolled up the last of its pages, the fact that she was to become a mother became visibly apparent. The breezes of autumn arrived, replete with humidity and the shadows of clouds, and every day I discovered something new from the world of my beloved wife. She had pride without being conceited, she loved to discuss things, she was a true believer, and she was possessed of a strength at which my heart rejoiced.

Perhaps the most extraordinary thing I encountered in my journey was Halba's type of Islam, in which there blazed the contradiction between outward and inward forms. "The difference between our Islam and yours," Samia said to me, "is that ours has not closed the door of independent judgment, and Islam without independent judgment means Islam without reason." What she said reminded me of the lessons of my old master.

However, I was in love with what was feminine in her and with her comeliness, which was so satisfying to my deprived natural impulses. I hungrily pursued that comeliness, heedless of anything else, though her personality was too strong and sincere to be dissolved in the beauty of a ripening woman. I found myself face to face with a brilliant intelligence, an enlightened mind, and exceptional goodness. I was convinced she was superior to me in many things, and this troubled me—I who had not seen woman other than as an object of enjoyment for man. My ardent love for her was commingled with fear and caution. Nevertheless reality demanded that I come to terms with the new situation and meet it halfway, in order to preserve both it and the happiness I had been granted.

"It is a mystery," I said to myself, "that she should give herself to me with such generosity. I am truly fortunate."

Disguising my inner fears, I once said to her, "Samia, you are a priceless treasure."

She told me openly, "And the idea of a traveler who sacrifices security in the cause of truth and goodness intrigues me a great deal, Qindil."

She brought to mind my slumbering project, wakening me from a sleep of honeyed ease, of love, of fatherhood and a civilized life. As though I were spurring on a person anesthetized to reality, I said, "I shall be the first person to write about the land of Gebel."

"Perhaps you will find it more remote than the dream," she said, laughing.

"Then I shall be the first to dispel the dream," I said resolutely.

Autumn passed and winter came in. Its cold was no more severe than that of my homeland, but the rainfall was heavy and one saw the sun but rarely. The winds would blow strongly and noisily, and the thunder would roar loudly and would engrave itself deep within one's soul. People talked of the war, which did not want to come to an end. I shared their feelings with sincerity and wished that freedom might gain the victory over the god-king and that my child might be born in the arms of freedom and security. Then one evening Samia joined me at home after work. She was aglow with a joy that brought to life that bloom of hers undermined by pregnancy. "Rejoice—it's victory!" she exclaimed.

She took off her overcoat, saying, "Haira's army has surrendered, the god-king has committed suicide, and Haira and Mashriq have become an extension of Halba. Freedom and civilization are now destined for their peoples."

Joy entered my heart, though some of the fears engendered by experiences of the past made me inquire, "Will they not pay the price of defeat in some manner?"

"The principles of the Authority are clear," she said enthusiastically. "There is no obstacle in the path of freedom apart from the land of Aman."

"At any event," I said innocently, "it did not double-cross you while you were enduring a long war."

"That's true," she said sharply, "but it is an obstacle in the way of freedom."

The day of the return of the victorious army was a memorable one. All of Halba, men and women, turned out to welcome it and pelt it with flowers, despite the cold weather and the pouring rain. Celebrations of every sort continued for a whole week. I soon noticed, on the way to work, that a strange state of affairs, incompatible with the festivities, was spreading strongly, unhesitatingly. Rumors were flying about as to the number of dead and wounded, rumors that were accompanied by sadness and disquiet. Pamphlets were distributed accusing the state of having sacrificed the sons of the people, not in order to liberate the peoples of Mashriq and Haira, but in the interests of the landowners, industrialists, and merchants; they said that it was a war of convoys of goods, not of principles. Another leaflet I received accused the publishers of the previous ones of being enemies of freedom and the agents of Aman. As a result of this there were noisy demonstrations attacking Aman and challenging the agreement to surrender the water wells. The head of state met with the experts and a unanimous decision was issued nullifying the agreement on the wells and regarding them as jointly owned by Halba and Aman, as they had been before. The people once again began talking about a possible war between Halba and Aman.

Sheikh al-Sabki and his family came to lunch with me, and we sat talking and exchanging views. "If this disturbance," I protested to the sheikh, "is as a result of a decisive victory, what would things be like if it were the result of defeat?"

"This is the nature of freedom," he said, smiling.

"It reminds me of anarchy," I said frankly.

"It is so for someone who has not had dealings with freedom," he said, laughing.

"I thought you were a happy people," I said bitterly. "But you are torn apart by invisible conflicts."

"The only remedy is yet more freedom."

"And how do you judge, morally, the nullifying of the agreement on the wells?"

"Yesterday I was visiting the sage Marham al-Halabi," he said earnestly, "and he told me that the liberation of human beings is more important than such superficialities."

"Superficialities!" I exclaimed. "One must admit of some moral basis, otherwise the world would be transformed into a jungle."

"But it was and still is a jungle," said Samia with a laugh.

"Look, Qindil," said the imam, "your homeland is the land of Islam, and what do you find there? A tyrannical ruler who rules to please himself, so where is the moral basis? Men of religion who bring religion into subjection to serve the ruler, so where is the moral basis? And a people who think only of the morsel which will fill their stomachs, so where is the moral basis?"

Something seemed to stick in my throat, so I remained silent. Once again I was seized by the memory of my journey. "Will war break out soon?" I asked.

"Only," said Samia. "if one of the two sides feels that it is stronger or if it is overcome by despair."

"Maybe you are thinking of the journey?" inquired my mother-in-law.

"First of all," I answered, smiling, "I must feel assured that Samia is all right."

At the end of the winter Samia had her first child, and instead of preparing myself for traveling I gave myself over to the soft life I led between work and home. I immersed myself in the life of Halba, in love, in a high standard of living, in fatherhood, in friendship, and in the treasures of the sky and the parks, which were endlessly beautiful. I dreamt of nothing more delightful than that this state of affairs should continue.

And with the passage of time I became a father to Mustafa, Hamid, and Hisham. However, I refused to admit defeat and would say to myself in shame, "Oh, my homeland! Oh, land of Gebel!"

I was recording some figures in the accounts book at the shop when I found Arousa in front of me. It was no dream, no illusion, but Arousa, dressed in a short skirt and a shawl embellished with pearls, of the sort worn by high-class women in summer. She was no longer young, no longer going about naked, but was still possessed of a decorously dignified beauty. It was as if she were a miracle come out of nowhere. She was turning over in her hands a coral necklace while I looked at her aghast. She happened to turn to me, and her eyes came into contact with my face and grew wider and wider. She forgot herself, and I myself.

"Arousa!" I called out joyfully.

In a daze she answered, "Qindil!"

We stared at each other till we decided, at one and the same time, to recover from our stupor and return to reality. I went to her and we shook hands, oblivious of the astonishment that had overtaken my partner.

"How are you?" I asked her.

"Not bad, everything's fine."

"Are you living here in Halba?"

"Since I left Haira."

"On your own?" I asked after some hesitation.

"I'm married to a Buddhist. And you?"

"Married and a father."

"I didn't have children."

"I hope you are happy."

"My husband is a remarkable and pious man and I have embraced his religion."

"When did you get married?"

"Two years ago."

"I gave up all hope of finding you."

"It's a large city."

"And how was your life before you married?"

She gave a gesture of displeasure. "It was a time of hardship and torture," she said.

"It's unfortunate," I muttered.

"It was for the best," she said, smiling. "We shall journey to Aman, and from there to the land of Gebel, then to India."

"May the blessing of God be with you wherever you may be," I said warmly.

She stretched out her hand and I clasped it, then she took up what she had bought and left. I found myself required to cast some light on the scene which had been enacted in front of my partner. However, I continued my work and kept my emotions to myself, though I knew for certain that everything had come to an end. I told Samia what had occurred, straightforwardly and with apparent indifference. I was not devoid, though, of a feeling of guilt about the excessive interest that flamed in my breast. It was violently shaken and there welled up in it springs of sadness and nostalgic yearnings. Warm gushings from the past flooded over it till it was submerged. While it was not unlikely that the old love had raised its head, had been resuscitated, the new reality was more weighty, more powerful than to succumb to such winds. Nevertheless the hidden desire to undertake the journey awoke in splendor, springing to the fore and searching out the morrow with firm and unrelenting resolve. Fearing that I would rush off to put it into execution, I invented doubts about it and took a decision to postpone it for a year, though during that year I would pave the way by preparing people to accept it.

And so it happened.

My beloved wife gave me permission, neither enthusiastically nor rapidly. I appointed the sheikh to replace me in the business until I should return, and I allocated such dinars for the journey as would give me a good life. I promised that I would return to Halba immediately after the journey and that I would then accompany my wife and children to the land of Islam, where I would compose the book of my journey and find those of my family who were still alive; after this we would return to Halba.

I bade Mustafa, Hamid, and Hisham a hearfelt farewell, as also my wife, Samira, who was bearing within her a new life.

Translated by Denys Johnson-Davies

from *Before the Throne*, 1983

This work was published in 1983 with the subtitle "A Debate with Egypt's Men from Menes to Anwar Sadat." The piece dealing with Abdel Nasser appears here.

Horus called out, "Gamal Abdel Nasser!"

A tall man entered; his features were strong and his personality powerful. He continued to stride forward until he stood before the throne.

Osiris asked him to state his case.

"I come from the village of Beni Murr, in the districts around Asyut," Abdel Nasser said proudly. "I was raised in a poor family, from the popular classes, and endured the bitterness and hardships of life. I graduated from the War College in 1938, and took part in Wafdist demonstrations. I was besieged along with the others at Falluja in 1949. The loss of Palestine dismayed me, but what disturbed me even more was the depth of the defeat's roots inside the homeland.

"Then it dawned on me that I should transfer the fight to within, where the real enemies of the nation were hiding in ambush. Cautiously and in secret, I formed the Free Officers' organization. I watched as events unfolded, waiting for the right moment to swoop down upon the regime in power. I realized my objective in 1952, then the Revolution's achievements—such as the abolition of the monarchical system, the completion of the total withdrawal of British troops from the country, the breaking up of the big landed estates through the law of agricultural reform, the Egyptianization of the economy, and the planning for the comprehensive revamping of both farming and industry to benefit the people and to dissolve the divisions between the classes—came one after another. We erected the High Dam while creating the public sector on the path to building socialism. We built a powerful, modern army. We spread the call for Arab unity. We assisted every Arab and African revolution. We nationalized the Suez Canal. In all this we were a beacon and a model for the entire Third World in its struggle against foreign colonialism and domestic exploitation. In my time of rule, working people enjoyed strength and power not known to them before. For the first time, the way was made for them to enter the legislative assemblies and the universities as well, when they could feel that the land was their land and the country their country.

"But the imperialist forces lay waiting to spring upon me—and then the detestable defeat of June 5, 1967 descended upon me. The great work was shaken to its foundations, and I was doomed to what seemed like death three years before I actually expired. I lived a sincere Egyptian Arab, and died an Egyptian Arab martyr," Abdel Nasser ended his opening statement.

"Allow me to convey to you my vast love and admiration," gushed Ramesses II. "What is my affection for you but an extension of my love for myself ? For look how much we resemble each other. Both of us radiate a greatness that filled up our own country till it spilled over her borders. Both of us fashioned a surpassing victory from a defeat, while neither of us was satisfied with his own glorious accomplishments, raiding the deeds of our predecessors as well. To my good fortune, I sat on the throne of Egypt when she was supreme among nations, while you ruled when she was a tiny band of believers straggling among titans. The God bestowed strength of spirit and body upon me through all my long life, while begrudging you but a little of these things, hastening your demise before your time."

"Your interest in Arab unity was higher than your interest in Egypt's integrity," bemoaned Menes, "for you even removed her immortal name with one stroke of the pen. You compelled many of her sons to migrate abroad, such as happened only in fleeting moments of subjugation."

"I am not to blame if some Egyptians see Arab unity as a catastrophe for themselves," disputed Abdel Nasser, "nor if I accomplish majestic things that those who came before me were too weak to achieve. For in truth, Egyptian history really began on July 23, 1952."

A hubbub arose among those present, continuing to build until Osiris called out, "Order in the court! Ladies and gentlemen, you must allow everyone to express their opinion freely."

"Permit me to hail you in my capacity as the first revolutionary among Egypt's poor," began Abnum. "I want to testify that the wretched did not enjoy such security in any age—after my own—as they did in yours. I can only fault you for one thing: for insisting that your revolution be stainless, when in fact the blood should have run in rivers!"

"What is that butcher raving about now?" objected Khufu, scowling.

"Do not forget that you are no longer sitting upon your throne," Osiris berated him. "Say you are sorry."

"I am sorry," said Khufu sheepishly.

"Despite your martial upbringing," Thutmose III lectured Abdel Nasser, "and though you have proven your outstanding ability in many other fields, none of them were military. Nor were you a military leader in any serious sense of the term."

"One must forgive my defeat by an army equipped by the most powerful state on the face of the earth!"

"Your duty was to avoid war and to refrain from provoking superior powers!" Imhotep, vizier to King Djoser, rebuked him.

"That conflicted with my goals, while I was deceived more than once!" Abdel Nasser complained.

"An excuse worse than the offense," snapped Ptahhotep.

"You attempted to blot my name from existence, along with the name of Egypt," said Saad Zaghloul. "You said about me that I rose on the crest of the 1919 Revolution. Let me tell you about the meaning of leadership. Leadership is a divine gift and a popular instinct. It does not come to a person either by blind luck or chance. The Egyptian leader is the one to whom all Egyptians pledge their allegiance, regardless of their differing faiths—or he will never be leader of the Egyptians. He may also be an Arab or Islamic leader—for which, in any case, I don't reject your claim. I consider your slander against me but a youthful indiscretion, that perhaps could be tolerated in view of the glorious services you have rendered. The Urabi Revolution was a noble struggle that was thwarted most painfully. The 1919 Revolution was one of the great exploits bestowed by history, but its enemies grew more and more numerous until it was wiped out with the burning of Cairo. Then your revolution came, and you put paid to its enemies as you completed the message of the two earlier uprisings. And though it began as a military coup, the people nonetheless blessed it and gave it their loyalty. It was in your power to build its base among them and to establish an enlightened, democratic form of government. But your delusive impulses toward autocracy were responsible for all the drawbacks and disasters of your rule."

"We needed a period of transition to fix the foundations of our revolution," Abdel Nasser asserted.

"That is a feeble dictatorial claim that we always hear from the nation's enemies," Mustafa al-Nahhas, Zaghloul's successor as head of the Wafd Party, retorted scornfully. "You had at your disposal a popular Wafdist fundament which you crushed with your tanks. You were incapable of creating an alternative to it, and the country suffered in a vacuum instead. You stretched out your hand to the criminals of the land, falling into an unfortunate contradiction between a reforming project whose spirit had come from the Wafd, and a style of rule inspired by the king and the privileged elites—until this way of running things frustrated all your fairest designs."

"True democracy to me," swore Abdel Nasser, "meant the liberation of the Egyptians from colonialism, exploitation, and poverty."

"You were heedless of liberty and human rights," al-Nahhas resumed his attack. "While I don't deny that you kept faith with the poor, you were a curse upon political writers and intellectuals, who are the vanguard of the nation's children. You cracked down on them with arrest and imprisonment, with hanging and killing, until you had degraded their dignity and humiliated their humanity, until you had eradicated their optimism and smashed the formation of their personalities—and only God knows when their proper formation shall return. Those who launched the 1919 Revolution were people of initiative and innovation in the various fields of politics, economics, and culture. How your high-handedness spoiled your most pristine depths! See how education was vitiated, how the public sector grew depraved! How your defiance of the world's powers led you to horrendous losses and shameful defeats! You never sought the benefit of another person's opinion, nor learned from the lessons of Muhammad Ali's experience. And what was the result? Clamor and cacophony, and an empty mythology—all heaped on a pile of rubble."

"I moved my country from one condition to another, just as I shifted the Arabs and the course of helpless nations. The problems will be treated until they disappear. In time, they will be forgotten, while what was helpful to humanity will remain. Then the people will affirm my true grandeur."

"If only you had been more modest in your ambitions, if only you had stuck to reforming your nation and had opened the windows of progress to her in all areas of civilization. The development of the Egyptian village was more important than the world's revolutions. Encouraging scientific research was more urgent than the campaign in Yemen. Combating illiteracy was more imperative than confronting global imperialism. Unfortunately, you wasted an opportunity that had never appeared to the country before. For the first time, a native son ruled the land, without contention from king or colonizer. Yet rather than curing the disease-ridden citizen, he drove him into a competition for the world championship when he was hobbled by illness. The outcome was that the citizen lost the race, and himself, as well."

Here Isis had her say.

"My joy at the return of the throne to one of my children cannot be contained!" she exclaimed. "His magnificent accomplishments would need all the walls of the temples in order to record them. As for his faults, I do not know how to defend them."

Osiris then announced his verdict.

"If our trial here had the last word in your judgment," he declared, "we would be compelled to give long and difficult consideration to arrive at justice. Certainly, few have performed so many services to their country as you have for yours, nor brought down so many evils upon it as you have, as well. However, in your case, being the first of Egypt's sons to occupy her throne since olden times, and the first to devote himself to the laboring people's welfare, we will suffer you to sit with the Immortals until this tribunal ends. Afterward, you shall go to your final trial with an appropriate recommendation."

Translated by Raymond Stock

from *Akhenaten, Dweller in Truth*, 1985

This short novel about the great prophet-king marks Mahfouz's successful return, after some forty years, to that period of Egypt's history with which he began his writing career.

Ay

Ay was the sage and former counselor to Akhenaten, and father of Nefertiti and Mutnedjmet. Old age had settled in the furrows of his face. I met him in his palace overlooking the Nile in south Thebes. He told me the story in a serene voice without letting his face reveal any emotion. I was in awe of his solemnity and dignity, and the richness of his experience. "Life, Meriamun, is a wonder," he began. "It is a sky laden with clouds of contradictions." He contemplated a while, surrendering to a current of memories. Then, he continued.

The story begins one summer day when I was summoned to appear before King Amenhotep III and Great Queen Tiye.

"You are a wise man, Ay," the queen said. "Your knowledge of the secular and the spiritual is unrivaled. We have decided to entrust you with the education of our sons Tuthmosis and Amenhotep."

I bowed my shaven head in gratitude and said, "Fortunate is he who will have the honor of serving the king and queen."

Tuthmosis was seven years old, Amenhotep was six. Tuthmosis was strong, handsome, and well built, though not particularly tall. Amenhotep was dark, tall, and slender, with small, feminine features. He had a tender yet penetrating look that made a deep impression on me. The handsome lad died and the weak one was spared. The death of his brother shook Amenhotep and he wept for a long time.

One day he said to me, "Master, my brother was pious, he frequented the temple of Amun, received his charms and fetishes, but still he was left to die. Master and Sage, why don't you bring him back to life?"

"Son," I replied, "one's soul is immortal. Let that be your solace."

That was the beginning of our many discussions on life and death. I was sincerely pleased with his insight and understanding in spiritual matters. The boy was clearly ahead of his years. I often found myself thinking that Akhenaten was born with some otherworldly wisdom. Even in secular subjects, he quickly mastered the skills of reading, writing, and algebra. I said to Queen Tiye, "His abilities are so extraordinary that he is beginning to intimidate his master."

I looked forward to lessons with him and wondered what his mind would produce when he reigned over the empire of his forefathers. I was certain that the greatness of his empire would surpass that of his father's.

Amenhotep III was a great and powerful ruler. He was merciless with his enemies and those who disobeyed him. In peaceful times he indulged himself with women, food, and wine. He became so thoroughly consumed by those pleasures that he soon fell victim to all kinds of ailments, and spent his last days in agony, suffering excruciating pains. As for Queen Tiye, she came from an honorable Nubian family. She proved to be a woman of such power and wisdom that she outshone even Queen Hatshepsut. Because of the death of her eldest son and her husband's infidelity she became very attached to the young Amenhotep. It was as if she were his mother, his lover, and his teacher. She was so passionate about politics that she sacrificed her feminine heart to nourish her ambition for power. The priests falsely accused her of being responsible for her son's perversity. The truth is that she wanted him to be abreast of all religions. Perhaps she wanted Aten to replace Amun and become the deity to whom all others owed allegiance, for Aten was the sun god who breathed life everywhere. His subjects were united by faith and not merely by force. She hoped to use religion as a political instrument that could bring about the unity of Egypt. It was not her intention that her son believe in the religion and not the politics, but Akhenaten refused to put religion in the service of anything. The mother had contrived a clever political scheme, but the son believed in the means, not the end. He devoted himself to his religious calling, jeopardizing the country, the empire, and the throne.

Ay remained silent for a while. He tightened the sash around his shoulders. His face looked rather small under the thick wig. When some time had passed in silence, he continued.

I am still amazed at the young boy's intelligence. It was as if he had been born with the mind of a high priest. I often caught myself arguing with him as though he were my equal. By the time he was ten, his mind was like hot springs, sparkling with ideas. His weak body harbored such strong will and perseverance that I took him as living proof that the human spirit could be stronger than the most exercised muscles. He was so devoted to his religious instruction that he spent no time preparing himself for the throne. He would not accept any idea without questioning and argument, and he never hesitated to express his doubts about many of our traditional teachings. I was taken aback when, one time, he said, "Thebes! A holy city! Isn't that what they claim? Thebes, Master, is nothing but a den of rapacious merchants, debauchery, and fornication. Who are those great priests? They delude people with superstition, and take from the poor what little they have. They seduce women in the name of the deities. Their temple has become a house of harlotry and sin. Accursed Thebes."

I was greatly concerned when I heard him speak these words. I could see accusing fingers pointed at me, his teacher.

"Those priests are the foundation of the throne," I replied.

"Then the throne is built on lies and dissolution."

"Their power is no less than that of an army," I warned him.

"Bandits and thugs are powerful, too."

It was clear from the very beginning that he disliked Amun, who reigned in the holy of holies. He favored Aten, whose light shone throughout the world.

"Amun is the god of priests, but Aten is God of heaven and earth."

"You should be loyal to all deities."

"Should I not trust my heart to show me the difference between right and wrong?" he asked.

"One day you will be crowned in the temple of Amun," I said in an attempt to persuade him.

He spread his slender arms and said, "I would rather be crowned in the open air, under the light of the sun."

"Amun is the deity that empowered your ancestors and gave them victory over their enemies."

He remained quiet, thinking, then said, "I cannot understand how a god could allow anyone to massacre his own creation."

I grew more worried but continued my efforts to dissuade him. "But we, the subjects of Amun, cannot always understand his holy wisdom."

"The sunlight of Aten does not discriminate between people when it shines down upon us."

"You must not forget that life is a battleground."

"Master," he replied sadly, "do not speak to me of war. Have you not seen the sun when it rises above the fields and the Nile? Have you not seen the horizon when the sun goes down? Have you heard the nightingale sing, or the doves coo? Have you never felt the sacred happiness buried deep in your heart?"

I knew that there was nothing I could do. He was like a tree and I could not stop him from growing. I conveyed my fears to the queen, but she did not share my concerns.

"He is still an innocent child, Ay," she said. "He will learn more of this life as he grows. Soon he will begin his military training."

The pious young prince started his military training along with the sons of the nobles. He detested it, possibly because of his physical weakness. Soon he rejected the training, thus admitting a failure not befitting a king's son.

"I do not wish to learn the fundamentals of murder," he said bitterly.

The king was saddened by his son's decision. "A king who cannot fight is at the mercy of his commanders," he said.

The crown prince and the king had several confrontations. Most likely, this strife was the seed of the malice the boy harbored against his great father. I do believe, however, that the priests of Amun stretched this fact when they accused him of avenging himself by erasing his father's name from all the monuments. He only wanted to eradicate the name of Amun. He even changed his own name from Amenhotep to Akhenaten for the same purpose. Then came the night that condemned him to a life of seclusion. He had been waiting for the sunrise in the dark royal garden by the bank of the Nile. I learned all the details when I met him in the morning. I believe it was spring time. The air was clear of all dew and dust. When I greeted him, he turned to me with a pale face and mesmerized eyes.

"Master, the truth has been revealed to me," he said without returning my greeting. "I came here before sunrise. The night was my companion, its silence my blessing. As I bid darkness farewell, I felt that I was rising with the air around me. It was as though I was retreating with the night. Then there was a marvelous light, and I saw all the creatures that I had seen or even heard of gather before my eyes and greet each other in delight. I had overcome pain and death, I thought. I was intoxicated with the sweet scent of creation. I heard his clear voice speaking to me: 'I am the One and Only God; there is no God but I. I am the truth. Dwell in my kingdom, and worship me only. Give me yourself; I have granted you my divine love.' "

We stared at each other for a long while. I was overcome by despair and could not speak.

"Do you not believe me, Master?"

"You never lie," I replied.

"Then you must believe me," he said in ecstasy.

"What did you see?"

"I only heard his voice in the merry dawn."

"My son," I hesitated, "if you saw nothing, that means there was nothing."

"This is how he reveals himself," he replied firmly.

"Perhaps it was Aten."

"No. Not Aten, not the sun. He is above and beyond that. He is the One and Only God."

I was mystified. "Where do you worship him?"

"Anywhere, anytime. He will give me the strength and love to worship him."

Ay was silent. I wanted to ask him if he believed in Akhenaten's god, but I remembered my father's advice and remained silent. Ay, along with many others, had left Akhenaten when things were at their worst. Perhaps he had been forced to deny his faith for the rest of his life.

I had to tell the king and queen. A few days later, I found the crown prince waiting for me in his favorite part of the garden.

"You reported me as usual, Master," he smiled reproachfully.

"It is my duty," I replied calmly.

He laughed and said. "The confrontation with my father was rather interesting. When I recounted my experience to him, he grimaced and said, 'You must be examined by Bento, the physician.' I replied politely that I was in good health. 'I have yet to see a mad man confess to insanity,' he said. Then he continued, this time in a threatening tone, 'The deities are the foundation of Egypt. The king must believe in all the deities of his people. This god that you spoke of is nothing. He does not deserve to join our deities.' I told him that he was the Only God; that there is no other god. 'This is heresy and madness,' he cried. I repeated that he was the One and Only God. He became extremely angry and said, 'I command you to renounce these absurd ideas, and to honor the heritage of your ancestors.' I did not say any more so as not to show him disrespect. Then my mother said, 'All we ask of you is to honor and respect a holy duty. Let your heart love what your heart wishes to love, until you return to the right path. Meanwhile, do not neglect your duty.' I left them feeling sad, but more determined."

"My dear Prince," I said earnestly, "the pharaoh is a product of ancient and holy traditions. Do not ever forget that."

From that moment, I was sure that there were troubles ahead such as Egypt had never seen or imagined before. The great family of pharaohs that had liberated the country and created an empire was now standing at the edge of an abyss. Around that time—perhaps it was earlier, I am not quite certain of the chronology—I was summoned to a closed meeting by the high priest of Amun.

"You and I have known each other for a very long time, Ay," he said. "What is all this that I hear?"

As I say, I do not recall whether this meeting took place after it became known that the prince was inclined toward Aten, or after he declared his faith in the One and Only God. In any event, I replied, "The prince is a fine, sensible young man. Only, he is still too young. At such a sensitive age, one tends to follow one's imagination indiscriminately. He will soon mature and return to the right path."

"How could he renounce the wisdom of the best teacher in the country?"

"How can one control the flow of a river during the flood season?" I said in an effort to defend myself.

"Our duty, as the elite of this country, is to put our religion and empire first."

I had endless discussions with my wife, Tey, and my daughters, Nefertiti and Mutnedjmet, trying to make sense of the confusion that rattled in my mind day and night. Tey and Mutnedjmet accused the prince of heresy. Nefertiti, on the other hand, had no qualms about supporting him. Indeed she liked his ideas. "He speaks the truth, Father," she whispered. Nefertiti was about the same age as Akhenaten and, like the prince, had matured beyond her years. Both girls had completed their basic education and homemaking training. Mutnedjmet was good at writing and recitation, algebra, embroidery, sewing, cooking, painting, and ritual dance. Nefertiti excelled in the same subjects, but was not content with them. She developed a strong interest in theology and logic. I noticed her fondness for Aten, and later, when she declared her faith in the One God, I was aghast. "He is the only god able to rescue me from the torture of confusion," she announced.

Tey and Mutnedjmet were furious, and accused her of apostasy.

At that time, we were invited to the pharaoh's palace to celebrate thirty years of his reign. It was the first time our daughters had entered the palace, and by a stroke of fate, Nefertiti won the love of the crown prince. Everything happened so quickly thereafter. We could still hardly believe it, when Nefertiti and Akhenaten became husband and wife. I was summoned once more by the high priest of Amun. This time, as I stood before him, I felt that he regarded me as a potential enemy.

"You have become a member of the royalty, Ay." His voice was filled with apprehension.

"I am but a man who has never strayed from the course of duty."

"Only time can prove the true merits of men," he said calmly.

He asked me to arrange for a conference with Nefertiti. Before the appointed time I spoke with my daughter and armed her with advice. I must say though that Nefertiti had no need of counseling—her own wisdom aided her more than any advice she received. She answered the high priest's questions eloquently, without revealing secrets or making commitments. I believe that the priests' hostility toward my daughter started with that encounter.

"Father," she reported, "it may have seemed an innocent meeting on the surface, but in reality we were fighting an undeclared war. He claims that he is concerned for the empire when in fact he is only worried about his share of the goods that flow into the temple. He is a crafty, wicked man."

When the conflict grew between the pharaoh and his son, the king called me in and said, "I think we should send the prince on a tour of the empire. He needs experience, and must learn more about people and life." At that time, the king was enjoying his last days with a bride young enough to be his granddaughter—Tadukhipa, daughter of Tushratta, the king of Mitanni.

"It is a sound idea, my Gracious King," I replied sincerely.

So Akhenaten left Thebes accompanied by a delegation of the best young men in the country. I, too, was chosen to go with him on that memorable journey. In the provinces, the subjects had expected to see a powerful, invincible being, a high and mighty god looking down upon them. Instead, the crown prince greeted them humbly as he walked among them in public gardens and on their plantations. Priests and religious scholars were invited to convene with him. He denounced their faiths. What god, he asked, is so bloodthirsty that it cannot be worshiped without the sacrifice of human souls? He proclaimed his One God, the only creator of the universe. He told them that God regarded all his creation indiscriminately with love, peace, and joy; that love was the only law, peace was the ultimate end, and joy was the gratitude offered to the creator. Everywhere he went he left behind a whirlwind of confusion and frenzied excitement. I became extremely alarmed.

"My dear Prince," I said, "you are pulling out the roots of the empire."

He laughed. "When will you believe, Master?"

"You have slandered all the religions of our ancestors, religions we have learned to believe in and respect. Equality . . . love . . . peace . . . all this means nothing to the subjects but an open invitation to rebelliousness and strife."

He thought a while, then asked, "Why do wise men like yourself believe so firmly in evil?"

"We believe in reality."

"Master," he said with a smile, "I will forever dwell in truth."

Before we were able to visit all the provinces as planned, a messenger from the palace reached us with the news that the Great Pharaoh was dead.

Ay recounted the details of their return to Thebes, the grand entombment ceremony, and the crowning of the prince on the throne of Egypt. Akhenaten became King Amenhotep IV, and his wife, Nefertiti, the Great Queen. As was the custom, the new king inherited his father's harem. Although he treated them kindly, he abstained from any pleasure they offered him.

Ay then told me how Akhenaten summoned the noble men of the country and urged them to join his religion. Thus, he was able to select his men from those who declared their faith in the One and Only God. Mae was appointed commander of the armed forces; Haremhab became chief of security; Ay was chosen for the position of adviser to the throne.

"You will hear conflicting reports on why we declared our faith in Akhenaten's god," Ay told me. "But no one knows what the heart really holds." Feeling that I was after the secret of his heart, he told me, "I believed in the new god as a deity to be worshiped along with all the other deities. But I also believed that everyone should have the freedom to worship whichever god they chose."

Akhenaten continued his reform throughout the empire. He reduced taxes, and abolished all punitive measures. "My King," Ay advised him, "if public servants are no longer afraid of punishment, they will soon become corrupt, and the poor will be their sorry prey." The king shrugged and replied confidently, "You are still wavering, Ay, and your faith is not strong enough. You will soon see what wonders love can do. My God will never let me down." Meanwhile, relations between the new king and the priests of Amun had become so strained that Akhenaten resolved to build a new city and move the throne.

Thus we moved to Akhetaten, a city of unrivaled beauty. Upon arrival we held the first prayer in the grand temple that was erected in the center of the city. Nefertiti played the mandolin. She was like a jewel, radiant with youth and beauty as she sang:

O Precious Lord, Sole Creator,
You fill the universe with thy beauty.
There is no love greater than thine.

Each passing day was a sweet dream, filled with happiness and love. The blossom of the new religion was growing rapidly in our hearts. But the king did not forget his mission. In the name of love and peace, the pharaoh fought the most ferocious war Egypt had witnessed. He decreed the closing of temples, confiscated all the idols, and erased their names from the monuments. It was then that he changed his name to Akhenaten. Then he toured the country proclaiming his religion. People received him with amazing love and eagerness. In the past, they had heard about pharaohs without ever seeing them, but now the image of Akhenaten and Nefertiti in their public appearances became engraved on their memories forever.

Translated by Tagreid Abu-Hassabo

from *The Day the Leader Was Killed*, 1985

The day in the title is the day in 1981 on which Anwar Sadat was assassinated. The short novel is told through the mouths of three characters and describes a time when Egyptians were facing a period of change and difficulty.

Elwan Fawwaz Muhtashimi

Let this be a festive occasion and let's forget our worries for an hour or so. But how when there are a hundred chinks in the door? What is the River Nile trying to intimate? And the trees? Listen carefully. They're saying, Elwan, you poor fellow, trapped within four walls, Randa is coming back to you in the guise of friendship and small talk, in the guise of undeclared love resting on twin pillars of steel and despair, and shrouded in vague dreams. No persecution from family, no hope, and no despair! March at a brisk military pace, for today is soldiers' day. The café is packed with wordmongers. Here there's no satisfaction and no action. A transistor radio, brought along for the occasion, is placed on one of the tables between us. Just like on the day the late president broadcast his defeat in June 1967. The late president was greater in his defeat than this one in his glory, was the first thing I heard. This reminds me of what my grandfather once said: We are a people more given to defeat than to victory. The strain that spells out despair has become deeply ingrained in us because of the countless defeats we have had to endure. We have thus learned to love sad songs, tragedies, and heroes who are martyrs. All our leaders have been martyrs: Mustafa Kamel, martyr to struggle and sickness; Muhammad Farid and Saad Zaghloul, both martyrs to exile; Mustafa al-Nahhas, martyr to persecution; Gamal Abd al-Nasser, martyr to June 5. As for this victorious, smug one, he has broken the rule: his victory constituted a challenge which gave rise to new feelings, emotions for which we were quite unprepared. He exacted a change of tune, one which had long been familiar to us. For this, we cursed him, our hearts full of rancor. And, ultimately, he was to keep for himself the fruits of victory, leaving us his *Infitah*, which only spelled out poverty and corruption. This is the crux of the matter.

We were caught up in the heat of arguments as the loudspeaker and transistor radio broadcast the details of Victory Day celebrations to whoever cared to listen. And, as usual, time got the better of us until, suddenly, strange voices could be heard.

"The traitors . . . the traitors," cried the broadcaster's voice.

Tongues grew paralyzed and eyes were averted as heads crowded around the transistor radio. The broadcasting of the celebrations came to a sudden halt, and then some songs started to be broadcast.

"What happened?"

"Something unusual."

"He said: 'The traitors, the traitors, the traitors!' "

"An invasion!"

"Of whom?"

"Honestly, what a stupid question!"

"The songs being broadcast indicate that . . ."

"Since when has logic meant anything?"

"A little patience!"

We had no desire to go back home. We all just huddled up in an urge to remain all together in the face of the unknown. We had a quick meal of macaroni for lunch and then sat there waiting. Following a brief but violent period of time, the broadcaster announced that there had been an abortive attempt on the president's life, that the president had left, and that the security forces were in full control of the situation. And, once again, there were songs on the radio.

"This, then, is the truth."

"The truth."

"Think a little."

"Certain facts cannot be concealed."

"But they can be delayed."

"Who are the assaulters?"

"Who but those involved in the religious movement?"

"But he was sitting in the very midst of soldiers and guards."

"Listen, they've started to broadcast national hymns."

Suddenly, there was a new broadcast announcing that the president had been slightly injured and that he was getting full medical attention at the hospital. Our hearts leaped up at the thought of increased chances of new possibilities. Time came to a halt, changed its tune, and emerged with a brand-new look on its face.

"The man has been injured. What then?"

"Get ready for prison."

"A definite return to terrorism."

"He'll survive and seek revenge."

"Will we be hearing the Quran after the hymns?"

We whiled away the time that was weighing heavily upon us. Jokes were cracked and then the recitation of the Quran began. At first, we turned pale. It's true then. Amazing! Actually true!? The man's finished? Who would've believed? Why do we sometimes get a feeling that the impossible is actually possible? Why do we imagine that there exists a reality other than death in this world? Death is the true dictator. The official announcement comes to us like a final statement. I wonder what people are saying? I'd like to hear what is being said around us in the café. I pricked up my ears. There is no power or might save in God. To him alone is permanence. The country is in obvious danger. He doesn't deserve this end, whatever his misdeeds. On his day of glory? A plot. Surely there's a conspiracy. No doubt. The hell with him! Death saved him from madness. Anyhow, he had to go. This is what happens to those who imagine that the country is nothing but a dead corpse. No, it's a foreign conspiracy. He doesn't deserve this end. It was the inevitable end. He was a curse on us. He who kills will ultimately be killed. In a split second, an empire has collapsed. The empire of robbers. What is the Mafia thinking about right now? I returned to my seat, torn by conflicting feelings of despair, fear, and joy. Vague hopes hovered overhead, hopes of unknown possibilities, hopes that the prevailing lethargy and routine would, at last, be shattered, and that one could start soaring toward limitless horizons. Tomorrow cannot be worse than today. Even chaos is better than despair, and battling with phantoms is better than fear.

This blow has rocked an empire and shaken fortresses.

By evening, I realized I had started dozing off. All this talk had exhausted me. I felt like talking a walk. There's a trace of death on every passerby. Suddenly, there I am in front of Gulstan's villa. Anwar Allam's car

is parked there, awaiting its owner. Sexual desire of every sort takes possession of me and, with it, an irrepressible urge to kill.

Translated by Malak Hashem

from *Morning and Evening Talk*, 1987

This book consists of sixty-seven sketches of different characters, of which I have chosen one about a man and one about
a woman. It was the novelist's last chronicle of Cairo and has
been described as one of his most innovative contributions to
the Arabic novel.

Salim Hussein Qabil

The last child of Samira Amr and Hussein Qabil, he was born and
grew up on Ibn Khaldun Street. His father died when he was only
a year old so he was brought up in a disciplined climate, nothing
like the comfortable lifestyle his family had enjoyed when he was just a
glimmer on the horizon. He was good looking like his mother and tall like
his father, and had a large head and intellect like his brother Hakim. His
obstinacy and stubbornness, as well as his talent in school, came to light in
childhood. His sister Hanuma watched over him closely with her piety and
strict morality, and for a long time he believed he was learning the truth
about the Unknown from the lips of his grandmother Radia. He loved football and was good at it, enjoyed mixing with girls in al-Zahir Baybars
Garden, and hated the English. Dreams of reform and the perfect city toyed
constantly with his imagination. He did not incline to any one party, deterred
by his brother Hakim, who rejected everything outright. He once heard
Hakim say, "We need something new," and replied automatically, "Like
Caliph Omar ibn al-Khattab."

His own temperament and Hanuma's influence prompted him to turn to
the religious books in his brother's library. His dream of the perfect city vanquished football and girls. He was in secondary school for the July

Revolution and welcomed it eagerly, like deliverance from annihilation. The role his brother Hakim played in it strengthened his commitment and, for the first time, it seemed to him the perfect city was being built, brick by brick. He thought that by joining the Muslim Brotherhood he could immerse himself further in the revolution, but when the revolution and the Brothers came into conflict his heart remained with the latter. Disagreement emerged between him and his brother. "Be careful," Hakim said.

"Caution can't save us from fate," Salim replied.

He entered law school and his political—or rather religious—activities increased. But none of his family imagined he would be among the accused in the great case against the Muslim Brothers. Hakim was dismayed. "It's out of our hands!" he said to his anxious mother. Salim was sentenced to ten years in jail. Samira reeled at the force of the blow; Hakim's shining star could not console her for his brother's incarceration. She secretly despised the revolution, and Radia invoked evil on it and its men.

Salim was released from prison a year before June 5, completed the remainder of his studies, earned a degree, and started work in the office of an important Muslim Brotherhood attorney. He saw the great defeat as divine punishment for an infidel government. He did not sever links with his accomplices but conducted his business with extreme secrecy and caution. He found relief in writing and devoted years of his life to it. His labors bore fruit in his book, *The Golden Age of Islam*, which he followed with a work on the steadfast and pious. At the same time, he achieved considerable success as a lawyer and, with the sales of his two books, his finances improved, especially after Saudi Arabia purchased a large number of them. When the revolution's leader died, he recovered a certain repose. Samira said to him, "It's time you thought of marrying." He responded eagerly, so she said, "You must see Hadiya, your aunt Matariya's granddaughter through Amana."

Hadiya was the youngest of Amana's children. She had recently returned from the Gulf after teaching there for two years and had purchased an apartment in Manshiyat al-Bakri. He went with Samira to Abd al-Rahman Amin and Amana's house on Azhar Street and saw Hadiya, a fine-looking teacher in the prime of youth, whose beauty was very much like her grandmother Matariya's, the most beautiful woman in the family. Samira proposed to her on his behalf, she was wedded to him, and he moved to her apartment in Manshiyat al-Bakri. He had a lovely wife and flourishing career. He knew love and compassion under Sadat and had no cause for worry other than the new religious currents that had emerged within the Brothers, cleaving new paths surrounded by radicalism and abstruseness. "There is a general Islamic awakening, no doubt about it. But it is also resurrecting old differences which are consuming its strengths to no avail," he said to his brother Hakim. However, Hakim had other priorities and, despite his personal feelings, saw what befell the regime on June 5 as an absolute catastrophe; the nation was moving into uncharted territory. As the days went by, God granted Salim fatherhood, material abundance, and satisfaction on the day of victory. Yet none of this jostled from his heart his deeply rooted belief in, and eternal dream of, the divine perfect city. He swept Hadiya along in his forceful current until she said, "I was lost and you showed me the right way. Praise be to God."

Salim became a propagandist writer for the Muslim Brotherhood's magazine and, like the rest of the group, was filled with rage at Sadat's reckless venture to make peace with Israel. He reverted once more to vehement anger and rebellion, and when the September 1981 rulings were issued he was thrown back in jail. When Sadat was assassinated he said, "It's a divine punishment for an infidel government."

He could breathe freely in the new climate but had lost confidence in everything except his dream. It was for this that he worked and lived.

Shahira Mu'awiya al-Qalyubi

She was the second daughter of Sheikh Mu'awiya and Galila al-Tarabishi. She was born and grew up in the old family house in Suq al-Zalat in Bab al-Sha'riya. The hallway of the house was her playground, between the stove, well, and family sofa, where she, Radia, Sadiqa, and Baligh would congregate. There sounded her father, the sheikh's, exhortations, and there circulated Galila's mysteries of times past. From the beginning, Shahira showed no interest in religion or religious duties. Yet she eagerly embraced popular heritage and would add to it from her abundant imagination. In body and face she resembled Radia, though she was fairer, remarkably blunt and impudent, and eccentric to the point of insanity. Two years after her father died, one of his students, a Quran reciter with a sweet voice, nice appearance, and ample means, sought her hand in marriage. She was wedded to him in his house in Bab al-Bahr, not far from the family residence. She gave birth to a fine-looking son, whom his father called Abduh because he thought the name of the man whose voice he adored, Abduh al-Hamuli, would be a good omen. The marriage prospered in spite of Shahira's irascibility and impudence. "It's the spice of married life," the husband, Sheikh Ali Bilal, would joke.

Sheikh Ali Bilal made friends with Amr Effendi and his family, and whenever he visited the house on Bayt al-Qadi Square, Amr would ask him to bless it with one of his recitations. Thus, he would sit cross-legged in the reception room after supper, drinking coffee, and recite something easy from the Quran in his sweet voice. He was impelled by his voice and friends to recite eulogies to the Prophet at festivals. His livelihood grew and his admirers multiplied. Before long he was invited to enliven weddings with his panegyrics. Amidst the festive atmosphere and pleasant evenings, he got into the habit of smoking hashish. Eventually one of the composers suggested he try singing, foreseeing a rosy future in it for him. The sheikh met the invitation with a merry heart. He saw nothing wrong in abandoning the holy suras of the Quran to sing "Don't Speak to Me, Papa is Coming," "Draw the Curtains so the Neighbors Can't See," and "Yummy Scrummy Fried Fish," and was remarkably successful in so doing. He made recordings, which were circulated in the market, and people started talking about him. Amr clapped his hands together. "What a comedown!"

The temptations of the new milieu made Shahira anxious about her position as wife. "You were a blessed sheikh when I married you," she said. "Now you're a chanteuse!"

The man was intoxicated by his success and became the organizer of many a hashish gathering. He was soon drinking heavily and the house would be filled with horrid trenchant fumes at the end of the night, reminding Shahira of the tragedy of her brother, Baligh. The sound of her upbraiding and scalding him with her vicious tongue would drown the dawn muezzin. Then reports of him flirting with singers reached her ears. She pounced on him with a savagery that flung open the gates of hell upon him and he made up his mind to divorce her. But one night, before he could put his decision into action, he overdid the drinking and singing and had a heart attack. He died among friends, plucking the strings on his lute.

Shahira performed the rituals of mourning without emotion. She leased the house and the shop below and returned with Abduh to the old house to share her loneliness with her mother, Galila. "Let Abduh be your eye's delight," said Radia. But Abduh was snatched away in a fever, as though in a dream. By this time his mother was already known as Umm Abduh about the quarter, and the eponym would stick for the rest of her life. She became passionate about breeding cats and dedicated her time to looking after them until they filled the gap in her life and crowded the old house. She started to believe she could understand their language and the spirits that inhabited their bodies, and that through them she was in touch with the Unknown. She found her best friend in Radia. Whenever they met up, whether in Bayt al-Qadi or Suq al-Zalat, a curious session invariably ensued during which they would exchange anecdotes about the realm of the jinn, the Unknown, and the offspring of mysteries. In such things they were of one heart and one mind, despite Radia's misgivings and suspicion that Shahira begrudged her her children and happy marriage. Shahira was famous in Suq al-Zalat for her inscrutable, fearful personality and impudent tongue. She was not known to perform any religious duties and would prepare her meal at sunset in Ramadan saying, "People don't need religious duties to bring them closer to God." After her mother died she was wholly immersed in solitude, submerged to the top of her gray head in a world of cats. Her brother, Baligh, saw to her upkeep. He would invite her to visit his sublime mansion, but she hated his wife for no real reason, and only ever left her cats to visit Sidi al-Sha'rani or Radia. She fell victim to the cholera epidemic of 1947 and moved to the fever hospital after instructing a neighbor to go to Radia for the cats' care. She died in hospital, leaving some forty cats behind. Radia's sons and daughters mourned the aunt whom they had laughed at in life.

Translated by Christina Phillips

Short Stories

The Return of Sinuhe, 1941

A single story, "The Return of Sinuhe," has been chosen from the five tales set in ancient Egypt that make up the volume *Voices from the Other World.*

The incredible news spread through every part of Pharaoh's palace. Every tongue told it, all ears listened eagerly to it, and the stunned gossips repeated it—that a messenger from the land of the Amorites had descended upon Egypt. He bore a letter to Pharaoh from Prince Sinuhe, who had vanished without warning all of forty years before—and whose disappearance itself had wreaked havoc in people's minds. It was said that the prince had pleaded with the king to forgive what had passed, and to permit him to return to his native land. There he would retire in quiet isolation, awaiting the moment of his death in peace and security. No sooner had everyone recalled the hoary tale of the disappearance of Prince Sinuhe, than they would revive the forgotten events and remember their heroes—who were now old and senile, the ravages of age carved harshly upon them.

In that distant time, the queen was but a young princess living in the palace of Pharaoh Amenemhat I—a radiant rose blooming on a towering tree. Her lively body was clothed in the gown of youth and the shawl of beauty. Gentleness illuminated her spirit, her wit blazed, her intelligence gleamed. The two greatest princes of the realm were devoted to her: the then crown prince (and present king) Senwosret I, and Prince Sinuhe. The two princes were the most perfect models of strength and youth, courage and wealth, affection and fidelity. Their hearts were filled with love and their souls with loyalty, until each of the two became upset with his companion—to the point of rage and ruthless action. When Pharaoh learned that their emotional bond to each other and their sense of mutual brotherhood were about to snap, he became very anxious. He summoned the princess and—after a long discussion—he commanded her to remain in her own wing of the palace, and not to leave it.

He also sent for the two princes and said to them, with firmness and candor, "You two are but miserable, accursed victims of your own blind self-abandon in the pursuit of rashness and folly—a laughingstock among your fellow princes and a joke to the masses. The sages have said that a person does not merit the divine term 'human' until he is able to govern his lusts and his passions. Have you not behaved like dumb beasts and love-struck idiots? You should know that the princess is still confused between the two of you—and will remain confused until her heart is inspired to make a choice. But I call upon you both to renounce your rivalry in an ironbound agreement that you may not break. Furthermore, you will be satisfied with her decision, whatever it may be, and you will not bear anything toward your brother but fondness and loyalty—both inwardly and outwardly. Now, are you finished with this business?"

His tone did not leave room for hesitation. The two princes bowed their heads in silence, as Pharaoh bid them swear to their pact and shake hands. This they did—then left with the purest of intentions.

It happened during this time that unrest and rebellion broke out among the tribes of Libya. Pharaoh dispatched troops to chastise them, led by Prince Senwosret, the heir apparent, who chose Prince Sinuhe to command a brigade. The army clashed with the Libyans at several places, besetting them until they turned their backs and fled. The two princes displayed the kind of boldness and bravery befitting their characters. They were perhaps about to end their mission when the heir apparent suddenly announced the death of his father, King Amenemhat I. When this grievous news reached Prince Sinuhe, it seemed to have stirred his doubts as to what the new king might intend toward him. Suspicion swept over him and drove him to despair—so he melted away without warning, as though he had been swallowed by the sands of the desert.

Rumors abounded about Sinuhe's fate. Some said that he had fled to one of the faraway villages. Others held that he had been assassinated in Libya. Still others said that he had killed himself out of desperation over life and love. The stories about him proliferated for quite a long time. But eventually, the tongues grew tired of them, consigning them to the tombs of oblivion under the rubble of time. Darkness enveloped them for forty years—until at last came that messenger from the land of the Amorites carrying Prince Sinuhe's letter—awakening the inattentive, and reminding the forgetful.

King Senwosret looked at the letter over and over again with disbeliev-
ing eyes. He consulted the queen, now in her sixty-fifth year, on the affair.
They agreed to send messengers bearing precious gifts to Prince Sinuhe in
Amora, inviting him to come to Egypt safely, and with honor.

Pharaoh's messengers traversed the northern deserts, carrying the royal
gifts straight to the land of the Amorites. Then they returned, accompanied by
a venerable old man of seventy-five years. Passing the pyramids, his limbs
trembled, and his eyes were darkened by a cloud of distress. He was in
bedouin attire—a coarse woolen robe with sandals. A sword scabbard girded
his waist; a long white beard flowed down over his chest. Almost nothing
remained to show that he was an Egyptian raised in the palace of Memphis,
except that when the sailors' songs of the Nile reached his ears, his eyes
became dreamy, his parched lips quivered, his breath beat violently in his
breast—and he wept. The messengers knew nothing but that the old man
threw himself down on the bank of the river and kissed it with ardor, as though
he were kissing the cheek of a sweetheart from whom he had long been parted.

They brought him to Pharaoh's palace. He came into the presence of
King Senwosret I, who was seated before him, and said, "May the Lord bless
you, O exalted king, for forgiving me—and for graciously allowing me to
return to the sacred soil of Egypt."

Pharaoh looked at him closely with obvious amazement, and said, his
voice rising, "Is that really you? Are you my brother and the companion of
my childhood and youth—Prince Sinuhe?"

"Before you, my lord, is what the desert and forty years have done to
Prince Sinuhe."

Shaking his head, the king drew his brother toward him with tenderness
and respect, and asked, "What did the Lord do with you during all these forty
years?"

The prince pulled himself up straight in his seat, and began to tell his tale.

"My lord, the story of my flight began at the hour that you were informed
of our mighty father's death out in the Western Desert. There the Devil
blinded me and evil whispers terrified me. So I threw myself into the wind,
which blew me across deserts, villages, and rivers, until I passed the borders
between damnation and madness. But in the land of exile, the name of the

person whose face I had fled, and who had dazzled me with his fame, conferred honor upon me. And whenever I confronted trouble, I cast my thoughts back to Pharaoh—and my cares left me. Yet I remained lost in my wanderings, until the leader of the Tonu tribes in Amora learned of my plight, and invited me to see him.

"He was a magnificent chief who held Egypt and its subjects in all awe and affection. He spoke to me as a man of power, asking me about my homeland. I told him what I knew, while keeping the truth about myself from him. He offered me marriage to one of his daughters, and I accepted—and began to despair that I would ever again see my homeland. After a short time, I—who was raised on Pharaoh's famous chariots, and grew up in the wars of Libya and Nubia—was able to conquer all of Tonu's enemies. From them I took prisoners, their women and goods, their weapons and spoils, and their herds, and my status rose even further. The chief appointed me the head of his armies, making me his expected successor.

"The gravest challenge that I faced was the great thief of the desert, a demonic giant—the very mention of whom frightened the bravest of men. He came to my place seeking to seize my home, my wife, and my wealth. The men, women, and children all rushed to the square to see this most ferocious example of combat between two opponents. I stood against him amidst the cheers and apprehension, fighting him for a long time. Dodging a mighty blow from his axe, I launched my piercing arrow and it struck him in the neck. Fatally weakened, he fell to the ground, death rattling in his throat. From that day onward, I was the undisputed lord of the badlands.

"Then I succeeded my father-in-law after his death, ruling the tribes by the sword, enforcing the traditions of the desert. And the days, seasons, and years passed by, one after another. My sons grew into strong men who knew nothing but the wilderness as the place for birth, life, glory, and death. Do you not see, my lord, that I suffered in my estrangement from Egypt? That I was tossed back and forth by horrors and anxieties, and was afflicted by calamities, although I also enjoyed love and the siring of children, reaping glory and happiness along the way. But old age and weakness finally caught up with me, and I conceded authority to my sons. Then I went home to my tent to await my passing.

"In my isolation, heartaches assailed me, and anguish overwhelmed me, as I remembered gorgeous Egypt—the fertile playground of my childhood and youth. Desire disturbed me, and longing beckoned my heart. There appeared before my eyes scenes of the Nile and the luxuriant greenery and the heavenly blue sky and the mighty pyramids and the lofty obelisks, and I feared that death would overtake me while I was in a land other than Egypt.

"So I sent a messenger to you, my lord, and my lord chose to pardon me and to receive me hospitably. I do not wish for more than a quiet corner to live out my old age, until Sinuhe's appointed hour comes round. Then he would be thrown into the embalming tank, and in his sarcophagus, the Book of the Dead—guide to the afterlife—would be laid. The professional women mourners of Egypt would wail over him with their plaintive rhyming cries. . . ."

Pharaoh listened to Sinuhe with excitement and delight. Patting his shoulder gently, he said, "Whatever you want is yours." Then the king summoned one of his chamberlains, who led the prince into his wing of the palace.

Just before evening, a messenger came, saying that it would please the queen if she could meet with him. Immediately, Sinuhe rose to go to her, his aged heart beating hard. Following the messenger, nervous and distracted, he muttered to himself, "O Lord! Is it possible that I will see her once again? Will she really remember me? Will she remember Sinuhe, the young prince and lover?"

He crossed the threshold of her room like a man walking in his sleep. He reached her throne in seconds. Lifting his eyes up to her, he saw the face of his companion, whose youthful bloom the years had withered. Of her former loveliness, only faint traces remained. Bowing to her in reverence, he kissed the hem of her robe. The queen then spoke to him, without concealing her astonishment, "My God, is this truly our Prince Sinuhe?"

The prince smiled without uttering a word. He had not yet recovered himself, when the queen said, "My lord has told me of your conversation. I was impressed by your feats, and the harshness of your struggle, though it took me aback that you had the fortitude to leave your wife and children behind."

"Mercy upon you, my queen," Sinuhe replied. "What remains of my life merely lengthens my torture, while the likes of me would find it unbearable to be buried outside of dear Egypt."

The woman lowered her gaze for a moment, then raising up to him her eyes filled with dreams, she said to him tenderly, "Prince Sinuhe, you have told us your story, but do you know ours? You fled at the time that you learned of Pharaoh's death. You suspected that your rival, who had the upper hand, would not spare your life. You took off with the wind and traversed the deserts of Amora. Did you not know how your flight would injure yourself and those that you love?"

Confusion showed on Sinuhe's face, but he did not break his silence. The queen continued, "Yet how could you know that the heir apparent visited me just before your departure at the head of the campaign in Libya. He said to me: 'Princess, my heart tells me that you have chosen the man that you want. Please answer me truthfully, and I promise you just as truthfully that I will be both contented and loyal. I would never break this vow.' "

Her Majesty grew quiet. Sinuhe queried her with a sigh, "Were you frank with him, my queen?"

She answered by nodding her head, then her breath grew more agitated. Sinuhe, gasping from the forty-year voyage back to his early manhood, pressed her further.

"And what did you tell him?"

"Will it really interest you to know my answer? After a lapse of forty years? And after your children have grown to be chiefs of the tribes of Tonu?"

His exhausted eyes flashed a look of perplexity, then he said with a tremulous voice, "By the Sacred Lord, it matters to me."

She was staring at his face with pleasure and concern, and said, smiling, "How strange this is, O Sinuhe! But you shall have what you want. I will not hold back the answer that you should have heard forty years ago. Senwosret questioned me closely, so I told him that I would grant him whatever I had of fondness and friendship. But as for my heart . . ."

The queen halted for a moment, as Sinuhe again looked up, his beard twitching, shock and dismay bursting on his face. Then she resumed, "As for my heart—I am helpless to control it."

"My Lord," he muttered.

"Yes, that is what I said to Senwosret. He bid me a moving good-bye—and swore that he would remain your brother so long as he breathed.

"But you were hasty, Sinuhe, and ran off with the wind. You strangled our high hopes, and buried our happiness alive. When the news of your vanishing came to me, I could hardly believe it—I nearly died of grief. Afterwards, I lived in seclusion for many long years. Then, at last, life mocked at my sorrows; the love of it freed me from the malaise of pain and despair. I was content with the king as my husband. This is my story, O Sinuhe."

She gazed into his face to see him drop his eyes in mourning; his fingers shook with emotion. She continued to regard him with compassion and joy, and asked herself: "Could it be that the agony of our long-ago love still toys with this ancient heart, so close to its demise?"

Translated by Raymond Stock

Zaabalawi, 1962

While Naguib Mahfouz is thought of primarily as a novelist, with his contemporary Yusuf Idris being regarded as the genius of the short story, Mahfouz contributed no less than sixteen volumes of short stories. Some of his stories, in particular "Zaabalawi" and the short "Half a Day," have made their way into numerous anthologies. The following five stories are drawn from the collection *The Time and the Place*.

Finally I became convinced that I had to find Sheikh Zaabalawi. The first time I had heard his name had been in a song:

Oh what's become of the world, Zaabalawi?
They've turned it upside down and taken away its taste.

It had been a popular song in my childhood, and one day it had occurred to me to demand of my father, in the way children have of asking endless questions:

"Who is Zaabalawi?"

He had looked at me hesitantly as though doubting my ability to understand the answer. However, he had replied, "May his blessing descend upon you, he's a true saint of God, a remover of worries and troubles. Were it not for him I would have died miserably—"

In the years that followed, I heard my father many a time sing the praises of this good saint and speak of the miracles he performed. The days passed and brought with them many illnesses, for each one of which I was able, without too much trouble and at a cost I could afford, to find a cure, until I became afflicted with that illness for which no one possesses a remedy. When I had tried everything in vain and was overcome by despair, I remembered by chance what I had heard in my childhood: Why, I asked myself, should I not seek out Sheikh Zaabalawi? I recollected my father saying that he had made his acquaintance in Khan Gaafar at the house of Sheikh Qamar, one of those sheikhs who practiced law in the religious courts, and so I took myself off to his house. Wishing to make sure that he was still living there, I made inquiries of a vendor of beans whom I found in the lower part of the house.

"Sheikh Qamar!" he said, looking at me in amazement. "He left the quarter ages ago. They say he's now living in Garden City and has his office in al-Azhar Square."

I looked up the office address in the telephone book and immediately set off to the Chamber of Commerce Building, where it was located. On asking to see Sheikh Qamar, I was ushered into a room just as a beautiful woman with a most intoxicating perfume was leaving it. The man received me with a smile and motioned me toward a fine leather-upholstered chair. Despite the thick soles of my shoes, my feet were conscious of the lushness of the costly carpet. The man wore a lounge suit and was smoking a cigar; his manner of sitting was that of someone well satisfied both with himself and with his worldly possessions. The look of warm welcome he gave me left no doubt in my mind that he thought me a prospective client, and I felt acutely embarrassed at encroaching upon his valuable time.

"Welcome!" he said, prompting me to speak.

"I am the son of your old friend Sheikh Ali al-Tatawi," I answered so as to put an end to my equivocal position.

A certain languor was apparent in the glance he cast at me; the languor was not total in that he had not as yet lost all hope in me.

"God rest his soul," he said. "He was a fine man."

The very pain that had driven me to go there now prevailed upon me to stay.

"He told me," I continued, "of a devout saint named Zaabalawi whom he met at Your Honor's. I am in need of him, sir, if he be still in the land of the living."

The languor became firmly entrenched in his eyes, and it would have come as no surprise if he had shown the door to both me and my father's memory.

"That," he said in the tone of one who has made up his mind to terminate the conversation, "was a very long time ago and I scarcely recall him now."

Rising to my feet so as to put his mind at rest regarding my intention of going, I asked, "Was he really a saint?"

"We used to regard him as a man of miracles."

"And where could I find him today?" I asked, making another move toward the door.

"To the best of my knowledge he was living in the Birgawi Residence in al-Azhar," and he applied himself to some papers on his desk with a resolute movement that indicated he would not open his mouth again. I bowed my head in thanks, apologized several times for disturbing him, and left the office, my head so buzzing with embarrassment that I was oblivious to all sounds around me.

I went to the Birgawi Residence, which was situated in a thickly popu-lated quarter. I found that time had so eaten away at the building that nothing was left of it save an antiquated façade and a courtyard that, despite being supposedly in the charge of a caretaker, was being used as a rubbish dump. A small, insignificant fellow, a mere prologue to a man, was using the cov-ered entrance as a place for the sale of old books on theology and mysticism.

When I asked him about Zaabalawi, he peered at me through narrow, inflamed eyes and said in amazement, "Zaabalawi! Good heavens, what a time ago that was! Certainly he used to live in this house when it was habitable. Many were the times he would sit with me talking of bygone days, and I would be blessed by his holy presence. Where, though, is Zaabalawi today?"

He shrugged his shoulders sorrowfully and soon left me, to attend to an approaching customer. I proceeded to make inquiries of many shopkeepers in the district. While I found that a large number of them had never even heard of Zaabalawi, some, though recalling nostalgically the pleasant times they had spent with him, were ignorant of his present whereabouts, while others openly made fun of him, labeled him a charlatan, and advised me to put myself in the hands of a doctor—as though I had not already done so. I therefore had no alternative but to return disconsolately home.

With the passing of days like motes in the air, my pains grew so severe that I was sure I would not be able to hold out much longer. Once again I fell to wondering about Zaabalawi and clutching at the hope his venerable name stirred within me. Then it occurred to me to seek the help of the local sheikh of the district; in fact, I was surprised I had not thought of this to begin with. His office was in the nature of a small shop, except that it contained a desk and a telephone, and I found him sitting at his desk, wearing a jacket over his striped gallabiya. As he did not interrupt his conversation with a man sitting beside him, I stood waiting till the man had gone. The sheikh then looked up at me coldly. I told myself that I should win him over by the usual methods, and it was not long before I had him cheerfully inviting me to sit down.

"I'm in need of Sheikh Zaabalawi," I answered his inquiry as to the purpose of my visit.

He gazed at me with the same astonishment as that shown by those I had previously encountered.

"At least," he said, giving me a smile that revealed his gold teeth, "he is still alive. The devil of it is, though, he has no fixed abode. You might well bump into him as you go out of here, on the other hand you might spend days and months in fruitless searching."

"Even you can't find him!"

"Even I! He's a baffling man, but I thank the Lord that he's still alive!"

He gazed at me intently, and murmured, "It seems your condition is serious."

"Very."

"May God come to your aid! But why don't you go about it systematically?" He spread out a sheet of paper on the desk and drew on it with unexpected speed and skill until he had made a full plan of the district, showing all the various quarters, lanes, alleyways, and squares. He looked at it admiringly and said, "These are dwelling-houses, here is the Quarter of the Perfumers, here the Quarter of the Coppersmiths, the Mousky, the police and fire stations. The drawing is your best guide. Look carefully in the cafés, the places where the dervishes perform their rites, the mosques and prayer-rooms, and the Green Gate, for he may well be concealed among the beggars and be indistinguishable from them. Actually, I myself haven't seen him for years, having been somewhat preoccupied with the cares of the world, and was only brought back by your inquiry to those most exquisite times of my youth."

I gazed at the map in bewilderment. The telephone rang, and he took up the receiver.

"Take it," he told me, generously. "We're at your service."

Folding up the map, I left and wandered off through the quarter, from square to street to alleyway, making inquiries of everyone I felt was familiar with the place. At last the owner of a small establishment for ironing clothes told me, "Go to the calligrapher Hassanein in Umm al-Ghulam—they were friends."

I went to Umm al-Ghulam, where I found old Hassanein working in a deep, narrow shop full of signboards and jars of color. A strange smell, a mixture of glue and perfume, permeated its every corner. Old Hassanein was squatting on a sheepskin rug in front of a board propped against the wall; in the middle of it he had inscribed the word "Allah" in silver lettering. He was engrossed in embellishing the letters with prodigious care. I stood behind him, fearful of disturbing him or breaking the inspiration that flowed to his masterly hand. When my concern at not interrupting him had lasted some time, he suddenly inquired with unaffected gentleness, "Yes?"

Realizing that he was aware of my presence, I introduced myself. "I've been told that Sheikh Zaabalawi is your friend; I'm looking for him," I said.

His hand came to a stop. He scrutinized me in astonishment. "Zaabalawi! God be praised!" he said with a sigh.

"He *is* a friend of yours, isn't he?" I asked eagerly.

"He was, once upon a time. A real man of mystery: he'd visit you so often that people would imagine he was your nearest and dearest, then would disappear as though he'd never existed. Yet saints are not to be blamed."

The spark of hope went out with the suddenness of a lamp snuffed by a power-cut.

"He was so constantly with me," said the man, "that I felt him to be a part of everything I drew. But where is he today?"

"Perhaps he is still alive?"

"He's alive, without a doubt. . . . He had impeccable taste, and it was due to him that I made my most beautiful drawings."

"God knows," I said, in a voice almost stifled by the dead ashes of hope, "how dire my need for him is, and no one knows better than you of the ailments in respect to which he is sought."

"Yes, yes. May God restore you to health. He is in truth, as is said of him, a man, and more. . . ."

Smiling broadly, he added, "And his face possesses an unforgettable beauty. But where is he?"

Reluctantly I rose to my feet, shook hands, and left. I continued wandering eastward and westward through the quarter, inquiring about Zaabalawi from everyone who, by reason of age or experience, I felt might be likely to help me. Eventually I was informed by a vendor of lupine that he had met him a short while ago at the house of Sheikh Gad, the well-known composer. I went to the musician's house in Tabakshiyya, where I found him in a room tastefully furnished in the old style, its walls redolent with history. He was seated on a divan, his famous lute beside him, concealing within itself the most beautiful melodies of our age, while somewhere from within the house came the sound of pestle and mortar and the clamor of children. I immediately greeted him and introduced myself, and was put at my ease by the unaffected way in which he received me. He did not ask, either in words or gesture, what had brought me, and I did not feel that he even harbored any such curiosity. Amazed at his understanding and kindness, which boded well, I said, "O Sheikh Gad, I am an admirer of yours, having long been enchanted by the renderings of your songs."

"Thank you," he said with a smile.

"Please excuse my disturbing you," I continued timidly, "but I was told that Zaabalawi was your friend, and I am in urgent need of him."

"Zaabalawi!" he said, frowning in concentration, "You need him? God be with you, for who knows, O Zaabalawi, where you are."

"Doesn't he visit you?" I asked eagerly.

"He visited me some time ago. He might well come right now; on the other hand I mightn't see him till death!"

I gave an audible sigh and asked, "What made him like that?"

The musician took up his lute. "Such are saints or they would not be saints," he said, laughing.

"Do those who need him suffer as I do?"

"Such suffering is part of the cure!"

He took up the plectrum and began plucking soft strains from the strings. Lost in thought, I followed his movements. Then, as though addressing myself, I said, "So my visit has been in vain."

He smiled, laying his cheek against the side of the lute. "God forgive you," he said, "for saying such a thing of a visit that has caused me to know you and you me!"

I was much embarrassed and said apologetically, "Please forgive me; my feelings of defeat made me forget my manners."

"Do not give in to defeat. This extraordinary man brings fatigue to all who seek him. It was easy enough with him in the old days, when his place of abode was known. Today, though, the world has changed, and after having enjoyed a position attained only by potentates, he is now pursued by the police on a charge of false pretenses. It is therefore no longer an easy matter to reach him, but have patience and be sure that you will do so."

He raised his head from the lute and skillfully fingered the opening bars of a melody. Then he sang:

I make lavish mention, even though I blame myself, of those I love,
For the stories of the beloved are my wine."

With a heart that was weary and listless, I followed the beauty of the melody and the singing.

"I composed the music to this poem in a single night," he told me when he had finished. "I remember that it was the eve of the Lesser Bairam.

Zaabalawi was my guest for the whole of that night, and the poem was of his choosing. He would sit for a while just where you are, then would get up and play with my children as though he were one of them. Whenever I was overcome by weariness or my inspiration failed me, he would punch me playfully in the chest and joke with me, and I would bubble over with melodies, and thus I continued working till I finished the most beautiful piece I have ever composed."

"Does he know anything about music?"

"He is the epitome of things musical. He has an extremely beautiful speaking voice, and you have only to hear him to want to burst into song and to be inspired to creativity. . . ."

"How was it that he cured those diseases before which men are powerless?"

"That is his secret. Maybe you will learn it when you meet him."

But when would that meeting occur? We relapsed into silence, and the hubbub of children once more filled the room.

Again the sheikh began to sing. He went on repeating the words "and I have a memory of her" in different and beautiful variations until the very walls danced in ecstasy. I expressed my wholehearted admiration, and he gave me a smile of thanks. I then got up and asked permission to leave, and he accompanied me to the front door. As I shook him by the hand, he said, "I hear that nowadays he frequents the house of Hagg Wanas al-Damanhouri. Do you know him?"

I shook my head, though a modicum of renewed hope crept into my heart.

"He is a man of private means," the sheikh told me, "who from time to time visits Cairo, putting up at some hotel or other. Every evening, though, he spends at the Negma Bar in Alfi Street."

I waited for nightfall and went to the Negma Bar. I asked a waiter about Hagg Wanas, and he pointed to a corner that was semisecluded because of its position behind a large pillar with mirrors on all four sides. There I saw a man seated alone at a table with two bottles in front of him, one empty, the other two-thirds empty. There were no snacks or food to be seen, and I was sure that I was in the presence of a hardened drinker. He was wearing a loosely flowing silk gallabiya and a carefully wound turban; his legs were stretched out toward the base of the pillar, and as he gazed into the mirror in rapt contentment, the sides of his face, rounded and handsome despite the fact that he was approaching old age, were flushed with wine. I approached quietly till I stood but a few feet away from him. He did not turn toward me or give any indication that he was aware of my presence.

"Good evening, Mr. Wanas," I greeted him cordially.

He turned toward me abruptly, as though my voice had roused him from slumber, and glared at me in disapproval. I was about to explain what had brought me when he interrupted in an almost imperative tone of voice that was nonetheless not devoid of an extraordinary gentleness, "First, please sit down, and second, please get drunk!"

I opened my mouth to make my excuses, but, stopping up his ears with his fingers, he said, "Not a word till you do what I say."

I realized I was in the presence of a capricious drunkard and told myself that I should at least humor him a bit. "Would you permit me to ask one question?" I said with a smile, sitting down.

Without removing his hands from his ears he indicated the bottle. "When engaged in a drinking bout like this, I do not allow any conversation between myself and another unless, like me, he is drunk, otherwise all propriety is lost and mutual comprehension is rendered impossible."

I made a sign indicating that I did not drink.

"That's your lookout," he said offhandedly. "And that's my condition!"

He filled me a glass, which I meekly took and drank. No sooner had the wine settled in my stomach than it seemed to ignite. I waited patiently till I had grown used to its ferocity, and said, "It's very strong, and I think the time has come for me to ask you about—"

Once again, however, he put his fingers in his ears. "I shan't listen to you until you're drunk!"

He filled up my glass for the second time. I glanced at it in trepidation; then, overcoming my inherent objection, I drank it down at a gulp. No sooner had the wine come to rest inside me than I lost all willpower. With the third glass, I lost my memory, and with the fourth the future vanished. The world turned round about me, and I forgot why I had gone there. The man leaned toward me attentively, but I saw him—saw everything—as a mere meaningless series of colored planes. I don't know how long it was before my head sank down onto the arm of the chair and I plunged into deep sleep. During it, I had a beautiful dream the like of which I had never experienced. I dreamed that I was in an immense garden surrounded on all sides by luxuriant trees, and the sky was nothing but stars seen between the entwined branches, all enfolded in an atmosphere like that of sunset or a sky overcast with cloud. I was lying on a small hummock of jasmine petals, more of which fell upon me like rain, while the lucent spray of a fountain unceasingly sprinkled the crown of my head and my temples. I was in a state of deep contentedness, of ecstatic serenity. An orchestra of warbling and cooing played in my ear. There was an extraordinary sense of harmony between me and my inner self, and between the two of us and the world, everything being in its rightful place, without discord or distortion. In the whole world there was no single reason for speech or movement, for the universe moved in a rapture of ecstasy. This lasted but a short while. When I opened my eyes, consciousness struck at me like a policeman's fist, and I saw Wanas al-Damanhouri peering at me with concern. Only a few drowsy customers were left in the bar.

"You have slept deeply," said my companion. "You were obviously hungry for sleep."

I rested my heavy head in the palms of my hands. When I took them away in astonishment and looked down at them, I found that they glistened with drops of water.

"My head's wet," I protested.

"Yes, my friend tried to rouse you," he answered quietly.

"Somebody saw me in this state?"

"Don't worry, he is a good man. Have you not heard of Sheikh Zaabalawi?"

"Zaabalawi!" I exclaimed, jumping to my feet.

"Yes," he answered in surprise. "What's wrong?"

"Where is he?"

"I don't know where he is now. He was here and then he left."

I was about to run off in pursuit but found I was more exhausted than I had imagined. Collapsed over the table, I cried out in despair, "My sole reason for coming to you was to meet him! Help me to catch up with him or send someone after him."

The man called a vendor of prawns and asked him to seek out the sheikh and bring him back. Then he turned to me. "I didn't realize you were afflicted. I'm very sorry. . . ."

"You wouldn't let me speak," I said irritably.

"What a pity! He was sitting on this chair beside you the whole time. He was playing with a string of jasmine petals he had around his neck, a gift from one of his admirers, then, taking pity on you, he began to sprinkle some water on your head to bring you around."

"Does he meet you here every night?" I asked, my eyes not leaving the doorway through which the vendor of prawns had left.

"He was with me tonight, last night, and the night before that, but before that I hadn't seen him for a month."

"Perhaps he will come tomorrow," I answered with a sigh.

"Perhaps."

"I am willing to give him any money he wants."

Wanas answered sympathetically, "The strange thing is that he is not open to such temptations, yet he will cure you if you meet him."

"Without charge?"

"Merely on sensing that you love him."

The vendor of prawns returned, having failed in his mission.

I recovered some of my energy and left the bar, albeit unsteadily. At every street corner I called out "Zaabalawi!" in the vague hope that I would be rewarded with an answering shout. The street boys turned contemptuous eyes on me till I sought refuge in the first available taxi.

The following evening I stayed up with Wanas al-Damanhouri till dawn, but the sheikh did not put in an appearance. Wanas informed me that he would be going away to the country and would not be returning to Cairo until he had sold the cotton crop.

I must wait, I told myself; I must train myself to be patient. Let me content myself with having made certain of the existence of Zaabalawi, and even of his affection for me, which encourages me to think that he will be prepared to cure me if a meeting takes place between us.

Sometimes, however, the long delay wearied me. I would become beset by despair and would try to persuade myself to dismiss him from my mind completely. How many weary people in this life know him not or regard him as a mere myth! Why, then, should I torture myself about him in this way?

No sooner, however, did my pains force themselves upon me than I would again begin to think about him, asking myself when I would be fortunate enough to meet him. The fact that I ceased to have any news of Wanas and was told he had gone to live abroad did not deflect me from my purpose; the truth of the matter was that I had become fully convinced that I had to find Zaabalawi.

Yes, I have to find Zaabalawi.

Translated by Denys Johnson-Davies

The Conjurer Made Off with the Dish, 1969

"The time has come for you to be useful," said my mother to me. And she slipped her hand into her pocket, saying, "Take this piaster and go off and buy some beans. Don't play on the way and keep away from the carts."

I took the dish, put on my clogs, and went out, humming a tune. Finding a crowd in front of the bean seller, I waited until I discovered a way through to the marble counter.

"A piaster's worth of beans, mister," I called out in my shrill voice.

He asked me impatiently, "Beans alone? With oil? With cooking butter?"

I did not answer, and he said roughly, "Make way for someone else."

I withdrew, overcome by embarrassment, and returned home defeated.

"Returning with the dish empty?" my mother shouted at me. "What did you do—spill the beans or lose the piaster, you naughty boy?"

"Beans alone? With oil? With cooking butter?—you didn't tell me," I protested.

"Stupid boy! What do you eat every morning?"

"I don't know."

"You good-for-nothing, ask him for beans with oil."

I went off to the man and said, "A piaster's worth of beans with oil, mister."

With a frown of impatience he asked, "Linseed oil? Vegetable oil? Olive oil?"

I was taken aback and again made no answer.

"Make way for someone else," he shouted at me.

I returned in a rage to my mother, who called out in astonishment, "You've come back empty-handed—no beans and no oil."

"Linseed oil? Vegetable oil? Olive oil? Why didn't you tell me?" I said angrily.

"Beans with oil means beans with linseed oil."

"How should I know?"

"You're a good-for-nothing, and he's a tiresome man—tell him beans with linseed oil."

I went off quickly and called out to the man while still some yards from his shop, "Beans with linseed oil, mister."

"Put the piaster on the counter," he said, plunging the ladle into the pot.

I put my hand into my pocket but did not find the piaster. I searched for it anxiously. I turned my pocket inside out but found no trace of it. The man withdrew the ladle empty, saying with disgust, "You've lost the piaster— you're not a boy to be depended on."

"I haven't lost it," I said, looking under my feet and round about me. "It was in my pocket all the time."

"Make way for someone else and stop bothering me."

I returned to my mother with an empty dish.

"Good grief, are you an idiot, boy?"

"The piaster . . ."

"What of it?"

"It's not in my pocket."

"Did you buy sweets with it?"

"I swear I didn't."

"How did you lose it?"

"I don't know."

"Do you swear by the Quran you didn't buy anything with it?"

"I swear."

"Is there a hole in your pocket?"

"No, there isn't."

"Maybe you gave it to the man the first time or the second."

"Maybe."

"Are you sure of nothing?"

"I'm hungry."

She clapped her hands together in a gesture of resignation.

"Never mind," she said. "I'll give you another piaster but I'll take it out of your money box, and if you come back with an empty dish, I'll break your head."

I went off at a run, dreaming of a delicious breakfast. At the turning leading to the alleyway where the bean seller was, I saw a crowd of children and heard merry, festive sounds. My feet dragged as my heart was pulled toward them. At least let me have a fleeting glance. I slipped in among them and found the conjurer looking straight at me. A stupefying joy overwhelmed me; I was completely taken out of myself. With the whole of my being I became involved in the tricks of the rabbits and the eggs, and the snakes and the ropes. When the man came up to collect money, I drew back mumbling, "I haven't got any money."

He rushed at me savagely, and I escaped only with difficulty. I ran off, my back almost broken by his blow, and yet I was utterly happy as I made my way to the seller of beans.

"Beans with linseed oil for a piaster, mister," I said.

He went on looking at me without moving, so I repeated my request.

"Give me the dish," he demanded angrily.

The dish! Where was the dish? Had I dropped it while running? Had the conjurer made off with it?

"Boy, you're out of your mind!"

I retraced my steps, searching along the way for the lost dish. The place where the conjurer had been, I found empty, but the voices of children led me to him in a nearby lane. I moved around the circle. When the conjurer spotted me, he shouted out threateningly, "Pay up or you'd better scram."

"The dish!" I called out despairingly.

"What dish, you little devil?"

"Give me back the dish."

"Scram or I'll make you into food for snakes."

He had stolen the dish, yet fearfully I moved away out of sight and wept in grief. Whenever a passerby asked me why I was crying, I would reply, "The conjurer made off with the dish."

Through my misery I became aware of a voice saying, "Come along and watch!"

I looked behind me and saw a peep show had been set up. I saw dozens of children hurrying toward it and taking it in turns to stand in front of the peepholes, while the man began his tantalizing commentary to the pictures.

"There you've got the gallant knight and the most beautiful of all ladies, Zainat al-Banat."

My tears dried up, and I gazed in fascination at the box, completely forgetting the conjurer and the dish. Unable to overcome the temptation, I paid over the piaster and stood in front of the peephole next to a girl who was standing in front of the other one, and enchanting picture stories flowed across our vision. When I came back to my own world I realized I had lost both the piaster and the dish, and there was no sign of the conjurer. However, I gave no thought to the loss, so taken up was I with the pictures of chivalry, love, and deeds of daring. I forgot my hunger. I forgot even the fear of what threatened me at home. I took a few paces back so as to lean against the ancient wall of what had once been a treasury and the chief cadi's seat of office, and gave myself up wholly to my reveries. For a long while I dreamed of chivalry, of Zainat al-Banat and the ghoul. In my dream I spoke aloud, giving meaning to my words with gestures. Thrusting home the imaginary lance, I said, "Take that, O ghoul, right in the heart!"

"And he raised Zainat al-Banat up behind him on the horse," came back a gentle voice.

I looked to my right and saw the young girl who had been beside me at the performance. She was wearing a dirty dress and colored clogs and was playing with her long plait of hair. In her other hand were the red-and-white sweets called 'lady's fleas,' which she was leisurely sucking. We exchanged glances, and I lost my heart to her.

"Let's sit down and rest," I said to her.

She appeared to go along with my suggestion, so I took her by the arm and we went through the gateway of the ancient wall and sat down on a step of its stairway that went nowhere, a stairway that rose up until it ended in a platform behind which there could be seen the blue sky and minarets. We sat in silence, side by side. I pressed her hand, and we sat on in silence, not knowing what to say. I experienced feelings that were new, strange, and obscure. Putting my face close to hers, I breathed in the natural smell of her hair mingled with an odor of dust, and the fragrance of breath mixed with the aroma of sweets. I kissed her lips. I swallowed my saliva, which had taken on a sweetness from the dissolved 'lady's fleas.' I put my arm around her, without her uttering a word, kissing her cheek and lips. Her lips grew still as they received the kiss, then went back to sucking at the sweets. At last she decided to get up. I seized her arm anxiously. "Sit down," I said.

"I'm going," she replied simply.

"Where to?" I asked dejectedly.

"To the midwife Umm Ali," and she pointed to a house on the ground floor of which was a small ironing shop.

"Why?"

"To tell her to come quickly."

"Why?"

"My mother's crying in pain at home. She told me to go to the midwife Umm Ali and tell her to come along quickly."

"And you'll come back after that?"

She nodded her head in assent and went off. Her mentioning her mother reminded me of my own, and my heart missed a beat. Getting up from the ancient stairway, I made my way back home. I wept out loud, a tried method by which I would defend myself. I expected she would come to me, but she did not. I wandered from the kitchen to the bedroom but found no trace of her. Where had my mother gone? When would she return? I was fed up with being in the empty house. A good idea occurred to me. I took a dish from the kitchen and a piaster from my savings and went off immediately to the seller of beans. I found him asleep on a bench outside the shop, his face covered by his arm. The pots of beans had vanished and the long-necked bottles of oil had been put back on the shelf and the marble counter had been washed down.

"Mister," I whispered, approaching.

Hearing nothing but his snoring, I touched his shoulder. He raised his arm in alarm and looked at me through reddened eyes.

"Mister."

"What do you want?" he asked roughly, becoming aware of my presence and recognizing me.

"A piaster's worth of beans with linseed oil."

"Eh?"

"I've got the piaster and I've got the dish."

"You're crazy, boy," he shouted at me. "Get out or I'll bash your brains in."

When I did not move, he pushed me so violently I went sprawling onto my back. I got up painfully, struggling to hold back the crying that was twisting my lips. My hands were clenched, one on the dish and the other on the piaster. I threw him an angry look. I thought about returning home with my hopes dashed, but dreams of heroism and valor altered my plan of action. Resolutely I made a quick decision and with all my strength threw the dish at him. It flew through the air and struck him on the head, while I took to my heels, heedless of everything. I was convinced I had killed him, just as the knight had killed the ghoul. I did not stop running till I was near the ancient wall. Panting, I looked behind me but saw no signs of any pursuit. I stopped to get my breath, then asked myself what I should do now that the second dish was lost? Something warned me not to return home directly, and soon I had given myself over to a wave of indifference that bore me off where it willed. It meant a beating, neither more nor less, on my return, so let me put it off for a time. Here was the piaster in my hand, and I could have some sort of enjoyment with it before being punished. I decided to pretend I had forgotten I had done anything wrong—but where was the conjurer, where was the peep show? I looked everywhere for them to no avail.

Worn out by this fruitless searching, I went off to the ancient stairway to keep my appointment. I sat down to wait, imagining to myself the meeting. I yearned for another kiss redolent with the fragrance of sweets. I admitted to myself that the little girl had given me lovelier sensations than I had ever experienced. As I waited and dreamed, a whispering sound came from behind me. I climbed the stairs cautiously, and at the final landing I lay down flat on my face in order to see what was beyond, without anyone being able to notice me. I saw some ruins surrounded by a high wall, the last of what remained of the treasury and the chief cadi's seat of office. Directly under the stairs sat a man and a woman, and it was from them that the whispering came. The man looked like a tramp; the woman like one of those Gypsies that tend sheep. A suspicious inner voice told me that their meeting was similar to the one I had had. Their lips and the looks they exchanged spoke of this, but they showed astonishing expertise in the unimaginable things they did. My gaze became rooted upon them with curiosity, surprise, pleasure, and a certain amount of disquiet. At last they sat down side by side, neither of them taking any notice of the other. After quite a while the man said, "The money!"

"You're never satisfied," she said irritably.

Spitting on the ground, he said, "You're crazy."

"You're a thief."

He slapped her hard with the back of his hand, and she gathered up a handful of earth and threw it in his face. Then, his face soiled with dirt, he sprang at her, fastening his fingers on her windpipe, and a bitter fight ensued. In vain she gathered all her strength to escape from his grip. Her voice failed her, her eyes bulged out of their sockets, while her feet struck out at the air. In dumb terror, I stared at the scene till I saw a thread of blood trickling down from her nose. A scream escaped from my mouth. Before the man raised his head, I had crawled backward. Descending the stairs at a jump, I raced off like mad to wherever my legs might carry me. I did not stop running till I was breathless. Gasping for breath, I was quite unaware of my surroundings, but when I came to myself I found I was under a raised vault at the middle of a crossroads. I had never set foot there before and had no idea of where I was in relation to our quarter. On both sides sat sightless beggars, and crossing from all directions were people who paid attention to no one. In terror I realized I had lost my way and that countless difficulties lay in wait for me before I found my way home. Should I resort to asking one of the passersby to direct me? What, though, would happen if chance should lead me to a man like the seller of beans or the tramp of the waste plot? Would a miracle come about whereby I would see my mother approaching so that I could eagerly hurry toward her? Should I try to make my own way, wandering about till I came across some familiar landmark that would indicate the direction I should take?

I told myself that I should be resolute and make a quick decision. The day was passing, and soon mysterious darkness would descend.

Translated by Denys Johnson-Davies

The Answer is No, 1989

The important piece of news that the new headmaster had arrived spread through the school. She heard of it in the women teachers' common room as she was casting a final glance at the day's lessons. There was no getting away from joining the other teachers in congratulating him, and from shaking him by the hand too. A shudder passed through her body, but it was unavoidable.

"They speak highly of his ability," said a colleague of hers. "And they talk too of his strictness."

It had always been a possibility that might occur, and now it had. Her pretty face paled, and a staring look came to her wide black eyes.

When the time came, the teachers went in single file, decorously attired, to his open room. He stood behind his desk as he received the men and women. He was of medium height, with a tendency to portliness, and had a spherical face, hooked nose, and bulging eyes; the first thing that could be seen of him was a thick, puffed-up mustache, arched like a foam-laden wave. She advanced with her eyes fixed on his chest. Avoiding his gaze, she stretched out her hand. What was she to say? Just what the others had said? However, she kept silent, uttered not a word. What, she wondered, did his eyes express? His rough hand shook hers, and he said in a gruff voice, "Thanks." She turned elegantly and moved off.

She forgot her worries through her daily tasks, though she did not look in good shape. Several of the girls remarked, "Miss is in a bad mood." When she returned to her home at the beginning of the Pyramids Road, she changed her clothes and sat down to eat with her mother. "Everything all right?" inquired her mother, looking her in the face.

"Badran, Badran Badawi," she said briefly. "Do you remember him? He's been appointed our headmaster."

"Really!"

Then, after a moment of silence, she said, "It's of no importance at all—it's an old and long-forgotten story."

After eating, she took herself off to her study to rest for a while before correcting some exercise books. She had forgotten him completely. No, not completely. How could he be forgotten completely? When he had first come to give her a private lesson in mathematics, she was fourteen years of age. In fact not quite fourteen. He had been twenty-five years older, the same age as her father. She had said to her mother, "His appearance is a mess, but he explains things well." And her mother had said, "We're not concerned with what he looks like; what's important is how he explains things."

He was an amusing person, and she got on well with him and benefited from his knowledge. How, then, had it happened? In her innocence she had not noticed any change in his behavior to put her on her guard. Then one day he had been left on his own with her, her father having gone to her aunt's clinic. She had not the slightest doubts about a man she regarded as a second father. How, then, had it happened? Without love or desire on her part the thing had happened. She had asked in terror about what had occurred, and he had told her, "Don't be frightened or sad. Keep it to yourself and I'll come and propose to you the day you come of age."

And he had kept his promise and had come to ask for her hand. By then she had attained a degree of maturity that gave her an understanding of the dimensions of her tragic position. She had found that she had no love or respect for him and that he was as far as he could be from her dreams and from the ideas she had formed of what constituted an ideal and moral person. But what was to be done? Her father had passed away two years ago, and her mother had been taken aback by the forwardness of the man.

However, she had said to her, "I know your attachment to your personal independence, so I leave the decision to you."

She had been conscious of the critical position she was in. She had either to accept or to close the door forever. It was the sort of situation that could force her into something she detested. She was the rich, beautiful girl, a byword in Abbasiyya for her nobility of character, and now here she was struggling helplessly in a well-sprung trap, while he looked down at her with rapacious eyes. Just as she had hated his strength, so too did she hate her own weakness. To have abused her innocence was one thing, but for him to have the upper hand now that she was fully in possession of her faculties was something else. He had said, "So here I am, making good my promise because I love you." He had also said, "I know of your love of teaching, and you will complete your studies at the College of Science."

She had felt such anger as she had never felt before. She had rejected coercion in the same way as she rejected ugliness. It had meant little to her to sacrifice marriage. She had welcomed being on her own, for solitude accompanied by self-respect was not loneliness. She had also guessed he was after her money. She had told her mother quite straightforwardly, "No," to which her mother had replied, "I am astonished you did not make this decision from the first moment."

The man had blocked her way outside and said, "How can you refuse? Don't you realize the outcome?" And she had replied with an asperity he had not expected, "For me any outcome is preferable to being married to you."

After finishing her studies, she had wanted something to do to fill her spare time, so she had worked as a teacher. Chances to marry had come time after time, but she had turned her back on them all.

"Does no one please you?" her mother asked her.

"I know what I'm doing," she had said gently.

"But time is going by."

"Let it go as it pleases, I am content."

Day by day she becomes older. She avoids love, fears it. With all her strength she hopes that life will pass calmly, peacefully, rather than happily. She goes on persuading herself that happiness is not confined to love and motherhood. Never has she regretted her firm decision. Who knows what the morrow holds? But she was certainly unhappy that he should again make his appearance in her life, that she would be dealing with him day after day, and that he would be making of the past a living and painful present.

Then, the first time he was alone with her in his room, he asked her, "How are you?"

She answered coldly, "I'm fine."

He hesitated slightly before inquiring, "Have you not . . . I mean, did you get married?"

In the tone of someone intent on cutting short a conversation, she said, "I told you, I'm fine."

Translated by Denys Johnson-Davies

Half a Day, 1989

I proceeded alongside my father, clutching his right hand, running to keep up with the long strides he was taking. All my clothes were new: the black shoes, the green school uniform, and the red tarboosh. My delight in my new clothes, however, was not altogether unmarred, for this was no feast day but the day on which I was to be cast into school for the first time.

My mother stood at the window watching our progress, and I would turn toward her from time to time, as though appealing for help. We walked along a street lined with gardens; on both sides were extensive fields planted with crops, prickly pears, henna trees, and a few date palms.

"Why school?" I challenged my father openly. "I shall never do anything to annoy you."

"I'm not punishing you," he said, laughing. "School's not a punishment. It's the factory that makes useful men out of boys. Don't you want to be like your father and brothers?"

I was not convinced. I did not believe there was really any good to be had in tearing me away from the intimacy of my home and throwing me into this building that stood at the end of the road like some huge, high-walled fortress, exceedingly stern and grim.

When we arrived at the gate we could see the courtyard, vast and crammed full of boys and girls. "Go in by yourself," said my father, "and join them. Put a smile on your face and be a good example to others."

I hesitated and clung to his hand, but he gently pushed me from him. "Be a man," he said. "Today you truly begin life. You will find me waiting for you when it's time to leave."

I took a few steps, then stopped and looked but saw nothing. Then the faces of boys and girls came into view. I did not know a single one of them, and none of them knew me. I felt I was a stranger who had lost his way. But glances of curiosity were directed toward me, and one boy approached and asked, "Who brought you?"

"My father," I whispered.

"My father's dead," he said quite simply.

I did not know what to say. The gate was closed, letting out a pitiable screech. Some of the children burst into tears. The bell rang. A lady came along, followed by a group of men. The men began sorting us into ranks. We were formed into an intricate pattern in the great courtyard surrounded on three sides by high buildings of several floors; from each floor we were overlooked by a long balcony roofed in wood.

"This is your new home," said the woman. "Here too there are mothers and fathers. Here there is everything that is enjoyable and beneficial to knowledge and religion. Dry your tears and face life joyfully."

We submitted to the facts, and this submission brought a sort of contentment. Living beings were drawn to other living beings, and from the first moments my heart made friends with such boys as were to be my friends and fell in love with such girls as I was to be in love with, so that it seemed my misgivings had had no basis. I had never imagined school would have this rich variety. We played all sorts of different games: swings, the vaulting horse, ball games. In the music room we chanted our first songs. We also had our first introduction to language. We saw a globe of the Earth, which revolved and showed the various continents and countries. We started learning the numbers. The story of the Creator of the universe was read to us, we were told of His present world and of His Hereafter, and we heard examples of what He said. We ate delicious food, took a little nap, and woke up to go on with friendship and love, play and learning.

As our path revealed itself to us, however, we did not find it as totally sweet and unclouded as we had presumed. Dust-laden winds and unexpected accidents came about suddenly, so we had to be watchful, at the ready, and very patient. It was not all a matter of playing and fooling around. Rivalries could bring about pain and hatred or give rise to fighting. And while the lady would sometimes smile, she would often scowl and scold. Even more frequently she would resort to physical punishment.

In addition, the time for changing one's mind was over and gone and there was no question of ever returning to the paradise of home. Nothing lay ahead of us but exertion, struggle, and perseverance. Those who were able took advantage of the opportunities for success and happiness that presented themselves amid the worries.

The bell rang announcing the passing of the day and the end of work. The throngs of children rushed toward the gate, which was opened again. I bade farewell to friends and sweethearts and passed through the gate. I peered around but found no trace of my father, who had promised to be there. I stepped aside to wait. When I had waited for a long time without avail, I decided to return home on my own. After I had taken a few steps, a middle-aged man passed by, and I realized at once that I knew him. He came toward me, smiling, and shook me by the hand, saying, "It's a long time since we last met—how are you?"

With a nod of my head, I agreed with him and in turn asked, "And you, how are you?"

"As you can see, not all that good, the Almighty be praised!"

Again he shook me by the hand and went off. I proceeded a few steps, then came to a startled halt. Good Lord! Where was the street lined with gardens? Where had it disappeared to? When did all these vehicles invade it? And when did all these hordes of humanity come to rest upon its surface? How did these hills of refuse come to cover its sides? And where were the fields that bordered it? High buildings had taken over, the street surged with children, and disturbing noises shook the air. At various points stood conjurers showing off their tricks and making snakes appear from baskets. Then there was a band announcing the opening of a circus, with clowns and weight lifters walking in front. A line of trucks carrying central security troops crawled majestically by. The siren of a fire engine shrieked, and it was not clear how the vehicle would cleave its way to reach the blazing fire. A battle raged between a taxi driver and his passenger, while the passenger's wife called out for help and no one answered. Good God! I was in a daze. My head spun. I almost went crazy. How could all this have happened in half a day, between early morning and sunset? I would find the answer at home with my father. But where was my home? I could see only tall buildings and hordes of people. I hastened on to the crossroads between the gardens and Abu Khoda. I had to cross Abu Khoda to reach my house, but the stream of cars would not let up. The fire engine's siren was shrieking at full pitch as it moved at a snail's pace, and I said to myself, "Let the fire take its pleasure in what it consumes." Extremely irritated, I wondered when I would be able to cross. I stood there a long time, until the young lad employed at the ironing shop on the corner came up to me. He stretched out his arm and said gallantly, "Grandpa, let me take you across."

Translated by Denys Johnson-Davies

A Long-term Plan, 1989

Yesterday the challenges were hunger and utter destitution; today the challenge is excessive wealth. An ancient house for half a million. Isam al-Baqli was born again, born again at seventy.

He enjoyed looking at his image in the old mirror: a decrepit image ravaged by time, hunger, and afflictions; the face a mold of protruding bones and repugnantly tanned skin, a narrow sunken forehead, and lackluster eyes with but a few lashes remaining; black front teeth and no molars; and a skinny, wrinkled neck. What is left of life after seventy? Yet despite everything the fortune that had alighted upon him carried an intoxication that would not evaporate. Innumerable things must be achieved. Isam al-Baqli, indigent loafer, was now Isam al-Baqli, millionaire. All those old friends who were still in the land of the living were exclaiming, "Have you heard what's happened to Isam al-Baqli?" "What's happened to the layabout?" "The house has been bought by one of those big new companies for half a million." "Half a million!" I swear it by the Quran!"

Consternation spread through Sakakini, Qubeisi, and Abbasiyya like a hurricane. The house, with its spacious courtyard, faced onto Qushtumur Street, He had inherited it from his mother, who had passed on ten years ago after old age had turned her into a wreck. She had clung doggedly to life until the threads had been ripped to pieces and she had tumbled down. He had not grieved for her—life had accustomed him not to grieve for anything.

The family had had nothing except for his mother's small pension and the roof over their heads. He had had no success at school, had learned no trade, had never done any work—a good-for-nothing loafer. He might win a few piasters at backgammon through cheating and the indulgence of numerous friends won at school, or friends who had been neighbors in the days of childhood, boyhood, and youth. He possessed a certain charm that made amends for his many bad attributes and made one forgive him his faults, and his extreme wretchedness and the hopelessness of his situation always excited people's sympathy. His father had been an employee in the post office, and his mother had inherited the one-story Qushtumur house with its spacious and neglected courtyard. He was entitled to say that he was the son of a good family but had been unlucky, though the fact was that he was stupid, lazy, and ill-mannered, and it was not long before he was expelled from school. Practically his whole life was spent in the Isis Café, either in debt or in the process of settling his debts through cheating and the generosity of friends. His friend the lawyer Othman al-Qulla thought about taking him into his office on Army Square, but al-Baqli, with his absolute loathing for work, refused.

When left on his own after his friends had gone off to their jobs, he would spend his time indolently daydreaming. At election festivities and at weddings and funerals, he would indulge himself a little. His whole life he had lived off his charm and his friends' generosity; he made a profession of poking fun, singing, dancing, and cracking jokes in order to earn himself a meal of beans, a piece of sweet basbousa, or a couple of drags of hashish.

His natural impulses had remained starved, repressed, crazed. The Qushtumur house knew no food but beans (and the various dishes made from beans), eggplant, and lentils. As for his dreams, they revolved around fantasies of mysterious banquets and repressed sex. There were stories about his affairs with widows, divorcees, and married women too, but no one believed him, though no one called him a liar. The story everyone did believe was of his affair with a widowed servant woman ten years his senior, an affair that had quickly turned to discord and strife when it became clear that she was of a mind to marry him. In fact she had also stipulated that he find himself a job because, as the saying goes, idle hands are unclean. The affair broke up after a row in which humiliating blows were exchanged. That was the only real affair he had had, and his neighbor Mr. Othman al-Qulla had been a witness to the fight and had recounted it at the café. "You missed a scene better than a circus. A woman as fat as a sack of coal bawling out our dear friend al-Baqli and making him a public spectacle in the courtyard of his gracious house and within sight and earshot of his gracious and dismayed mother. The battle wasn't over till he was at his last gasp and some kind folk had intervened—when right away a new battle started up with his mother herself!"

Apart from that dismal experience, he would become boggle-eyed as he gawked at the women walking in the street, his heart suffering emotional pain as his stomach suffered hunger. He found no one but his mother on whom to vent his fury and frustration, despite her great love for him, the love of an old woman for an only son. Whenever she urged him to take a job or pull himself together, he would challenge her, "And when are you going to depart this world?"

"May God forgive you," she would say with a smile. "And what would you do if my pension was no longer available to you?"

"I'd sell the house."

"You wouldn't find anyone to buy it for more than five hundred pounds, which you'd fritter away in a couple of months, and you'd then take up begging."

He never said a kind word to her. His friends advised him to change his manner so he would not kill her off with worry and grief and actually expose himself to beggary. They reminded him of God's words and of what the Prophet had said about respect for one's parents, but his feeling of utter hopelessness had plucked out the roots of faith from a heart brimful with hunger and afflictions. He stuck to his scoffing, embittered attitude toward the events that passed by him, such as the battles between the political parties and the World War, calling down upon the world, with exaggerated mockery and scorn, yet more ruin and destruction. His mother completely despaired of him and resigned herself to the will of God. Sometimes, overwhelmed by distress, she would say, "Why do you repay my love with disrespect?"

And he would say derisively, "One of the causes of ill-fortune in this world is that some people live longer than necessary."

The cost of living continued to rise. Was there to be further deprivation? And so he suggested to his mother that he should take in a person, or a family, as lodgers in his bedroom and that he should sleep on the couch in her room. "And open our house to strangers!" cried his mother in disbelief.

"Better than dying of hunger," he shouted at her. He cast a glance at the courtyard of the house and muttered, "It's like a football ground and it's good for nothing."

An agent brought along a student from the country, who took the room for a pound. Friends made a joke of the incident and said that the Qushtumur house had become a boardinghouse, and they gave his mother the name "Madame al-Baqli." But he did not try to evade their ridicule and would sing "Days arrive when a man of breeding is humiliated."

Unlike many he made light of the air raids. He never responded to the siren—he would not leave his seat at the café and did not know the way to the shelter. He did not mind this. What he did mind was that life was rushing past him and he was approaching his forties without having enjoyed a decent meal or a beautiful woman. He had not even been affected by the

Revolution. "It seems," he had remarked ironically, "that this Revolution is directed against us landlords!"

He never in his life read a newspaper, and got his information haphazardly at the gatherings of his friends. He became older, passed fifty. His mother became advanced in years; she grew frail and began to lose interest in things. She became critically ill. A doctor friend of his examined her and diagnosed a heart condition and prescribed medicines and rest. Rest, however, was out of the question, and medicines not feasible. In the meantime he continued to wonder how he would make out if he were to be deprived of her pension. Hour by hour she drew nearer to death, until one morning he woke up to find her dead. He looked at her for a long time before covering her face. He felt that he was recollecting dimmed memories from a distant past and that he was compelled to desist from his sarcasm and to recognize that that particular moment of the morning was a sad and melancholy one.

Right away he sought out the richest of his friends, Mr. Nuh, a dealer in property, who undertook to make the necessary arrangements for the burial of the deceased, and who also warned him against selling the house if he should find himself after a while down and out in the street. Isam al-Baqli wondered, though, how long cheating at backgammon and the letting out of the room would support him. Might there not be too a limit to one's friends' generosity? He made a venture into begging in the outskirts of the city, and it was not a barren exercise.

Days followed one upon the other, one leader died and another took his place, and then the 'open-door' policy came in when he was knocking on seventy, his seventieth year of desperation and the squandering of life. The cost of living continued to rise in real earnest, and the scales wavered perilously. Begging was no longer of any avail, the generosity of friends was suddenly cut off (some of his friends had, for his bad luck, departed this world, while the remainder had betaken themselves to a quiet old age in which they were happy to sit around and chat), and he plunged headlong into the abyss of ruin. What a wretched, desperate old man he was!

Then one day the darkness of his existence dissolved to reveal the face of the broker making his descent on angelic wings straight down from the heavens. In the presence of his two friends, the lawyer and the property dealer, the transaction was concluded and the fabulous sum deposited in the bank. The three of them then sat in a low-class café on al-Azhar Street, a café whose unpretentiousness was in keeping with the wretched appearance of the millionaire. Isam al-Baqli gave a deep sigh of satisfaction that dispensed with any words. For the first time in his life he was totally happy. Yet, feeling at a loss, he said, "But don't you two leave me on my own."

"From today on you're not in need of anyone," said Othman al-Qulla, the lawyer, laughing.

But Mr. Nuh said, "He's mad and needs someone to guide him at every step."

"You two," said al-Baqli gratefully, "are the best persons I've known in my life."

"There are certain priorities," said Mr. Nuh, "before we get down to any work—things that can't be put off. First and foremost, you must go to the Turkish baths and get rid of all that accumulated dirt so that you can show your true self."

"I'm afraid they won't know me at the bank . . ."

"And have a haircut and a shave, and today we'll buy you a ready-made suit and other clothes so that you can put up at a decent hotel without arousing suspicion."

"Shall I stay at a hotel permanently?"

"If you want to," said the lawyer. "You'll find full service and everything. . . ."

"A flat also has its merits," said Mr. Nuh.

"But a flat's not complete without a bride!" exclaimed al-Baqli.

"A bride?"

"Why not? I'll not be the first or last bridegroom at seventy!"

"It's a problem."

"Don't forget the bridegroom's a millionaire."

"That's a strong incentive, but only to the unscrupulous. . . ." said the lawyer, laughing.

"Scrupulous or not—it's all one in the end!" said al-Baqli scornfully.

"No, you might find yourself back at begging quicker than you imagined," said Nuh.

"Let's put that off for the time being," said the lawyer.

"The question of a woman cannot be put off," said Isam al-Baqli, "It's more important than the ready-made suit."

"There are plenty of opportunities, and nightclubs galore."

"My need of the two of you in this respect is particularly urgent."

"But we said goodbye to riotous living ages ago."

"How can I get along on my own?"

"Someone accompanied by money is never alone."

"We'll have another session," said Mr. Nuh, "after giving thought to the investing of the fortune. It would be wise to spend from the income and not from the capital."

"Remember," protested al-Baqli, "that I'm in my seventies and have no one to inherit from me."

"Even so!"

"The great thing is for us to make a start," said the lawyer.

When they got together in the evening, Isam al-Baqli had a new look and a new suit. But while the filth had vanished, the signs of the wretchedness of old age and former misery still remained.

"Valentino himself, by the Lord of the Kaaba!" said the lawyer, laughing.

As Othman al-Qulla was on friendly terms and had business with the manager of the Nile Hotel, he rented a fine room there for al-Baqli, and the latter at once invited his two friends to dinner. They had a few drinks before the meal and then sat together after eating, planning a meeting for the following day. Then al-Baqli accompanied them to Mr. Nuh's car but did not return to the hotel. Instead he took a taxi to Mohammed Ali Street and made straight for a restaurant famous for its Egyptian cooking. He did not consider what he had just eaten a meal, but merely something to whet his appetite. He ordered hot broth with crumbled bread and the meat of a sheep's head, and ate to his heart's content. He left the place only to pick and choose among such sweets as baseema, kunafa, and basbousa, as though afflicted by a mania for food. Just before midnight he returned to the hotel, so drunk with food he was nearly passing out. Locking his room, he experienced an unexpected feeling of sluggishness creeping through his limbs. Still with his trousers and shoes on, he threw himself down on the bed without turning off the light. What was it that lay crouched on his stomach, chest, and heart? What was it that stifled his breathing? Who was it that grasped his neck? He thought of calling for help, of searching for the bell, of using the telephone, but he was quite incapable of moving. His hands and feet had been shackled, his voice had gone. There was help, there was first aid, but how to reach them? What was this strange state he was in that wrested from a man all will and ability, leaving him an absolute nothingness? So, this is death, death that advances with no one to repulse it, no one to resist it. In his fevered thoughts he called upon the manager, upon Nuh, upon Othman, upon the fortune, the bride, the woman, the dream. Nothing was willing to make answer. Why, then, had this miracle taken place? It doesn't make sense. It doesn't make sense, O Lord.

Translated by Denys Johnson-Davies

Forgetfulness, 1984

The collection *The Seventh Heaven* contains thirteen stories, many of which deal with dreams. The following three stories are taken from this collection.

My searing imagination, its waves exploding in all directions, could never have conjured the endless city, sprawling as far as the eye can see. It was like a disorderly giant of infinite size, waving its thousands of limbs and appendages. Over it towered innumerable rows of massive buildings in the haughty, arrogant style of the age. Another kind, their colors fading, were clearly in the violent grip of time, while a third type was about to collapse in destruction, their residents hanging on in desperate resignation. In every quarter, the people brawled in an uproar, confronting each other in heedless tumult. Buses, cars, horse carriages, camels, and handcarts all followed each other, their noises clashing amidst the countless accidents, blaring weddings, shrieking funerals, bloody arguments, warm embraces, and throats hawking merchandise in the east and west, south and north, the groans of complaint blending with the soft cries of praise and contentment.

The communal home of the immigrants from our village was like a life vest in a stormy sea. The sheikh of the resettled tribe received me, saying, "Our new son—welcome to your family."

"Thank you, uncle," I said, kissing his hand.

I found my seat at the institute waiting for me too. I was well thought of, so the trip was crowned with success. I took a post in the government's Survey Department, musing, "Hard work has its reward." And after work I would slip off to the café to see my friends there, though I feared to spend like the other patrons did. My mind was filled with fantasies the way a fasting man dreams of food and drink—for in our residence there were many young flowers just beginning to bloom.

As the wheel of mornings, afternoons, and evenings kept revolving, something unremarkable occurred—a fleeting dream that one either remembers or ignores. Yet it must have shown in my expression, in a way that did not escape the attention of our sharp-eyed sheikh. As he sat cross-legged on his couch, mumbling the prayers of his rosary, he said to me, "Something is distracting you."

"A man has come to me in a dream," I confided. "He warned me against forgetfulness."

The sheikh thought for a while, then declared, "He's reminding you not to waste your youth."

I considered carefully what he was saying. In our abode of urban exile, no obstacles were placed between a man and his heart's desires—ours was a compassionate, brotherly tribe. A room was as suitable for a couple as it was for a single person. The bride was already waiting—and there were many kindly acts and favors to help ease the way.

"Let's stick to our holy traditions—with the blessings of God," said the sheikh.

The room was freshly painted and aptly furnished, as well. And so that city which pays no mind to anyone welcomed the new bride and bridegroom. Life in our home away from home was anchored in solidarity; many means were devised to triumph over the hardships of the times. Overwhelmed with happiness, I said to myself, "Our path was paved for us by so many glorious forebears."

Engrossed in love and marriage, in fatherhood and work, one day I told the sheikh, "This is all thanks to God—and to you."

"Our house is like Noah's ark," he answered benignly, "in the raging flood that engulfs us all."

"Uncle," I said, "people have the evil eye for us—they envy us."

"That only grows greater as time goes by," he replied.

I awoke one night with a start at the return of my dream. The same man warned me against forgetfulness. I saw him just as he appeared the first time, or so it seemed. The man was the same man, and the words were the same words.

The sheikh listened with concern. "We have grown used to you dreaming about your fears," he concluded.

"I am quite confident. I have no fears."

"Really?" he queried me. "You aren't concerned for the future of your family?"

"Happy today are those who prepare for their last day," I blurted in protest.

"What would you do tomorrow if the demands of this life should increase upon you?" he asked.

I paused in silent embarrassment.

"Do what many others are doing," he counseled. "Take an extra job."

Through his influence, I was able to start training in a center for plumbing skills. I excelled in a most praiseworthy way—and began to invest my new experience in it in the evenings after I finished my government toil each day. My profits kept growing, and my savings as well. The sheikh watched my success with satisfaction.

"This is surely better than illicit gain," he said. "These days require us to be like the cat with seven lives!"

A marvelous energy pervaded my limbs. I fell rapturously in love with life, disregarding its beating chaos all around us. All this prompted me to lease an apartment for which I paid a sizeable deposit. Inviting me for breakfast, my uncle told me, "This is how things are going these days."

I believed there was no security for any living being without work and money—and the most fortuitous thing that we gain in our world is a dependable future. I maintained my moderation as best I could; the only new things in my life were cigarettes, fatty meats, and oriental sweets. My sons and daughters graduated from foreign language schools, and with the passing days only the best things came to me. Amidst all this delicious abundance, one night my dream returned for the third time. The man warned me against forgetfulness, as he had before. I saw him just as I did the two previous times, or so it seemed: the man was the same man, and the words were the same words.

Astonished, I did not take it lightly. Unfortunately, the sheikh was not at hand to discuss it with me. Being so absorbed in business, I had stopped seeing him briefly, while I hated to visit him for any purpose other than just to say hello. Still, a feeling of unease assailed me, pervading all I did.

Suffering from it harshly, my wife scolded me, "Goodness comes from God, and evil from ourselves."

"What is it but a dream?" I said to her dismissively.

"I don't see you forgetting anything," she replied.

Yet I could not escape the hold of the amazing vision upon me. It was always chasing me, occupying my mind. Under its sway, I rushed from the sidewalk to cross the street, without paying attention to the traffic going by. Suddenly, without any warning, I found myself in front of a car that could not brake in time. Striking me, it threw me through the air like a ball. I lost consciousness completely, until I awoke in the hospital, where I learned there was no hope for my recovery at all.

Looking back with pity and sadness, the sheikh later told us:
He was taken to hospital under the dark clouds of death. There he underwent a desperate operation, while the investigation and the testimony of the eye-witnesses all confirmed that he had run into the road as if wanting to end his own life. The car's driver, therefore, was innocent of any fault. I sat next to my nephew's bed, knowing there was no chance that he would survive,

when the driver arrived in humble consolation, offering to render what assistance he could. He stayed for a while, then left on his own.

When he had gone, my nephew's eyelids fluttered, and I saw a familiar look on his face. I bent my head down close to his mouth. "That's the man," he muttered faintly, "the man in the dream!"

Those were the last words ever to leave his lips.

Translated by Raymond Stock

The Reception Hall, 1996

Today is my birthday. The feast of life renewed. We gather in the grand reception hall and our emotions warm it in the full force of winter. All that is delicious and delightful in food and drink and sweet song surrounds us. We come singly and in couples and in groups. Love guides us forward and good camaraderie binds us together. Differing moods and tempers blend in our hearts. We have no need to hire entertainers, for among us are excellent singers and glorious dancers—and what are these but our joy of life bursting out? Our joking evening banter is completely informal and unrestrained. The fragrance of flowers wafts through the room, which glitters with pleasure and contentment. The soirée stretches on till the coming of dawn, when we go out little by little, the same way we came in, eyelids sagging with satiety, throats hoarsened by laughter and loud talk, as dreams draw us on to happy slumber.

We are decreed from birth to be divided only by the Destroyer of Delights—but he seems quite far away. Security, it appears, is granted us. Of course, our numbers dwindle and faces disappear in the passing of days. The span of life has its dominion, and circumstances have their dominion, and what lasts forever but the One who is eternal? In the flood of pleasure and its warmth, we overlook the losses and savor what is fated for us, but with a deep sense of grief.

"That beautiful, bewitching face!"

"And her girlfriend who would never stop laughing!"

"And that self-important character who made himself the maestro at every party!"

We philosophize and say, "Well, that's life and we must take it as it is. It's been that way since the age of Adam, always treating people in the same fashion. . . . So where's the surprise?"

But the debate subsided as the hall was emptied of its heroes. Today, no one comes, not a man or a woman. I wait and wait in hope that maybe . . . but it's no use. I am tortured by loneliness, as my loneliness is tortured by me. I am unaware of what goes on beyond my sight. Nothing remains but mummified imaginings in the sarcophagi of memory. Sometimes I believe— and sometimes I do not. There was nothing in my heart but bruises and wounds, and affection for that One who dwells within me, when he asked me, "Shall I tell you the truth?"

"Please."

"They have all been arrested," he said. "The Guardian executes his duty, as you are aware."

"But they're all so different. How can he arrest them all without distinguishing between them?"

"He is not concerned with differences."

"Do you foresee when they will be released?" I asked, with intense distress.

"Not one of them shall be freed," he answered, his voice frigid with finality.

Ah! He means what he says. None of them shall be spared. The period of my loneliness shall linger and lengthen. But the matter didn't stop there. Motion is eternal and unceasing. I was watching a moth fluttering about my lamp when he breathed in my ear, "Be warned. . . . They are looking into you."

Really? No matter how long your voyage, your mission keeps growing with it, an old saying goes. But anxiety did not grip me as it did of yore. I listened to him as he whispered, "There is a chance for survival."

I heard without heed. He was goading me toward the impossible. He often teased me this way—but I felt neither fear nor a desire to protest. Nor was I without a certain strange pleasure.

"No," I told him.

And I occupied myself with packing my bag.

I alternate between packing my bag and amusing myself by watching the comings and goings.

I wrap myself in my robe against the cold of winter. I stand behind the windowpane, the glistening earth shaded by the boughs of trees, the sky obliterated by clouds. My eyes observe closely. More than once I spot him as he crosses the road, his tall, slender figure untouched by age. But he has not yet headed toward my house. In my youth I was deceived by his friendship with my father and his praise for him, and then . . . what was the result? That amazing man! During the days when I was deceived with what there was between him and my father, I came upon him unexpectedly on the street near my home. In all innocence, as courtesy demands, I invited him to visit us.

"Not today—thank you, my son," he said, smiling.

How often people are confused by his kind reputation and his sadistic acts! In an interview a woman journalist asked him about his preoccupations.

"That I execute my duty to perfection," he explained.

She pointed out examples of iniquity that sometimes occur.

"My work is carried out with perfect justice!" he rejoined.

"Have you never once loathed your duty?"

"Never—I execute a law that is absolutely just."

"Aren't there incidents that deserve explanation?"

"If we get into these legalistic details, the readers will lose all patience with me!"

And so the reporter ended the interview by noting his complete self-assurance.

Such is the man whose name breathes terror into hearts, who once declared publicly, "I do not go to people to arrest them. Rather, it is they who come to me by themselves."

He added, "Likewise I deny with vehemence all that is said about the torture practiced in prisons."

And so, here I am, looking out from behind the windowpane, during the brief moments in which I pause from packing my bag.

Translated by Raymond Stock

Traveler with Hand Luggage, 1996

O f an early morning the city appears quiet, clean, almost empty. Its sun, giving out heat, mitigates the winter weather. The family collected itself in the Fiat, the mother driving. He sat alongside her, an item of hand luggage between them. On the back seat were the two boys in school uniform. At his ease, the man looked out at the road.

"How overcrowding takes away from the dignity of the street," he said.

Making no comment, she drove the car at some speed until, a quarter of an hour later, they arrived at the school. The two boys got out and hurried off.

"To the chemist's," muttered the man, and the woman drove to the chemist's, which lay close by on the other side of the road. The man made his way to the shop, bought various medicines for himself and his wife, and returned.

"Please don't forget to take your medicine," he told her, seating himself.

Smiling as she drove off, she said, "To the bank, which is more important."

There was a flurry of movement in the road. It did not start gradually but with the sweeping suddenness of an earthquake: cars, buses, and lorries, all rushing forward as though in a race. The Fiat took a relatively long time to cover the short distance. The man got out and went to the bank, which he found half empty. Drawing out from his account, he stuffed a bundle of notes into his trouser pocket and hurried back. He put the bundle into his wife's handbag with the words, "Spend as much as you need in the time and leave me the rest."

"You're returning tomorrow?"

"Or the day after at the most."

She proceeded toward the station and stopped in front of the east entrance. "Shall I stay with you until the train goes?"

"No," he said quickly. "You've more urgent things to do. Till we meet again, dear."

It pleased him that the station never nodded off: always there was someone going in or coming out—a constant meeting place for those arriving and those departing. Under its high roof, sounds were magnified, echoes reverberated, while from the stationary trains emanated hot, noisy exhalations that triggered the latent beginnings of farewells. Despite being preoccupied with what he had left behind him and with what awaited him there, his heart throbbed. He brought to mind so many journeys, tears, and smiles. Then, with a thought that suddenly struck him, his tongue expressed his inner thoughts: "Glorified is He who possesses permanence."

There advanced toward him a group of passengers, among whom he discerned a woman of mature age who attracted his keen attention. He was intensely startled before he could recover his equilibrium: he was thinking that she had recently passed away. He could not recollect now how it was that this fact had lodged itself in his head. Perhaps it was through some erroneous similarity in names, or some item of news that he had misunderstood.

As she approached him, she in her turn saw him and smiled. Automatically, they shook hands.

"What a pleasant surprise!" he muttered.

"How long has it been? It seems like a lifetime."

They exchanged good wishes, then she went off. His heart beat wildly. He said to himself: If only I were some other man I would have had an affair with her, as in times past. He proceeded on his inevitable way toward the ticket window, from where he went towards the waiting train. A group of people were waiting to see someone off. But what was this?—he knew several of the faces. In fact there was not a strange face among them, all were relatives, neighbors, or colleagues! And here they were, making their way in his direction as though they'd come just to bid him farewell. What was it all about? After all, he would be away only for a day or two, and no one knew he was going on a journey. He was not used to anyone coming to say goodbye even when he went on long journeys. He found himself shaking one hand after another as he said, "What a coincidence that we should all be traveling on the same train!"

"We've come to say goodbye to you!" said more than one voice.

"How did you know I was traveling?" he said in amazement. "I'll only be away for a day."

No one paid attention to what he had said. Surrounding him with evident affection, they wished him a safe journey.

"How extraordinary of you!" he exclaimed with a laugh.

His uncle, the oldest of those there, said to him, "I wish I'd been able to travel with you."

"Thank you. Thank you," he said with intense feeling. "I'm sorry to put you all to this trouble—it's not all that important."

"Why didn't Ameena Hanem come along with you?" asked his maternal aunt.

"I'm going on business and the house can't do without her."

Still astonished, he inquired, "But how did you know of the news, and why have you gone to all this trouble?"

"What a thing to say!" said more than one voice.

The train let out a warning whistle, so he waved them goodbye and went up into the carriage. One of them went with him and put his bag on the rack, while he went down again and stood among them exchanging pleasantries. One by one they left. He closed the door, gave a sigh of satisfaction, and seated himself. For the first time he realized he was the only passenger in the whole carriage. How odd! It had never happened before that the train had left without all the seats being occupied. What had happened in the world that he should be taking an empty train—as though he were king of his time! It was certainly a day filled with surprises.

The train moved off. Slowly it glided along, leaving the station and those who had come to say goodbye. It increased speed, the monotonous rhythm sounding unceasingly. He would have time for contemplating and understanding what he had passed through. He sighed and asked himself, "What's the meaning of all this?"

Translated by Denys Johnson-Davies

The Rose Garden, 1999

A*ll of it happened such a long time ago. The sheikh of our alley told me the story as we sat one day in a garden full of roses. . . .*
Hamza Qandil was found after a long disappearance, a stiffened corpse lying out in the desert. He had been stabbed in the neck with a sharp

object. His robe was soaked with hardened blood, his turban strewn down the length of his body. But his watch and his money had not been touched—so clearly robbery had not been the motive. As the authorities began to look into the crime, word of what happened spread through the quarter like a fire through kindling.

Voices rang out from within Hamza's house. The neighbor women shared in the customary wailing, and people traded knowing looks. An air of tense drama spread out through the hara. Yet some felt a secret satisfaction, mixed with a certain sense of guilt. Uncle Dakrouri, the milk peddler, expressed some of this when he whispered to the prayer leader of our alley, "This murder went beyond what anyone expected—despite the man's pigheadedness and lack of humor."

"God does what He will," answered the imam.

The prosecutor's office asked about the victim's enemies. The question exposed an atmosphere of evasion, as his widow said that she didn't know anything of his relations with the outside world. Not a soul would testify that they had ever seen a sign of enmity between the murdered man and anyone else in the quarter. And yet, no one volunteered any helpful testimony. The detective looked at the sheikh of the hara quizzically, saying: "The only thing I've been able to observe is that he had no friends!"

"He got on people's nerves, but I never bothered to find out why," the sheikh replied.

The investigation revealed that Qandil used to cut through the empty lot outside of our alley on his way to and from work in the square. No one would accompany him either coming or going. When the traditional question was asked—"Did the folks here complain about anyone?"—the consistent response was a curt denial. No one believed anybody else, but that's how things went. But why didn't Hamza Qandil have a single friend in the alley? Wasn't it likely that the place held a grudge against him?

The sheikh of the hara said that Qandil had a bit more learning than his peers. He used to sit in the café telling people about the wonders of the world that he had read about in the newspapers, astounding his listeners, whom he held entranced. As a result, every group he sat in became his forum, in which he took a central place considered unseemly for anyone but local gang bosses or government officials. The neighbors grew annoyed with him, watching him with hearts filled with envy and resentment.

One day, tensions reached their peak when he talked about the cemetery in a way that went far beyond all bounds of reason. "Look at the graveyard," he grumbled. "It takes up the most beautiful place in our district!"

Someone asked him what he wanted there instead.

"Imagine in the northern part houses for people, and in the south, a rose garden!"

The people become angry in a way they had never been before. They hurled reproaches at him in a hail of rebuke, reminding him of the dignity of the dead and the obligation to be faithful to them. Most agitated of all was Bayumi Zalat; he warned him not to say anything more about the cemetery, shouting, "We live in our houses only a few years—but we dwell in our tombs till the Day of Resurrection!"

"Don't people have rights, too?" Qandil asked.

But Zalat cut him off, enraged. "Religion demands respect for the dead!"

With this, Zalat, who didn't know the first thing about his faith, issued his very own religious ruling. But later, after the battle began to cool, the sheikh of the hara came, bearing a decree from the governor's office. The order called for the removal of the cemetery by a fixed deadline—and for the people to build new tombs in the heart of the desert.

There was no connection between what Qandil had said and this decision, though some thought there was—while others believed, as the Quran says, that it's wrong to suspect someone unless you have proof. Meanwhile, most people said, "Qandil certainly isn't important enough to influence the government— but in any case, is he not like an evil omen?"

All in all, they blamed him for what happened, while, from his side, he made no effort to hide his pleasure at the decree. The people's frustration and anger kept getting stronger and stronger. Finally, they gathered before the sheikh of the hara, the men crying out and the women lamenting, and demanded that he tell the authorities that the government's order was void and forbidden: that it was against religion, and fidelity to the dead.

The sheikh replied that his reverence for those who have died was no less than theirs. Nonetheless, they would still be moved, in absolute compliance with the laws of God and of decency. But the people insisted, "This means that a curse will fall upon the hara, and upon all who live there!"

Then the sheikh called out to them that the government's decision was final, and charged them to ready themselves to carry it out. At this, Zalat pulled away from them. In a braying voice, he declared:

"We haven't heard anything like that since the age of the infidels!"

Their anger with the government mixed with their anger at Qandil until it became a single, seething fury. Then, one night, as Bayumi Zalat was returning from an evening out, he took a shortcut through the tombs in the cemetery. There, at the little fountain, a skeleton loomed before him, wrapped in a shroud. Zalat halted, nailed where he stood, while everything that had been in his head instantly flew out of it. Then the skeleton spoke to him:

Woe unto those who forget their Dead, and who neglect the most precious of all their possessions—their graves.

Zalat stumbled back to the hara, his heart filled with death's whisperings. And in truth, he didn't conceal from anyone that it was he who had killed Qandil. Yet no one divulged his secret, whether out of fear, or of loyalty. Gossip said that this fact had even reached the police commissioner himself. But he, too, had been against moving the cemetery in which his ancestors were interred. The blame was laid against a person unknown—and so Hamza Qandil's blood was shed unavenged.

The sheikh of the hara ended his talk on a note of regret, as we sat in the rose garden that—once upon a time—had been the graveyard of our ancient quarter.

Translated by Raymond Stock

Autobiographical Works

from *Echoes of an Autobiography*, 1994

During his last ten years of writing Naguib Mahfouz produced, among other publications, this outstanding work. It consists of what have been termed "aphoristic narratives" inspired by events in the author's life. Nine separate items from this book are given here. Each tells a brief story, giving us a slice of something learned by the author during his long life, much of which was spent looking back at the past and seeing what lessons it had to teach him.

The Next Posting

"I have come to you because you are my first and last refuge," he said urgently.

"This means that you come with a new request," said the old man, smiling.

"My transfer from the governorate has been decided upon as the next posting."

"Haven't you spent there the period as laid down by law? These are the conventions followed in your position."

"Being transferred would be harmful to me and my family," he entreated.

"I informed you of the nature of your work from the very first day."

"The fact is that the governorate has become like home to us, and we can't do without it."

"That is what your colleagues, past and yet to come, say, and you know that the time for your transfer cannot be put forward or back."

"What a cruel experience," he said in grief.

"Why did you not prepare yourself for it when you knew it was your inevitable destiny?"

Shortly Before Dawn

The two of them would sit cross-legged on the same sofa. They would chat in cheerful friendship: the widow in her seventies and her mother-in-law of eighty-five. They had forgotten a long period of time that had been filled with jealousy, rancor, and hatred. The deceased had been able to judge justly between people but had been unable to provide justice between his mother and his wife. He had also been unable to avoid taking sides. The man had departed and, for the first time, the two women had collaborated in something: the deep grief they felt for him.

Old age had tempered defiance and had opened windows to the breezes of wisdom.

The mother-in-law now prays for the widow and her offspring from the depths of her heart, for their health and long life, while the widow asks God to lengthen the life of the other woman lest she leave her alone and lonely.

Music

He stood in my way, smiling and extending his hand. We shook hands as I asked myself who this old man could be. He took me to one side of the sidewalk.

You've forgotten me?" he said.

In embarrassment I said, "Please forgive an old man's memory."

"We were neighbors when we were at primary school. In my spare time I used to sing to you in a beautiful voice, and you used to like those odes called tawashih, sung in praise of the Prophet."

Having totally despaired of me, he once again extended his hand.

"I mustn't delay you any further," he said.

I said to myself, "Such forgetfulness is like nonexistence! Rather, it is nonexistence itself. Yet I did and still do enjoy listening to tawashih."

A Man Reserves a Seat

The bus started on its journey from Zeytoun at the same moment that a private car set forth from the owner's house in Helwan. Each varied the speed at which it was traveling, speeding along and then slowing down, and perhaps coming to a stop for a minute or more depending on the state of the traffic.

They both, however, reached Station Square at the same time, and even had a slight accident, in which one of the bus's headlights was broken and the front of the car was scratched.

A man was passing and was crushed between the two vehicles and died. He was crossing the square in order to book a seat on the train going to Upper Egypt.

After You Come Out of Prison

The hall was packed with petitioners.

We sat down exchanging anxious looks and directing our gaze at the high door leading to the inside, which was covered with two halves of a giant green screen.

When would luck smile and my turn come? When would I be invited to the interview so that I could present my requirement and obtain hope? The door is open and turns away no one who goes to it, yet only the lucky ones achieve a meeting.

Thus the days proceed and I go with heart gladdened by hope, then return dejected.

A thought occurred to me: Why did I not disappear in some place in the garden until the evening party broke up and the man came out for his evening stroll, when I would throw myself at his feet. But the servants perceived that I had slipped in and they dragged me off to the police station, and from the police station to the prison, where I was cast into its darkness.

In vain did I attempt to clear myself.

How was it that I had gone aspiring to an honorable post and had ended up in prison?

Exchanged whisperings brought to our knowledge the fact that the important man would be visiting the prison and would investigate the conditions in it and listen to the complaints of those who had been unjustly treated.

I was astonished that I would achieve in prison what had been impossible for me in the outside world.

And this need of mine for his sympathy increased and grew more intense.

With bent head I told him my story.

He showed neither that he believed it nor that he disbelieved it.

"All that I wish," I said entreatingly, "is that I be allowed a meeting after I come out of prison."

About to depart, he said in a calm voice, "After you come out of prison."

Laughter

I stood above the opening to the grave, casting a farewell glance at the body of the loved one that they were preparing for its final rest. His ringing laughter came to me from the beautiful past, so I gazed around me but saw only the solemn faces of the mourners.

On the way back by the cemetery road, a friend whispered in my ear, "What about a moment's rest at the café?"

The invitation brought a tremor of delight to my nerves. I took off briskly to where there was someplace to sit, to the glass of ice water, the spicy coffee, and the intimate talk of those who are going to follow those who have gone before.

The Postman

On one of the Nights of the Cave there was a strong wind and a heavy downpour of rain. Gusts of air penetrating through from the entrance played with the wispy flames of the candles, and hearts beat violently. Eyes were directed at the entrance and they waited, hearts beating even more wildly.

One of them whispered, "They say that the night of this year is blessed."

Hearts were drawn toward the entrance with all the strength they possessed.

A whistling came to them from afar and they jumped to their feet. At that moment the postman entered in his familiar uniform and with his bag almost drenched from the water soaking his clothes.

Calmly he gave to each outstretched hand a letter, then left without uttering a word.

They broke open the envelopes and looked at the letters by the light of the candles. They found that they were blank pieces of paper with nothing on them.

Abd-Rabbih exclaimed, "The outcome will be known to those that are patient."

Freedom

Sheikh Abd-Rabbih al-Ta'ih said:

The nearest man comes to his Lord is when he is exercising his freedom correctly.

The Heartbeat

Sheikh Abd-Rabbih al-Ta'ih said:

There is nothing between the lifting of the veil from the face of the bride and the lowering of it over her corpse but a moment that is like a heartbeat.

Translated by Denys Johnson-Davies

from *The Dreams*, 2000

Following in the path of *Echoes of an Autobiography,* these two final books, *The Dreams* and *Dreams of Departure*, contain fragments of actual dreams as well as imagined dreams. Like *Echoes*, they make for delightful reading.

DREAM 1

I was riding my bicycle from one place to another, driven by hunger, in search of a restaurant fit for my limited means. At each one I found its doors locked, and when my eyes fell on the clock in the square I saw my friend at its foot.

He called me over with a wave of his hand, so I headed my bike in his direction. In view of my condition, he suggested that, in order to make my quest easier, I leave my bicycle with him. I followed his suggestion—and my hunger and my search grew even more intense, until I happened upon a family eatery.

Propelled by the need for food and by despair, I approached it, despite knowing how expensive it was. I saw the owner standing at the entrance before a hanging curtain. What could I do but to throw it open—only to find the place changed into a ruin filled with refuse in place of its grand hall readied with culinary delights. Dismayed, I asked the man, "What's going on?"

"Hurry over to the kabab-seller of youth," he answered. "Maybe you can catch him before he shuts down."

Not wasting any time, I ran back to the clock in the square—but found neither the bicycle there, nor my friend.

DREAM 6

The telephone rang and the voice at the other end said, "Sheikh Muharram, your teacher, speaking."

I answered politely with a reverent air, "My mentor is most welcome."

"I'm coming to visit you," he said.

"Looking forward to receiving you," I replied.

I felt not the slightest astonishment—though I had walked in his funeral procession some sixty years before. A host of indelible memories came back to me about my old instructor. I remembered his handsome face and his elegant clothes—and the extreme harshness with which he treated his pupils. The sheikh showed up with his lustrous jubba and caftan, and his spiraling turban, saying without prologue, "Over there, I have dwelt with many reciters of ancient verse, as well as experts on religion. After talking with them, I realized that some of the lessons I used to give you were in need of correction. I have written the corrections on this paper I have brought you."

Having said this, he laid a folder on the table, and left.

DREAM 7

What a stupendous square, crammed with people and cars! I stood on the station's sidewalk, waiting for the arrival of Tram Number 3. It was nearly sunset. I wanted to go home, even though no one waited for me there.

Evening fell, the darkness blotting the lights of the widely-spaced lamps, and loneliness seized me. I wondered what was holding up Tram Number 3? All the other trams came in, each carrying away those who had been waiting for it—yet I had no idea what had happened to Tram Number 3. Movement in the square diminished as traffic slowly ground to a halt, until I was left nearly alone in the station. I glanced around and noticed to my left a girl who looked like a daughter of the night. My sense of isolation and despair only increased when she asked me, "Isn't this the stop for Tram Number 3?"

I answered that it was, and thought of leaving the place—when Tram Number 3 quietly pulled into the station. The only people aboard were the driver and the ticket conductor. Something inside me told me not to get on—so I turned my back to it, staying that way until the tram had gone.

Looking about afterward, I saw the girl standing there. When she felt my eye upon her, she smiled and walked toward the nearest alley—and I followed her in train.

DREAM 15

A great hallway along which offices were arrayed. A government department, or perhaps a commercial agency. The employees were either sitting quietly at their desks, or moving about between their offices.

They were made up of both sexes, obviously working well together, lightly and openly flirting with each other. I seemed to be one of the newer functionaries here, with a suitably low salary, a fact that I felt profoundly. Yet this didn't prevent me from asking for the hand of a beautiful young lady of higher rank, who had worked here longer than me. In the event, she thanked me, but declined my request.

"We lack what we'd need for a happy life," she explained.

This pierced me with a wound in the seam of my psyche.

From that day onward, I grew wary of broaching any such subject with my female colleagues, though I was attracted to more than one of them. I felt the bitter suffering of loneliness and dejection. Then a new girl joined our service—and for the first time, I found myself in a superior position. I was an auditor, while she was a typist: my salary was twice as large as hers. She was not good looking, and, even worse, people gossiped about her immoral behavior. Out of despair, I decided to break through my isolation—so I flirted with her. She flirted back. So happy was I that I lost my head and asked her to marry me.

"I'm sorry," she replied.

Not believing my ears, I pressed on, "There's nothing wrong with my salary, especially when added with yours."

"Money doesn't concern me," she said.

I thought of asking what *did* matter to her, but she'd already walked away.

DREAM 17

The quarters of Gamaliya and Abbasiya passed before me, yet I seemed to be walking in only one place.

I imagined that someone was tailing me. I turned to look behind me, but the rain poured down more intensely than it had in years—so I scurried back to my home. I wanted to take off my clothes, but then had the uncanny feeling that a strange man was hiding in my house. His audacity infuriated me—so I screamed at him to give himself up. The door to the foyer opened and there appeared a man whose equal in size and strength I had never before seen. "Give *yourself* up," he said, in a quietly sarcastic voice.

A sense of feebleness and fear gripped me: I was certain that one blow from his elephant-sized hand would flatten me completely. Then he ordered me to give up my wallet and my overcoat. The overcoat was more important to me—yet I hesitated but a little before handing him both items. He shoved me, and I hit the ground. When I regained my feet, he had disappeared—and I wondered if I should call out to raise an alarm.

But what had happened was contemptible and shameful, and would make me an object of jokes and ridicule—so I did nothing.

I thought about going to the police station, but one of my friends was an officer from the detective bureau. Hence the scandal would spread one way or another.

I decided upon silence, but this didn't save me from worry.

I dreaded that I would run into the thief somewhere while he was walking happily about in my coat, and with my money.

DREAM 27

On a ship crossing the ocean, people of all colors and tongues were arrayed. We were expecting the wind to swoop down, and when it did, the horizon disappeared behind the angry waves. I became frightened: it was every man for himself. I felt alone in the depths of the sea. An inner fear told me there was no way to survive the all-encompassing terror—unless this really was just a nightmare, to be shattered by a fevered awakening on my bed.

The wind became violent as the boat was tossed back and forth on the waves. Suddenly, I saw before me Hamza Effendi, my math teacher, wielding his wicker rod. He fixed me with a look demanding to know if I had done my homework. If I hadn't, he would rap me ten times across my knuckles—

which made them feel as though they'd been pressed with a hot iron. My hatred grew with the memory of those days.

I wanted to grab him by the neck, but feared that any move would cause my demise. So, saying nothing about my humiliation, I swallowed it despite the dryness in my throat. I saw my sweetheart and scurried toward her, cutting my way through tens of confused onlookers. But she did not recognize me and turned her back, proclaiming her annoyance. Then she ran toward the ship's edge and threw herself into the storm—I thought she was showing me the way to deliverance. So I rushed stumblingly toward the side of the ship, but the old math teacher stood in my path, brandishing his stick of bamboo.

DREAM 42

The ship cut its way through the stately waves of the Nile. We were sitting in a circle, in the center of which reposed our teacher. Clearly we were taking the final exam, and our answers were rated excellent.

We dispersed for tea and cake. In the meantime, we received our diplomas.

The ship pulled up at the pier and we disembarked, each one bearing his degree in a giant envelope. I found myself walking down a wide street devoid of both people and buildings, when a lonely mosque loomed before me. I went toward it in order to pray and relax for a while, but when I went inside, it seemed to actually be an old house. I felt the urge to go back out, but a bunch of brigands surrounded me, taking my certificate, my watch, and my wallet, and raining a hail of blows upon me before disappearing into the recesses of the place.

I ran outside onto the street, not believing that I had survived. After walking a short way, I came across a patrol of policemen, and told their commander what had happened to me.

We all marched together to the house full of thieves. They rushed in with their weapons drawn—only to find it was a mosque where people were praying behind their imam. Confused, we beat a hasty retreat, and the patrol's commander ordered that I be placed under arrest.

I kept testifying over and over to what had befallen me, swearing the most sacred oath that it was true. But clearly they had begun to doubt my sanity—and I was no less perplexed than them.

DREAM 44

I found myself seated before the Minister of the Interior at his desk. A few days earlier, he had been my colleague in the newspaper: his selection as minister came as a surprise. I seized the opportunity to ask him for a meeting, and he received me with welcome and affection. Then I presented him with my request, to recommend me to a businessman known to be his friend, when I applied for a position in one of his companies.

He wrote out the requested letter by hand, and the meeting ended on a happy note. On the evening of the same day, as I promenaded on the banks of the Nile, a man whose name is bantered in the press accosted me. He pulled out a gun and robbed me of my money—roughly fifty Egyptian pounds.

Traumatized, I went back to my flat, yet took no action that would affect the appointment that the businessman had given me. The next morning, I was at his office. After a few minutes, he permitted me to enter. I handed him the reference, then froze where I stood.

"My Lord," I said to myself, in this moment of high anxiety—for he was the very thief who had robbed me, or his twin brother. The ground spun before me.

DREAM 73

Back in the old house in Abbasiya, I'm evidently annoyed because nothing came of my criticism, such as painting the walls or fixing the woodwork, the floors, and the furniture.

Then, from the far end of the flat, my mother's voice calls out in a sweet, pleasant tone that it's time I went out looking for a new apartment that would please me.

At this, the time and the place switch as I find myself in a reception hall, with many rooms and people. The way it looks reminds me of a government agency. This is confirmed by the arrival of my departed colleague, Mr. H.A., who informs me that the minister had sent a request to see me. Immediately I dashed to the minister's office, and, excusing myself, entered it—to find the man in other than his usual smiling state. He said that he had dreamed about my criticism of the revolution and its leader, which had wounded him grievously. I told him that I considered myself blindly infatuated with the principles of the revolution rather than being among those who opposed it— though I also always wished for its perfect completion, and for the avoidance of stumbles and setbacks.

Again I was taken through other times and places until I was a little boy meandering through Bayt al-Qadi Square. A friend my own age invited me to the wedding of his older brother. He said that his brother had invited Sa'd Zaghlul to officiate at the party and to give it his blessings—and that the great man had accepted, promising to attend. Utterly astounded, I told him, "Even more important than currently being prime minister, Sa'd Zaghlul is our nation's leader. What's more, you aren't among his relatives, or his comrades in the struggle."

"Sa'd truly is the nation's leader," the boy rejoined, "and singles out the simple people for his affection"—adding that I would see for myself.

At the appointed time I went to the feast in Crimson Lane, where my friend guided me into a room. There—in the place of honor—I saw Sa'd Zaghlul, wearing the suit of the master of ceremonies, sitting down with him. The two were engrossed in conversation, laughing hard together. I was so dazzled by what I saw that it rooted itself in my depths forever.

DREAM 81

At long last I went to the mansion. I asked the doorman to inform the eminent woman that the winner of her literary prize had come to present his thanks in person, if only she would permit him.

The man soon returned to bring me into the reception hall, whose beauty and vastness dazzled me. Before long a musical tune signaling welcome was played for me—and I spied the enchanting figure of the madam moving gracefully to its rhythm. I undertook to present my letter of thanks—but she, with a chic sweep of her hands, opened up her breasts, drawing from between them a neat little gun.

She pointed it at me. I forgot the letter—fainting away before she could pull the tiny pistol's trigger.

DREAM 84

I dreamed I was on the Street of Love, as I used to call it in my hopeful youth. I dreamed that I sauntered between grand houses and gardens perfumed with flowers. But where was the mansion of my worshiped one? Gone without a trace, its place had been taken by a huge mosque of majestic dimensions, magnificent design, with the tallest and most graceful of minarets. I was shocked. As I stood there in a stupor, the muezzin started the call for the sunset prayer. Without tarrying I went into the mosque, praying with the worshipers. When the prayers were finished, I moved slowly, as though not wanting to leave. Hence I was the last one departing to reach the door. There I discovered that my shoes had gone missing—and I had to find my own way out.

DREAM 92

There I was in a radiant reception hall. In my hands was a golden platter filled with all manner of delectable delights.

I was reminded of the brilliant evening companions among our lifelong friends who had left this world. I began to see them approaching, their resonant laughter preceding them. We traded salaams of greeting, as they began to praise the platter and what it presented. Yet my happiness was suddenly extinguished when I exclaimed that I could not partake with them, for the doctors had categorically forbidden me ever to smoke.

Surprise showed on their faces as they scrutinized me intensely. They asked dismissively, "Are you still afraid of Death?"

DREAM 100

This is a trial and this a bench and sitting at it is a single judge and this is the seat of the accused and sitting at it is a group of national leaders and this is the courtroom, where I have sat down longing to get to know the party responsible for what has befallen us. But I grow confused when the dialogue between the judge and the leaders is conducted in a language I have never before heard, until the magistrate adjusts himself in his seat as he prepares to announce the verdict in the Arabic tongue. I lean forward to hear, but then the judge points at me—to pronounce a sentence of death upon me. I cry out in alarm that I'm not part of this proceeding and that I'd come of my own free will simply to watch and see—but no one even notices my scream.

DREAM 104

I saw myself in Abbasiya wandering in the vastness of my memories, recalling in particular the late Lady Eye. So I contacted her by telephone, inviting her to meet me by the fountain, and there I welcomed her with a passionate heart.

I suggested that we spend the evening together in Fishawi Café, as in our happiest days. But when we reached the familiar place, the deceased blind bookseller came over to us and greeted us warmly—though he scolded the dearly departed Eye for her long absence.

She told him what had kept her away was Death. But he rejected that excuse—for Death, he said, can never come between lovers.

Translated by Raymond Stock

from *Dreams of Departure,* 2004

DREAM 117

I was sitting in the café, when, without seeking my leave, our neighborhood's chief bully sat down next to me.

As I welcomed him with distaste, he announced that he had chosen me to marry his daughter, a divorcee. My limbs trembling, I replied that I was going to wed my paternal uncle's daughter that weekend.

He answered with confident simplicity, "You're going to marry my daughter, and your uncle's daughter's going to marry me."

DREAM 132

She and I were going out as usual to one of our favorite nightclubs when I excused myself to stop briefly to buy some cigarettes.

When I returned, I didn't find her; I assumed that she'd gone to the agreed place before me. But when I got there, she was nowhere around.

So I went from club to club in search of her. I am still looking for her.

DREAM 142

This empty plot of land is my sole inheritance. I call it "the ruin," because it has been neglected for so long.

After making a bit of money, I thought of building on it. Yet I didn't make any progress, due to what I knew about the prevalence of fraud and financial corruption.

Finally, I asked a wise woman who lived next to me, "Is there an honest person left in the world?"

She answered that he existed indeed—but endless courage and resolve were needed in the ceaseless quest to find him.

DREAM 180

I dreamt of my mentor, Sheikh Mustafa Abd al-Raziq, when he was the head of al-Azhar.

As he entered the main office, I rushed to catch up with him, offering my hand in greeting. Walking along with him, inside I saw a sprawling, spectacular garden. He told me that he had planted it himself—half with native roses, the other half with Western ones.

He hoped the two would give birth to a wholly new kind—in form perfect, and in fragrance, sublime.

DREAM 189

I was a minister in the cabinet of Mustafa al-Nahhas. I began to think about a project to create elementary, primary, and secondary schools that would be cost-free, including tuition, for exceptional boys and girls whose parents were peasants and workers.

We would follow up by caring for them at university and in study missions abroad. I presented the idea to the chief, and he welcomed it, while adding some changes of his own. He wanted these schools for super-achieving children to be devoted to building the entire nation.

He asked me to propose the plan in the cabinet's next meeting, pledging his stalwart support.

DREAM 204

I was the director of cinema affairs when the actress "F" asked to be excused from working with actor "A." Annoyed, I pointed out that this would change our whole plan—but she stuck to her demand.

Next, "A" came to me, insisting that I put pressure on "F" to keep working with him, but I demurred. Meanwhile, "F" was telling the actors' ombudsman that I was forcing her to collaborate with my friend "A" against her wishes. Then my friend claimed that I had eased her release from work for some private purpose.

I cursed the day that I took this job.

Translated by Raymond Stock

Sources

Thebes at War, translated by Humphrey Davies (Cairo: The American University in Cairo Press, 2003). Copyright © 1944 by the estate of Naguib Mahfouz. English translation copyright © 2003 by Humphrey Davies.

Khan al-Khalili, translated by Roger Allen (Cairo: The American University in Cairo Press, 2008). Copyright © 1946 by the estate of Naguib Mahfouz. English language copyright © 2008 by Roger Allen.

Midaq Alley, translated by Trevor Le Gassick (Cairo: The American University in Cairo Press, 1985). Copyright © 1947 by the estate of Naguib Mahfouz. English translation copyright © 1975 by Trevor Le Gassick.

The Beginning and the End, translated by Ramses Awad (Cairo: The American University in Cairo Press, 1985). Copyright © 1949 by the estate of Naguib Mahfouz. English translation copyright ©1985 by the American University in Cairo Press.

Palace Walk, translated by William Maynard Hutchins and Olive E. Kenny (Cairo: The American University in Cairo Press, 1990). Copyright ©1956 by the estate of Naguib Mahfouz. English translation copyright © 1990 by the American University in Cairo Press.

Palace of Desire, translated by William Maynard Hutchins, Lorne M. Kenny, and Olive E. Kenny (Cairo: The American University in Cairo Press, 1991). Copyright © 1957 by the estate of Naguib Mahfouz. English translation copyright © 1991 by the American University in Cairo Press.

Sugar Street, translated by William Maynard Hutchins and Angele Botros Samaan (Cairo: The American University in Cairo Press, 1992). Copyright © 1957 by the estate of Naguib Mahfouz. English translation copyright © 1992 by the American University in Cairo Press.

Children of the Alley, translated by Peter Theroux (Cairo: The American University in Cairo Press, 2001). Copyright © 1959 by the estate of Naguib Mahfouz. English translation copyright © 1996 by Peter Theroux.

The Thief and the Dogs, translated by Trevor Le Gassick and M.M. Badawi, revised by John Rodenbeck (Cairo: The American University in Cairo Press, 1984). Copyright © 1961 by the estate of Naguib Mahfouz. English translation copyright © 1984 by the American University in Cairo Press.

Adrift on the Nile, translated by Frances Liardet (Cairo: The American University in Cairo Press, 1999). Copyright © 1966 by the estate of Naguib Mahfouz. English translation copyright © 1993 by Frances Liardet.

Miramar, translated by Fatma Moussa Mahmoud (Cairo: The American University in Cairo Press, 1978). Copyright © 1967 by the estate of Naguib Mahfouz. English translation copyright © 1978 by the American University in Cairo Press.

Mirrors, translated by Roger Allen (Cairo: The American University in Cairo Press, 1999). Copyright © 1972 by the estate of Naguib Mahfouz. English translation copyright © 1999 by Roger Allen.

Karnak Café, translated by Roger Allen (Cairo: The American University in Cairo Press, 2007). Copyright © 1974 by the estate of Naguib Mahfouz. English translation copyright © 2007 by Roger Allen.

Fountain and Tomb, translated by Soad Sobhi, Essam Fattouh, and James Kenneson (Boulder and London: Lynne Rienner Publishers, 1998). Copyright © 1975 by the estate of Naguib Mahfouz. English translation copyright © 1998 by Lynne Rienner Publishers. Reproduced by kind permission.

The Harafish, translated by Catherine Cobham (Cairo: The American University in Cairo Press, 1994). Copyright © 1977 by the estate of Naguib Mahfouz. English translation copyright © 1994, 2001 by Catherine Cobham.

Arabian Nights and Days, translated by Denys Johnson-Davies (Cairo: The American University in Cairo Press, 1995). Copyright © 1979 by the estate of Naguib Mahfouz. English translation copyright © 1995 by the American University in Cairo Press.

The Journey of Ibn Fattouma, translated by Denys Johnson-Davies (Cairo: The American University in Cairo Press, 1997). Copyright © 1983 by the estate of Naguib Mahfouz. English translation copyright © 1992 by the American University in Cairo Press.

Before the Throne, translated by Raymond Stock (Cairo: The American University in Cairo Press, 2009). Copyright © 1983 by the estate of Naguib Mahfouz. English translation copyright © 2009 by Raymond Stock.

Akhenaten, Dweller in Truth, translated by Tagreid Abu-Hassabo (Cairo: The American University in Cairo Press, 1998). Copyright © 1985 by the estate of Naguib Mahfouz. English translation copyright © 1998 by the American University in Cairo Press.

The Day the Leader Was Killed, translated by Malak Hashem (Cairo: The American University in Cairo Press, 1997). Copyright © 1985 by the estate of Naguib Mahfouz. English translation copyright © 1997 by the American University in Cairo Press.

Morning and Evening Talk, translated by Christina Phillips (Cairo: The American University in Cairo Press, 2007). Copyright © 1987 by the estate of Naguib Mahfouz. English translation copyright © 2007 by Christina Phillips.

"The Return of Sinuhe" is from *Voices from the Other World: Ancient Egyptian Tales*, selected and translated by Raymond Stock (Cairo: The American University in Cairo Press, 2006). Copyright © 1941 by the estate of Naguib Mahfouz. English translation copyright © 2000, 2001, 2002 by Raymond Stock.

"Zaabalawi," "The Conjuror Made Off with the Dish," "The Answer is No," "Half a Day," and "A Long-term Plan" are from *The Time and the Place and Other Stories*, selected and translated by Denys Johnson-Davies (Cairo: The American University in Cairo Press, 1991). Copyright © 1962, 1969, 1989 by the estate of Naguib Mahfouz. English translations of "Zaabalawi" copyright © 1967 and "The Conjuror Made Off with the Dish" copyright © 1978 by Denys Johnson-Davies; all others copyright © 1991 by the American University in Cairo Press.

"Forgetfulness," "The Reception Hall," and "The Rose Garden" are from *The Seventh Heaven: Stories of the Supernatural*, selected and translated by Raymond Stock (Cairo: The American University in Cairo Press, 2005). Copyright © 1984, 1996, 1999 by the estate of Naguib Mahfouz. English translations copyright © 1996, 1999, 2004, 2005 by Raymond Stock.

"Traveler with Hand Luggage" is from *Under the Naked Sky: Short Stories from the Arab World*, selected and translated by Denys Johnson-Davies (Cairo: The American University in Cairo Press, 2000). Copyright © 1996 by the estate of Naguib Mahfouz. English translation copyright © 2000 by Denys Johnson-Davies.

Echoes of an Autobiography, translated by Denys Johnson-Davies (Cairo: The American University in Cairo Press, 1997). Copyright © 1994 by the estate of Naguib Mahfouz. English translation copyright © 1996 by the American University in Cairo Press.

The Dreams, translated by Raymond Stock (Cairo: The American University in Cairo Press, 2004). Copyright © 2000 by the estate of Naguib Mahfouz. English translation copyright © 2004 by Raymond Stock.

Dreams of Departure, translated by Raymond Stock (Cairo: The American University in Cairo Press, 2007). Copyright © 2004–2006 by the estate of Naguib Mahfouz. English translation copyright © 2007 by Raymond Stock.

Modern Arabic Literature

The American University in Cairo Press is the world's leading publisher of Arabic literature in translation.

For a full list of available titles, please go to:

mal.aucpress.com